# THE COMMON DEFENSE

## ED RUGGERO

POCKET BOOKS

New York   London   Toronto   Sydney   Tokyo   Singapore

POCKET BOOKS, a division of Simon & Schuster Inc.
1230 Avenue of the Americas, New York, NY 10020

Copyright © 1992 by Ed Ruggero
Map designed by GDS/Jeffrey L. Ward

ISBN: 0-671-73009-6

First Pocket Books paperback printing September 1992

10  9  8  7  6  5  4  3  2  1

POCKET and colophon are registered trademarks of
Simon & Schuster Inc.

Cover art and design by Andrew Newman

Printed in the U.S.A.

# Praise for Ed Ruggero's

# THE COMMON DEFENSE

"A TAUT THRILLER . . ."

—*Milwaukee Sentinel*

"AN ENGAGING . . . STORY OF INTERNA-
TIONAL SUSPENSE . . . *THE COMMON DE-
FENSE* is action-packed. It raises good
questions about the vulnerability of the United
States to both terrorism and Mexican-based
drug activity. And it offers plenty of rumination
about the military's future in the new geopoliti-
cal scheme."

—*St. Petersburg Times* (FL)

"*THE COMMON DEFENSE* provides not only
a lot of action—ambushes, raids and a climactic
running gunfight at the end—but a good look at
how professional soldiers impart their skills to
others, all of this against a frighteningly believ-
able backdrop of political events that could very
well constitute tomorrow's headlines. . . . THE
WORST THING ABOUT ED RUGGERO'S
SECOND NOVEL IS THAT IT ISN'T LONG
ENOUGH."

—*Washington Times*

**Books by Ed Ruggero**

38 North Yankee
The Common Defense

Published by POCKET BOOKS

to Renee

and for Colin and Dealyn
*three people who make it all worthwhile*

It will come as no surprise to anyone who knows me that I relied on quite a few people to help me with this project. I'd like to thank Brock, for what made it in and what didn't; John, the multicultural golfer; Jay, perhaps the world's most patient listener; Domenick, who may yet wind up in Mexico; and all the people who gave of their time and expertise.

Thanks to Paul McCarthy, my hardworking and long-suffering editor, who has the guts to make the hard calls; and to Robert Gottlieb and his great staff at William Morris Agency.

And thanks to Renee, who rode the roller coaster and is buckled in for another go at it.

*We the People of the United States, in order to form a more perfect Union, establish justice, insure domestic tranquility, provide for the common defense, promote the general welfare, and secure the blessings of liberty to ourselves and our posterity, do ordain and establish this Constitution for the United States of America.*

It has to be said that a great victory is a great danger. Human nature finds it harder to endure a victory than a defeat; indeed, it seems to be easier to achieve a victory than to endure it in such a way that it does not in fact turn into a defeat.

—Nietzsche
*Untimely Meditations*

# THE
# COMMON
# DEFENSE

1

# northwest of Tampico, Mexico
## 19 February

THE HOT AIR BOILED OVER THE REAR RAMP AND INTO THE
aircraft as soon as the crew opened the door. Even before
he caught a glimpse of the skillet that was the Mexican
countryside waiting outside the plane, the smell of the dust
and the bright light reflected off the earth reminded him of
Saudi Arabia. He stood up next to the webbed jump seat,
shouldered his rucksack, checked to insure that his pistol
was in its holster, and turned to the rear of the C-130 Her-
cules cargo plane to wait for the signal from the air force
loadmaster that would release him from the smothering
belly of the aircraft.

As far as Isen knew, he was the only passenger getting
off at this remote airstrip, and as he looked out on the
bleached landscape through the rectangular frame of the
aircraft door, he began to feel as if he were being abandoned on the moon. He remembered what the briefing officer had told him before he left San Antonio on the last leg
of his journey south. *Where you're going isn't the end of
the world, but you can see it from there.*

Isen hoisted his rucksack high up on his back, where he
could already feel the blouse of his desert camouflage uniform plastered in sweat to his shoulders. He tucked his

elbows in tight to the ruck's aluminum frame and hustled off the ramp when the loadmaster pointed at him. The air force noncom said something to him as Isen went past, but he couldn't make it out over the roar of the engines. He jogged away from the plane, closing his eyes against the grit that shot out from the prop blast. When he opened them again in a squint to see where he was going, he spotted the dusty tops of two army-issue tents set down in a dry wash, trying in vain, it seemed to him, to hide from the windblown sand. The few hardscrabble trees along the edge of the wash offered no shade. He supposed the tents were the headquarters of what passed for an airfield out here.

He walked over to the streambed, where he found a private and a buck sergeant just beginning to stir from two bare cots in the middle of the smaller tent. Neither of them acknowledged him when he came in.

"Excuse me, Sergeant," Isen said after pausing a few seconds to let the soldiers notice him. "I'm Captain Isen, and I think I'm supposed to meet someone here."

"Yessir," the buck sergeant said without looking directly at him. He continued to lace up his boots as Isen waited for him to complete the sentence. He was a rangy man, with wicked red blotches on the skin of his throat and what Isen could see of his shoulders through the stretched-out neck of his T-shirt. *He's too fair skinned for this duty,* Isen thought.

"So, you know anything about it? Did you know I was coming in?" Isen continued patiently.

"Yessir, we heard." He seemed about to stop talking again and leave Isen hanging, but just as the captain made ready to press the point, the sergeant bent at the waist, down low enough to see out through the rolled-up door flap.

"I think that's your ride over there, Cap'n," he said at last. He stayed bent over, like a pointer, as if Isen wouldn't be able to see anything without his guidance. Isen bent over too and thought about how ridiculous they must look, the upper halves of their bodies pointing out from the heavy tent like twin signposts. Isen saw two pickup trucks about three hundred meters away. There was no one else in sight.

2

"Thanks for your help," Isen said sarcastically. He chided himself immediately. Whenever he joined a command, he made it a policy to be tolerant of anyone he hadn't met yet. You never knew if a soldier you chewed out was going to turn out to be the guy who processed your leave papers or handled your pay records.

He ducked out from under the tent just as the sergeant and his assistant left to sort through the supplies the plane had dropped off. All around him the canvas smelled as if it had been burned with a hot iron. He still couldn't see anyone as he neared the pickups, and he began to wish he had insisted on learning the name of the officer who was supposed to meet him out here. He walked up to the cab of the first truck and looked in. Nothing. He walked around back to the second, and as he approached something caught his eye. There was a man—a Mexican civilian—stretched out on the running board on the shaded side of the truck. Isen walked up to him.

"Pardon," he said, loud enough to wake the man. Nothing stirred. The sleeper's face was covered with a straw cowboy hat that was made up mostly of holes. Isen could see the hat move ever so slightly, so he knew the body was alive. He wasn't sure how the man would react to being woken in the middle of his siesta, but Isen had to find the American officer who was supposed to take him to his new job. He nudged the sleeper's foot and tried again. "Hey there."

This time he was rewarded with movement as the man slowly reached up and pulled the hat back from his eyes. He made no attempt to speak.

*"Americanos?"* Isen asked in what he hoped was an inquisitive tone. "Gringos?" Once again he had occasion to be angry at the assignment officer who had changed his orders, pulling him off the list for schooling at the Defense Language Institute and sending him directly to Mexico. *There's lots of folks who speak English down there; they need your skills as an infantryman right now,* the major had told him. As he stared down at the silent straw hat, which the driver had returned to his face, Isen wondered where all these bilingual natives were. He looked around,

squinting in the dazzling sunlight, wishing he had kept his sunglasses in his shirt pocket instead of burying them in his ruck. *Welcome to the war, boys,* he said to himself.

Mark Isen had, three days earlier, celebrated his thirtieth birthday with his wife in their home at Fort Benning, Georgia. He had just completed an intensive eight-week refresher course in small-unit tactics, guerrilla operations, and training techniques at the U.S. Army Infantry School, and he was about to bring that expertise, as well as what he had learned from his previous tours with infantry units, to this assignment as an adviser.

Although he considered himself well trained, Isen knew that the army believed his most important qualification was marked by the patch he wore above the left breast pocket of his uniform blouse, his Combat Infantryman's Badge, or CIB. There were all sorts of things his combat experience had taught him, and he could even imagine how some of these things would help him react better the next time around. But his most vivid memory was a sickening familiarity with death. He envied those who had not been to combat their ignorance of what it was like to see young men loaded into body bags—young men who had been alive and moving hours before, men who were under his command and for whose lives he was responsible to unnamed mothers and sweethearts, to wives and fathers and children not yet grown. That experience left him with an unshakable determination to do and say whatever he felt necessary—no matter who was offended—in order to accomplish a mission and take care of the soldiers.

Isen looked down at the straw hat and considered that his welcome was somewhat less than enthusiastic.

Just when he was about to try again to rouse the sleeper, the man stretched lazily and sat up. "Ride, Captain?" he said.

"You're my ride?"

"Captain Isen, si?" the man said, pointing to Isen's chest.

Isen nodded, and the driver indicated the bed of the pickup. Isen dropped his rucksack into the back and opened the passenger side door. There was no seat.

The Mexican got in the other door after pulling a wooden crate out of the back. He put the crate on the bare metal floor of the cab, just behind the steering wheel, climbed in, and adjusted the box so that he could reach the pedals. Then he looked over at Isen and motioned at the floor. Isen pulled his rucksack from the bed, set it on the truck's floor and perched on top of it, bracing himself against the rusty metal door as they began rolling over the rutted path. Just when he thought he might ask the driver where they were heading, the man grinned at him, the first expression of any sort he had offered.

"*Bienvenido a Mexico,*" the driver said.

Welcome to Mexico.

They had driven less than a mile when Isen spotted what looked like a U.S. Army vehicle coming at them from the other direction. He thought he could make out, at the leading edge of a rooster tail of dust, the boxy outline of an army jeep. Although the workhorse jeep had been replaced by a larger vehicle throughout the army, it still pulled yeoman duty for the National Guard and Reserve units, and scores of them had been sent to Mexico for this operation. The jeep seemed to be going very fast, but as they approached he realized that the impression came from the fact that it was bouncing crazily over the road. The driver of the pickup stopped, and Isen got out to flag down the other vehicle.

The jeep skidded to a stop, and the pursuing cloud caught up and engulfed Isen before he could get a good look at the two men under the canvas top.

"Quick, grab your shit and jump in," said a voice from inside the swirling, gritty cloud.

Isen reached into the pickup and grabbed the straps of his rucksack. By the time he turned around again, he saw that the voice he'd heard belonged to another GI who'd gotten out of the passenger side and pulled the front seat forward so Isen could climb in back.

"You're Isen, right?" the man asked.

"Yeah, Mark Isen."

As the dust continued to clear and the voice's owner

materialized, Isen became less sure that this was his welcoming committee. The other man certainly sounded like an American, but the rest was a puzzle. He wore at least a five-day growth of beard below the raccoon stripe across his eyes where his goggles had protected his face from the dirt and sun. His uniform may have once been army-issue but was now a sun-bleached brown, the color of the surrounding landscape. He wasn't wearing the conventional load-bearing equipment of pistol belt, suspenders, and holster that Isen wore. Instead he had a wide leather belt slung low across his hips, with what Isen took to be a Bowie knife sheathed on the left side. On the right he wore the standard-issue holster for the U.S. Army nine-millimeter pistol. His wide-brim cloth hat was ringed with a dark streak of sweat where it rested on his head.

"I'm Dave Gaspar," the mirage said, without putting out his hand. "But we ain't got time to talk, so jump in."

Isen did as he was told, and the vehicle skidded into a tight turn even before Gaspar was seated. *This is happening too fast,* Isen thought. *I don't even know where the hell we are.* He banged his head twice on the pole that propped up the canvas top in the few seconds before Gaspar turned around and shouted at him above the roar of the vehicle's fight with the washboard road.

"That old man was supposed to bring you out to me, but we had a change in plans and couldn't wait," Gaspar said. He pointed to the pistol at Isen's side. "Is that thing loaded?" he asked.

"No."

Gaspar tossed him two boxes of ammunition without further explanation, then turned to say something in Spanish to the Mexican soldier who was driving. Isen held the cardboard boxes in his hands for a moment, then realized Gaspar wasn't going to turn around and talk to him anymore.

"Shit," he said, as he tried to balance the pistol's magazines, the loose rounds, and the ammo boxes in the tossing, dusty backseat.

After an hour of tortuous driving, the vehicle swung off the barely visible track and into some sparse, stunted trees.

Isen figured that cross-country movement couldn't be any rougher, and at least the driver had to slow down. The young soldier sat well forward in his seat, straining to see the road in front of the vehicle's hood. The noise had abated somewhat.

"Where are we headed?" he tried again with Gaspar.

"The company you'll be with has a raid going down to-night," Gaspar said. "About thirty or thirty-five klicks from where you landed." He propped his arm on the seat back and turned to face Isen. "No better way to learn how to swim than jumping in the water, eh?"

Isen noticed that Gaspar was checking out the new arrival's uniform, taking in all the badges and awards that the army loved to plaster all over even the field uniforms. Isen referred sarcastically to this measuring-up process that went on between soldiers meeting for the first time as "measuring dicks." Isen didn't put too much stock in all the tabs and wings and patches; what mattered was how you did your job.

Except for his Combat Infantryman's Badge, Isen's peers in the course at Fort Benning hadn't seen him, at first, as a very impressive soldier. Isen had heard his own mother once describe him as "a plain-looking boy." He was just a shade over five feet nine inches tall, unremarkable in coloring, build, and feature, except for his eyes. His wife, who was, he conceded, a bit more literary than his mother, had told him he had a prophet's eyes: gray, but surprisingly expressive and beautiful in their intensity.

Although he was kind of bookish, he had shown almost no facility with languages in the course at Benning. He had completely exasperated the Spanish-speaking officers and noncoms who worked with the group trying to give the officers a crash course in basic Spanish. His score on the diagnostic physical fitness test given on the second day of the program had been in the bottom third of the class; and he was very quiet in the classroom instruction that filled up the training schedule for the first week. He began to shine only when the course turned to small-unit tactics. Mark Isen was a soldier all the way through, and he seemed to know instinctively things other men learned only after study, trial, and error.

Isen sat with his arms braced against the vehicle sides and wondered if Gaspar had arranged this to shake Isen up a bit. He had been in units where old hands pulled pranks on new arrivals to see if the novices rattled easily. Isen had even participated in such pranks as a lieutenant. But he had to admit that a combat patrol seemed a bit extreme.

"Any chance of me getting a map of the area we're in here?" Isen asked, trying to keep things low-key.

It was difficult to gauge Gaspar's reaction in the growing gloom. "I'll see if I can scare one up," he said finally.

They stopped the vehicle after drawing into what looked to be some sort of a grove where the trees were evenly spaced in rows about ten feet apart. The driver pulled up close under some overhanging branches.

Isen got out and stretched his back and legs. He rarely got motion sickness, but he was glad he had refused the last greasy box lunch the air force had offered. He took a long pull from one of his canteens as Gaspar walked off deeper into the grove. In a few minutes, the American returned with a Mexican officer. Gaspar addressed the smaller man in Spanish, then turned to Isen.

"This is Major Pablo Escobar," Gaspar said. "He is the commander of this company. He says you may go with us tonight."

Escobar was dressed in solid-colored fatigues, and even through the most recent layers of dust Isen could see that his fatigues were considerably cleaner than Gaspar's. He had a potbelly that shoved over a leather belt, and he carried only a small, perhaps thirty-eight caliber, revolver in his holster.

The three men stood still for a moment, an awkward pause. Escobar seemed to be waiting for something, so even though they were in the field, Isen saluted. Escobar offered his hand, and Isen stepped forward to take it. Escobar's handshake was firm, but his palms were too soft to belong to a field soldier. Neither man spoke, then the Mexican turned on his heel and headed back to the lengthening shadows amid the trees.

Isen hadn't expected to be welcomed as a savior, but he was surprised to find that he felt like an intruder. Isen was part of a small but growing number of American infantry officers and NCOs who were being assigned as advisers to the Mexican Army in a program called Operation Sentinel. After several years of ineffective attempts to close the border between Mexico and the United States to drug traffic, the U.S. government finally wised up enough to realize that the best way to accomplish the goal was with the assistance of the Mexican government. One of the goals of the program, as envisioned by the planners in Washington, was to train the various Mexican police organizations and the army to a point where they could take on the increasingly aggressive drug traffickers who were using Mexico as a staging area. Throughout the vast stretches of the country's inhospitable interior, smugglers had established tiny airfields where they dropped off cargo for the overland journey to the U.S., or where they refueled their long-range planes before they made end runs around the heavily patrolled southern border of the United States. In exchange, the United States planned to establish several ambitious programs to tie the Mexican and U.S. economies, and a somewhat reluctant Congress had agreed to ease immigration restrictions to allow Mexican workers greater access to the American labor market. It was this economic helping hand that finally overcame Mexican resistance to U.S. interference in their internal affairs.

The Mexican president and his party accepted the terms—the economic assistance helped guarantee the political status quo. But nearly everyone else resisted. The Mexican Army was insulted by the smug American presumption that they needed help. The various federal, state, and local police organizations in Mexico who competed with one another for the federal funds that were their only revenue, were not anxious to see rivals succeed. Cooperation among these agencies, rare at the best of times, had all but disappeared with the American presence.

All of these obstacles were still unknown to Mark Isen, because the lawmaking and economic machinery moved forward slowly. But the U.S. Army wasted no time in getting people on the ground in Mexico. By the time Isen was identified for the program, the army was attacking the problem vigorously, as if gearing up for battle. Isen had come to Mexico to fight a new kind of war, and he had no idea how it might compare to what he already knew of that terrible business.

Gaspar spit thoughtfully. "C'mon, let's go watch the follies."

The two Americans made their way to the edge of the grove, and Isen saw that the trees were rooted alongside a depression that might have been, except for the lack of water, a streambed. Down below, he could hear a dozen or so men talking. They weren't talking loudly, but neither did they appear all that concerned that the noise they were making might give away their location.

"Tell me about this mission," Isen said to Gaspar.

"We'll be walking from here; it's only a couple of klicks or so. There's an airstrip located in this little valley east of here. The druggies have been using it for a few weeks. They come in, set up for a while, then cut out before we can pin them down. They've only used this strip as a refueling point, so there won't be a lot of stuff on the ground, maybe a couple of trucks. From here they fly west, out over the ocean and up the West Coast. They stay pretty much offshore and don't approach the mainland again until they're near northern California, sometimes even Oregon or Washington." Gaspar lowered his voice as they approached a group of Mexican soldiers, and he and Isen kept walking slowly. "The drug operations here don't look like much on the ground, but they got some nice long-range planes."

Isen and Gaspar were now standing at the edge of the little group of men, some of whom were sleeping. Isen revised his estimate; there were upward of twenty soldiers in the little grove, waiting for darkness. Gaspar squatted down at the base of a tree, making sure the tree was between him and the Mexicans.

"I can predict what will happen. These guys will go over there and lay up in the brush for a while, waiting to see if they can snag one of the airplanes coming in. But they'll get tired of that fast, so they'll start shooting and wind up bagging a truck or two."

Isen sat on the ground next to Gaspar, who lowered his voice as he continued. "It'll be the biggest cluster-fuck you ever saw."

"I don't know; I've seen some pretty spectacular cluster-fucks," Isen said. "Have you had time to teach them anything about patrolling or raids?" Isen asked.

Gaspar snorted. "Nah. I got down here five months and twenty-three days ago, with the first planeload of GIs, and went to the field right away, just like you're doing. When we stood down after a couple of days, they all split for home. I saw the training schedule they sent to the Defense Ministry. It said they were doing training with the American advisers, but I didn't see any of them until the day before we went out to the boonies again."

Isen started to say something but sensed that Gaspar wasn't finished.

"It took me a while to figure out what was going on here. You see, the Mexican Army doesn't want to see this program succeed, because they've been saying all along that they don't want us around telling them what to do. Right?"

"I'm with you so far," Isen said.

"But the politicians, who stand to make some political hay from the American assistance, force it down the army's throat. So the generals get their revenge by sending us recruits to work with. They figure—and they're right—that we won't be able to get anything done out here with these guys. Operation Sentinel is doomed to failure."

"These guys are recruits?" Isen asked.

"Military service is compulsory here. When a boy turns eighteen, he has to go for a certain amount of military training, usually on weekends, usually right near home. These unlucky bastards got mobilized for their training and sent to us. They haven't a clue as to what's going on as far as soldiering is concerned."

"What about the noncoms and officers?" Isen asked.

"Most of them have been fired from other units, and this

11

is the end of the line. Every once in a while, we get a volunteer, like the second in command of this bunch.''

A few feet away, one of the sleeping soldiers began to snore.

"This has not only been a big waste of time, but a dangerous one at that," Gaspar said. "I spend all my time in the field making sure the motherfuckers don't leave me out in the desert when they make a truck move or something.''

Isen wanted to ask what kind of generals would send untrained men out on dangerous missions, but a few meters away, there was a stir at the edge of the grove.

Gaspar stood. "Looks like show time." He shouldered his own small backpack and motioned to Isen. "I hate to see you have to carry that big ruck, but if you leave it here, they'll not come back just out of spite."

Isen picked up his rucksack by the frame, slid one arm in, and swung the bulky nylon bag around to his other arm like a heavy coat. "How much is it going to cool off out here tonight?" he asked, remembering the temperature tricks the desert played at night.

"It'll get chilly," Gaspar said. "And these guys will be wrapped up in blankets and ponchos, sleeping as peacefully as boy scouts at camp.''

The earth was already darkening, though the western sky was still lit, a bright cowling that feathered into darkness overhead. The Mexicans started moving out of the gully, and Isen could see a one-quarter moon just beginning to make its way over the eastern horizon, where the edge of the earth was bent and crumpled with low mountains like balled up paper.

Gaspar didn't say anything else, so Isen just fell in behind him on the move. As they walked into the open Isen dropped back until he was about fifteen meters behind and to Gaspar's right. He had a natural aversion to walking right next to anyone when he moved tactically. He used to tell his soldiers to pretend they were all magnets, and they couldn't get close to one another. The old John Wayne movie cliché about "one grenade getting us all" really did apply, but up ahead, the Mexicans were merely walking in a file, following behind one another, heads down.

The land here consisted of narrow valleys flanked by low ridges bare of vegetation. The hills were skeletal fingers pointing generally north and south, and the patrol followed one of the valleys, heading north. The march sent up a cloud of dust, choking the men in the rear. Isen, suppressing the urge to cough, took a green bandanna from the cargo pocket of his trousers, wet it with his canteen, and wrapped it around his face bandit-style. It wasn't very comfortable, but it cut down on the dust he was dragging in.

He watched the lay of the land, estimating how wide the valleys were and how easily the patrol could be ambushed. He reminded himself that the enemy they were about to fight wasn't on the offensive, but he supposed that if anyone was listening, they would be able to hear the patrol approaching from quite a distance. Isen was surprised to hear the men in front of him carrying on intermittent conversations in the darkness; the officers and noncoms did nothing to quiet the soldiers. Isen decided not to ask Gaspar if this was their normal way of traveling.

They walked that way for about an hour, then Isen heard a small commotion up front. Eventually the column came to a halt. Isen discovered that they were on a small road that ran north and south on the valley floor. He moved off to the side of the track into the protection offered in a gully. Gaspar made no attempt to move to the front of the formation to find out what was going on; instead, he turned around and found Isen, then joined him in the ditch.

"I reckon we're near the place," he said as he sat down heavily and took out his canteen.

"Do you have a map?" Isen asked him.

"No."

Isen wanted to know how Gaspar, supposedly an adviser, could give anyone advice from the rear of the column and without a map. But he held his tongue.

"Mind if I go up there and watch what's going on?" Isen asked. Although Gaspar didn't seem interested in asserting himself with the Mexicans, he was still the adviser, Isen the new guy.

Gaspar sighed. "Go ahead." He raised his hand and indicated the front of the group. "Be my guest."

Isen made his way along the file of soldiers, most of whom had simply flopped down on the ground where they had stopped, making no attempt to provide all-around security for the patrol.

When he reached the front of the group, Isen saw the major and another man squatting over a map, looking at it by the light from a butane lighter Escobar held. Isen knelt down next to them. They ignored him and continued their desultory discussion in Spanish. When they seemed to reach some agreement, Escobar indicated Isen with a nod of his head as he talked to the other man.

"I am Lieutenant Cortizo," the other figure said in English. He had the voice of a young man, though it was hard to tell in the darkness. "The major says you are to stay with me." He didn't wait for Isen to answer but stood quickly and moved back along the line of men.

Isen followed him to the rear and watched as, along the way, the lieutenant spoke to a few of the men in the column. He realized that Cortizo, who must be the second in command, was probably talking to the small-unit leaders, the squad leaders. Cortizo spoke quietly to the men he addressed, leaning forward carefully and talking into their faces, making sure they understood the instructions. Cortizo moved like a soldier, as if the darkness were his natural element, while the other men moved clumsily in the gloom.

The column started moving before Isen and Cortizo reached the rear. The men stopped talking, and some who had been carrying their weapons slung over their shoulders moved them to the ready position. Others lifted their heads and stopped watching the ground. But other than that, there was no discernible difference in the way they moved. Except for the quiet, for all their attentiveness, they could have been a group of men looking for a lost dog. Isen wondered how close they were to their objective.

Soon they moved up a small slope and into some trees. The column stopped, then started, then stopped again. Isen heard voices up ahead of him, some of them exasperated and talking loudly. He figured that they were getting closer,

14

and that the leaders were placing their men into an assault formation.

Isen could see down into a small valley that lay on the eastern side of the ridge they were on. The moonlight filled the low ground like a bowl and highlighted a straight line on the valley floor that was lighter than the surrounding grasses. *An airstrip,* Isen thought. They had come at it almost perpendicularly, and across the narrow track Isen could see the dim outlines of at least three small trucks parked at the edge of the wood line. Within a few minutes, Escobar's men had stopped completely and lined up at the near edge of the clearing, parallel to the moonlit stripe. Since no one else moved, Isen did not move either. He got down in the prone position next to Cortizo, who had propped himself on his elbows and was intently watching the other side.

Isen felt a familiar queasiness in the pit of his stomach, a sickening anticipation that began just above his genitals that was, he knew, the first trace of fear. He had been through this before, this much and worse. But then he had been in charge and so had little time to think about personal danger. And he had always known the men around him, had always belonged to the unit. His alarm here had a new quality, a frightening tinge of ignorance. Here he had no idea how many men were across the strip, had no idea what Escobar's plan was or even if there would be any shooting. All he did know was that he was in a dark wood with a group of armed men who were looking to kill other men. And he was waiting. That was always the worst part.

He moved his eyes over the area on the other side where the trucks were parked, knowing that the best way to lose sight of something at night is to stare directly at it. He shifted his gaze, and his brain compiled the little snapshots, so that he could watch the area and the trucks for men moving. He could hear Cortizo's measured breathing next to him. Then he heard another sound off to his left. A man was snoring.

Cortizo twisted his head and snapped off a command in Spanish. A few meters away, Isen heard a muffled thud, followed by a grunt as someone woke the sleeper.

15

Isen wondered where Gaspar was. He wondered if Escobar had had the airstrip under surveillance or if he had simply walked up on it. He rolled over onto his back and strained his eyes against the darkness of the trees they had left. When he rolled back, he tapped Cortizo on the arm.

"Do we have any rear security?"

"What?" Cortizo asked, startled, as if he were surprised that Isen could talk.

"Do you have men behind us so that the bad guys can't come up and surprise us from the rear?"

Cortizo didn't answer him but turned his head to look behind where they lay, as if Isen were the first one to point out to him that they, too, could be attacked.

"Major Escobar says that the enemy does not move around after dark," Cortizo said, sounding unconvinced himself. He looked at Isen, waiting for some further comment, but Isen kept his mouth shut. The silence was too much for Cortizo.

"Wait here," he told Isen. He crawled away to the left, where most of the patrol lay, Isen was sure, asleep by now.

He returned in a few minutes. "I told the major that we should have men behind us, just in case," Cortizo said. Isen wondered if Cortizo had told his boss that the recommendation had come from one of the Americans.

In a few minutes, one of the noncoms moved along the line. Unlike Cortizo, this man was standing up and talking in a normal tone. Cortizo got up on his knees to tell the soldier to quiet down but never got a chance.

The scene along the line was suddenly lit by the muzzle blasts from automatic weapons fire—from behind them. Several men screamed as they were hit, and Isen scrambled forward a few feet out of the light before he turned—his back now to the airstrip—to see what was going on. The firing was coming from the woods behind the line. He pulled at his rucksack and tried to make himself smaller behind its doubtful cover. He tugged his pistol from its holster, wishing he had a rifle.

Incredibly, Cortizo was on his feet and moving to Isen's right, down the line of his men, firing his own weapon and exhorting the others to return fire. It took the Mexicans several seconds to get their first rounds out. Isen could see the muzzle flashes from two automatic weapons no more than twenty meters away, as the ambushers calmly fired at the surprised Mexicans. Isen doubted if the shooters could see any targets; they were probably firing at the sounds the soldiers were making. Isen brought his pistol up and rested his forearm on the bulk of his rucksack. Before he could fire, two men next to him stood and bolted across his front, running away from the fight. Isen could still hear Cortizo yelling.

As suddenly as they started, the automatic weapons stopped firing.

Isen slid down the small slope to his rear, toward the strip, and turned to look for the trucks. One of them pulled partway from the line and turned parallel to the runway.

"The trucks are getting away," he yelled. Up on the line, wounded men were screaming for help, and other men were just screaming. No one fired at the escaping vehicle, and Isen wasn't sure what he should do. Every professional instinct told him to take charge of what was going on, but he had to remind himself that he was an adviser and so had to work through the leaders already in place. By the time he thought about it, the trucks were gone.

It was over in less than two minutes. A few of the Mexicans had flashlights, which they used to check their own casualties and look for the ambushers.

Isen watched the lights bobbing around in the darkness for a while until he heard Gaspar's voice. He stood up and approached the other American.

"They lost two killed and have four wounded," Gaspar said when he spotted Isen.

"They didn't have any security out behind our position, did they?"

"No. They never do. They think it isn't macho to come sneaking up on a position." Gaspar spat on the ground, then dragged the edge of his boot through the dust. "They either want to avoid a fight altogether or stand and slug it out toe to toe with somebody; it doesn't really matter who."

"Did you know they didn't have security out?" Isen asked evenly.

"Yeah, I knew."

"Why didn't you tell them they needed it?" Isen could feel his anger rising. Off to the side, one of the wounded groaned as his comrades moved him.

"Look, Isen, they don't listen. They don't listen to me, they won't listen to you, and anything you try will be like pissing up a rope. So the best thing you can do is hang back and not get yourself killed."

*"I almost did get killed, you asshole,"* Isen said, leaning toward Gaspar, trying not to shout. "I was up on the line too."

Gaspar didn't answer, so Isen asked the obvious question.

"Where were you?"

"I was out of the way, man. And you would've been too if you hadn't charged up there to see what was going on with the fucking major."

There was anger in Gaspar's voice, and something else too. He knew he had done wrong, letting Isen hang out there without warning him, and the wheezing edge of that shame was in his voice. Isen was too disgusted to respond.

Gaspar took Isen's arm and led him away from the group before he continued. "The stupid motherfuckers don't want us down here. They couldn't care less if the whole fucking U.S. of A. went to hell on a cocaine highway."

Gaspar suddenly realized he was almost shouting at Isen and that he had tightened his hold on Isen's arm. "I'm sorry, man. I guess I'm getting nervous 'cause I'm about to rotate out of this shit hole." He tucked his hat under his arm and ran his hand through his hair.

"Do yourself a favor. Don't get too wrapped up in this thing. These guys are not only beyond help—they don't want our help."

Isen didn't answer him.

A few meters away, he could hear Cortizo giving directions to the men who would be stretcher-bearers for the wounded.

Isen and Gaspar separated from the Mexicans after unloading from the trucks that picked them up after the failed raid. Gaspar didn't seem interested in hanging around to see what the Mexicans were going to do, and since Isen had no idea where his billet was, he had to follow Gaspar. They climbed a small hill to an unlit cinder-block building with two rooms. Gaspar motioned to a cot in the front room and then disappeared into the back.

For an hour or more Isen lay awake, staring at the ceiling and trying to force from his mind the tension that the short fight brought on. He had dozens of questions for Gaspar, and he was filled with curiosity. His natural instinct was to be a little farther down the hill with the soldiers. There was nothing he could do there, but he had learned as a junior officer that very often an officer's job was just to be there when the troops were working, especially in the middle of the night. Being in bed when the soldiers were busy was wrong. Once he had made a mental list of things he wanted to do in the morning, he fell asleep, lulled by the sound of a gentle wind through the trees outside the house. He fell asleep thinking about the two dead men. He had no idea what they looked like.

Isen woke to the sound of a rooster crowing.

*That's something new,* he told himself.

He opened his eyes and saw that the room was still dark. There was an east-facing window over his head, and he could just make out a lighter slice of sky through the frame. He sat up, swung his feet out over the edge of the army cot, and took in his surroundings. The room held the cot he sat on, a U.S. Army field table—a folding wooden platform about two feet square—and two metal folding chairs. The floor was dirt. Light came through two windows, which were uncovered, and through the door, which was partly covered by a canvas curtain.

"Not exactly the Ritz," he said to himself.

Isen drew his boots on over dirty socks. His uniform was dusty and caked with a thin mud where dust had clung to sweat, but he didn't know when he would be able to wash his clothes, so he decided to save his clean uniforms and wear the dirty one another day.

He rummaged in his rucksack for his soap, towel, and toothbrush, then he stood, tucked his T-shirt into the top of his trousers, and started out the door in search of water. At the threshold, he stopped, turned back, and retrieved his pistol from the holster. He ejected the magazine, cleared the chamber, and stuck the weapon in the waistband of his pants in the small of his back. He had never been comfortable with the idea of a pistol, even an unloaded one, stuck in the front of his trousers.

He made a circuit of the small building and found that they were on a knoll on the western side of a ridge. The sun was already picking its way down from the top of the ridge toward the valley below. Farther down, he could see the scattered block buildings that he supposed housed the troops. There was no one stirring there. Down in the valley, perhaps a half mile away, there was a village of sixty or seventy buildings. He was too far away to hear anything, but he thought he could smell cooking.

Isen found a couple of five-gallon water cans and a basin. He filled the basin with water and splashed his face and arms. The water was cold from the night's cooling, and although it wasn't as good as a cup of coffee, it was invigorating. As he lathered his arms he looked back over his shoulder. The light was now picking out the next set of buildings below him. *I wonder where the soldiers are?*

Unconsciously, he began to sing to himself.

Inside the building, Dave Gaspar lay awake on his cot, listening to Isen, wondering how he was going to face his replacement this morning.

The night before, Gaspar had been off about seventy-five meters to the rear of the formation as Isen and the Mexicans lay in ambush. He was at the base of the small rise that Escobar and his men had climbed, sitting quietly at the foot of a tree, twirling his filthy hat in his hands. After a while, he heard something moving nearby, just a slow swishing in the darkness, not even the sound of footsteps, more like a disturbance in the air. He assumed it was one of the Mexicans, a soldier who had wandered off to relieve himself and was now stumbling around in the dark. Gaspar held himself very still as the sound grew closer.

Then two figures took shape in the darkness, black shadows only slightly darker than the surrounding night. And though he could see nothing, Gaspar knew quite suddenly that they were not soldiers from the ambush. These men moved too quietly, too cautiously; they were part of the night.

The two figures passed within six or seven feet of where Gaspar sat, fighting to control his breathing, trying to quiet even his heart and the sudden rush of blood through his body. He could have shot them handily after they passed him, but his pistol was in its holster. To get at it, he would have had to pull back the covering flap, and he was afraid of the noise it would make. He was sure the men would shoot him before he could get the pistol unholstered. He decided to wait until they were past him, looking the other way, before he moved.

He counted their steps after they passed. Five, six, seven. They were beyond him, maybe ten meters away. He still had time to draw on them before they disappeared in the blackness. He moved his hand toward the pistol and made to pull off the cover. But the brush of his fingers against the nylon was a crashing sound in the stillness. He was sure they heard him, sure that at any minute they would wheel and fire. And suddenly he thought about how soon he would be home, and by the time that thought passed, the figures had been swallowed by the gloom, and Gaspar was left with the sickening metallic taste of mortality and the realization of what he had done.

Later, he had tried not to look at the dark bundles, the bodies of the soldiers who were killed. But he felt their hot blood on his hands. He had reacted angrily when Isen confronted him, only as a way of masking what he really knew. But now, in the full light of day, he wasn't sure how he was going to salvage what self-respect he had left.

"Morning," Isen said to Gaspar as the other man came around to the back of the building. Isen had his T-shirt off and was drying his chest and shoulders with an olive drab towel.

"Good morning." Gaspar studied Isen's face for something of the anger that was there last night, but Isen seemed unguarded.

"I haven't seen any of the troops stirring down there," Isen said. "I figured that those are barracks or something." His hands were in the towel, and he pointed with his elbow at the buildings just below them on the slope. "Did we miss something? I mean, have they already left to go somewhere?"

"Chances are most of them didn't even spend the night there," Gaspar said. "They probably split for the ville as soon as they could."

Tampico, the nearest town of any size, was a good thirty miles to the southeast, so Isen figured that Gaspar was referring to the little collection of buildings they could see from the hill. "Do they have families down in the village?"

"Just a couple of them, the older ones," Gaspar said as he shook the other water cans to see if there was any water left. "They go down there to eat all the time and to get away from Escobar when they can."

"I thought I might walk down there," Isen said, not sure what he was supposed to make of Gaspar's revelation. "Is there a chow hall or anything?"

"There's a mess hall, outfitted a while back with U.S. Army equipment, field ranges and stuff like that. But nobody's ever cooked anything there, far as I know. I usually head down to the village at midmorning and get something to eat down there."

Isen looked as if he was at a loss, so Gaspar continued. "Why don't you go down and see if you can find Cortizo, Lieutenant Cortizo, the second in command of this outfit. He might be down near the barracks. He actually sleeps there. I'll join you in a while."

Isen went inside and shook out his shirt. He kept an extra pistol belt and holster in his ruck so that he wouldn't have to wear the complete load-bearing equipment all the time. He strapped this belt on and wiped down the pistol with a cleaning rag. Just before he left, he spread some sun protectant on his exposed skin.

There were five buildings on the small level place just below the cube the two Americans were in. These were made of the same impoverished-looking cinder block, with tar-paper roofs. Isen had the impression of a construction site, though it didn't look as though anyone were going to make any improvements here.

One of the buildings was a long rectangle, and Isen took this for a barracks. He stepped up to the doorway and pushed aside the canvas curtain that hung here. He could see the whole interior at a glance: there were steel bunk beds lined up along each wall, in the style, Isen imagined, of barracks the world over. Only a few of these had mattresses on them, and those were filthy. The floor was concrete and was littered with piles of military equipment, old newspapers, and pornographic magazines. Dust motes twisted slowly in the morning light burning in through the eastern windows.

Isen thought he saw someone sleeping on a bunk at the far corner of the room. He walked in and made his way between the unevenly spaced rows of bunks. There was a man sleeping on one of the mattresses, but he wasn't a soldier. He looked to be around seventy years old, and he was wrapped in a dirty blanket that had once been red. He woke before Isen reached him and smiled up at the stranger, revealing a lone tooth that clung precariously to his upper gums.

*Why do I always get the sleeping guides?* Isen asked himself.

He couldn't remember the word for lieutenant, so he said "Cortizo?"

The old man rolled away from Isen without even attempting to answer, and that's when Isen noticed the weapons. There were at least three dozen rifles and grenade launchers piled on the floor between the old man's bunk and the wall that was about two feet away. A long chain, not much thicker than what a kid might use to secure a bike in a schoolyard, was looped through the carrying handles, and the chain's ends were padlocked to the leg of the

ED RUGGERO

bunk. Some of the rifles still had magazines in place, meaning that they hadn't even been unloaded. All of them were dirty.

Isen was flabbergasted. The Mexicans had apparently simply piled the weapons up after they reached the barracks early in the morning. Isen had a sharp mental picture of his own company at Schofield Barracks, the men sitting on the porches and balconies of their 1930s-style barracks, shielded from the Hawaiian sun, cleaning their weapons after a field problem. Even after five days in the hot, dry wastes of the Kahuku training area, no one could get a shower until his weapon was cleaned and inspected by the NCOs in his chain of command.

"Captain Isen?"

Isen turned around. He hadn't heard Cortizo come up behind him.

"I was just going to start looking for you," Isen said, studying the other man in the daylight. Cortizo was much younger than he would have guessed, perhaps no more than twenty-two. He was several inches shorter than Isen and carried a spare tire of flesh around his middle. He had a trim little mustache and delicate features that made him look like a banker or a teacher. But his sharp, dark eyes locked on Isen's own. His boots were shined, his uniform freshly laundered and pressed; Isen suddenly felt very dirty.

Isen decided to get right to the point. "Do you always store your weapons this way?"

"Ah, the weapons." Cortizo put his hands behind his back and rose up slightly on his toes, then rocked back to his heels. He repeated the movement nervously—up, forward, back, up, forward, back. "Yes. Well . . . I suppose I will have the men come back and clean them."

Isen thought Cortizo was deliberately understating the problem, perhaps to save face.

"Perhaps today," Cortizo went on.

*Perhaps?* Isen thought.

"Where are your men?" Isen asked, trying not to sound like an inquisitor.

"Most of them sleep down in the village," Cortizo began.

24

"There is not much to keep them up here, you see." He let one hand slip from behind his back to make a small gesture at the filthy room.

"I see," Isen said. He looked around for Gaspar. It would have been a lot easier to find all this out from the other American, but Gaspar seemed to make a habit of being out of sight. Isen thought it might be easier to sit down with Cortizo over coffee and discuss the shape the company was in.

"Do you have a mess hall?"

Cortizo frowned, and Isen assumed that he didn't know the term.

"I mean, a dining facility, a place to eat?"

"Come with me," Cortizo said, stepping past Isen.

They went out the door at the narrow end of the room, opposite where Isen had come in, and crossed a narrow dirt trail into another block building. This one had a screen door, though the screen had a slash down the center. Cortizo pushed open the door.

"This is our mess hall."

The room was all but empty. There were no tables or chairs, no sign of any stoves or serving tables in the single room. In the far corner, Isen saw a stack of what looked like cases of U.S. Army MREs (for Meal, Ready to Eat), the standard field ration for U.S. troops. Isen wasn't sure what to say, so he walked over to the familiar boxes. They were unopened.

"The dried food is no good here. The men do not like them because they take too much water," Cortizo offered. He rocked on his feet again, up, forward, back. Neither he nor Isen wanted to address the obvious question: Where was the mess hall?

The awkward silence stretched out for what felt to the two men like many minutes but had been only seconds, when Gaspar walked into the room.

"I see you've found our four-star dining facility," he said.

Cortizo appeared to shrink just a bit.

"I thought these units got complete mess hall outfits from Uncle Sam as part of this deal," Isen said.

Cortizo looked down at the floor, and Isen sensed that he had just put his foot in his mouth. One look at Gaspar confirmed it. The senior adviser was looking from Cortizo to Isen and back again, with what could only be described as a stupid grin on his face. He reminded Isen of a cruel child who reveled in another's discomfort.

"Yeah, the stuff got as far as this here building," Gaspar said, taking a melodramatic turn about the room, as if to emphasize its emptiness. Then he stopped right in front of Cortizo.

"Then it all disappeared one night. Stoves, trays, pans, utensils, even the fucking hot mitts were gone. Ain't that right, Lieutenant?"

Isen would have had to be deaf and blind to miss the implication, but there was nothing he could do to save Cortizo now. The little lieutenant said nothing.

Gaspar tired of his game quickly. He dropped his arms and thrust his hands into his pockets as he continued. "Anyways, the troopies all go down to the ville to eat. Oh, and the major eats . . . where does the major eat, Señor Cortizo?"

"Major Escobar was called to Tampico," Cortizo said.

"Ah, yes," Gaspar said. Then he turned to Isen and smiled, his mouth a thin line.

"Excuse me, gentlemen," Cortizo said formally, pulling himself up to full height. Isen wouldn't have been surprised if he'd clicked his heels. He turned and walked out of the room, leaving the two Americans and the dusty boxes of food.

"What the hell was that all about?" Isen asked.

"Cortizo's just a toady for Escobar," Gaspar said, seemingly relieved to have it out. "Escobar stole all this shit, all the mess hall stuff, and sold it somewhere else in the state."

"How do you know?"

"Are you kidding? The troops told me everything. Escobar made them load the stuff right onto a private truck that he had brought down here. They know he stole the shit, only Cortizo won't admit it to me."

"Did you report him?" Isen asked.

Gaspar whistled through his teeth. "Nah. That's the norm down here. Everybody expects to get ripped off. Even the troops—who don't have a place to eat now—are philosophical about it. I guess they figure that they'll do it if they ever get the chance. At least they're honest about that. Except for fucking Cortizo."

Isen looked out through one glassless window to where Cortizo had stopped at the edge of the hill, looking out over the town. "Is he in on it too?"

"No, he's up on a high horse or something," Gaspar said.

"I don't get it," Isen said. "You're pissed off at Cortizo because he's honest?"

"No; I'm pissed because he won't admit that everyone else is dirty."

Isen looked hard at Gaspar, whose face was in profile against the gray wall. He wondered where Gaspar had been the night before when the ambush hit them. He wondered how dirty Gaspar was.

"So where can I get something to eat?" Isen said finally.

Gaspar directed Isen to a café in the village, where the newcomer ate alone, a fried egg served with a tortilla and beans. It was only after his food was served that he remembered that he hadn't eaten since before the plane flight. Was that only yesterday? He ate with gusto and concentrated on his food, though he knew some people were staring at him. He thought some of the younger men who passed through the café might be soldiers, but they weren't in uniform and didn't have the recognizable haircuts that U.S. soldiers had, so he couldn't be sure. Isen was drinking bitter black coffee out of a glass tumbler when Cortizo walked up to him.

"May I join you, Captain?" he said formally.

"Please do." Isen pushed the chair opposite his own away from the table with his foot.

Cortizo sat down, tugging at his trouser legs as he did so, as if trying to preserve the crease. Isen wasn't sure where to start. Cortizo started for them.

"How did you come to this assignment?"

27

"I volunteered for it," Isen answered. *That's only half true*, he reminded himself. "Actually, the army offered me this job and one other one, so I took this one."

"What was the other job?" Cortizo asked stiffly. Isen wondered if Cortizo meant to be confrontational, or if he simply picked up the tone in translating to English.

"I was supposed to go work in the Pentagon, in Washington. But I didn't want to sit behind a desk, so I took this job. Besides, I think fighting druggies is more important than chasing down coffee for a bunch of generals."

"You don't mind being away from your family?" Cortizo asked.

Isen had a sudden picture of Adrienne, his wife of eight years. Just a few nights before, at a fancy dinner in Columbus's antebellum historic district, they'd had an argument over his staying in the service. He had wanted to avoid a scene, but the more he kept his voice low, refusing to become agitated, the madder she had become. They had finally eaten that beautiful meal in stony silence.

To Mark Isen, family separations were part of the price he had to pay for being in the army. His own father, a career noncom, had spent several long stretches of time away from home—including two tours in Vietnam—as well as a double handful of month-long separations every few years. His father and his father's friends always reserved the right to complain about things: the new commander or skimpy pay raise or lack of training time, but they taught Isen practical lessons about service every time they volunteered their off-duty time to coach the kids' soccer league or to take the scouts to camp. Isen took his lessons to heart, and when he chose the army, he did so with his eyes open, fully aware of the sacrifices and the rewards.

"Yeah, but this is only for six months to a year. In Washington I'd be working twelve hours a day, spending an hour in traffic each way, and taking a couple of dozen trips a year away from home. And that would have been a four-year stint. I figure this is better in the long run. Besides, this is what I know how to do."

*That sounded lame*, Isen thought. If Cortizo thought that

last comment egotistical, he did a good job of hiding his reaction.

"Did you know that a lot of people here would resent you?"

Isen was surprised at the lieutenant's candor. "Yes, I guess I knew that. I mean, I know a lot of your politicians think we're using the Mexican Army to fight our war."

"It's actually worse than that, Captain Isen," Cortizo said crisply.

"What do you mean?" Isen asked.

Cortizo raised his hand and signaled the proprietor, asking for more coffee.

"The truth, Captain?"

"We might as well get started on the right foot," Isen said, hoping that he wouldn't regret it.

"We know that your Congress is willing to use the American military as a quick way to fix the drug problem. You have this big, successful military, and the people are saying 'Look, it worked before in Panama and Iraq. Why not use it to stop the flow of cocaine?' "

Cortizo pressed the tips of his fingers together in front of his face. "But of course, it is not such an easy thing to do, as you will learn down here. Still, it is easier to send in the wonderful American army than it is to teach Americans not to use drugs."

Isen shifted uncomfortably in his seat. His first reaction was defensive—he thought he should be insulted. But it dawned on him that even though Cortizo was speaking in generalities, he was mostly right.

"I am sorry, Captain Isen," Cortizo said, smiling. "I do not mean to offend you. This is not the truth, but only the truth as I see it. And as always with difficult questions, there are many truths.

"One is that my country needs the economic concessions and assistance that the United States has offered us for cooperation in this venture. We must establish a viable economy of our own, or Mexico will be ripe for revolution and anarchy. Our people cannot go on living in abject poverty forever." He leaned forward, resting his forearms on the table. Isen thought he was going to rise up out of his seat. "But I do not like the fact that we are prostituting ourselves."

The old man brought two more glasses of the boiling coffee, and Cortizo's accusation hung in the air with the steam. Isen could already hear the rumblings in his stomach from the unfamiliar brew, but he picked up the glass Cortizo had bought him.

"So how do we work out this . . . arrangement between us? Between Major Escobar, you, and me?"

"Well, you already have an advantage. Captain Gaspar never accepted that we did not like him. He could not work with us—he thought we had to love him, thought we had to accept him with open arms like some sort of savior. You are much more pragmatic."

*Gaspar was afraid for his life out there, afraid that Mexican incompetence would get him killed,* Isen thought. *I wonder if he was right?*

"I have nothing against you personally, Captain Isen," Cortizo said, sipping carefully from his glass. "I am just unhappy about your country's presence here, that is all. I recognize that you are much better trained in the tasks we are to master, so I am willing, anxious, even, to learn from you."

Isen shifted uncomfortably in his seat. No one at Fort Benning had told him about this; no one had prepared him to handle the delicate politics involved with being an adviser. He was an infantryman; that's what he knew how to do. And suddenly it wasn't enough; all the questions were instantly larger than he had anticipated.

The army did not routinely prepare its officers for service as advisers. Even the Special Forces, which did train with indigenous groups, went little further than telling officers not to piss off the guerrilla leaders. Somehow Isen had been maneuvered into a position where he was representative of a policy worked out between two heads of state but which was unpopular—to say the least—on the ground. His role was no longer just that of an infantry adviser, or even a trainer. He had somehow crossed over into the realm of being a diplomat. There was no issue of his liking it or not.

Gaspar hadn't liked it, and Gaspar had apparently failed in his mission. Isen wasn't going to give up easily.

"So where do we go from here?" Isen asked.

"Well, we need to work out a training program for the missions we're supposed to be able to do," Cortizo said.

"I know that," Isen said. "I'm talking about my role. If I'm to be effective at all, you must be willing to listen to my advice."

Cortizo narrowed his eyes ever so slightly.

"And I must understand," Isen continued, "that you will not accept *all* of it. Listening must be enough."

"Agreed."

Finally, even this journey would begin with a single step.

"Maybe we'll start," Cortizo said, "by getting those weapons cleaned up."

# 2

## along the Rio Soto La Marina, Mexico
### *12 March*

AS HE WATCHED THE SOLDIERS GO THROUGH THE MOTIONS of assaulting a bunker, Isen thought of a volleyball team he'd played with at Fort Leavenworth. The players were in it strictly for fun, and to prove the point they'd had a shirt printed that sported the team logo: *Start Slow, Taper Off.*

Below him, a noncommissioned officer was yelling for the privates to move faster, motioning frantically with his arm as he did so. The sergeant might as well have been in another state for all the soldiers were listening to him. Isen sighed. *I've seen dead people move faster,* he thought. He looked up at the sun and wondered what it would be like to be out here in July.

"You do not like what you see, Captain Isen?"

It was Cortizo. The Mexican officer had come up behind him and was now sharing the little hill Isen was using to observe training.

In the three weeks he'd been in-country, Isen had used every tactful stratagem he could dream up to light a fire under the Mexicans' training. So far, nothing seemed to be working. He decided it was time to stop dancing around the problem.

"I've seen people move faster."

"They are not happy about being here," Cortizo said, stating the obvious. "They are conscripts. . . ."

"Yes, yes, I know all that," Isen came back. "But I don't think that's the problem," Isen said. He watched his counterpart closely for some hint as to how he was reacting to the criticism. Cortizo stood quietly, unreadable as a sphinx.

"One of the big problems is that the training is boring," Isen said. "It isn't challenging enough."

Cortizo leaned forward stiffly and clasped his hands behind his back.

"We have the same problems with our soldiers," Isen said. "They get bored with training exercises, so we go to great lengths to make the training realistic and stressful."

Cortizo turned away from the field below, where another team of four men was making its desultory way toward the bunker with their practice hand grenades. He faced Isen. "And your soldiers respond to that?"

"It's the only kind of training they respond to. Soldiers want to do hard training; they don't join the service because they want to be bored. They like to use their skills."

Isen thought about how he used to take his light infantry company on extended road marches while other units were still recovering from field training exercises. "Besides, it gives them bragging rights."

"What is 'bragging rights'?" Cortizo asked.

"Oh, you know, 'Our company is better than your company because we train harder. We stay in the field, you sleep in tents; we walk, you ride,' that sort of stuff."

"I don't know that these men will respond to this hard training; they do not see the end," Cortizo said. It was not a final pronouncement, so Isen figured that Cortizo was talking out loud, plumbing for ideas to apply to training his company. He'd inherited command from Escobar shortly after the debacle of the ambush.

"We can try to make the training more challenging, set up a series of rewards. Competitions, maybe, between squads. We can use live ammunition in these battle drills;

realistic training will make it easier for them to imagine what it will be like in the real thing.''

Cortizo rocked forward on his toes. Just once, then he settled down. "That is what I mean. There may be no 'real thing' for these soldiers.''

Now it was Isen's turn to stare. "What about the drug-interdiction mission?''

Cortizo rolled forward on his toes, rocked back. "Well, yes, as I said, that is our mission, and, uh, I expect that we *might* be called upon. . . .''

Isen did not respond. Cortizo rocked back and forth.

"The truth is, Captain Isen,'' Cortizo said, delaying again. "The truth is that I don't think there are any plans for committing these forces in anything more serious than a halfhearted effort at a raid, such as you saw on your first night here.''

Cortizo seemed relieved that it was out, and Isen was reminded of his initial impression of the man. Here was a professional soldier—a bit stuffy, to be sure, but a pro nonetheless—who was trying to do the best job he could with very limited resources, and all the while trying to preserve his country's dignity by putting on a good face for the foreigners.

"This is part of the plan to sabotage Operation Sentinel?'' Isen asked. *Since we're being open about all this,* he thought.

"In a way. The poor training of these soldiers will be enough to sabotage it. Their enlistment period will be up before they are ready for anything more sophisticated. Then the American advisers, they will have to train a new bunch, and the cycle will go on. Every once in a while, a few soldiers may be killed, as they were in that ambush, and that will just allow the army to point and say, 'See, they are not ready.' ''

Isen considered the implications of this confession. "You volunteered for this duty?'' he asked.

Cortizo was disoriented for a second by the change of subject. "Pardon? Yes, oh, yes, I did volunteer.'' He smiled a small, ironic smile. "I was aware of the politics involved, but I naively thought that my government was going to try to do something about the drugs, which are a curse."

"So, no matter what is going on at the head shed, the bottom line is that you'd really like to see this unit used. Is that correct?"

"What is 'head shed'?"

"Sorry. I mean up at headquarters. No matter what they say, your goal is to get these people doing something worth their time?"

"Yes," Cortizo said. He had stopped rocking and seemed more relaxed now. Perhaps he had expected Isen to be angry with the revelation that the Mexican government was toying with him and wasting his talents.

"Then it seems to me we have two things to do," Isen said. He was a big believer in plans and milestones and organization, and he liked to think of tasks as logical steps in a process with predictable outcomes.

"First, we have to get these people trained up to standard, and that's going to take some real salesmanship on your part and mine. We'll make the training more realistic and challenging; we'll put them in tough spots so we can identify the leaders. Then we tell them that they are going to be committed to the fight."

"Why would we tell them that?" Cortizo asked, intrigued now.

"That brings me to my second step: we have to get the people upstairs to buy that this is an important and well-trained unit; that it is imperative that these people be committed as soon as possible."

"How do we do that?" Cortizo asked.

"That I haven't figured out yet."

Mark Isen was no stranger to the difficulties of training soldiers to work as a team, but he underestimated the job before him. He and Cortizo started right in with massive changes to the schedule, introducing physical training and group sports to build cohesion, road marches and classes in weapons maintenance, first aid, and radio procedures. They arranged to bring in helicopters for mock air assaults, they fired weapons at night and in the daytime, singly and in groups, while attacking mock targets. But still the program threatened to die of its own weight.

When it was still touch and go, Isen stepped back and looked again at what they were doing. He decided that they needed a more fundamental change: he and Cortizo were going to have to change the company's mental state.

One morning before physical training, which usually consisted of a run followed by push-ups and sit-ups, Cortizo got up in front of all the soldiers and talked to them. It was such a departure, they recognized, for their commander to talk to them informally, that they stood in rapt attention.

"You are no longer individual trainees," he told them, "but part of this unit." He was terribly conscious of avoiding the kind of empty rhetoric they had all heard before, and he knew that he had only a moment or two to reach them. "Each of you has a job to do, and the rest of us depend on you to do that job well. If any one of you fails, the group will be the worse for it."

A man below him coughed, and Cortizo looked around. He was surprised to see that they were listening to him. He knew that his men thought he was cold and distant, and he suspected that Isen agreed with that. But he sincerely wanted to reach them this time.

"We are going into a fight here. It may be tomorrow, more than likely it will be in some weeks. We have a good reason to fight," he said. He wanted to imply that they weren't fighting for Americans but could think of no way to do it diplomatically. "These drug smugglers violate our country, and if they gain a foothold here, Mexico will become like Colombia, with no safety for the decent citizens."

He wasn't sure how long he'd been talking, so he decided to wrap up. "But out here, *Mexico* is an abstraction. Soldiers do not fight with thoughts of their country in mind. You should do things the right way because you have people depending on you." He gestured dramatically, palm upraised. "These people around you."

Then he introduced Isen. The American climbed up on the back of the jeep where Cortizo had been standing. The

# THE COMMON DEFENSE

soldiers looked at him curiously; they knew he spoke very little Spanish.

But he said nothing. Instead he pulled from his shirt a bundle he'd had his wife send down from Fort Benning, a roll of light blue cloth. Isen grasped the corners and shook out a guidon, a forked cloth flag of the kind that marks company-size units in the United States Army. This one was in infantry blue and was decorated with crossed rifles of white cloth. Cortizo handed him a pole he'd cut a few days earlier, and Isen tied the flag to the shaft. Then he handed the flag over to Cortizo.

It wasn't much, but it was a beginning.

A week later, Isen and Cortizo were both convinced that, in fact, the soldiers were showing more interest in their training. Cortizo was still worried about how he and Isen were going to make good on their promise that the unit would be committed to action.

"Don't worry about that," Isen said, smiling and showing more enthusiasm than he had a right to. "Let's get them ready first."

Isen left the unit for two days at the beginning of April, disappearing to some stretch of the river with three villagers he hired to take him out. He refused to tell Cortizo what he was up to, and the secrecy had the effect he wanted. By the time he came back, the Mexican lieutenant was overcome with curiosity. On the evening Isen returned, he took Cortizo out in the jeep to a site along the Rio Soto.

"There it is," Isen said as they pulled up in a swirl of dust.

Cortizo saw a few big wooden poles lashed together into a framework, some over the land, some over water.

"What is it?" he asked.

"We call it the Log-Walk, Rope-Drop, Slide-for-Life Confidence Obstacle Course," Isen said proudly.

Cortizo didn't follow; he merely looked at the American. Isen, as excited as if he'd just found the contraptions growing along the riverbed, doffed his shirt. His arms were brown from the bicep down, white above a line where his shirt sleeves ended.

"Watch," he said.

He ran to an upright pole that had a rude ladder attached. As he climbed, Cortizo had to smile at his energy. The change in the company had wrought a change in Isen; Cortizo wished Gaspar were around to see the difference.

The first obstacle consisted of three upright poles: the first on the bank, the second and third in line out in the river. A horizontal pole connected the first two, the second and third were tied by a rope stretched parallel to and twenty-five feet above the water. There was a small wooden platform, no more than a few feet square, at the top of the ladder Isen was climbing, some twenty feet above the muddy bank. Reaching this, Isen perched uncertainly, hesitating for only a few seconds before hurrying across the log stretched in front of him. At the center of this he was obliged to step over a wooden box about a foot high, which he did without slowing down.

Cortizo sucked in his breath as he thought about the English words Isen had used to describe this thing. *He expects the soldiers to do this.*

At the middle pole Isen climbed on top of the rope and shimmied out to the center, one foot hooked behind him, one pointing to the water for balance. When he reached the center, he grabbed hold with both hands and let his body swing below the rope. He executed one perfect pull-up, then called to Cortizo.

"When they get here, they have to holler something," Isen shouted from fifty feet away.

"What?"

"THEY HAVE TO SHOUT SOMETHING THAT SHOWS A LITTLE SPIRIT."

Cortizo shrugged.

Isen looked straight ahead. "RANGERS LEAD THE WAY." That done, he dropped to the water and knifed below the dark surface. When he came up, he was smiling from ear to ear.

"Whaddya think?" He emerged from the water, his boots squishing brown with each step. Cortizo thought the American had lost his mind.

"Why do you want the soldiers to do this?" he asked.

"It's a confidence builder," Isen explained. "If you can get a kid to do this, you've gone a long way to convincing him that he can do more than he thought he was capable of."

"I can hardly wait to see what this other one is for," Cortizo said skeptically.

The other one was a thirty-foot pole, complete with ladder and tiny platform, though this deck had a railing of sorts. There was a heavy cable stretched over the platform and across the river to an anchor in the water about a hundred and fifty feet away.

"This one is the Slide-for-Life; it's really great," Isen said.

"I can only imagine," Cortizo said.

Isen had been hoping that Cortizo would be more enthusiastic, but on reflection he figured that expecting an instant convert was unrealistic.

"Okay, I'll show you how this one works. When we run the soldiers through, we'll have a guy on the far bank with signal flags. The soldier climbs to the top and hangs on to this pulley, which slides down the rope with the soldier underneath it. When the signal guy raises the flags, the soldier pulls his legs up to a sitting position; then he lets go when the guy with the flags lowers them. When he turns loose the handles, he'll be doing around twenty miles an hour."

Cortizo had no comment, so Isen climbed the pole and demonstrated. Once again, he yelled something—unintelligible to Cortizo—on the way down. He was going very fast when he hit the water, and he skidded across the top for a few meters before going in.

"This looks like an amusement park ride," Cortizo said.

"It's a scream," Isen maintained. "And it really does do a lot for someone's physical confidence."

"What if someone drowns? What if they get up there and freeze—it would be humiliating."

"First of all," Isen explained, "only soldiers who can swim will do this. We'll have people below with hooks to yank them out if need be. Second, peer pressure will make most of them go. The ones who won't will just have to live with themselves."

"This is dangerous." Cortizo's resistance seemed to be stiffening.

Isen sat down on the ground and took off his sopping boots.

"Look, I know that this looks like it's a bunch of fun and games, and it is fun, but that isn't the point." He drained muddy water from one boot, then went to work on the other. "Your soldiers are developing the skills they need. But in order to put those skills together, they have to develop confidence in themselves; they have to believe they can do difficult things. Since we cannot simulate the danger of battle, we must come up with something else that at least appears dangerous."

He paused for a moment to let that settle in. He had invested a lot of time in this riverside project, and he didn't want to see it fail. "This will give them some of the confidence they need; it will help them come together as a team."

Cortizo looked out at the river, which swirled by in brown eddies the color of the landscape.

"We will try it."

Isen brought six NCOs out the day before the scheduled training, hoping to run them through the course quickly so that they could act as safeties. Two of the men flatly refused to participate, one more pretended that he didn't understand the instructions Isen gave. Isen finally coaxed two men through, then ran through again himself to show the last holdout how it was done. He had allowed an hour and a half to get the NCOs up to speed; it took him three, and he didn't even get them all through.

*This does not bode well for tomorrow,* Isen thought as they bounced back to their encampment in the darkness.

Whatever he might say about Cortizo's reluctance, Isen thought, the man knew what it meant to be a leader.

The Mexican lieutenant gave the safety brief Isen had drawn up for him, standing before a group of soldiers as somber as any Isen had ever seen outside of a combat zone. When Cortizo got to the part about nonswimmers being excluded, there were several hoots of relief, but these were quickly swallowed up by the tenor of the rest of the crowd.

Isen couldn't tell, of course, since he didn't speak Spanish, but he didn't think Cortizo gave any great words of encouragement. Nor did he try to lighten the moment with a little humor, but that would have been out of character. Nevertheless, when he was finished, he marched over to the first pole as stiffly as if he were approaching a gallows. He stripped off his shirt, folded it neatly, and laid it on the ground, then he turned to the first safety and asked permission to climb. When the NCO gave him the go-ahead, Cortizo climbed deliberately to the top.

Isen was on the nearby platform of the Slide-for-Life, above the crowd and even with Cortizo. He could see the lieutenant's face, unsmiling, his gaze fixed on the top rungs of the ladder.

The man was terrified.

*How stupid can I be?* Isen thought.

Cortizo hadn't said anything to Isen about his being afraid of heights, but now Isen understood some of his reluctance to agree to the training. He could easily have refused to bring his company out here; Isen hadn't even consulted him before he built the thing. And Isen was sure that Cortizo remained unconvinced that this confidence-building thing would really work. Nevertheless, here he was trying to go through with it. Then it occurred to Isen that Cortizo might freeze at the top. And that would be the end of his commanding this company.

Isen suddenly believed that this wasn't such a good idea. Cortizo was the only thing these soldiers had going for them. He was hardworking and concerned, and he was a patriot in the best sense of that slippery word. He was fundamentally a good man.

*What if someone freezes at the top?* Cortizo had asked.

Isen cringed when he thought about his smug answer. *The ones who don't make it will just have to live with themselves.*

41

Cortizo was at the top now. To his credit, he recognized that hesitating on the tiny platform would be the wrong thing to do. He set right out across the plank that was fixed to the top of the horizontal pole, though he shuffled his feet along, never lifting either one off the plank to place it in front of the other. When he got to the obstacle in the center, he lifted one foot gingerly and placed it on the box.

Isen had not planned for the box to hold a soldier's weight; they were supposed to step over it. He wanted to look down at the crowd below to see what they were doing, but he was riveted on the lieutenant, wondering if the little box was going to come off, sending Cortizo and his pride crashing into the water below.

The box held.

Cortizo made it to the end, where he grasped the line with a death grip. The trick here was that one had to lean out over the water far enough to lie on the rope. Cortizo had both hands wrapped around the cable, and he inched them forward a tiny bit at a time, as if he could fool himself into thinking that he wasn't really moving. Finally, he was on the rope. He shimmied out slowly, and Isen could see that his trail leg, the one hanging out for balance, was shaking, but he didn't think the soldiers could see it. Cortizo let himself down suddenly, facing the wrong way. The idea was to face the shore so that the others, waiting in line, could see the agony of whoever was on the rope drop. Cortizo was facing Isen, looking across the gap, his eyes a perfect advertisement of fear. But his voice was steady.

"Permission to drop, Sergeant?" he yelled.

It took Isen a second or two to realize that Cortizo had said it in English, probably because he was facing Isen. The safety below didn't know what to do, so Isen, stifling a laugh in spite of everything, answered.

"Drop."

Cortizo screwed his face up as he fell, but his terror was short-lived, and he hit the water neatly.

He was up in a second, and a few of the soldiers, looking surprised that he came out of the dark water, began to cheer him on. Cortizo raised his arm in bare acknowledgment as he climbed from the water and jogged around to the base of the pole where Isen waited.

Isen lost sight of Cortizo when the lieutenant reached the bottom of the ladder, but he could feel the vibrations through the platform as Cortizo climbed. When the lieutenant stuck his head over the edge of the deck, Isen noticed that his eyes were all but shut.

"You have to open your eyes, Lieutenant, to climb up over the edge," Isen whispered.

Cortizo struggled up, clawing at the boards with his fingernails in fear of falling backward.

"That's it, that's it," Isen coached. "Just stand up now." He was holding the little pulley mechanism that Cortizo would ride down to the water. There were two metal wheels that rode the cable and a handle that hung from the frame. "Just stand up and grab this," Isen said.

Cortizo got to his knees and looked up as if the bar were a hundred feet away.

"You can do it," Isen said. "You watched me do it; it isn't hard. As a matter of fact, it's a lot easier than what you just did over there," Isen said, pointing to the rope drop. He was chattering away like a catcher encouraging a pitcher.

"Yes, I saw you do it, but you have done all this many times before," Cortizo said. He was still on his knees. Below them, Isen could hear some of the soldiers calling to their commander, encouraging him to go on. Isen thought he might lose him here.

"Look, I'm scared every time I do this," he said. "I didn't look scared because you were watching me and I wanted to appear brave. That is what you are doing now."

Cortizo considered the bar above his head, then glanced across at the flag man, who was waving his green signal flags gently back and forth, back and forth, as if he had all the time in the world.

"C'mon," Isen said.

Cortizo stood, grabbed the handle, nodded to the safety across the water, and did a half pull-up. Isen gave him a gentle shove and the pulley rolled on the line until Cortizo was speeding down the inclined rope toward the water at twenty miles an hour. The flag man raised his flags above his head, and Cortizo raised his legs to a sitting position. When the flag man dropped the flags, Cortizo let go of the handle and bounced into the water.

The soldiers below broke out in loud cheering, and in a few seconds Cortizo was above the surface of the water, one fist raised in a salute to his men.

As the other soldiers in the company began to negotiate the obstacles, Isen felt a deep elation. He had known a few moments like this before, when suddenly all the sacrifices seemed worthwhile. He enjoyed showing young men that they were capable of doing things that they were afraid of; he liked to watch them grow, and each of their steps was a small victory for him. He stood up in the sun and the air, happy to be making a difference. For Mark Isen, this is what it meant to be a leader.

# THE COMMON DEFENSE

## U.S. Navy Admits Mishap on Nuclear Cruiser
## European Protest Turns Violent

by Stephen Pryzbylkowski
*Philadelphia Inquirer*

Rome, March 23—American military installations and diplomatic posts throughout Europe became targets for protesters this week as public reaction to last week's near-disaster on board an American naval vessel in the Mediterranean Sea continues.

U.S. Navy spokesmen in Washington confirmed that the cruiser USS *Texas,* now in port in Naples, Italy, had a malfunction in its cooling system last week while on routine naval maneuvers as part of a Sixth Fleet Task Force. When the cooling system for the ship's nuclear reactor failed, engineers switched to a backup system that uses seawater to control reactor temperatures. Although the main cooling system is closed—that is, the heated water is run through a cooling apparatus on board—the heated seawater used in the backup is jettisoned overboard. Navy officials insisted again today that there was no danger of nuclear contamination, as the reactor remained stable and no radioactive material escaped into the cooling system.

The incident has become a rallying point for various European political groups, from those who oppose all forms of nuclear energy to those who want all American military forces out of Europe. One environmental group claimed to have proof that the *Texas* had contaminated seawater with radioactive material. Several thousand Italian protesters blocked entry to the pier in Naples where the *Texas* was docked. The Sixth Fleet commander ordered the *Texas* to stand off from the port, though he allowed other ships to stay docked while hundreds of American sailors continued their shore liberty in this normally hospitable city.

Italian authorities confirmed reports that three U.S. sailors were attacked in a bar frequented by American servicemen. But neither the Italians nor the Sixth Fleet spokesman would say whether the attack was in response to the *Texas* incident. In Rome a small but angry crowd outside the U.S. Embassy set fire to a van attempting to make a delivery to the compound.

In Germany, protesters splattered red paint on cars belonging to American servicemen in Heidelberg, while in France, opposition party members called for an international committee of nuclear scientists to investigate the incident.

3

# Heidelberg, Germany
## 5 *April*

HEINRICH WOLF PUT ON A PRACTICED SMILE AS HE CLOSED
the gap between himself and the American woman.

"Do you need some help with that?" he asked. She was
struggling with a double-size baby stroller and its cargo of
twin boys, who looked to be about a year old. The woman
had one foot locked behind a stroller wheel and the other
leg bracing open the car door as she lifted a squirming
toddler to the backseat. She seemed startled, Wolf thought,
probably because he'd come from behind her, but she
quickly regained as much of her composure as she was
going to get back.

"Why, yes. Thank you, that would be very nice." She
tried to stand up straight, but the car door started to slip.
Wolf grabbed the handle, moving closer to her and looking
directly into her eyes. He thought he saw her guard slip a
bit.

Heinrich Wolf was very much aware of his good looks.
His lean five-eleven frame was topped with a thick mass of
dark curly hair, which he wore long on top and in the back,
short on the sides, as was the fashion. He had a close-
cropped beard and deep, wide-spaced eyes of a startling
blue, now locked on the young mother.

47

"I have two children of my own," Wolf said, smiling at her again. "Of course, they're not twins, like these handsome young men. But they're close in age, so I have an idea of how much work this is." At first she was just glad for the help, but now she seemed happy to have found someone who understood her problems.

"I wish my husband knew how much work these guys are," she blurted. She dropped her eyes, apparently embarrassed at her admission.

"Why don't you let me put this in the trunk for you?" Wolf said, grasping the handles of the stroller.

"That would be great. I want to get these guys home in time for their nap. They miss that and they're cranky all evening."

Wolf watched her as he pushed the buggy to the back end of the car. She was neatly dressed, for an American, but she'd already gone big in the hips and would probably stay that way for the two or three years she and her husband were in Germany.

"You live on the *Kaserne?*" he asked, referring to the housing area provided for soldiers serving at the nearby U.S. Army headquarters. When she did not answer, Wolf thought that perhaps she hadn't heard him. He looked up and found her looking at him directly, and she suddenly seemed capable of suspicion. *Perhaps her husband has warned her to be careful in the wake of these anti-American protests,* Wolf thought.

"I'm sorry," he said, dropping his eyes. "I didn't mean to be too forward."

When he glanced at her again, the American housewife was smiling, her fears quieted. She had convinced herself that this handsome German was making a pass at her.

"I'll just put this in the trunk," Wolf said, pulling the stroller. It took him a few seconds to figure out how to close the huge contraption, but he got it folded before she had the first boy strapped into the car seat. Wolf popped the trunk lid and lifted the carriage into the luggage compartment. Bent over and shielded by the lid, he slipped his shoulder bag off into the deep well behind one of the rear wheels. He quickly unzipped the bag and pulled out a parcel the size of a shoebox, which he hid under some cleaning cloths at the bottom of the well. He stood and closed the trunk just as the woman shut the rear door. Inside the car, one of the twins was yelling for his mother.

"As a matter of fact, I do live on the *Kaserne*," she said, moving toward Wolf. Her voice had changed, and Wolf supposed she was being playful. "Do you ever have occasion to visit?"

Wolf leaned on the car and put his hands in his pockets, flexing his shoulders as he did so, pushing down on his jeans. "No, I have no reason to go there, but I eat lunch here two or three times a week," he said, tossing his head toward the restaurant across the sidewalk.

"Well, perhaps I will see you here," the woman said, smiling nervously.

Wolf shrugged and pushed off the car. "You'd better get these boys home," he said, nodding toward the babies in the backseat. "It sounds like they're ready for a nap."

"Thanks for the help," she said.

"My pleasure," Wolf said. He checked his watch as she drove away. *Three hours,* he thought. *She should be at home by then, eating dinner with her husband in their snug little apartment.* Wolf walked down the street to a *Gasthaus* and ordered a beer. It was a little early for him, not quite two, but he was celebrating a great beginning.

Wolf was an unlikely candidate for the terrorist files of the German Federal Police. The most antisocial thing he might be accused of was that he spent seven of his thirty-one years in university—on his parents' money—without taking a degree. As far as the police were concerned he was a model citizen. He had been very careful to ensure that there was no record of his four-month-old association with the NDP—the Neu Deutschland Party—the newly reconstituted right-wing political group that was absorbing so many of the politically disenfranchised of the old East and West. When Germany had become one again, Wolf was just one of many young Germans who believed the government should be bolder in defining the new nation's world role. He was one of a smaller group who sought to mold a new movement that would goad the German government to take the commanding lead in European and world affairs. And, as he sat drinking his beer and waiting for the first blow of his campaign, he knew he was the first to take action.

When news of the *Texas* accident had broken in Europe, Wolf had wanted the NDP to ride the wave of antinuclear and anti-American anger to a position of power in Europe. But the group leader, a tired old man by the name of Zeitler, resisted Wolf's ideas. So Wolf arranged to meet one on one with the military attaché from the Soviet Embassy, the man through whom the NDP got its financial backing. In a two-hour session on a park bench in Bonn, Wolf managed to convince the minor official that he could offer the Soviets an inexpensive victory that would weaken the United States' military position in Europe. Wolf had done his homework, and he knew that the Soviet military was deeply worried about its own shrinking budget. The Soviet Army had been driven from Europe, and the navy was quickly disappearing from the seas. Wolf knew that nothing could help the Soviet economy bring back the Cold War budgets for ships and aircraft. But he convinced the contact that he could shake up the United States Navy in the Mediterranean, so that the Americans would consider withdrawing of their own accord. Having fewer American ships around wasn't as good as having more Soviet ships, but it was better than nothing.

The Soviets agreed to provide him with money and some other hard-to-come-by support: three fake passports with a set of credit cards for each identity. They also helped him obtain the weapons he planned to use. Once he had secured the promise of financial backing from the Soviets—on a mission-by-mission basis—Wolf murdered Zeitler, the man who welcomed him into the NDP. Now he was about to strike a highly public, if not particularly damaging, blow against the dwindling American presence in Germany. Wolf's ultimate goal was not the demilitarization of Europe as much as it was the consolidation of his own power. He was in a position to single-handedly cause the withdrawal of the United States Navy from the region; such a coup would help him win control of the splinter groups now operating with impunity in a Europe no longer haunted by secret police. Dissatisfied with slow economic reform, these groups were avid for a single leader with the clout to make governments bend. If he forced the hand of the U.S. president, Wolf thought, who else could resist him?

Now, as he sipped the last of his beer and held up a finger for another, he awaited the outcome of the next battle.

Wolf watched the time carefully, pacing himself through a second and third beer. When it was time to leave, he walked to his hotel, stopping at a pharmacy to purchase a pair of inexpensive shears, a disposable razor, and some shaving cream.

The owner of the small hotel, a fat woman with a ready smile, was behind the desk when he entered the lobby.

"*Guten Tag,*" she said, showing bad teeth.

"*Guten Tag,*" Wolf said, smiling. "I will be leaving within the hour. May I clear my bill now and leave the key in the room?"

"Of course," the woman said. "But I will be sorry to see you go." She smiled again at him, suggestively, but Wolf was done here. He returned a colorless grin.

The woman totaled the bill, which Wolf paid in cash.

"Make sure you stop to say good-bye," the woman tried again. "I will have a surprise for you."

"Thank you very much," he said. He thought about offering his hand but decided against it. *Better for her to forget me.*

On the way up the stairs, he checked the back door on the first landing, which was unlocked during the day. He would not go through the lobby again. Back in his room, Wolf packed his meager bag, then stripped to the waist and spread a towel over his shoulders. He cut his own hair, an awkward bowl cut that he would have a barber fix while he waited for the train. He used the shears to cut most of his beard as well. Once he got close to the skin, he lathered his face and began scraping away at the rest of the thick growth of hair. The skin under the beard, which hadn't been shaved in months, was very sensitive, and Wolf cringed each time he drew some of his own blood.

He was finished in thirty minutes. He got on his hands and knees to clean the bathroom floor, then he checked the room again to make sure he hadn't left anything behind. He wrapped the contents of the trashcan, including all the hair clippings, in a newspaper and stuffed that in his bag as well. He was ready to leave by the time the evening news began. He pulled one of the two stuffed chairs in front of the television set and sat with his day-planner book open in his lap. As he expected, the story headlined the local news.

The videotape of the car showed the back end twisted under the rest of the vehicle, like a frightened dog trying to tuck its tail. But the car seemed to be on a road. That would never do. He had planned for it to be in a parking lot on the *Kaserne;* the whole point was that the explosion had to be on the American military base. Wolf reached over and turned up the sound.

> *. . . an American woman and her two children, twin boys a year old. A neighbor said the woman was going to pick up her husband, an American army officer.*

The screen filled with a picture of a woman, her face sagging and tearstained. The face began to speak in English, and then there was a German voice-over.

> *I offered to keep the babies while she went to pick up her husband, but she said the boys would enjoy the ride.*

The newscaster came back on, the photo of the twisted car nestled in the corner of the screen behind her.

> *The bomb exploded just as the car was passing the Military Police checkpoint at the gate. One American Military Police officer was killed at his post, while two more were seriously injured. One of the wounded men is not expected to make it through the night.*

Wolf reached across the space between him and the television and turned down the sound. He flipped his book open to the day's sheet and pulled an index card from a paper clip there. He dialed the number noted in pencil on one side of the card, then flipped it over so that he could read the few lines of text printed neatly on the back.

"Military Police, Desk Sergeant."

Wolf waited until he heard the *click-beep* of the tape machine that recorded all calls to the Military Police desk. Then he spoke, in slow and careful English. "This is Neu Deutschland," Wolf said, unhurried. "The American government did not listen to the public outcry for the withdrawal of the naval forces, and now four people are dead. Our demands are simple: the United States must announce plans to withdraw its naval forces from the Mediterranean within seven days. If it does not, more will die." He paused, ever so slightly. "This is not a threat, but a promise."

Wolf placed the phone back in its cradle and looked around the room. The American woman had almost blown his plan to have the bomb go off on the base by going out again after she said her babies would be napping. *Tough luck for her,* Wolf thought.

He put the index card with the number and message in an ashtray on the sill of the open window and lit the end with a disposable lighter. He watched the thin flames, then peered out at the sky over the roof of the building across the street. He would soon leave Germany again to take his war closer to the enemy. So far, everything was going as he had planned, and he expected to return, if not in legitimate power, at least in real power.

Heinrich Wolf watched the small flames and breathed in the heady smoke of his own dreams.

# 4

## near the Rio Soto La Marina, Mexico
## Training Camp #7
### 16 April

MARK ISEN SHIVERED AND SEARCHED THE EASTERN SKY once again for the first trace of light. He checked his watch and saw, out of the corner of his eye, Lieutenant Cortizo do the same. Three minutes more and they'd spring the ambush. He worked his elbows under him and rocked forward, trying to see through the gloom to where fifteen soldiers of this patrol were hidden along the assault line. They were invisible. He checked to his right where, twenty-five meters away, the two machine-gun teams of the fire support element were set up at the rough edge of a gully. He thought he saw the barrel of one gun begin to take shape as the sky lightened imperceptibly. He heard the soft scraping of gravel behind him and knew that Cortizo was using the tug cord to make sure his men were alert.

The tug cord had been Isen's idea, but he had really intended for them to use it only in the early stages of their training. He had the men put one wrist through a loop in a long piece of communication wire that ran along the line where the patrol lay. The leader could then pull on this cord, and each man would pass the signal down to the next. It was crude but effective. In the beginning of their training, Cortizo had had to pull rather vigorously on several occa-

54

sions to overcome the inertia of the sleeping men he had
been tied to. But Isen and Cortizo had achieved some sort
of breakthrough with the intensified training begun a month
ago.

Looking back on it now, Isen thought that the soldiers
had left behind—perhaps at the water's edge by the confidence obstacle course—the timidity that had been holding
them back. It did not happen magically, or all at once,
but the indicators of change were there. These men were
becoming soldiers. They stayed awake, even out here on
ambush, one of the most tedious missions they practiced.

Down the line, they responded to the signal tug on the
wire. Some of them were even far enough along in their
development as soldiers to anticipate the pulls. These were
the ones Cortizo had his eye on to recommend for promotion to noncommissioned officers.

Isen looked back to the horizon. *The sky is so big here,*
he thought to himself again. The world out here on the flat
plain seemed to be made of two shallow plates. One was
the earth, brown and right side up, and one was the sky,
inverted and matched at the edges with the earth. At night,
the sky was a brilliant swirl of stars, so many lights that it
looked like daylight glimpsed through black cloth. At this
high elevation and this far from artificial illumination, the
stars revealed themselves, a gift for anyone hardy enough
to shiver through a desert night. During the day, the sky
was malevolent, a flat furnace that rested just above the
head and turned the landscape white hot.

This time of the morning was the most tranquil. For an
hour or so the heat would be bearable, even welcome for
the relief it brought. There would be color along the edges
of the visible world, along the horizons as the light chased
away the dark. Isen appreciated the peacefulness, even
though it gave the lie to what they were about to do.

A few feet away, Cortizo looked at him, nodded, then
pressed with both hands the firing device for the mines.
The blast rolled over them like heavy surf, and the machine
guns off to the right were hammering away at the target
area even before the last sound of the explosion had left
their ringing ears.

The gun teams were doing well, firing a choreographed fire that wouldn't overheat the barrels, but kept a steady stream of lead on the target. Isen then heard the seemingly insignificant tapping sound of the rifles and the compressed-air *ploop* of the grenade launchers. He stole a glance at the kill zone. Tracers from the assault team and the support team, which were firing at right angles to each other, formed a deadly thatchwork of white over the area. The forty-millimeter grenades burst like dangerous white flowers, appearing and disappearing across the tumult.

*It's working,* Isen allowed himself. *It's coming together.* He listened in his imagination and heard the machine operating as designed. *Click, click, click.*

Cortizo came to a kneeling position and held the aluminum tube of a hand-fired signal flare out in front of him. He struck the bottom of the tube with the palm of his hand, and a red streak jumped out of the other end and cut across the kill zone. This was the signal for the fire-support team to shift fire. Isen looked over at the machine guns, and the gunners dutifully swung their weapons away, off to the far side of the kill zone. The theory was that they would hit anything trying to get out of the ambush on that side, or anyone trying to reinforce the enemy.

*Great, great,* Isen thought. *Click, click, click.*

Cortizo was on his feet now. He stood and fired a few rounds from a standing position. Then he rushed forward into the kill zone. The assault line also stood, and the fifteen other men swept across the area, quickly but under control, firing as they moved, keeping the correct interval between them, sweeping the objective and stopping in a skirmish line on the far side. Cortizo called for the search team, and four soldiers dropped off the line and entered the kill zone again from the far side, ready to search the dead.

Cortizo gave the signal for cease-fire, and Isen stood up and hit the stop button on his chronometer.

"Good job, good job," he said enthusiastically. "That was only ninety seconds from start to finish."

Most of the soldiers couldn't understand him, but there was no mistaking the upbeat tone, and in the now trustworthy light of predawn, they could see his face and gauge his reaction to the training mission. Cortizo could understand him, but Cortizo didn't hang on Isen's approval. He valued Isen's experience and listened carefully to the lessons the American combat veteran had to offer, but he clearly had his own agenda. And, as much as Isen wished the lieutenant would take everything offered as gospel, he respected Cortizo's independence.

"Yes, this much went well," Cortizo said as he cleared the chamber of his weapon. "And of course a quick withdrawal from here is as important as anything else."

"What are the parts of the withdrawal?" Isen quizzed him.

Cortizo was a proud young man, but he accepted Isen as his teacher and considered it a point of pride that he was able to answer these questions. They gave him a chance to prove that he had read and assimilated the information in the U.S. Army Field Manuals Isen had given him.

"I check for friendly casualties, then move out of the objective area to await pickup. I take with me any prisoners, and I must make sure that I have accounted for all my men."

Cortizo was working off a set of assumptions that Isen was trying to fight against. The Mexican officer was preparing for battle only with an enemy that would not fight back after the initial contact, an enemy who would never use a reaction force, would never attempt more than an unsophisticated counterambush. He was preparing to fight all the old battles again—after all the rules had changed.

All across the country, other American advisers were attempting the same things Isen was, and none were meeting with any great success. Yet this was the mission the U.S. Army had been given, and as with every mission, the work was being carried out by individuals, often overworked, attempting to apply a mix of imagination, skill, and persistence where it looked as if giving up was the thing to do.

Even with all the progress the soldiers had made with their skills, there was still a tremendous inertia on the part of the leaders, starting with Cortizo, who refused to think that the coming fight would present any new challenges, and ending with the Mexican Army brass in Mexico City, who were still intent on limiting the effectiveness of the American advisers. Isen could make progress on the small stage peopled by this one company, but he was not going to gain wide acceptance, nor was he likely to get the Mexicans to see that they were engaged in something new.

The reality of the situation was that Cortizo's men were training to take on drug smugglers who were, with increasing frequency and boldness, using Mexico as a staging area for shipments into the United States. But even after the counterambush that Isen had seen on his first day in-country, even after mounting evidence that the druggies were not going to give up easily but were willing to stand and fight it out with the Mexican authorities, including small units of the Mexican Army, Cortizo and most of his supervisors continued to think of them as mere bandits who would melt away at the first sign of a serious threat. Isen wasn't convinced this was the case, and he certainly thought the assumption dangerous.

"You can't ease up just because you've assaulted the objective. You've got to conduct your searches, account for your people, and get out of the area as quickly as possible. If you have indirect fire assets, you'll call for fire on this kill zone as soon as you're clear."

Cortizo couldn't resist disagreeing. He lowered his head to hide, halfway, his patronizing smile.

"Captain Isen, we are not going to have to use mortar fire against these people. This is not open warfare against a modern army. We are dealing with *banditos*. I believe we have nothing to fear from them as long as we surprise them."

Isen resisted bringing up the night at the airstrip. He had mentioned it only once before and found it to be a tremendous sore point. Apparently, Major Escobar, Cortizo's supervisor in that operation, had covered up what had happened. And Gaspar, the long-gone American adviser, hadn't mentioned it to anyone for fear of uncovering his own poor showing.

Isen and Cortizo had been over this ground before, but

Isen wasn't about to let it rest. He was nothing if not tenacious and believed that a large measure of his success as a commander in combat came from his unrelenting insistence on doing things correctly. That didn't always mean doing it by the book, but it did mean always rejecting the half-effort, refusing to settle for appearance over substance. His philosophy had earned him, among his own soldiers, a reputation as a hard trainer. And the men he had trained had earned their own reputation as good fighters.

"If you train for the most difficult mission, then you can handle anything. If you train only for the easy mission, the *expected,*" Isen emphasized, "you may be caught short if the enemy is more resourceful than you anticipated."

As he always did when this topic came up, Cortizo listened respectfully but offered no other comment. He looked at Isen blankly, as someone might indulge the stories of a senile elder, and in his eyes Isen saw the great unchangeable weight that would resist whatever the Americans tried to accomplish. When Isen was finished talking, Cortizo looked around to where the men were forming up for the march back to the barracks.

"We had better get moving, Captain Isen. We don't want to be walking when the sun is up in earnest."

Isen walked at the rear of the little march column, off to one side so he could avoid most of the dust the men kicked up. As they moved, one soldier began singing a marching song. Others picked it up, and the group got into step, matching the cadence of their march with the cadence of their song . . . left, right, left.

In a moment Isen heard the unmistakable long-legged stride of his assistant, an American NCO named Worden. Jack Worden was a staff sergeant, a twenty-eight-year-old career infantryman with ten years of service, eight of them with line units. Assigning NCO assistants was something new, another attempt by the American army to strengthen Operation Sentinel. Worden had come down shortly after Isen had taken the Mexicans through the confidence obstacle course. Cortizo later told Isen that the Mexican soldiers thought the two Americans made a funny-looking pair.

Where Isen was of average height and plain features, Worden made a quick and lasting impression on whomever he met. The sergeant stood six feet five and a half inches tall. He had a head of bright red hair, and his rail-thin arms and legs were liberally sprinkled with freckles. He was loud and friendly, almost a stereotype, and he had made an immediate impact on the unit. He had taken it upon himself to teach the Mexican noncoms everything he knew about being a noncommissioned officer, which was considerable. Isen had heard him several times telling his charges the overused, but no less true for that, dictum that officers plan things and NCOs run the army. Worden was positive and cheerful and willing to do anything that the Mexican soldiers had to do. In response, the Mexicans took an immediate liking to him, and they clustered around him on and off duty. Even the ones who couldn't speak English listened to his stories, told in a mixture of Spanish and English and unrolled in the deep timbre of his native Oklahoma, laughing whenever he did and basking in the glow of this immensely likable American.

"Hey, sir," Worden addressed Isen as he always did. "Why'd they stop after actions at the objective? Why didn't they do the drill all the way through to the end, pulling off and stuff?"

"They still think the bad guys are always going to die in place or run away with their tails between their legs when the army shows up," Isen said.

"Well, you have to admit that it would take a pretty good sized gang to stand up to an infantry platoon in an open firefight."

"That's not the point," Isen said. "We're supposed to be training them to be soldiers, according to how soldiers do things in our army. And we do it all the way through." The argument sounded straightforward enough when he said it out loud, but Isen and Worden both knew that it wasn't as simple as that.

"From what I've seen, we're asking them to make some major adjustments, though, sir," Worden offered. "First of all, even though these guys are fairly well motivated, the bottom line is: they want to do their year and get out. They aren't well trained, and they got sent down here"—Worden glanced around to see who might hear—"as a way of fucking with us. Then, we're asking them to be policemen too."

"I know, I know," Isen said. He unsnapped his canteen cover and pulled the sweating plastic bottle from its quilted holder. "And I know that this is only the beginning of the problems they have." Isen took a long drink from the canteen, letting some of the water run down his chin and throat, luxurious and cold, being wasteful only because he knew they would be able to fill up again in camp in an hour or so.

"Still, we've already overcome a lot of problems here, sir," Worden said. "I mean, they stay awake now when they're getting ready to attack. And they keep their weapons and equipment clean. When I got here, I'd be willing to bet there were guys around here who didn't fire their weapons in a fight because they didn't want to have to clean them. Know what I'm saying, sir?"

"Yeah, you're right, I guess," Isen said, wiping his face with his shirt sleeve. "At least we got the higher-ups to issue more ammo so we could run these live-fire training exercises," Isen said.

Worden chewed the inside of his lip. *I should've come clean sooner,* he thought. *Now it'll bring the old man down worse.* He considered staying quiet but decided to plunge ahead.

"That's not exactly what happened, sir."

Isen didn't even look at him, and there was a second's hesitation before he spoke. "Oh?"

*Here goes,* Worden thought.

"I kind of finagled the ammo . . ."

Isen looked at him now.

". . . by trading off with one of the other companies." Worden swallowed. "Well, two other companies. We have three companies' worth of ammo out here," he said.

"Does Cortizo know about this?" Isen asked.

"No. Me and the supply sergeant are keeping it quiet." Worden grinned. He was proud, thinking he had anticipated all the angles.

Ordinarily, it might have worked: the Mexican brass

61

wasn't all that interested in backdoor trading among NCOs. But someone had recently decided that a good way to keep the Americans in check was to tighten up on the ammo. Worden had reacted to this latest move, but Isen couldn't help but feel that someone was watching.

"Don't you think that the brass will find out eventually? They keep records just like we do of where the ammo goes, who gets what. Don't you think that Cortizo might say something at his next meeting? Maybe ask the other commanders how their live-fire training went?"

Worden looked down at his boots. "We could get into hot water, I know, but we gotta be ready to fight." He looked up, resolved now to speak. "The more live fires we do, the more ready we'll be to fight the druggies."

Worden looked at Isen, a trace of a grin on his face. "And it's turning out that we have to fight the Mexican brass, too, for training resources. I figure I won this round."

Isen thought there was something humorous about this: the Mexicans did have something to worry about if there were a half-dozen GIs in the country as resourceful as Worden. Isen shook his head and felt the familiar sense of frustration. He'd been sent down here to train soldiers, and he had been confident all along that he could do that job. In spite of language barriers and the Mexicans' lack of basic training in things such as marksmanship and weapons maintenance, in spite of poor logistical support and the inhospitable climate, in spite of the fact that the hierarchy of the Mexican Army was conspiring against them, he and Worden had accomplished a great deal. But there were still some nagging points. Isen sometimes felt sympathetic to the Mexicans; he could understand their resentment. For the most part, however, he was frustrated.

Mark Isen had spent his adult life preparing for war, and he had spent a part of his time in the army actually fighting a war. But that had been against an enemy that fought back, an enemy who wore different uniforms and used tactics that were recognizably similar to what Isen knew. Now he felt as if he were in some sort of limbo. He had expected Operation Sentinel to be a kind of guerrilla war, and he'd devoted a good deal of time while he was at Fort Benning to reading up on the U.S. Army's experiences fighting insurgents, from Vietnam, back through the Philippine campaigns at the turn of the century, to the Indian wars, and even as far back as the French and Indian War. He had believed, on the day he left for Mexico, that he could make the transition. But it was harder than he'd thought. Here he was, a soldier, goading reluctant men to fight criminals who belonged to no state, who recognized no single leader, who didn't even have a common goal—except making money. All the lines were blurred, the rules of doubtful use. It reminded Isen of the old Chinese curse: *May you live in interesting times.*

As they walked along Isen looked up at the distant mountains visible to the west. From here they looked like a low, dark blue wall that began and ended in hazy light. He thought of the mountains running their thousands of miles deep into South America, the great ranges that made up the spine of the two continents. Somewhere to the south, within sight of those mountains and sometimes in the mountains themselves, were the men who made this fighting necessary, the processors and the growers and the shippers and the monied overseers like feudal lords.

All along that spine were countries that had been treated poorly by their rich neighbors to the north; now they reveled in the problems the U.S. was having. There were South American politicians, Isen knew, who were glad to see the American president come, hat in hand, asking for help from their own impoverished nations. There were others among them who feared the presence of the American military, men who had long memories and would not forget that the U.S. had invaded southern neighbors before. Some of the countries cooperated, Isen believed, out of fear that the gringos would come in force to smash those poor countries at the source of the flow of drugs. The Mexican resentment seemed to be mostly a matter of pride.

Some of Isen's peers scoffed at those notions, at the idea that sovereign countries had anything to fear from the U.S. They pointed out that the invasion of Panama had been brought about only after the dictator in that country had kept the duly elected government from power. But the evidence was *here,* Isen thought, as he looked down at his feet shuffling through the Mexican sand. *I am here,* he thought, *an American soldier armed and within sight of those mountains. Who's to say that more won't come behind me?*

"I had a buddy killed in Panama," Worden said to Isen as they walked. "And I was pretty pissed off, you know; 'cause the Panamanians probably could have done the job themselves a few months earlier if we'd helped them. You don't have time to second-guess the politicians when you're strapping on the 'chute at Fort Bragg, waiting for the word to load up." Worden paused, and Isen had the feeling that he was weighing what he was going to say next. "But we do think about it," Worden said, "later, I mean."

"The British used to call little scraps like this one 'brushfire wars,' " Isen said. "I think that, in spite of what happened in the Gulf, this kind of stuff"—he gestured vaguely out to the distant mountains, and his sweep included the Mexican soldiers toiling up the slope before them—"is what the army is going to be doing from now on."

"Yeah," Worden agreed, suddenly silent. He was thinking about his friend, who'd been buried the day after Christmas while Operation Just Cause was just winding down in Panama. "Weird as shit, ain't it?"

Isen nodded. Off to the west, the blue mountains marched in a solid line toward South America.

That evening, Isen was propped up on his cot, holding a heavy paperback over his head as he read by the light of a battery-powered lamp. He dozed as he read, and the threat of the book crashing down on his nose kept jarring him awake. He had just about decided to put the book on his chest and give in to the tiredness when he heard someone outside.

"Cap'n Isen?" It was Worden.

"Come on in," Isen said, rubbing his eyes as he swung his feet off the cot. Worden was a night person. On more than one occasion, he'd stayed in Isen's hootch talking animatedly even as Isen's eyes drooped. The man had incredible energy.

"I got these in the mail today," Worden said as he pushed back the canvas curtain that served as a door. "Thought you might like to see this." He snapped one of several newspapers from under his arm, holding the front page out to Isen. The paper was the Columbus, Georgia, *Ledger-Enquirer,* which served the city outside Fort Benning. Worden's wife and two children were living at Benning—the sergeant's last posting—while he was away. Isen's eyes were drawn to the banner headline: *Sailors Murdered by Terrorists in "War" on U.S.*

As fast as Isen could read, Worden narrated. He seemed to have the article committed to memory.

"Somebody killed these three sailors while they were on liberty in Italy," Worden said before Isen could get through the first paragraph. "Said it was because we didn't respond within a week after that bombing on that *Kaserne* in Germany—when that lady and her kids got blown away."

Worden dumped what looked like a week's worth of newspapers on Isen's cot.

"They said they want the navy out of the Med," Isen said. "I guess they were serious."

Isen shuffled through the papers. The three sailors, none of them from the USS *Texas,* had been sitting in an outdoor café in Naples when a gunman on a motor scooter drove up and sprayed them with automatic weapons fire. They didn't have a chance to react. A group calling itself the Neu Deutschland—for New Germany—Party claimed responsibility and said that the people of Europe demanded that the U.S. military leave the Mediterranean and Europe.

"Did you get to the part about us having to withdraw within two weeks?" Worden said, incredulous, agitated.

Isen read farther. "Actually, this NDP group said that we have a week to announce *plans* for getting out."

"And all the antinuke granola crunchers are coming out of the woodwork," Worden added.

Isen had turned the page to an article about related demonstrations in the United States. "At home too. It says that fifteen thousand people marched in Washington, protesting anything connected with nuclear power.''

"They're on the side of the cocksuckers who killed those sailors?'' Worden flared.

Isen looked up. "The protest took place before the murders.''

"I hate all those marchers, anyway,'' Worden said. "They're always looking for a way to shit on the military.''

"Protest is a fundamental right in America,'' Isen said. Then he realized he was preaching, so he shut up. Worden knew the score; he was just letting off steam.

Worden showed Isen a photo buried inside another edition. White pieces of tables and chairs lay scattered on a wet street. "Can you beat this?'' Worden said. "Those three sailors were sitting around drinking beer, and somebody blows them away just because they're Americans.'' He shook his head, perplexed. "At least when you're in a war you know to keep your head down,'' he said.

Isen looked around at the bare concrete blocks, at the holstered pistol tucked at the head of the cot. "It's only a little better down here,'' Isen said. "We're getting it at both ends too.''

He hadn't meant to make the analogy obscene, but now it seemed appropriate. "The druggies will shoot, and the Mexicans are just as likely to pull the rug out from under us any chance they get.''

Worden piled his remaining papers on the cot for Isen to peruse. "I'm watching my back, sir. You can bet on that.''

# 5

## near Tampico, Mexico
### 20 April

FINALLY, IT WAS JACK WORDEN'S IDEA THAT BROKE THEM, in his phrase, out of the minors and into the bigs.

Worden came into Isen's hootch on a Sunday morning. Isen was sleeping in.

"Captain Isen," he called from the door. "Yo, sir."

"What is it?" Isen's face was under the nylon poncho liner. He'd been having a dream about Adrienne. The two of them had been at the beach, and Mark was rubbing suntan oil on her shoulders as she lay facedown, talking to him about getting out of the army. When this dream-Adrienne rolled over onto her back, she'd become Kathleen Turner. And since the characters who populated Mark Isen's dreams never questioned the logic of what was happening, he had just leaned over to kiss her when Sergeant Worden's voice chased it all away.

"Can I come in, sir?"

"Sure." Isen rolled over onto his stomach. No sense in advertising what he'd been dreaming about.

"Sorry to bother you this early, sir," Worden said, not without sincerity. "But I just saw Lieutenant Cortizo down the hill, and he told me we're going to have a visitor, some general."

Isen sat up. "Right now?"

"No, sir, tomorrow."

Isen fell back on the cot again. "So why are you waking me up now?"

"Thing is, sir, I know how you and Lieutenant Cortizo have been racking your brains to figure out how we can get the Mexican Army to commit this company to an operation. Well, I came up with an idea."

Isen sat up on the edge of his cot, pulling the poncho liner around his middle. He was still a little fuzzy around the edges from sleep, and with Sergeant Worden, it always paid to be sharp. "Go ahead."

"Lieutenant Cortizo says the only reason this general is coming is because the Mexican president is leaning on the army big time—he wants something done. Apparently one guy told the president that none of these units were really ready. But then the president found out that none of the brass had even been around to visit; you know, get a first-hand glimpse of things. So the boss picks this real hard-charger of a general, a guy with political ambitions, maybe, to come out and make an assessment."

"Yeah?" Isen offered.

"So this guy is practically on our side already."

As Worden talked Isen went through a range of reactions. At first he was flabbergasted that Worden would suggest something as wild as he'd cooked up that morning. Isen didn't interrupt, but only out of respect for the NCO. As he listened he realized that although the ethics of the scheme were a bit questionable, it wasn't as dangerous as he'd thought initially. While Worden talked, Isen nodded his head.

"If we give this a try," Isen said, "there are lots of things that can go wrong that would embarrass us."

"Yes, sir, but even if we worst-case it—say, for instance, that the Sentinel commander got wind of it—we can always say that we were just trying to get the Mexican Army to do what they had agreed to do all along, which is to commit these units. We've been down here for weeks, and whenever we make any progress, they think of ten ways to beat us back down—like those bullshit ammo restrictions. You heard those other guys at the meeting: all of the American teams are in the same boat, and the boat is making no headway. If we don't do something, we won't do anything. That's not what we were sent here for."

Isen smiled. Worden was an optimist, first, last, always. Several times over the last week or so, Isen had thought he detected a dulling of that enthusiasm, a winding down brought about by all the sitting around, the repetitive training, the lack of free time. He wondered if he weren't agreeing to this just so Worden would feel encouraged again.

It was true that the other American advisers, with whom Isen met monthly in Tampico, were expressing the same concerns. And no one was doing anything about it. *What the hell*, he thought. *I'm in charge; I'm the one who'll take the rap if there is one.*

"Okay, let's try it," Isen said.

"Good. We've got 'til tomorrow at noon to get ready," Worden said. "It'll work, sir, you'll see."

*Famous last words,* Isen thought.

He lay back down on his cot, hoping that Kathleen Turner was still roaming around in his subconscious, waiting for him to return.

Brigadier General Xavier Manuel Acata de Querros and his staff came wheeling up in two shiny, decidedly unmilitary four-wheel-drive vehicles that sent clouds of dust off the road and out over the small valley below the camp. When the general stepped from the front seat of the lead vehicle, Isen was surprised at what he saw. Querros looked no more than forty years old. He was fit and trim, with the build of a long-distance runner, and Isen was a bit ashamed that he had assumed the general would be fat and slow moving. This energetic officer looked like a picture-postcard general.

Cortizo had his men formed up on a dirt square down by the road. He and Isen had arranged for the general to make a tour of the billets area, completely overhauled since Worden's arrival, then they would watch Cortizo's soldiers run through a bayonet-assault course and some recently completed squad battle-drill lanes they'd begun using only the week before.

As Cortizo trooped the line with the general, Isen could see that the lieutenant had pressed his lips together in a tight line that might have been a grin; with Cortizo such a sign meant he was fairly overcome with emotion.

"And this is our American adviser, Captain Mark Isen," Cortizo said as the general moved to Isen's position in the back of the formation.

"I am very happy to meet you, Captain," Querros said. His English wasn't as clear as Cortizo's, but as always, it was better than Isen's Spanish. "We are happy to have you in our country, and I am sure that there is a most helpful exchange of ideas going on here."

Isen had prepared himself for the cold shoulder. This sarcasm was worse. He knew that Querros had come out here to see how much progress the Americans were making with these companies. Maybe he would see things clearly; maybe he would dream up new ways to pull the plug on Operation Sentinel.

"Thank you, sir. I am happy to be here."

Cortizo seemed too distracted to notice that Worden was missing. He was trying to steer the general along without appearing to steer. "I would like to take you through the billets here, General."

"That will be fine," Querros said imperially.

As Cortizo and Querros walked away and the NCOs took charge of the troops to get them ready for the next part of the demonstration, Isen got a look at Querros's entourage. There was a sprinkling of captains and majors, none of whom showed any interest in talking to the American. What caught Isen's eye was the photographer. The young man ran ahead of Querros and Cortizo and snapped pictures continuously as they talked, and all the while the general beamed pleasantly.

*A publicity hound,* Isen thought. *How handy.*

Worden waited at the bayonet-assault course. With him were two American men in civilian clothes, one of them festooned with cameras and camera bags. Isen got there ahead of the general's party, just about the same time that the first troops were getting ready to run through.

The course consisted of three parallel lanes, each about two hundred and fifty meters long with various obstacles along the way. The idea was for the soldier to run along one lane, negotiating the obstacles as fast as he could. Each time he encountered a dummy obstacle, he had to stop and engage it using the bayonet fighting skills that Worden and the Mexican NCOs had taught out on the field below the troop barracks. It was a completely exhausting few minutes and a wonderful photo opportunity.

The general's photographer got there ahead of the rest of the party. He nodded politely to the other photographer, then trotted out onto the course to set up some shots. Isen wondered if the general would pose with a bayonet, perhaps stab a few targets.

Cortizo arrived with Querros in tow, and there were a few seconds of confusion as the general's group sorted itself out, looking for a place to stand that would afford each the chance to see what was going on, with the higher-ranking officers closer to the throne. Isen pulled Cortizo aside.

"We have an American reporter and photographer here to do a story about your company's combat readiness."

"What?"

It was obvious to Isen that Cortizo did not consider this a pleasant surprise.

"Look, over there, with Sergeant Worden."

Cortizo looked over, and Worden grinned widely at him. The two men with him waved as if they knew Cortizo.

"What is going on here?" Cortizo demanded.

Isen hadn't anticipated that he would become angry at the surprise. He put the answer as straightforwardly as he could.

"Your general will have a chance to appear in the American press," Isen said.

Cortizo considered that a moment. He seemed to want to say more to Isen, but the NCO who was running the course called to him that everything was ready. Cortizo turned away and nodded at the general and the NCO. The latter sent the lead soldiers running to begin their assault.

Over his shoulder, Cortizo said, "We'd better tell the general."

The soldiers were very enthusiastic in their assault, and Cortizo had to raise his voice and lean close to Querros to make himself heard. Isen watched the men in the course, trying to appear uninterested in the American reporters and whatever it was that Cortizo was reporting to Querros. The general raised his hand and said something to Cortizo, and the lieutenant called to the NCO at the trench. A few seconds later, the troops at the beginning of the course were held up. Isen looked over to Querros, who was beaming and gesturing to Worden and the two men with him.

"Come here, please, Sergeant Worden," Cortizo called.

Worden raised a broad smile and led his two charges over to the general's circle. Isen edged closer.

"General Querros, this is Sergeant Worden, another one of our advisers," Cortizo said.

Worden snapped a salute, then took the general's offered hand. "Pleased to meet you, sir." Worden did a half turn to include the men behind him in the circle.

"This is Mr. Jon Welch of *The Washington Post*," Worden said. "And this is Mr. Kurt McClusker who is, as you can see, a photographer. He also works for the *Post*."

*Geez,* Isen thought to himself, *couldn't you have picked something a little less conspicuous?*

Brigadier General Querros was suddenly quite animated.

"Ah, yes," Querros said. "Tell me about your story."

Isen had never laid eyes on the man Worden introduced as Jon Welch, but he was impressed immediately.

"Well, General . . . is that Q-U-E-R-O-S?" Welch asked, snapping out a notebook. Isen cringed; the notebook was a green army memo book.

"Two *r*'s" Querros said.

"Well, we're doing a story about the combat readiness of these units participating in Operation Sentinel. Sergeant Worden here tells me that this company in particular has made great strides under your guidance."

"Yes, yes, that is true," Querros said.

Now it was Cortizo's turn to grimace. General Querros, who was responsible for this training in all the states of northern Mexico, had never before visited Cortizo's company or any other company assigned to Operation Sentinel.

The general held his hand up, Caesar-like, and the NCO at the start line yelled for the soldiers to resume the assault. Querros kept talking to the reporter, but Isen couldn't hear what was being said because of all the shouting and firing of blank ammunition. He watched the men go through the obstacles, and he had to admit they showed as much spirit as he'd seen at any such training in the United States. He was musing on how much progress they'd made since his first night in the field when Cortizo, still following the general at close range, caught Isen's eye and made a *Come here* signal with one hand.

Isen waved back.

Now General Querros was down at the very beginning of the course, holding a rifle, with bayonet attached, in his clean hands. The last of the soldiers were still running through the course, though no one was paying them any attention. The entourage had moved in a small cloud behind the general and was now clustered around, hanging on every word he said. As the noise from the soldiers died down, Isen could hear them.

"The Mexican people are very proud, very nationalistic," Querros was saying. "And that aggressive spirit is carried over to our army. We are not a big army," he said, pausing a bit with the English. He said something in Spanish to Cortizo, who supplied him with the word he was looking for. "But do not underestimate us."

Welch was scribbling down every word Querros uttered.

"I know that the American people are glad to have you on our side in this epic struggle," Welch said.

Isen wished he'd quit pouring it on so thick.

"Could we get a picture of you, sir," Welch asked, "attacking one of these . . . what do you call them? Targets?"

"They're called dummies," Worden said helpfully.

Querros obliged, smiling as he stuck the bayonet into the first of the dummies on the course. He warmed to the sound of the shutter snapping, and he stabbed it a second time, then a third. On the fourth thrust, he let out a yell of some sort. "Eee-yup!"

Welch and McClusker couldn't have been more pleased. The photographer was snapping pictures at a rapid-fire pace; Welch was scribbling away as Querros talked. Cortizo stood woodenly in the back, watching the whole thing suspiciously.

"So tell me, General," Welch said, looking up from his pad. "When do you think this company will actually be committed to the fighting?"

The general paused for a moment, then looked down at the rifle in his hands as if he wasn't sure what he was holding.

"I'm not sure I can say," Querros answered.

*He's going to sidestep this one,* Isen thought.

But Welch was good.

"Oh, of course I know you can't tell me when this particular company will be going into action. But on the average, say, how long does it take before these units are ready?"

One of the general's entourage was flipping through a notebook he carried, probably looking for something to give the American reporter that would deflect this line of questioning.

"You said that these men were well trained, sir," Welch persisted, flipping back a page or two in his notes to make sure. "I was just wondering how long they'll have to wait before they are committed. Don't soldiers get stale sitting around waiting for something to happen?" As he said this, Welch looked around for someone to agree with him. The general's straphangers backed away or looked down at their feet, as if Welch had just asked who wanted to fight.

*This is it,* Isen thought. *He can make a big splash here and come down publicly on the side of the president and what the president wants to have happen—or he can side with the old guard in the army and tell us to go fuck ourselves.*

"Yes, Mr. Welsh," Querros said, mispronouncing the name for the first time. "I did say these men were ready, and so they are."

Querros climbed back across a shallow-trench obstacle and motioned for Cortizo. The lieutenant came forward, moving stiffly as ever.

"You have done a good job here, Lieutenant," Querros said. "This is the best camp and the best-trained unit I have seen in all of northern Mexico."

Querros took Cortizo's hand and shook it. As he did, he looked for the photographer. McClusker obliged him by snapping a few more pictures.

"You are ready to proceed to the next step in our plan to rid Mexico of these drug smugglers." Querros spat to emphasize his disgust. "This way," he said, smiling broadly again, "all of these American soldiers can return home to their families."

It was clear that Cortizo had no idea what was going on, and neither could Isen assess exactly what it was the general was saying, but he figured there would be time for that later.

Querros and his party went to their shiny jeeps straight from the bayonet course. He let McClusker take a few more shots of him alongside his vehicle, and Welch obligingly looked inside at all the appointments. Just before he drove off, Querros had one of his aides give Welch the address of his headquarters.

"You be sure to send me copies of whatever you publish," Querros said. "I know you will tell the American people the truth about what you have seen down here." He waved again—a gentle, papal gesture this time—as the first vehicle drove off.

Isen looked over at Worden, who had stayed a safe distance away.

"I think it worked, Captain," Worden said happily.

Isen gave him a stern look to quiet him, then looked for Cortizo. The lieutenant was getting some instructions from a major who remained behind with the second of the general's jeeps.

When Worden was closer, Isen said "Let's keep a lid on it for a few minutes until we see how our friend reacts."

Welch and McClusker stood by, looking quite proud of themselves. Cortizo walked up to the four Americans, holding a sheet of notepaper in his hand.

"Who are these men?" he said to Worden.

Worden looked at Isen for help. Cortizo looked as ruffled

as Isen had ever seen him: his mouth was a thin line, and he gripped the balled up paper in a white-knuckled hand. Isen nodded to Worden.

"These here are some friends of mine from the headquarters down in Tampico," Worden said.

Cortizo's mouth dropped open, but Worden didn't miss a beat.

"This is Staff Sergeant McCallum . . ."

The photographer stepped toward Cortizo and nodded his head. "Sir."

"And this is Sergeant First Class Wagers."

The Welch character, the one who'd done all the talking, stepped forward. "You don't have to thank us, sir. We know how hard you all been working up here, and we're just glad to be able to help out."

Isen shook his head. He should have guessed that anybody with enough balls to impersonate a reporter from one of the nation's most prestigious newspapers, then to bamboozle a general from the host country—and he had insisted that Querros commit himself—would say anything to a lieutenant like Cortizo.

Isen bit his lip. He had hoped to carry the ruse far enough to fool Cortizo, but that hadn't worked. He had risked the relationship he'd built up over the last two months, all in a harebrained scheme to force the hand of the Mexican Army. *I must be out of my fucking mind,* he thought to himself.

Cortizo, his face the same inscrutable mask it always was, unfolded the paper in his hand.

"The general's chief aide tells me that I must report to his headquarters in Mexico City next week with a plan for using my company as a reaction force for all of Tamaulipas State."

"Hot damn!" Worden whooped, slapping Welch/Wagers hard on the back. "We'll be moving now!" Worden saluted happily and the three NCOs walked off together, no doubt to do some celebrating down in the village.

"I'm sorry we didn't ask you about this beforehand," Isen said. "But I figured you probably wouldn't go along with it."

"You are no doubt correct there, Captain," Cortizo said. "But I know it is frustrating for you, encountering resistance at every turn."

Cortizo was too much of a professional to say anything more damning of his own army to an outsider. But in the awkward silence, he and Isen shared the knowledge that this first battle, against the intransigence of the Mexican Army, was a necessary first step to the work still ahead.

"Perhaps I should take a lesson or two from you Americans," Cortizo said.

Down the hill, Worden, Wagers, and McCallum were laughing and shouting, and McCallum was pretending to take pictures of the other two as they walked and ran.

"That took *cojones*," Cortizo said.

"Or lack of brains," Isen added. "And if I were you, I'd be selective about the lessons you learn from us."

# 6

## Neu-Ulm, Germany
## 20 April

ERNST JUNGER SAT ON HIS COAT, WRAPPED THE EMPTY
sleeves around his middle, and settled farther into the
wooden bench seat.

*"Damn drafty in here,"* he thought to himself. *"Why
can't old Dufte keep this place heated properly?"*

He looked out the window at the next building on the
street. Before the American exodus from Germany, it had
been an officer's club for a nearby U.S. Army base. For
years he'd watched raucous lieutenants and captains and
their overdressed wives gather there for lunch. Off to the
right, he could see the wall that marked the far bank of the
Donau River that separated Neu-Ulm—New Ulm—from
the medieval city of Ulm on the opposite shore. He
couldn't see, from this angle, the tower of the great cathedral, but he was comforted just knowing it was there, lit
by the early morning sun, four hundred years old, steady,
imperturbable. *The cathedral stood above this river long
before there was such a thing as America,* he told himself
again. *And it will be here when they are completely gone.*

He turned back to the interior of the *Gasthaus*, the local
café, and caught the proprietor's eye. He raised his empty
teacup, and the man nodded. Dufte knew exactly how he

took his tea. Ernst Junger had been coming to this same *Gasthaus* for eleven years. Only rarely did he use it for meetings, but this was to be one of those days. He was to meet Wolf here and give him the good news and the bad about Ernst's trip to Italy.

"Ernst."

Junger turned away suddenly from the window and his reverie.

"Hello, Heinrich. Sit down and join me. Would you like some tea?"

Wolf slid onto the wooden bench, his back to the wall. "You look well," he said.

Junger smiled. "The sun probably did me some good."

Wolf watched in silence as an old woman brought over two cups of tea, set them on the table, and turned away, without saying a word.

"The old lady is not happy about being here this early in the morning," Junger said. "Her husband and I have been friends for years, and I asked him if I could use the place this morning. They do not open for another few hours—I didn't expect him to send her along to serve us."

Wolf took a sip of the hot, sweet tea. "So tell me about your trip," Wolf said.

Wolf had read all about the murder of the three sailors in Italy—Wolf's idea, carried out by Junger. The older man traveled to Italy, hired the gunmen, and made the payments. Wolf had seen the results in the papers and on the television news; now he wanted Junger's version.

"The operation went off pretty much like clockwork," Junger said. "It was easier than I anticipated to find men for this kind of work. Perhaps Italy is full of gangsters, just like in the movies." He smiled awkwardly at the joke.

Wolf obliged him with a smile in return. Junger did not have a great mind, but he had several qualities that Wolf valued: he was loyal, he carried out instructions, and he believed that Heinrich Wolf was a true leader. Wolf had plans to use the middle-aged man sitting before him; nothing violent, but Junger would make a good courier. Wolf even considered leaving Junger in charge of the NDP's affairs in Europe when it came time for Wolf to go away.

"That incident has done a great deal to focus attention on the problem of America's nuclear-powered fleet," Wolf said.

Junger nodded enthusiastically. "The move to enlist the concern of all the antinuclear groups was nothing short of brilliant," he said.

Wolf would have been suspicious of flattery from anyone else. He let the comment go. "So everything else went well?"

"Not exactly," Junger said. He looked down at the table, then around the empty room. "I had a bit of trouble with the payment."

Wolf had a sudden inkling that perhaps he had been wrong about Junger. He had given the man cash to pay the assassins; perhaps Junger, who certainly had never had so much money before, had used some of it on himself. "Oh?" Wolf said.

"The day after the shootings, one of the men I had met with approached me and said they wanted more money." Junger hesitated, watching Wolf's face for a reaction. Wolf remained impassive.

"He said that once they saw the news, they realized that this should have been a much more expensive hit."

"But the business was concluded," Wolf said. "Did he threaten you?"

"Oh, no. I guess he figured I wouldn't have the money with me. But he said I had to return by the end of the month or he would expose me."

Wolf watched the older man carefully for some sign that he was lying. *Could I have been wrong about Junger's loyalty?* Wolf lifted the cup in front of him, then set it down carefully without drinking. He was about to speak when Junger interrupted.

"I know what you must think," Junger said.

*Here it comes,* Wolf thought. *Protestations of his innocence.*

"I'm sure I could have handled it better. I just didn't know what to say to the man. I thought later that, if I had been armed, perhaps I could have killed him."

Wolf looked up at this. Although Junger was an accessory to murder, Wolf doubted the older man was capable of killing someone with his own hand.

"And I suppose I could go back for that," Junger said halfheartedly. "Although I doubt I could get the better of a professional."

Wolf could see that Junger was afraid—not just of being sent back to Italy, but of what Wolf might think. He decided to put aside questions of Junger's loyalty for a moment.

"What do they know?" Wolf asked.

"Besides what they read in the paper about the NDP, the only other thing they have is the name I used at the hotel. And the man who met me said they had some photographs of our second meeting, the one where I paid them."

"Is that possible?" Wolf asked.

Junger looked at him.

"Were you in a place where you might have been photographed?"

"I'm afraid so."

Wolf was about to suggest that perhaps Junger was making up this story to extort money when the door to the *Gasthaus* opened.

"I thought you said this place was closed," Wolf said.

Junger turned toward the door and raised a hand to the old man who'd let himself in. Turning back to Wolf, he said, "It is. That is my friend, Johann. He is the owner."

Johann looked much older than his wife. Wolf smiled and stood as the old man shuffled up to the table.

"How are you today, my friends? Please, sit down, sit down," he said to Wolf.

Junger made no effort to introduce Wolf, which was a relief. Instead, the two older men launched into some gossipy chatter to catch up on the time since they'd last seen each other. Wolf studied Junger's face in profile. By the time the two old friends interrupted themselves—apologizing to the younger Wolf for ignoring him—Wolf had decided that Junger was loyal. He had no proof, but seeing the man talk to his ancient friend had convinced him nonetheless.

"I am sorry for the interruption," Junger said as the owner shuffled off. "Johann and I go back many years."

"It is good to see old friends get together," Wolf said warmly. "Perhaps you can introduce me."

"What about our business?" Junger asked.

"I need some time to think about our response," Wolf said.

Junger seemed relieved. He stood away from the table. "You know, this morning I was afraid that you might think that I made up this story," Junger said.

"Why would I think that?" Wolf asked. The two men were walking side by side toward the door at the back of the *Gasthaus*. Wolf could hear the deaf old couple in the back, each shouting to be heard.

"I thought you might think I was trying to get money for myself," Junger said, a nervous flutter in his voice.

"Nonsense," Wolf said, clapping the older man on the shoulder. "How could anyone as solicitous of friends as you are be anything but loyal?"

"I am so relieved," Junger said. "I am loyal." He pulled himself up to his full height of five eight. "And I am willing to go back to Italy to straighten this mess out."

Wolf let Junger lead them into the back room, which was an office. A door to the right opened into the kitchen. Wolf pulled the door shut behind him, then stepped to the side to shut the kitchen door. As Junger began to introduce him to the couple, shouting as he did so they could hear him, Wolf turned to face them. The old man and woman were sitting side by side at a large desk; Junger was standing on the other side of the desk.

Wolf reached into his jacket pocket and pulled out a twenty-five-millimeter automatic. He brought the pistol up, centered the barrel on the old man's face, and pulled the trigger. The woman turned her head toward her husband, unable to comprehend in the second or two before Wolf shot her in the side of the head what was happening. Wolf then turned toward Junger, who had taken a step back toward the door. The first shot hit Junger in the throat, sending a bright jet of blood down his shirt. The second round struck home right where Wolf aimed, just above the nose in the center of the forehead.

Wolf tucked the pistol away and began ransacking the

office. He did not expect to find any money, but he wanted to make it look like a robbery. When he pulled the bottom drawer of the desk free, a metal cash box clanged to the floor. Wolf forced it open and grabbed the money and checks inside. Then he stepped over Junger and put his hand on the door handle, listening before he opened the door.

"I'm sure you were loyal," he said to the wide-eyed corpse at his feet. "But they must not know who I am."

Wolf stepped out into the *Gasthaus* and let himself out the back door. There was no one on the street.

## Congressman Assails Pentagon Over
## Military Travel Restrictions,
## Says Families Are Trapped in Europe

Washington, D.C., April 21—Congressman Thomas Gerigan (R-GA) blasted Pentagon travel rules that are keeping military families "trapped in Europe when they want to come home." Citing a "significant terrorist threat" against the families of U.S. military personnel, Rep. Gerigan said he sympathized with constituents who have contacted him because they are unable to get the military to return them to the United States.

According to a Pentagon spokesman, the armed services routinely pay moving expenses for military families when the service member is assigned overseas, and military personnel may elect to send their families back to the United States before the end of the tour. The problems cited by Rep. Gerigan stem from a recent rush of families wanting to leave Europe after the recent attack on U.S. civilians.

"We are just overwhelmed with people who want to move immediately," said one spokesperson for the U.S. Military Traffic Command. "The system isn't designed to handle all this."

But Rep. Gerigan maintains that the military is deliberately dragging its feet. "They don't want to admit that they are unable to protect family members over there," Mr. Gerigan said, referring to the recent murder of an American woman and her two children near Heidelberg.

Pentagon spokesmen were quick to respond, saying that the U.S. Army Criminal Investigation Division reported that the bomb used in that attack had a time-delay fuse. "The bombers almost certainly did not anticipate that this woman would still be in her car at the exact moment of detonation," the report said.

Still, military families are fearful and divided over the issue. "I want my wife to go home now," said one commander, who asked to remain anonymous. "She says it would look bad for her to go running home when there are many other people over here still."

One enlisted soldier pointed out that the system is unfair. "Officers can afford to send their families home on commercial flights. My family's gotta stay here until the army says they can go home."

Rep. Gerigan said that the U.S. military would bear the responsibility for any further deaths or injuries to family members. "We are abandoning these people when they need us most," Gerigan said.

# 7

## near Tampico, Mexico
### 22 *April*

SATISFIED HE'D KEPT UP AN ENERGETIC APPEARANCE DURING
the two days spent doing airmobile training with Cortizo's
men, Mark Isen didn't care who saw him drag himself,
head down, up the little hill to his hootch. He didn't notice
the two extra duffel bags propped against the outside wall
until he had his hand on the door curtain. The bags were
standard U.S. Army-issue, remarkable only because they
were brand-new and not stenciled with the owner's name.
Isen pushed the curtain aside and entered the small room;
a tall man in desert battle-dress uniform was inside with
his back to Isen.

"Can I help you?" Isen asked.

When the man turned around, Isen could see that he was
a major in the U.S. Army. Crossed rifles on his left collar
point further identified him as an infantry officer, and his
name tag read "Spano." He wore no badges or flashes to
identify his unit. Major Spano was holding one of Isen's
books, pulled from the wooden battery-crate-turned-book-
case at the head of the single cot.

"Captain Isen? Mark Isen?" the major asked. He pro-
nounced the name *izzen*.

Isen said, "Yessir. But it's Is-en, like ice cream, ice-en."

"I'm Major Ray Spano," the tall man said.

"Pleased to meet you, sir," Isen said, taking the offered hand.

"Hope you don't mind me looking at your books," Spano said. "I've been here a number of hours." Without waiting for an answer, Spano held up the volume in his hand, a collection of Emily Dickinson's poems. "You really read this stuff?"

Isen didn't think the question deserved an answer. It was his bunk, and those were his books. "Yessir," Isen said again. He didn't think he was interested in pursuing small talk with this guy. "What brings you out here, sir?"

"I guess that means nobody sent you a message to expect me, right?" Spano said.

Isen shook his head slightly.

"Great." Spano sat down heavily on Isen's bunk, which looked as if it might collapse. He was a big man, about six foot one, Isen guessed, with the broad shoulders of a swimmer or gymnast. He was also another gringo who was going to burn in the Mexican sun. He had a thick shock of blond hair, and his pale skin was lightly freckled across the bridge of his nose.

"I came down here from Fort Bragg to learn what I could about your operation," Spano said.

"You with the Eighteenth Airborne Corps, sir?" Isen asked. The XVIII Airborne Corps was the headquarters element that controlled the 82nd and 101st Airborne Divisions, the 24th Mechanized Division, and a host of supporting units.

"Not exactly," Spano said. Although his superiors at Bragg had told him to give a full briefing to his American point of contact in-country, Spano was still a little hesitant about showing his hand. Major Raymond Anthony Spano was a member of the Delta Force, the U.S. Army's elite and very secretive antiterrorist unit. During his six years with that outfit, he had made it a habit not to talk about his job.

"I'm with the JSOC," Spano said. Technically, this was true. The Delta Force was controlled by the Joint Special Operations Command, jay-sock, in army jargon. Since

Spano had laid eyes on Isen only a minute earlier, he felt no need to tell him more, not yet, anyway.

"Are you guys going to be joining Operation Sentinel?" Isen asked.

"I'm here to see if the special ops community can help down here, though it wouldn't necessarily have to be as part of your operation," Spano said. "I'm sorry that you didn't get a heads-up about my coming, and I hope it's not a big problem. I'm going to be around a week or two, and I'd like to tag along during training and on any missions that go down while I'm here."

"Okay. You can bunk in the room on the other side," Isen said, pointing to the wall that separated his room from what had been Gaspar's space.

Spano put the book of poems down on Isen's cot and went outside. Isen dropped his field gear and stepped through the curtain to give him a hand with the bags.

"You ever been down here before, sir?" Isen asked.

"No. But I've been out in the desert before, and I know I'd better get some sunscreen on my lily-white self, or I'll look like a burnt hot dog in about an hour."

While Spano unpacked his gear, Isen filled the canvas bag he'd rigged up as a shower on the side of the building. He stripped off his filthy uniform and stood under the water dripping from the spout. Spano didn't seem overly friendly, but Isen was happy to have the additional company.

Spano came out a few minutes later and sat down on a water can. Isen's sense of modesty had long ago been eliminated in countless army field latrines and mass shower points, and in the old World War II–style barracks with the toilets lined up side by side along the latrine wall. In Isen's ROTC summer training, the cadets would sit and pass sections of the newspaper back and forth to one another. Nevertheless, Isen felt a bit self-conscious as he stood patiently under the trickle of water dripping from the shower bag. He'd been taking a beating down here, from the sun and the field work and the long foot marches he'd recommended to get Cortizo's men in shape. His arms were bruised and his elbows scabbed, and he could count most of his ribs. It had occurred to his thirty-year-old captain more than once in the last few weeks that it was a good thing that infantry platoon leaders were usually in their early twenties.

If Spano thought Isen looked beat-up, he didn't say anything about it.

"Would you mind telling me about your end of the operation down here?" Spano said.

"Not at all, sir."

Isen supposed later that he was just glad to talk without having his guard up. He had talked to Worden about the operation, of course, but the fact that Worden worked for him influenced the limits of what he might say to the NCO. Cortizo was friendly enough, and Isen suspected that the Mexican officer even liked him. But Isen was constantly aware of his status as observer, evaluator, adviser, outsider. Not so when he spoke with Spano. He talked freely about what he'd found when he got to Mexico, about the problems with Gaspar and Cortizo's predecessor, the one who'd sold off the mess hall equipment. He talked about the soldiers' indifference toward the drug smugglers, about their antipathy to the American presence. He talked about the mental strain on the dozens of American officers and NCOs spread throughout the northern part of the country at lonely outposts such as this one, a mental strain exacerbated by the Mexicans' less than hospitable attitude. He talked about the Mexican brass erecting obstacles at every turn: restrictions on ammo, on building materials, on training time. He told Spano how they'd had to bamboozle the general to get any sort of commitment from headquarters. He talked about the contradictory nature of what they were doing—half in war, half out.

Every week it seemed, Operation Sentinel headquarters, sensitized to an extreme by the Mexican Army's hostility, sent out a barrage of instructions that insulted the intelligence of the advisers: don't give orders directly to Mexican soldiers, don't argue with the hosts, don't carry anything other than a pistol, and never fire it except in self-defense. He talked about his frustration with the infantry school and how they didn't really prepare men for this duty. He talked while he showered and while he dried off. He was still talking when he was dressed, and he kept it up as he soaked his dirty uniform in a tub full of water. Finally, it occurred to him that Spano might want to ask a question.

"I'm sorry, sir, for running off at the mouth. I just haven't had the chance to tell anyone what I think is wrong with the program. I didn't think it would be right to unload all of this on Sergeant Worden."

"No problem," Spano said.

"Let me ask your opinion on something, sir. This kind of mission is exactly what the Special Forces does—training the local army and supervising their operations. Why do you think they have run-of-the-mill grunts like me doing this stuff?"

Spano chewed his lip for a moment. "It might have something to do with what's going on with the Special Forces," Spano said. "After the war the guys up in the Pentagon really had to look at what kind of army we're going to take into the next century." Spano stood and Isen noticed that he had his nine-millimeter pistol stuck in the waistband of his pants in the small of his back. "You might remember that just before the invasion of Kuwait, the army was considering cutting the mechanized infantry and armor forces by a third. Obviously the assumptions behind that plan— that without the Russians to worry about we didn't need an armored force—were proven wrong in the desert. Now we're in the process of drawing up new plans, and in the interim, missions are being handed out differently."

Isen didn't answer. He had both hands in a washbasin full of dirty uniforms, and he was pushing the mess up and down in the brown water.

"Do you agree with that?" Spano said.

"I guess I have more of a Machiavellian reading," Isen answered. He pulled his hands out and dried them on his trousers. "I think the people behind the light infantry concept are afraid their sun is setting."

"What do you mean?"

Isen had a quick flash that Spano might be one of the people hoping to get the army *more* involved in the drug war. Isen hadn't even had time to call his superiors to see if this guy was for real, although he couldn't imagine why someone would come out to this desolate spot unless he was ordered. *What the hell, I'm just shooting my mouth off,* Isen thought. *Nobody said I couldn't have opinions.*

"The armor and mechanized infantry guys got a shot in the arm after Iraq—more money for weapons development, modernization, all that. The people who think the army needs more light forces are looking for ways to prove that we *need* light infantry. In other words, they're looking for missions suited for us light fighters so they can point and say, 'See? We need more money.' I think we're going to see the army more and more involved in these weird missions, stuff that's short of war but a little more than police work."

Spano dropped his eyes to the ground between his feet. "The people back home are afraid that the druggies are winning."

"They should be afraid," Isen said. "But I'm wondering about the effect of all this infighting on the army." He looked around reflexively, then pulled another water can over and sat down next to Spano. "Some of the guys down here in Sentinel didn't get to the Persian Gulf, and they're anxious to make a name for themselves because they know we have two armies now: everybody who fought Iraq, and everybody else. And as the force gets smaller, the guys without the combat patches are worried that their tour at Fort Ord or West Point or East Jesus, Idaho, Recruiting Command during that war will be a discriminator . . . will make them miss a promotion or something. When they start tossing people, they might just start with the ones who weren't in the desert." Isen paused to see if Spano had some reaction. There was nothing, so he went on.

"Anyway, you send these guys down here, and they're all hungry to make a name for themselves, and they're looking for any way possible to get in a big fight with the druggies. They push the Mexicans and take stupid chances and generally piss people off, and that's not good."

"That's an interesting theory," Spano said, looking at his boots. "So they're assholes. What's that got to do with the whole army?"

"If we come down here and forget our mission, start

focusing on kills or body counts or some such nonsense, then this becomes a trade school for grunts. And then we've forgotten what we're about. *That's* bad for the army.''

Spano was watching Isen closely now, though dusk was making it hard to pick out features. ''Could be, I suppose. The next six months will tell a lot. By that time we should have a handle on how Sentinel is working.'' He stood and stretched his arms above his head. ''I think I'm going to turn in,'' Spano said. ''What time you get started here in the morning?''

''Someone will come by at five o'clock and wake us up,'' Isen answered.

''I'll see you then,'' Spano said.

''Yes, sir. I'll see you in the morning,'' Isen replied. He watched the tall shadow of Spano's frame retreat into the hootch. *They've sent me a real rocket scientist here. Nice enough guy, but I hope he doesn't forget how to work the zipper on his sleeping bag.*

In the small room on the opposite side of the block building, Spano was writing out a message to his boss, requesting that he be allowed to spend all three weeks in-country with Isen.

> *He's a smart guy, and he's thought about this mission quite a bit. I'd like to be able to pick his brain for a while and, unless we don't go anywhere, I can't imagine a better place to spend my limited time.*

Spano hadn't expected to find an Isen here—a guy who was obviously smart and working hard to make a go of this. Everything he'd heard about Operation Sentinel was unflattering: the units weren't well-trained, they weren't getting out to the field, they weren't hitting the smugglers. These perceptions, as prevalent on Capitol Hill and in the media as in the military, did nothing to help the already unpopular program. The public didn't like the idea, culled from the media, of American GIs spreading havoc through the Mexican countryside.

The special operations community had lobbied for a role

in the action—the only game in town—arguing as they did in every case that their specialized training made them perfect for the job. They planned to come on strong and take out the smugglers quickly, violently, and with direct U.S. action. The thinking at the Pentagon was that this approach might give the Mexicans less to complain about.

But now Spano saw that the regulars down here, the men like Isen, weren't buffoons. They were being asked to fight a two-front war: one with the druggies and one with the Mexican Army.

He'd learned a lot in a few hours, though much of it had been through the filter of Isen's experience. He read over what he'd written and thought about adding, *He's a talkative devil*, but he let it slide. Spano had let Isen talk for quite a while, partly because he was in Mexico to learn and his father had once told him, *You never learn anything while your mouth is running*. But listening had also seemed like the right thing to do. Isen was wound pretty tight, and Spano's surprise visit had given him the opportunity to relax a bit. Spano figured he hadn't said two dozen words the whole time the captain talked. As he unrolled his sleeping bag and pulled out a balled up fatigue shirt to use as a pillow, Spano wondered what Isen must think of him, dropping out of the sky with some hush-hush mission.

*I guess I'll know tomorrow if he leaves me stranded back here.*

The first shotgun blast jolted Ray Spano awake, and by the time the second and third reports reached him seconds later, he was on the floor next to his cot, pistol in hand, crawling for the door. It took him a few seconds to get oriented, but by the time he reached the canvas flap that covered the door, he had already determined that the shots had come from someplace down the hill. He gingerly pushed the curtain with the muzzle of his weapon. As far as he could tell, there was no one immediately outside the little building he and Isen shared. Spano raised himself to a crouch and rocketed through the door, hitting the ground a few meters away and rolling for the shelter at the lip of the hill. There he paused again, checking around him first, then scanning the trail that led to the rest of the compound below.

"Shit," he muttered. "My first goddamn night here and I'm getting shot at." His breath was coming in gulps, and though he could feel the scrapes and cuts he'd inflicted on his bare back when he rolled in the gravel, it was a relief to know he hadn't been shot.

In the light of the half moon, Spano could see what looked like a bundle of some sort lying in the middle of the trail. He scanned the darkness on either side of the trail between himself and that bundle, opening his mouth to equalize the pressure in his ears so that he could hear better. He saw nothing there.

Spano decided to back up, away from the bundle, to see if he couldn't get around the building and link up with Isen, who was probably on the other side of the hootch. He turned toward the little block structure, its outline visible less than ten meters away from where he hid on the slope of the hill. Spano saw movement. There by the door he'd just burst through, a figure just darker than the surrounding blackness was moving along the wall. At first Spano thought it might be Isen, but then the figure lowered the barrel of a rifle or shotgun as if preparing to fire into the room. Spano watched in amazement as it occurred to him that he was the one being stalked. Then he wondered if Isen, who slept on the other side of the hootch, was already dead.

The dark figure stepped away from the wall and pulled the weapon shoulder high. Spano tensed for the blast, but it never came. Instead he saw the winking muzzle flash of a pistol on the far side of the figure. The attacker staggered at the first shot, dropping the weapon that was trained on Spano's room. Two more rounds and the figure by the door went down.

"Spano."

It was Isen's voice, coming from the far side of the hootch. He'd been the one doing the shooting.

"I'm, over here," Spano said aloud. "I'm okay. Are you?"

"Yeah." Isen spoke as he cleared the shadows; Spano

could see him check out the body by the door. Spano got up to join him there, but Isen turned and trotted down the barely visible path to the bundle Spano had spied earlier. Spano supposed it was another attacker, and he jogged after Isen, careful to stay in the shadows off the light-colored sand of the track.

"What the hell happened?" Spano said as he tried to keep up with Isen. Spano was barefoot, and the sharp rocks in the wash by the side of the trail gave him considerable difficulty. He was looking down, trying to pick his way along, when another muzzle blast split the darkness. Spano went down again, but not before he saw Isen, barely visible in the faint moonlight, sprint for the brush from which the shots had come. At first Spano thought Isen was confused about the directions in the dark, and he started to shout a warning. Then he realized Isen was pursuing the attacker.

Spano left the questionable shelter by the side of the trail and found that the bundle he'd seen was a Mexican soldier, unarmed, in uniform, and wounded in the chest and arms. The man was breathing raggedly, and he grabbed hold of Spano's leg as the American tried to determine the extent of the wounds. By the time he pulled the man's shirt open, he'd been joined by half a dozen other soldiers—these were armed—all of them talking to him excitedly in Spanish. When a soldier came up with a flashlight and a medic's bag, Spano backed off. He went back to his hootch, where two more Mexican soldiers were examining the body outside his door.

"Who did this?" Spano asked in English. The Mexican soldiers responded, but only because they'd heard the tone of a question in his voice. Spano watched them for a few more minutes before deciding to wait at the hootch for Isen to return. He sat down on a plastic crate and leaned up against the wall in the shadows. The Mexicans carried away the body. He could hear lots of activity below him—apparently the soldiers were sweeping the area for the attackers—but no one bothered with him for the hour until Isen returned.

"You okay, sir?" Isen asked as he walked up the hill.

"Yeah, I'm fine. Are you okay? You're the one who went tearing off into the brush chasing the shooters."

"Oh, I'm okay. Just pissed off, I guess. The bastards got away—except for the dead guy, of course."

"Do you know what happened?" Spano asked.

"Not for sure," Isen said. "But if I had to guess, I'd say the druggies want us dead . . ."

Isen seemed to leave the sentence unfinished, as if he were going to add another clause.

"Or?" Spano pressed him.

"Well, I wanted to catch one of them alive to see who they were working for," Isen answered.

Spano couldn't see the captain's face, but he felt as if a lot was going unsaid.

"Do the Mexicans have any ideas?" Spano wanted to know.

Isen shrugged, a *Who knows?* gesture, and Spano realized that there was now enough light to see by.

The two men heard, before they saw, someone walking up the hill on the trail. A few seconds later, a short Mexican in a pressed short-sleeve shirt and trousers took shape from the gloom.

"Major Spano, this is Lieutenant Cortizo," Isen said. Spano stood and shook hands with Cortizo, noting that the three of them made an odd trio: Cortizo was dressed neatly, even though he'd no doubt been startled out of bed like the rest of them; Isen wore his boots, olive drab boxer shorts, and dog tags; Spano, who towered above the other two men, wore army-issue gym shorts and his ID tags.

"I am afraid the others got away, Captain Isen," Cortizo said. "We will post guards throughout the compound from now on."

"Okay," Isen said.

"I will ask the local authorities for help in identifying the one you shot here," Cortizo said to Isen.

"Okay," Isen answered tersely. Spano thought he was still tense from the shootout, but now it seemed to him that Isen was holding something back from Cortizo.

The Mexican officer saluted, turned, and made his way down the hill. Isen walked away without looking at Spano.

Just before he turned the corner of the hootch, he said over his shoulder, "I'll see you in about an hour, sir."

Spano watched Cortizo's back and wondered what was going on here.

*Well,* he said to himself. *This is going to be one hell of an interesting time down here.*

When Isen stepped outside exactly an hour later, Spano was shaved, fully dressed, loaded, and ready to go.

"Morning, sir," Isen said. "Now maybe we can start a normal day."

"Good morning, Mark . . . Okay if I call you Mark?"

"Sure," Isen answered.

"I want to thank you for watching out for me last night," Spano said. He was still pretty keyed up from the firefight, and he hoped Isen would talk about it. "I was already out of the hootch when that bad guy was about to open up on my side, but I appreciate your help."

"No sweat, sir," Isen answered, wanting to be done with it. He surreptitiously checked Spano's gear. The major had removed the metal clips from his web gear and replaced them with short pieces of five-fifty cord, the multistrand five-hundred-and-fifty-pound test line used to hold a parachute to a jumper's harness. Spano was evidently an old airborne soldier; Isen had seen paratroopers make the same adjustment to their load-bearing equipment. The metal connectors that came with the suspenders and belt could get wedged between the jumper's body and the very tight parachute harness, whereas the little pieces of cord were just as strong and not as uncomfortable. He wondered how much Spano would tell him about the mission for JSOC.

"The NCO I work with is an old paratrooper too," Isen offered, changing the subject.

Spano raised his eyebrows a bit. "Oh, yeah?"

Isen wasn't sure if the change in tone was an admission about Spano's history or not.

"His name's Jack Worden. Staff sergeant, soon to be sergeant first class. Good man."

A few moments later Worden joined them on the trail that led off the hill. Isen did the introductions.

"Major Spano, this is Staff Sergeant Jack Worden."

"Nice to meet you, Sergeant Worden," Spano said, extending a hand.

"Helluva reception last night, sir," Worden said. "I went out and beat the bush with a patrol for a while," Worden said, apparently to Isen. "Whoever it was got away clean."

Isen was still quiet, so Worden turned back to Spano. "You going to join us, sir?"

Spano evidently thought Worden was talking about the day's operation. He replied, "Thought I'd tag along."

But Isen recognized Worden's directness. Jack Worden wanted to know if he had a new boss. When Worden didn't say anything further, Spano caught on.

"Oh. You mean am I going to be working with you and Captain Isen. No, I'm just down here for a while to learn what I can about the operation," he said.

"Major Spano came from Fort Bragg," Isen offered.

Worden's face lit up. "You from the Eighty-deuce, sir?"

Isen smiled. He'd never had the opportunity to serve in an airborne unit like the 82nd Airborne Division, and he was always amazed at the esprit that lived in those men. At times he might even admit to being a bit jealous.

"No, I'm from behind the fence," Spano said.

Isen had heard the expression "behind the fence" used to describe the special operations community. When you asked where someone was currently assigned and got the answer, "Oh, he's behind the fence," that meant that the person had disappeared into the shadowy world of the Delta Force, or Task Force 160, the special ops flight unit, or the navy SEALS, or one of the other units that fell under the multiservice control of the Joint Special Operations Command. Isen hoped the sergeant would ask Spano if that meant Delta Force. Spano had told Isen he was with JSOC; to ask again would imply that Isen didn't believe the first answer. But Sergeant Worden hadn't been privy to that conversation, and he was nothing if not direct.

But Worden dropped the line of questioning. "You want to know what I've found out, sir?" Worden said to Spano as the three men reached the bottom of the hill. He was suddenly chatty, like a young soldier being interviewed by a journalist, and Isen remembered how he himself had bent Spano's ear the night before. "When they told me about this job, they said I was going to be an instructor, a teacher, you know? But since I've been down here, I've figured out that the stuff I'm teaching is pretty simple compared to what I'm learning from all of this."

Isen smiled at the sergeant; he and Worden got along well because they were intellectual equals. The noncom didn't have the education Isen did, but he had one of the sharpest minds Isen had encountered in a while. To his credit, Spano was listening intently.

"What do you mean?" Spano asked.

"I thought I was going to learn to speak Spanish a little better, and that would be it. But this is turning out to be an eye-opener." Worden adjusted the straps of his load-bearing equipment and looked at Isen, as if asking if it was okay to go on. Isen said nothing, so Worden continued. "These guys come from backgrounds about as different from yours and mine as possible. They're really cynical about their own government's programs—especially this one, but they'll put out if they're well lead. But the thing that surprised me the most was that, in spite of the killing going on, they don't see this as their fight. Yet if you listen to the stuff coming out of Mexico City, this is a life-and-death struggle to maintain control of the country."

"I believe the Mexican government is afraid that what happened in Colombia could happen here," Isen added. "Down there the druggies run the show. They even got the government to give them guarantees that they wouldn't be extradited . . . this after murdering hundreds of civilians, police officers, and government officials."

"Maybe last night will change some of that attitude," Spano said.

"Maybe," Isen said. "Or maybe the common soldiers will just stay clear while the druggies try to off the GIs."

The three of them walked quietly for a short distance, each of them thinking about the players in the game, wondering if there were new rules.

"The thing that gets me is that nobody up at the infantry school is letting on about how complicated this mess is,"

Worden continued. "It's tough advising people who don't want us around."

They paused long enough to let a jeep go by on the narrow, dusty trail.

"I'm not sure it's as simple as putting a couple of briefings into the program at Benning," Isen said. "I mean, there's more to it than resentment." He was looking at his boots as he walked, scuffing along in the dust like a schoolboy. He'd had a nagging feeling about their role for some time; last night, with Spano listening, he'd tried to articulate what he thought the trouble was. But he wasn't quite there yet.

"These guys," Isen said, pointing to indicate the Mexican soldiers who were joining their morning formation at the bottom of the hill, "are caught between a rock and a hard place. Their government really does fear the smugglers, who have already made a mockery of Colombian sovereignty, and they also want U.S. economic assistance. But the soldiers kind of sympathize with the growers down south, the little guys, most of whom are just trying to feed their families. And they're wary of what might happen as the U.S. becomes more desperate to shut off the flow of drugs. It isn't as if we've never stomped on anybody's rights to get what we want."

"That's exactly what I'm talking about, sir," Worden agreed enthusiastically. He was nodding at Spano. "Somebody needs to tell all this to the guys who'll be following us. Up at Benning, all they're learning is the correct pronunciation of *The patrol must maintain security at all times.*"

Isen laughed, but he knew Worden was right. Isen's father, a Vietnam veteran, had told him stories of how the young GIs in that war knew nothing about the culture they were supposedly trying to preserve. Their ignorance bred frustration and even more suffering in a country wracked by tragedy. Isen knew that to do the same thing in Mexico—send untutored Americans to fight alongside men they didn't understand and in circumstances unlike anything their training had prepared them for—was to court disaster. Mark Isen also believed that the United States couldn't afford to lose this war. Gaspar, his predecessor, had been frustrated by the same things. Unprepared for the role he was supposed to play, Gaspar had adopted the outward appearance of his hosts but had remained apart from them fundamentally. Isen had made some headway but was far from satisfied with his efforts. His tactical knowledge was not enough. He had no way of understanding, to the satisfaction of his hosts, what it was like to be Mexican.

Cortizo had told him once, "You have a good heart, Captain Isen, but you will always have American eyes."

"But you'll be happy to know, Captain," Worden said, turning his attention to Isen and putting his hand on the captain's shoulder in a way that was part joke, mostly serious, "that your trusted sidekick has hit upon a plan to correct this situation."

"I can hardly wait to hear it," Isen said, rolling his eyes. Spano hadn't said two words, and Isen was trying to draw him into the conversation to set him up for the request he thought Worden was about to make: Spano could carry the gospel back to the States.

But Worden didn't take his eyes off Isen. "I think you should write a couple of letters to the *Army Times*," Worden said, referring to the widely distributed private newspaper that catered to the Army.

Isen stopped walking. "What?"

"Look, sir, if you write to the head of the infantry school, what will happen to your letter?"

"I'm not sure I follow," Isen said, looking at Spano and wondering how the newcomer had gotten off the hook.

Worden patiently continued the Socratic questioning. "I mean, what will physically happen to the letter at Fort Benning?"

Isen saw what Worden was getting at. "Some captain working in the chief's office will probably open it . . ."

"And shitcan it," Worden finished. "But if you write to the newspaper, everyone will see it, at least everyone in the army will," Worden said. "You'll be able to spread the good word, and you might even rustle up a couple of replacements for you and me."

Isen laughed again. "So you do have an ulterior motive," he said.

"I prefer to believe that I'm just a couple of steps ahead of everybody else," Worden said.

"Sounds like you are," Spano said at last.

Worden was right, Isen knew. Somebody had to tell the guys at Benning that they wouldn't be able to sweep in with their technology and American know-how and in short order fix everything that the *Americans* thought was wrong with Mexico. Isen felt a responsibility to warn those men still at Benning to pack some measure of humility in their duffel bags, but he was not sure he was up to the task. He pushed the thoughts to the back of his mind as he turned to the easier task of briefing Spano.

"Lieutenant Cortizo, the guy you met this morning, commands this company. He's really coming into his own as a ground commander and as a tactician," Isen said. "His company has been relieved of the pretty mundane mission of continuous patrolling and has been made a reaction force for Tamaulipas State."

As he thought about his counterpart it occurred to Isen that Cortizo should have been given his captaincy. He had hoped that the U.S. Army was the only military outfit that promoted people based almost exclusively on their time in service—in the case of officers, the year they were commissioned—and not on the work they did. Nevertheless, Cortizo was the only lieutenant in the state allowed to operate with this degree of autonomy.

Worden left Isen and Spano and made his way to the troop formation, while the officers headed for the small building that served as Cortizo's quarters and office. Cortizo was there, engrossed in some typewritten notes sent the night before from higher headquarters.

"Lieutenant Cortizo, this is what Major Spano looks like in his clothes," Isen said when Cortizo noticed his visitors. Cortizo stood but didn't smile at the joke.

"Yes, sir. I am sorry, once again, for what happened this morning, and I can assure you that we will get to the bottom of this," Cortizo said.

"Okay," Spano said.

There was a moment of awkward silence before Cortizo turned to the maps he'd been poring over.

"The reports I am receiving tell me that this area"—
Cortizo pointed to a spot he'd marked with grease pencil—
"east of Ciudad Mante, between the Tampesi River and
the Inter-American Highway, has suddenly become interesting to our friends."

Cortizo always referred to the smugglers they hunted as
"our friends." And although he never cracked a smile
when he said this, Isen thought he was doing it to be humorous. Whenever they were talking about an individual on
the other side, Cortizo, in speaking to Isen, would call him
"*your* friend."

"There has been an increase in overflights of this area."

"Is that info from the air defense sites?" Isen asked.

Part of the increased commitment of the United States
military to the interdiction mission had been the deploy-
ment of an extensive series of radar sites throughout the
countryside. Although there weren't enough units to cover
the whole length of Mexico (its longest axis, of about twenty-one hundred miles, is equal to the distance from San
Diego to Atlanta), there were enough to make a difference.
With advice from the army military intelligence planners,
the Drug Enforcement Agency had put together a clearing-
house for intelligence from all sources. There, reports from
agents on the ground in South America were compared to
data collected from informants at both ends of the pipeline.
This allowed the hunters to narrow the number of sites that
had to be watched. The radar units, most of them highly
mobile stations from the U.S. Army's air defense community, were then transported by helicopter and aircraft to
suspect locations. In just the time since Isen had come on
board in Mexico, the new system had accounted for a dramatic increase in the number of aircraft seized.

"Yes," Cortizo said, "but they are getting wise to us.
They know that we are waiting for them, and they have
taken steps to counter our efforts." Cortizo reached into
the leather pouch that he used as a briefcase and pulled out
a sheaf of black-and-white photographs. "They are buying
aircraft capable of making landings on unimproved run-
ways. If they have a series of these fields to choose from,
the pilot can pick his field at the last moment. Even the

pilot does not know, until he is in the air, where he will land, and that is the best way to keep a secret. Even though they have people on the ground waiting for the planes, they just send out more ground crews than they need—so even the ground crews don't know if a plane will land. The locations are kept secret, and that reduces the possibility for advance warning from our intelligence net."

Isen was surprised once again at the wealth commanded by these bandits. They were investing in *fleets* of aircraft, and when one type proved less than successful, they bought another fleet. They had also established a fairly sophisticated command-and-control system that could give course changes to planes already in the air and direct widespread ground operations.

"You'll have to be pretty mobile to catch up with them," Spano said.

"Exactly," Cortizo agreed. Summoned by General Querros, Cortizo had traveled to Mexico City with two plans of his own, and he'd left Isen behind to avoid any embarrassing questions about the American reporters. "That is what I told the army staff. We can no longer sit on the ground waiting. Our friends will simply avoid us."

Isen expected Cortizo to be noticeably pleased that the army staff had accepted the recommendation, but the lieutenant leaned forward, his forearms on the table. "Our friends now have thermal-sensing devices that allow them to spot our soldiers hiding in ambush near the airstrips."

"Whew." Isen blew out a long breath between his teeth. "So all they have to do is fly around looking for a cold airstrip." The technique was one that had long been in use in the American army. The pilot or copilot looked through a thermal-sensing device that could pick out the signature body heat from a man at a great distance. At night, figures on the ground looked like glowing animated characters. Even against the hot landscape of central Mexico, it was easy to spot the forms of several dozen soldiers lying in ambush. It was obvious that the soldiers could no longer wait in an ambush position. Cortizo, anticipating that the army would respond to new pressures from the Presidential

Palace—pressures that developed after Querros's visit—came up with new plans. And so the seesaw war went on.

"I presented the two plans I worked out," Cortizo told Isen. "The staff went for one of them, but the commander went for the other." He smiled at Isen, his beautiful white teeth doing nothing to hide the mischief in his heart.

"Let me guess. The old man went for the hairy one."

"Ah, yes," Cortizo said to Spano, adding more of an accent to his English. "Captain Isen is becoming a good judge of the Mexican character."

Cortizo had devised two plans, one of them prudent, cautious, the other considerably more dramatic and resource intensive. The second one—the one Isen referred to as the "hairy" one—appealed to Querros. It called for split-second timing and coordination between the radar sites and the air and ground forces involved. Thanks to a painstaking monitoring of the reconnaissance flights the smugglers had flown over the potential airstrips, the joint intelligence center had built up enough data to make reasonable predictions as to where landings would most likely take place. There was a tremendous amount of ground to cover, and the intelligence was perishable, but the smugglers had made the mistake of falling into a pattern.

When a suspicious aircraft crossed into Mexican airspace, the sites on the ground got a fix on its heading and course, and the plane was then picked up by on-call aircraft of the Drug Enforcement Agency. These planes were versions of the corporate jets used by big companies to shuttle executives, and they could keep up with any plane the smugglers had used so far. More important, and unlike the high-performance aircraft of the air force, these planes could slow down enough to track smaller airplanes. When the suspect made a landing, propeller-driven aircraft, newly outfitted with machine guns, would close in on the airstrip, ready to force the smuggler down again if he tried to take off. Meanwhile a helicopter-borne strike force, Cortizo's grunts, would race to the field.

The difficult part came if the smugglers were alerted to the fact that someone was following them. They could ditch their cargo or take evasive action; they could even prepare a nasty reception for the infantry.

"So when do we get to try out our new approach?" Isen asked Cortizo.

"Well, if you remember your first night here in Mexico," Cortizo said, inclining his head toward Isen, "you know that we don't like to leave new arrivals in suspense, Captain Isen."

Isen looked carefully at Cortizo, who didn't seem to be kidding. The lieutenant went on. "I think the general is anxious to test us, perhaps to see if we will fail."

Isen turned to Spano. "Looks like you're going to see your first mission as part of Operation Sentinel, Major. We'd better go get our weapons."

# 8

## near Tampico, Mexico
### 24 April

IN SPITE OF CORTIZO'S PLAYFUL EXCITEMENT, THE FIRST TWO nights of the new mission were uneventful, and Isen, Spano, and Cortizo spent them in the tent alongside the airstrip where the U.S. Army Blackhawk helicopters waited in the dusk and dim. There were several alerts, but the ground-based radars weren't able to guide the aircraft on station quickly enough for the pilots to get a fix on the targets. Cortizo was discouraged and began to think that his violation of the dictum that Isen said applied to all planning—keep it simple—had come back to haunt him. Isen did his best to encourage the lieutenant, but he had several long, dusty days and chilly nights in which he was reminded that boredom is a chief ingredient of the soldier's life. On the third night, as midnight passed into those long hours when it is hard to keep alert, Isen also began to wonder if they should scrap the plan.

Then the bank of radios came to life.

"Romeo two-two, this is Bravo niner-one, over."

Isen was tilted back on a metal folding chair, and he almost lost his balance as he tried to wake up and force the chair forward at the same time.

"Romeo two-two, this is Bravo niner-one, over."

"This is Romeo two-two, over." The soldier manning the radio was another American, part of the flight unit that had traveled south from Fort Campbell, Kentucky, on a six-month temporary duty stint to support operations in Mexico. The caller was the central control for a series of air defense radars deployed only the day before to an area along the Tampesi River north of Tampico.

"This is Bravo niner-one. Stand by for message traffic, over."

Spano had been lying on the ground in the corner, shielding his eyes with the bottom flap of the tent. He rolled over quickly and got to his feet, and he and Isen watched as the soldier who was receiving the transmission put on a set of headphones to free his hands. Isen hadn't been watching the youngster, a private first class from New York, but if the kid had been half asleep, as Isen had, he was showing no signs of it now. The soldier had out his map as well as the Plexiglas board that showed the code words he would use to communicate with the control radar site.

"Go ahead, niner-one."

Isen and Cortizo were both standing behind the soldier now, waiting to see if they had a live one.

"We have code yellow at square seven-one-seven. ETA five mikes. The hammer is in position. No sign of contact or alert, over."

Cortizo watched as the soldier copied the location, using a grease pencil to make notes on the Plexiglas. Cortizo pulled his own map out of his pocket, turned, and walked unhurriedly out the tent door.

"Understand code yellow at seven-one-seven," the operator said. Isen was responsible for the highly stylized jargon they were using. After the first American units had arrived in Tamaulipas, they had all but abandoned their discipline of radio security and had lapsed into using call signs that identified units and even referred to locations in the clear. The druggies, of course, had radios and could listen in whenever it struck their fancy. Isen had had to throw a tantrum to get his way, but all of the Americans involved in this operation now observed the strictest security measures. Even if the other side were listening, the chances of their divining the location of square seven-one-seven were slim, since Isen had made up the system using random numbers, and the designations changed twice during each twelve-hour shift.

*Code yellow* meant that they had a contact that was going to ground, about to land on one of the strips under surveillance. The *ETA,* or estimated time of arrival, was the trail plane's best guess as to when the quarry would land. The *hammer* was the armed aircraft that would force the smuggler down if he got wise and tried to escape. So far, there was no sign that the hunted aircraft had any inkling as to what was going on.

By the time Isen got outside, he heard the high whine of the dual-engined Blackhawks revving up for takeoff, saw the shadows of the wide blades moving eerily across a half moon above the eastern horizon. Spano appeared a few seconds later, and after their eyes adjusted to the darkness the two men walked to the edge of the strip near the lead aircraft, where Cortizo was briefing his sergeants off one of the drawings local authorities had provided him of the possible airstrips in the region. The paper was mimeographed, and Cortizo had hastily drawn in a sketch to show his men what they were going to do. Isen and Spano stood behind his group. One of the soldiers held a flashlight on the paper, which was beginning to flap wildly in the wash from the chopper blades.

The strip pointed northwest and southeast and was bordered on the northern edge by a fairly deep streambed and some small trees. The southern end would make the better approach, so Cortizo had sketched in a rectangular strip with that in mind. West of the strip a series of uneven fields moved off to the southwest—lots of open ground, but not usable for airplanes. East of the strip was a stand of trees and some intermittent clearings that would provide a good hiding place for the aircraft and the trucks needed to refuel it. Cortizo had marked the east side with an *X*.

"I think they will hide the plane in here," Cortizo said, pointing to the spot he'd marked. "If we continue to make good time, we should be there while they are refueling. My plan is to land on the airstrip, so that they can't use it right away. It should only take us a few minutes to deploy, and we can quickly shut down the operation."

Cortizo drew a hasty sketch in the dirt and used his finger to trace the approach he wanted to take. His subordinates listened intently.

Isen thought the plan was a good one. He and Spano left the group and found Sergeant Worden talking to a helicopter crew chief. As Isen approached he could see, through the open doors on both sides of the aircraft, the Mexican soldiers huddled in a small group on the far side of the helicopter. The crew chief was showing Worden something on the door gun, a 7.62-millimeter machine gun suspended from straps in the doorway of the helicopter, designed to give the crew chief some limited ability to suppress ground fire. Worden turned to Isen and shouted above the increasing noise.

"He's gonna let me ride shotgun," Worden yelled. "If that's okay with you, sir."

Isen looked at him incredulously. Worden's philosophy, Isen knew, was ask anything and you'll eventually win a few concessions. But this was too much. Every message from a jumpy Sentinel headquarters reminded them to keep their weapons holstered except in extreme circumstances.

"Negative," Isen shouted, trying to keep a handle on the sarcasm in his voice. "We can't shoot except in self-defense, remember?"

Worden shrugged. He knew the rules—established by civilians in the State Department and desk jockeys at the Pentagon—as well as Isen.

Isen reached down to his holster and patted his pistol, checking out of force of habit to make sure it was there. He climbed into what would be the lead aircraft of the flight, where he and Cortizo could talk to the senior pilot, who was the flight commander. He'd asked Spano to ride in the trail aircraft. Major or not, the grunts had to get there first, and Cortizo figured he was already sacrificing two seats—for Isen and Worden—to the Americans.

Along both sides of the strip, the soldiers responded as one when the crew chiefs waved them over to the helicopters. They moved in good order, hurrying without losing

control in their haste. Isen thought about the soldiers doz-
ing in the ambush position on his first night as he watched
this group climb confidently aboard the helicopters and
buckle themselves in as the aircrews made their last
checks. They'd come a long way, but the real test would
come if there was a fight at the airstrip.

Isen glanced into the cockpit as Cortizo clambered in.
The pilot and copilot were wearing the lastest model night-
vision devices. The glasses were wonderfully clear and not
nearly as awkward as those aviators had to suffer back
when Isen was a lieutenant. These new sets had proven
themselves in combat in Panama and Iraq, where pilots
were able to fly night missions with all the confidence of
daylight flying. The copilot turned to look at the crew chief,
swiveling his head like some cumbersome cyclops, a big
electronic eye growing out of his forehead.

It had been only a few minutes since the radio call had
come in, and Isen had not even had time to think about
what they were going off to do. It wasn't until they were
airborne that he began to experience the first tinkling of
worry, like the ringing of a distant telephone. He worried that he and Cortizo had missed something in the
planning. He worried about the pilots' navigation. He
worried that the communications might break down between the controlling center and aircraft already on station. He worried that the smugglers might run. He
worried that they would stand and fight. He worried
about the soldiers and about the impetuous Worden,
armed only with a pistol. And finally, he even had time
to worry that he might get hurt.

His thoughts were interrupted by the crew chief, who
motioned to the headset Cortizo had dangling around his
neck. The lieutenant picked it up and listened, then nodded his head. The copilot, who was manning the radio,
glanced back again, and Cortizo gave him a thumbs-up.
They were twenty minutes flying time away from their
objective, and Cortizo switched on his penlight to show
Isen the sketch once more.

"The spotter plane says that our friends have landed,"
Cortizo yelled, struggling to be heard over the roar and

wide slapping of the blades in air. He was screaming in Isen's face, close enough for Isen to feel the spittle. "We will get there while they are doing their business."

Isen looked at the quick sketch again. Cortizo wanted to land almost on top of the smugglers, and Isen understood his reasoning. He wanted to give them no time to react, and he expected light resistance. Still, it was a dangerous maneuver.

"If we land a little farther away, we'll have room to maneuver if they try anything," Isen answered, his voice going hoarse almost immediately.

"I want to land on their heads," Cortizo said. Then the Mexican officer smiled at Isen with a smile that Isen had come to recognize. *Thank you, Captain Isen,* the smile said, *but I have made up my mind.* As if to underscore the fact that the point wasn't open to debate, Cortizo clicked off the small flashlight, and they were once again in darkness in the plunging bird.

Twenty-six miles away, a group of fourteen men watched the sleek fuselage of a light six-seater as the plane rolled to a stop on the dirt runway. A few of these men, one German, one Israeli, and two Libyans, had been soldiers before, in other armies, in other times. Even under their heavy burdens of automatic weapons, rocket launchers, and machine guns, the former soldiers moved quickly and efficiently. The remainder of the small force, Colombian peasants who had been recruited in the poorest districts of Medellín and Bogotá, were not soldiers at all but had made a good living up to this point as hired bullies. These men, used to fighting close to home and always in situations where their prey was nearly defenseless, moved awkwardly. They carried, in addition to the boxes of ammunition and bulky weapons, a heavy load of fear.

One of the Libyans was the commander. The other foreigners, having done some soldiering, had a grudging respect for his skills. To the Colombians, he was merely the man put in charge by those who paid their salaries, and so they were compelled to listen to him. There was no mutual respect in this group. There was fear of retaliation against

112

any man who balked, and for the Colombian peasants that threat extended to their families. There was the promise of booty to be had. And for those who loved violence—and there are such men everywhere—there was the promise of battle.

These men had been sent here to turn the tables on the Mexican and American interdiction efforts, which were slowly but surely becoming more effective. In the months since the advent of Operation Sentinel, overland drug traffic between Mexico and the southwest United States had been cut by one third, and the air traffic that passed through Mexico had been cut by one fifth. The men behind the scenes, the men hiding on the palatial ranches in the South American mountains, the men who were a law unto themselves, had decided that the best defense was a good offense. It had worked in Colombia, and they expected it to work in Mexico. They were taking the war to the drug fighters, and the leaders, as well as these men waiting in ambush, were sure it would be a surprise.

The Libyan had kept his men hidden several hundred meters away from the strip, to avoid detection by the American or Mexican scouting planes. Now that the bait, in the form of the smugglers' plane, had arrived, he hurried his men to the northern edge of the airstrip, through some trees there, and into the wash. Hunched over like beggars, they scuttled down the rut, tripping in the gully at the bottom, until they were in a position across the short end of the airstrip. Here they set up their weapons: two Soviet-made medium machine guns that had come by way of Cuba, three RPG-7 antitank grenade launchers, and two SA-7 Grails, which were shoulder-fired, short-range antiaircraft missiles. The Grails were manned by the Israeli and the German. The Colombian veterans had the machine guns, while the peasants were placed in security positions along the flanks. All of the weapons were aimed to place enfilading fire across the length of the dirt airstrip from north to south.

The Libyan checked the men quickly, moving without speaking to them. Out on the runway before them, a half-dozen small cans of fuel burned along the edges of the strip, crude landing lights the airplane had found easily enough, now beckoning to unsuspecting quarry.

The helicopters went into a sharp turn when the pilots spotted the lights burning on the ground below. They swung so that Cortizo and Isen could get a glimpse of the landscape. Cortizo sized up the situation quickly and spoke into the mouthpiece of his headset. The aircraft dropped even lower to the ground and pivoted again, this time more sharply, diving for the lights.

The helicopters landed directly on the airstrip, blocking its use, so that the plane could not escape when the smugglers tried to run. The smugglers always tried to run.

Isen could see the yellow loam in the moonlight as it rushed up to meet him. His bird touched down first, a solid jolt of the big wheels against the dirt strip. He bolted from the door and took a few steps before he hit the ground, skinning elbows and knees. Everything was happening quickly now, and Isen felt the familiar heady rush that visited him in combat, when there were hundreds of things to sort out and decide all at once, and everything happened at twice normal speed. There was a razor sharpness to these moments, a clarity that one could forget about in peacetime, and it seized him now as fresh and frightening as the first time. He brushed against fear as he wondered if the plan would come together, and suddenly there it was, ahead of him, the moonlight glint off the airplane that had drawn them here.

It was parked at the northern corner of the strip, in between two clumps of trees, a fat target and still.

Isen turned to Cortizo, who was just a few feet away and up on his hands and knees, craning to get a better view. Beyond the lieutenant, Isen saw the dark forms of soldiers, moving quickly, sure of their actions, but dangerously backlit by the landing lights. Isen wished someone would douse those torches. A split second later, he wondered why the smugglers hadn't done so when they landed.

The first rounds smashed into the windshield of the lead aircraft, tearing through the sensitive cockpit electronics. The ship buckled and the nose came down, so that the pilot and copilot were looking, just before they crashed, into the wash at the northern end of the strip, where the ambushers were hidden.

Isen turned to the north and saw the yellow tongue of flame from the Grail and knew what it was even as the missile found the howling engines of the second Black-hawk. There was a burst of white light above the bird, which lurched forward and tumbled into the first aircraft. The two of them exploded in a tremendous roar, lighting the whole airstrip, catching the Mexican assault team out in the open.

Isen rolled away from the light, got up on his feet and sprinted, in a low crouch, for the dark edge of woods on the east side of the LZ. When he reached the trees, which provided no cover but at least were in shadow, he looked back out to the open area. Amid the explosions, he hadn't yet heard the machine gun, but now he could see the red tracers, the deadly finger of light, searching for targets among the soldiers who hadn't made cover. At last three rumpled forms littered the open space.

Both aircraft were down, and he had no idea where Cortizo was. He figured he was only a few dozen meters from the smugglers' plane. He turned north, thinking he might catch another glimpse of its sleek hull to get his bearings, and was rewarded with a hail of gunfire that chopped splinters of wood from the tree just above his head.

There was a security team in the woods near the plane. Isen flattened out in the dirt, the left side of his face feeling the heat from the fire out on the strip. He couldn't hear the Mexicans, didn't know how many of them had been hit; he might be the only one left, for all he knew. He took a few seconds to gather his thoughts. In the careful placement of the security team to protect the airplane, Isen saw the evidence of a well-planned ambush.

Even given the disaster that was unfolding, Cortizo still felt somewhat in control. When the firing started, even before the second helicopter had been hit, he felt a wavering among the men, a shaky, uncertain lean toward panic. But it passed quickly, and when he commanded, they responded just as they had been trained. If he'd had a second or two to articulate it, he might have thought, *They are good men.* For now, he moved, and they moved with him.

He hustled his men off the southern end of the airstrip, intending to attack around the right in a sweep that would keep them clear of the huge circle of light from the flames.

Things were bad, but he was reacting. He remembered laughing the first time Isen had used one of those epigrammatic sayings that Americans are so fond of, *Don't Do Nothing.* It meant, of course, to take action. He had taken action and was now figuring out how to gain the advantage over the ambushers. Isen would be pleased.

Cortizo had fifteen men with him in the darkness at the southern edge of the strip, including two of the Americans, Spano and Worden. Here, the ground sloped down from the landing lights, and they were protected from the ambushers, who were below ground on the opposite end. He knew there were at least three men out on the strip, dead or wounded. That left three unaccounted for, including Isen. Cortizo felt a small pang of guilt, for he cared about his soldiers a great deal, when he realized that he hoped Isen wasn't one of the men down.

Cortizo split the group into two squads, and since one of the missing men was a squad leader, he decided to command one group himself. The Americans, armed only with pistols, split up between the two formations. The airstrip sat on the flat top of a low, nearly circular hill. He planned to move around that circle to the right, keeping below the level of the field, heading north until they hit the low ground and the wash where the ambushers were. They would cross over the dry bed and get behind the enemy, using the light from the burning helicopters to silhouette the smugglers. As he briefed the other squad leader, Cortizo noticed that the men around him were all quietly facing outward, securing their position as Isen had stressed to them so many times. The soldier nearest him had his rifle at the ready, but shook visibly. Cortizo put a hand on the man's arm to steady him.

"I will be all right," the soldier said.

"We will all be fine," Cortizo said loud enough for a few of the men to hear.

The two teams moved out, Cortizo's in the lead.

The Libyan commanding the ad hoc force of ambushers had anticipated this scenario, though he thought it the least likely. He had killed the helicopters, but because he hadn't initiated the ambush immediately, and because the Mexicans had moved faster than he had expected them to, the soldiers were able to get out of the aircraft. Now there were at least a dozen enemy out on the ground unaccounted for—and they would be looking for him. In an uneven fight, such as an ambush, he was not reluctant to take on the Mexicans. He was less thrilled about sparring with them in the darkness on more even terms. There was something about this group, about the way they had moved from the helicopters, that made him think twice about his chances and the contingency plan he had thought up.

The Libyan climbed out of the wash and made his way over to the plane. He lay beneath the wheels and called to the four men he had in the security position on the south side of the aircraft. He knew only one by name, an older man, perhaps forty, he had placed in charge.

"Raoul." Pause. "Raoul."

"I am here," the man whispered back. "They are in front of us, on the other side of these woods." There was a trace of panic in Raoul's voice, and the Libyan wondered if the old Colombian could be right. Perhaps they were already being flanked.

"How many?" the Libyan called.

"I know we shot one of them," Raoul answered.

The quavering in the old man's voice made the Libyan wonder if his plan to use these four would work.

"Raoul, I want you to advance straight ahead," the mercenary leader said. He paused, waiting to see if Raoul would answer. "We killed most of them on the far side of the strip." The Libyan turned to gauge whether Raoul could see enough of the open space to know he was lying. "Some of the wounded dragged themselves off into the

117

woods in front of you. All you have to do is walk forward and shoot them.''

There was no movement from the woods in front of him. The Libyan strained, in the glow from the fire, to see where he had placed the security team.

"Raoul."

"This one was not wounded."

"What?" The Libyan stalled, trying to think of another way to use these four—he thought of them as expendable—to flush the Mexicans.

"The one we saw was not wounded. There may be more out there, and now they wait for us. We cannot move."

The Libyan resorted to his trump card.

"Raoul, you must move forward now, or I will come looking for *you*."

The commander watched the woods, and it was nearly a minute before he saw anything, but finally the four men stirred themselves and began to move away from the aircraft. He figured they had a better than even chance of stumbling into the enemy and getting killed, but he wasn't concerned with the lives of these men; his only objective was to find out where the Mexicans were.

Isen heard the whole conversation in Spanish from his vantage point only thirty meters away from the security team. He had no idea what they were saying but figured something was up and so took care to conceal himself. Then four men stood upright and walked toward him, all of them talking nervously among themselves. Because he didn't know where Cortizo was, he assumed that the four were looking for him. His pistol felt very light in his hand.

Cortizo's men had now worked their way almost to the wash and were heading due north, only about sixty meters away from where Isen lay tense in the underbrush. Excited and barely able to contain himself, Cortizo had moved all the way up in the formation to a position just behind the point man. The mix of exhilaration and fear made him feel extraordinarily alive, as if he were breathing pure oxygen through the very pores of his skin. Off to his left, the burning helicopters still blotted out the moonlight.

Isen thought at first that the men would pass him without seeing him. The four figures, lit by the fire, were bunching together and would pass to Isen's right. It would be close, but he would be all right.

Then one of the men—Isen recognized the voice from the conversation—turned to the others and snapped some command. Isen watched and knew that he had told them not to bunch up. One of the figures turned around a tree and walked directly toward him.

The man was twenty-five feet away, pushing through the scant brush, his head down, holding his rifle carelessly, with his arms fully extended, so that the stock was across his thighs. He was small, maybe five feet tall, Isen guessed, and hatless. He shuffled forward, walking some invisible line to Isen. There was nowhere the American could go. If he stood, they would all see him; if he moved, at least the closest one would see him.

Isen thumbed the safety on his weapon.

The man was fifteen feet away.

Isen decided that he would shoot first, before the bandit could get off a shot. He wondered where the other three were, for he would have to shoot them too, but he couldn't take his eyes off the man approaching him. The dark figure dragged his feet through the brush, laboring under a death sentence he knew nothing about.

Isen brought the pistol up, braced his firing hand with his left, and drew a bead on the man's face.

The little man stopped and bent over.

Isen was not breathing.

When the ambusher stood again, not ten feet away, he looked directly at Isen, and in the unsure light, Isen thought he saw the eyes widen almost imperceptibly.

He pulled the trigger.

The sudden flash and roar stunned even Isen, and he did not see, through the muzzle flash, the man fall. Isen immediately turned to his right, where he imagined the other three were. One of the bandits fired blindly into the night, and Isen swung his locked arms around to where the muzzle flash cut the dark, giving away the firer's position. He squeezed off two rounds and saw the shooter go down.

Isen turned and crawled furiously back to the south, in the same direction these hunters had been going. He was breathing in short grunts now; the noise startled him, and he wondered if they would hear him. He raised himself to a crouch and ran awkwardly, arms and hands scraping the ground like an ape. He rushed a few meters before stopping to see if anyone was chasing him, but the woods behind him were silent, heavily laced with the smell of shooting.

His first thought was *I made it,* and then, *Where the hell is everybody?*

When he heard the firing to his left, Cortizo halted his patrol. He guessed, correctly, that the ambushers were looking for him. He stopped the forward movement of his men, placed them on line facing the small woods where the firing had come from, then crawled forward to see what was going on.

The Libyan was startled by the shots, coming as they did so quickly after he sent the four men forward. He decided to move his men left, around to the eastern side of the woods. He motioned for them to get up, and the little band moved out of the wash, trying to find the advantageous position. The commander, mistaking the location of Isen's shooting for the position of the Mexicans, estimated that his quarry must be just south of the airplane at the edge of the woods. He hurried the men along, and they moved efficiently, but with no evident desire to close with the enemy. These mercenaries were happy to ambush a group, but mistrusted one another too much to chance a stand-up fight.

When they cleared the wash and the small open space that held the still undisturbed airplane, the bandits formed two wedges and sliced into the small woods. The Libyan judged that they needed to stay about ten or fifteen meters east of where they heard the firing.

He was off by a good bit.

\* \* \*

Major Ray Spano held his battle dressing—torn from a pouch on his suspenders—against his calf. He'd fallen like a sack on the airstrip, feeling as if someone had kicked him hard on the fleshy part of his calf. He made it off the strip and found that his pants leg was torn and sticky. He couldn't risk turning on a flashlight to examine the wound, but he thought he'd taken a round through the muscle there. He pressed hard and looked around.

Spano was concerned about Isen. He'd seen Worden in the other squad-size group Cortizo had formed, but not Isen, and he wondered if Mark was one of the dark forms he had seen out on the runway. Spano was on line with the other Mexican soldiers Cortizo commanded. He crawled forward a few painful inches and gasped in surprise at what he saw next in the light from the still-burning aircraft. Eight or nine men walked in between their position and the fire, passing from right to left, and even among the small trees they silhouetted themselves against the light. At least one of them was struggling with a heavy weapon, perhaps a machine gun. A few feet away, Spano could just make out Cortizo. The lieutenant took a second to look left and right along his line. His men were alert, all of them looking at the targets that had so obligingly walked between their rifles and the light. Cortizo raised his weapon and pulled the trigger.

Isen froze when the edge of the wood erupted in fire, and he pressed himself to the ground, wishing he could burrow beneath the soil. Stray rounds passed over his head, *thwacking* against the small trees and ripping the air. The firing swelled rapidly, then fell away to a few shots in less than a minute. He heard some movement off to the east, and then, incredibly, he heard his name being called.

"Captain Isen. *Captain Isen.*"

He didn't trust his ears completely, but he thought it sounded like Cortizo. He waited until his head stopped ringing, then he crawled around to face the sound of the voices. Soon there were teams of Mexican soldiers moving through the bush, calling his name even as they looked for more of the enemy.

"Captain Isen."

After the terrible loss of the aircraft, his side had won this skirmish.

Isen found Cortizo and Spano near the smugglers' airplane. Spano was sitting against a tree, his leg wrapped in something bloody.

"This is turning out to be a helluva visit," Spano said to Isen.

"You gonna be all right?"

"Yeah. It just went through the meaty part. Course, my days as a world-class marathoner are over."

In the diminishing light from the fire, Isen could see two other ambushers, probably the pilot and copilot, kneeling on the ground with their hands behind their heads. Cortizo was looking over a wooden case of extra ammunition in the doorway of the plane.

"I am glad to see you are in one piece, Captain," Cortizo said formally.

Isen tried to talk but found his mouth incredibly dry. Cortizo handed him a canteen, and he took a long, luxurious pull. He tried to screw the cap back on, but his hands were shaking. Cortizo took it back with the cap still open.

"They got the drop on us somehow," Isen said finally.

"Yes." Cortizo looked as if he wanted to say more. "There are a lot of things wrong with this little war. There is too much money involved. They hire mercenaries . . ." he motioned at the two prisoners, then left the thought unfinished. "They simply have too much money."

Shaken as he was, Isen noticed something in Cortizo, something similar to what he had seen when Gaspar, Isen's predecessor, had talked plainly about how corrupt Cortizo's old boss had been. There were some things that pride would always keep Isen and Cortizo from sharing.

"But you," Cortizo said with sudden enthusiasm, "you were wonderful. *You* kept us from taking more casualties." Cortizo was suddenly animated, effusive. He stepped away from the plane and walked toward Isen, his arms wide, taking in the whole scene.

"What are you talking about?" Isen asked him.

A large figure walked up out of the darkness. Sergeant Worden.

"Those were your shots that warned us of the bandits' position, correct?" Cortizo went on.

"I shot . . ." Isen was about to say *first,* then thought about his warning to Sergeant Worden. He had violated the rules of engagement but believed that the facts would speak for themselves; besides, Cortizo deserved the truth. "I shot one of them just as he was about to walk on me."

Cortizo nodded, grasping the situation immediately. "Don't worry," he said. "Come with me."

He and Isen walked toward the airstrip, where his soldiers had collected the bodies of the bandits killed. Isen's eyes were drawn to the still-burning heaps that had been the two Blackhawks. He would be the one to report the deaths of those crews to their commander. Someone else, someone far away and yet unsuspecting, would have the job of telling the families.

"Look here," Cortizo said, pointing at the corpses. "These two we dragged from the woods."

Isen looked down, but could see very little. Cortizo split the merciful darkness with his pocket flashlight. One of the bodies was a man, shot in the side. Isen recognized the entry wounds as being from his pistol. *This was the second one I shot, the one who gave away his position by firing blindly,* Isen thought. The other body was very small, a young man, maybe even a teenager. The boy's mouth was wide open. There was a small hole above the right eye, where Isen's round had entered the skull.

One of the soldiers nearby said something in Spanish, and Cortizo laughed mildly. He shined his flashlight on the dead boy's eyes, which were crossed grotesquely. Cortizo repeated the joke in English.

"He was watching the bullet up until it hit," the lieutenant said, only smiling now.

Isen bent down to look closely at the face of his enemy.

Isen spent the twelve hours after the ambush at the crash site, waiting for the Mexicans to remove the bodies, then waiting for someone in his chain of command to relieve him of having to stay with the wreckage. Early the following afternoon, an officer from the U.S. Army aviation unit that had supplied the crews and Blackhawks took over the work of recovering the aircraft. By the time he reached Cortizo's base camp, Isen was in turmoil about what he'd seen and done. He attended Cortizo's second debriefing—the first had been right after they returned from the mission—and wrote his report about what had happened. He did not write that he had fired first, but skated around what was quickly becoming—in his mind at least—a dangerous hole in the ice.

*I engaged one of the attackers who had discovered me in my hiding position,* he wrote, imagining how someone reading the report would take that line. He told himself that the feeling of unease came with being a survivor: it would take more than an army report to put to rest the dead men and the questions he had about their mission.

Isen had two notebooks in the personal effects that Adrienne had sent down to him. He used one of them for writing letters, because he didn't like the cramped pages of standard letter tablets. He liked to write long missives, liked to see the words spread out on the page, to feel the weight of the thoughts he was sending, as if they could be measured by the space he filled up. Mostly, he liked to write because it helped him think, helped him sort out the confusing welter of ideas. And thus he decided to write to the *Army Times* about Mexico.

But as he sat on an overturned washtub outside his sleeping quarters the next day, Isen found the empty white page daunting. He was suddenly terrified of the work before him. He had to write something that would tell the other Americans coming down what was going on here, without appearing condescending to either side. One of the greatest problems with his fellow officers, Isen understood, was that they too often thought they knew everything. He somehow had to explain to them that this was a new venture that was at once war *and* politics, even for foot soldiers. He had to tell them that in the modern United States Army, it was no longer enough to be a warrior. Even captains had to be statesmen.

He had to convey the deadly seriousness of what they were about, both out of respect for the soldiers he'd just seen die and out of necessity for those who would be following. This was no game. He had to think also of his superiors; he could not write honestly without mentioning the problems with the program, but he could not make his writing an indictment. He had to be positive, forthright and cautious, informative and engaging. He had to pick the correct tone but had not yet even imagined his audience. He had to write legibly enough so that he could send it to Adrienne, back in that part of the world where there were typewriters. And he was worried about all these things before he even put the pen to the paper.

Not surprisingly, Mark Isen drew a blank.

He looked out over the camp. Down the hill the soldiers were cleaning their weapons. They were spread out under the shade of a half-dozen thin trees, hats off, some of them sitting on the ground, their legs splayed like children. Isen could just hear the notes of conversation. These boys who had little or no say in their being here were learning the grim truths that all soldiers must eventually face. Off to the side, Isen could see Cortizo, standing, hat on, because he was the commander and so had to lend his support, even if that simply meant being present as the young men—his soldiers—adjusted to the absence of some of their own and to the new presence: sudden, violent death. And Isen began to write.

*Lieutenant Cortizo, the commander of the company I advise, has an odd habit of rocking back and forth on his toes whenever he is intent on something. He is intent a lot.*

He tried to tell his audience of American soldiers what it meant to be a Lieutenant Cortizo—a conscientious professional caught between mammoth opposing forces: the seemingly unstoppable, greed-driven smugglers; an American electorate that assumed its successful army could stop the flow of drugs by applying enough force (in someone else's backyard); and the struggling government of Mexico, riddled with drug-money bribes and scared of becoming a battleground, or worse, another Colombia. But he got through only those two sentences before the little black marks failed him. He could never force mere letters to contain what it felt like to lose men in battle, what it felt like to make mistakes that cost other men their lives. And even though his own moment of fear—when he thought the bandits were going to find and kill him first—had been as sharp and dense as a diamond, he could not get that tiny speck onto the paper and still retain all of the truth.

He tore the top sheet off the pad, balled it up, dropped it at his feet. He wondered if he should remind Cortizo not to mention, in the report the Mexican would file, the fact that Isen shot first.

A few days after the battle at the landing zone, Mark Isen was sitting on a camp stool, cleaning his pistol, when he heard footsteps approach. He didn't bother to look up, expecting Cortizo or Sergeant Worden, so he was surprised to hear an unfamiliar American voice.

"Captain Isen?"

Isen shaded his eyes and looked up. The voice belonged to a captain, also dressed in desert camouflage, who stood with a notebook in his hands.

"Yeah," Isen said, standing. The other officer put out his hand, and Isen shifted the pistol and cleaning rag to his left hand to shake. "Mark."

"Pleased to meet you. My name's Eric Cartson. I'm with the Public Affairs Office down in Mexico City."

Cartson, who looked young for a captain, Isen thought, was an infantry officer. But his uniform and boots were too clean to be from anywhere but headquarters. On closer inspection, Isen noticed that the holster that depended from his belt was empty.

"What can I do for you?" Isen said, sitting back down and resuming his work.

"I have a reporter here from Los Angeles. He's doing some interviews around the countryside, talking to Operation Sentinel people, and he'd like to talk to you."

Isen felt a small unsettling, but then he remembered that

Cortizo hadn't mentioned, in his official report, that Isen had fired first at the ambush site. *Don't get paranoid, now,* he told himself. Cartson's mundane briefing put him further at ease; this was all pretty standard.

"You can talk about anything that's unclassified, as long as you don't speculate about future operations. You can also end the interview any time you begin to feel uncomfortable or unsure of what's going on. I'll stand by and will be glad to listen in if you want; it's up to you."

"Okay," Isen said, checking the action on his reassembled weapon. "Where is this guy?"

"He's down there talking to some of the soldiers," Cartson said, indicating with his head the Mexican barracks just down the hill.

Isen didn't hide his concern well. "He's talking to the Mexican soldiers?"

"He was," Cartson answered. "That's him coming up the hill now." He turned back to Isen. "He's from Los Angeles, a native. Speaks fluent Spanish, although he tells me he has trouble every once in a while understanding what some of the soldiers are saying."

Isen stood, his pistol held loosely by his side and watched the figure approach.

"Captain Mark Isen," Cartson said, standing to introduce the two men. "This is Jorge Perreira."

Before they even shook hands, Perreira dropped his bomb. "So this is the American marksman," he said.

Cartson stayed around for the rest of the show, at Isen's request. Isen did his best to contain the damage, explaining how he'd had no choice but to fire on the smugglers. Perreira nodded sympathetically, but the tenor of his opening remark left little doubt as to how the story would play. When they were finished, Cartson walked the reporter back to their vehicle, then returned to where Isen was still standing by the camp stool.

"Well?" Isen said.

"He could write it a lot of different ways," Cartson said. "The Mexican soldiers did their best to convince him that you were a hero out there."

"But he could make it sound bad too," Isen said.

"There's always that possibility," Cartson admitted, "when you're dealing with these guys." He scuffed his clean boots in the dust. "I guess I have to let them know about this down in Mexico City."

Isen looked at him. He'd expected as much but wanted to hear Cartson's reasons.

"We can't shut down this story, not for certain, anyway. And it's better to give the general a heads-up before the story is printed."

"I agree," Isen said.

He watched the two men drive away in the dusty rented jeep. Then Isen picked up his weapon-cleaning gear and his camp stool and went inside his hootch. He looked around at the stuff on the floor, two-duffel-bags-worth of uniforms, some candy wrappers from junk food Adrienne had mailed him. He sat down on the cot and leaned close to a picture of Adrienne taped to the wall.

"At least if I get fired, I'll get to see you soon, baby," he said aloud.

# THE COMMON DEFENSE

## No More Yellow Ribbons:
## The Nation Looks for a Common Cause

by J. Cox
Special to *The New York Times*

May 1—The millions of yellow ribbons that decorated everything from front doors to huge office buildings during the Persian Gulf War have given way to something that is, sadly, more familiar on the American landscape: a frustrating lack of consensus as the nation faces another challenge.

The recent terrorist attacks on Americans in Europe have provoked an angry response from all sectors of the population. Everyone decries the crimes, but no one is sure how to proceed from here.

Some groups within the political body, though anxious to distance themselves from the terrorists, are using the current crisis to point out the folly of a large American military presence in Europe. At a recent Greenpeace rally in the nation's capital, one speaker pointed out that "keeping American service members and their families in Europe simply exposes these innocent people to attack. There is no reason the United States should maintain current troop strengths in a Europe no longer threatened by the Soviet Union."

Yet other groups are quick to point out that times of crisis call for strengthened resolve. "We must not bow to the demands of outlaws," a U.S. senator recently told a convention of the Veterans of Foreign Wars. "We must stand up to our enemies."

For most Americans, the problem does not seem to be whether or not we should "stand up" to our enemies; the question is: How do we strike? Who do we strike?

C. T. Luding, a professor of international relations at Duke University, said in an interview that the problem is the lack of a target. "In 1986, when the U.S. claimed it had airtight evidence linking the Libyans to the bombing of a bar favored by American soldiers in West Berlin, President Reagan responded by bombing

Libya. There is no such clear objective this time, no state to target. We—as a nation—are getting beaten up, and we don't have anyone we can hit back."

Retired Marine Lieutenant General Richard Bokmeyer, who fought in Vietnam and who now works for the Rand Corporation, suggested that these problems are not new. "The frustration we are seeing now is not unlike what we saw in Vietnam. When you can't pin down the enemy, when you feel like you're fighting ghosts, the frustration mounts. There is no national consensus, and that makes it hard to give the military a definable mission."

This lack of a national objective may be reflected in the polls indicating the President's approval ratings, which have risen and fallen dramatically with every new development or presidential announcement.

Or the problem may be more accurately defined in the remarks of Staff Sergeant Mark Bond, a U.S. Army cavalryman stationed in Germany. Sergeant Bond recently put his family on a plane back to the States, saying that "they're safer at home." As he made ready to leave the bustling Frankfurt Airport, Sergeant Bond told a reporter, "You know, we went over and kicked Iraq's butt when they messed around and didn't take us seriously. I hated every day I spent in the desert over there," Sergeant Bond said as he lit a cigarette. "But I'd do it again to fight these people who are killing GIs and families—if we only knew who to fight."

# 9

## Mexico City, Mexico
### 3 May

HEINRICH WOLF DROVE ALONE OUT OF MEXICO CITY IN A small American-made car, the ineffectual air conditioner going full blast, the windows shut tight against the heat and the queasy odors of the city. He had been in-country only two days and had stayed busy since his plane had touched down at Benito Juárez International Airport. If he stuck to his tight schedule, he'd finish everything well before the deadline he'd set for himself. He expected this next phase to take longer than the two weeks he'd mentioned in his last threat, but that was part of the psychological game he was playing. He would always make a threat; sometimes he would strike before the deadline, sometimes after. They would always know something was coming, but they would never be able to say exactly when—that would give them too much control.

Flush with excitement, he tapped his hands against the hot black plastic of the steering wheel. With the very first stroke of his plan—the bombing in Germany—he had managed to focus the considerable attention of the world media on his demands. He'd had a few moments of fear at the airport when he left Germany; the police attention had been extraordinary. But Wolf had covered his tracks well. The

131

BKA, or *Bundeskriminalamt,* the agency responsible for antiterrorist and antinarcotic work in Germany, was certain to be looking for him. But he was fairly certain that they did not yet know his identity and had no way of tracing his move to North America. The first rounds had gone well, Wolf allowed.

Mexico was the logical jumping-off point for the next stages of his war. In order to convince the Soviets that he was serious and could deliver the promised results, Wolf had to hit hard. A few strikes against U.S. installations in Europe would not be enough. Wolf wanted to strike the Americans where they hadn't been hit before: at home. It was easy to get into the U.S. from Canada, but tough to get into Canada. It was a bit more difficult to cross the southern border into the U.S., but a great deal easier to move men and materiel into Mexico. When he considered that there already existed a complex system for moving contraband north from Mexico into the U.S., the choice of a staging area was easy.

Wolf had spent an entire day sorting out the various bank accounts in Mexico City to which his Soviet military contact would wire funds. He had allowed himself to hope that these Mexican banks—many of which helped move drug money to offshore accounts—would be easy to deal with. He was not disappointed, and three of the banks he chose indicated that they were eager to accept large deposits on his behalf. No one bothered to ask his line of work.

On this last day before joining the battle again, he traveled alone out of the city to a small hotel where he was to meet the only non-German who had anything to do with his scheme. He found the street easily enough, but missed the hotel on his first pass. When he checked the address again, he pulled his car over and walked back along the tiny sidewalk until he found the place. A shaky wooden staircase rose from a trash-filled courtyard to the second floor. Wolf picked his way through the garbage, then went up slowly, glancing back down the street from the top. When he put his foot on the last step he looked down at his right leg to see if the pistol showed. A small automatic, complete with a silencer, was strapped to the inside of his right ankle. The cold metal lump felt like a tumor. Satisfied that the piece was well hidden, he walked to the door where a long-gone and rusty 4 had left its mark in the chipped paint.

A short, dark man answered his knock, looked past Wolf to the stairway, then stuck his head out and checked the small landing. Convinced that Wolf was alone, he met the much taller German's eyes.

"What do you want?" the man said in English.

"I need directions," Wolf said. The man's gaze didn't flicker, and Wolf continued the code. "I am a long way from my home in Europe, and I heard you are also a traveler."

"Wait here."

The dark man turned his back on Wolf and walked into the room. Wolf glanced again at the courtyard and the street below, then back into the open room. He heard a woman's voice inside.

They were supposed to meet alone.

Wolf raised his leg and pulled the pistol from its strap and peered into the dark room, waiting for his eyes to adjust. The man was going through the pockets of a pair of pants that hung from a bedpost. On the bed, a small Mexican girl of about seventeen watched, then said something in Spanish. She was naked from the waist up, and she made no effort to cover herself when she noticed Wolf looking in. She picked up a bra from the mass of crumpled sheets and placed it—backwards—around her middle. Wolf stared. She hooked the bra in the front, then spun it around and slipped her arms in. The small man gave her some money and patted her bottom when she stood up. She put a flimsy shirt over her shoulders and, without bothering to button it, slipped past Wolf, who stood woodenly in the tiny doorway.

Wolf watched her go, remembering to fold his arms so that the pistol was hidden under one armpit. She didn't even look at him.

Wolf went inside and noticed for the first time that the man who'd answered the door was in his underwear. The room was larger than Wolf expected, though it was hard to tell just how large because of the gloom. It smelled of fried food, unwashed clothes, sex. Wolf looked at his contact, who shrugged and said, "I have been waiting for six days."

"Do you have my material?" Wolf asked.

"It is in the city," the man answered.

Wolf felt a small flutter of concern. He'd planned on killing this foreigner—a mere middleman—once he knew where his merchandise was, but if the messenger held on to the information, there was no way Wolf could get rid of him. Even if he could kill him here, there was a small chance that the whore might return to her customer to earn a few more pesos and wind up telling the police about the tall European she had seen.

But the man across from him, a Palestinian, didn't seem as suspicious as Wolf. In an automatic response that seemed easier on this continent, Wolf categorized him as another example of the inferior races.

"I rented a small garage in the city," the Palestinian said. "Everything you need is in there. I will give you the keys and directions as soon as I pack."

Wolf sat down on the single chair and tried not to watch the other man dress. He thought about the whore, wondered if she were diseased. He wondered how much it cost to have her, wondered how her brown body would move under his in the heat.

*Stop it,* he told himself. And with the snap of control came a physical revulsion—a palpable shudder at the thought of coupling with the whore after the Palestinian had mingled his sweat with hers.

Across the small space, the Palestinian pulled on a pair of dirty cotton trousers and a clean shirt, then threw a few things into a nylon bag. Wolf hated dark people, and he suddenly felt sick in the room, surrounded by the foreign smells.

"I thought devout Moslems shunned foreign women, unclean women," Wolf said. The Palestinian said nothing, but continued packing his few things.

*He is probably ashamed that I found him with that slut,* Wolf thought. *Or maybe he is too dull to even care.* Wolf felt the rise of a self-righteous anger. *And the Moslems go on and on about the infidel Westerners.* The man was nearly finished and still hadn't said anything.

Wolf pressed his point. "I said, I thought . . ."

"I heard what you said," the Palestinian snapped as he wheeled around. He had a large automatic in his hand, and the barrel was leveled at Wolf.

"Let me have that tiny pistol you carried in here," the Palestinian said.

Wolf had no choice but to hand over his weapon. He tossed the gun onto the bed, and the Palestinian picked it up and pocketed it. Wolf wanted to ask the Palestinian what was going on but thought he would sound stupid or, worse yet, frightened.

The dark man waved a piece of paper at Wolf. "I will leave the address of the garage here," he said, placing the soiled paper on the nightstand. Then he produced a set of keys from his pocket and dropped them on top of the note. "And the keys as well."

The man wasn't going to kill him but was merely guaranteeing his own escape. Wolf was too angry to feel relieved.

*I've been outsmarted,* Wolf thought, his face burning.

"You're not all that careful for a big international terrorist," the Palestinian said as he backed out the door. He grinned at Wolf, and only one side of his mouth turned up. "You'd better watch yourself."

Wolf fumed all the way back to the city. He had been humiliated by a whoremonger, an inferior, and it was only his pressing timetable that kept him from pursuing the little man and killing him. For several miles he entertained himself with mental pictures of his strangling hands around the Palestinian's throat.

By the time he reached the area where the rented garage was located, he was calm enough to have his guard back in place. As he always did when approaching a new spot, he drove around the area a few times to look for police activity. But this neighborhood, like so many in Mexico City, was desperately poor, and Wolf doubted that the police came to this sector often.

The garage was off a narrow alley, which, Wolf noted,

might make loading difficult. He parked the car near the mouth of the alley and walked the few meters down the narrow passage to the door he sought. There was a shiny new lock on the hasp, looking out of place against the cracked and peeling paint, once green, that caked the wooden door. He opened the lock with one of the keys on the ring and swung the door up.

The garage was empty.

Wolf, thinking he'd been had, felt a dangerous welling of anger rise inside him. He was about to slam the door down when he noticed a smaller door at the back of the room. He climbed over stacks of garbage, rusty cans, pieces of metal, old newspapers, and a single child's shoe, and tried the remaining key in the lock on the back door. This one opened onto a smaller room that was barely big enough to stand in. Wolf bent over and peered into the gloom. He felt something on his face—a spider?—and pulled back quickly, banging his head on the doorframe.

It was only the string from an overhead light.

He tugged at the string with one hand as he rubbed the back of his head with the other. The light showed a wooden packing crate in the corner. Its forged markings declared that it had come through Cuba from Hong Kong. Wolf knew it had actually come straight from the Mediterranean through Cuba to Mexico.

He pulled at the wooden top, prying loose the one nail that held the lid on the already opened container. The squeak was loud in the small space. Wolf reached in and pushed aside the straw packing, wondering if there might be spiders in here.

The first thing he found was a radio cassette player wired to what looked like a plastic-wrapped block of artist's clay. Under that, his hand felt something cold, and he pushed the straw aside more vigorously until he uncovered the top of a metal tank, like something a hospital might use to hold oxygen. He felt a shiver of pleasure and fear this close to the weapon, but he forced his hands down deeper in the straw until he could count the metal bottles in the crate.

There were six of them.

Wolf removed the cassette player and put it into a blue

nylon bag he'd brought along. Then he closed the crate and locked the inner door. In the dark garage he allowed himself a smile of self-congratulation.

He had worked the whole plan out ahead of time, in great detail, which satisfied his penchant for orderliness and gave the campaign—in his mind at least—a certain weight, an importance, an aura of the irresistible. Wolf could easily imagine the whole affair, laid out before him in the coming months on the neat blocks and lines of his calendar, all of it pointing to an apocalyptic ending somewhere in the United States. And now the pieces were beginning to fall into place with a satisfying sound, like the dropping of tumblers in the lock of the garage door.

*Now the battle begins in earnest,* Wolf thought.

# 10

## Benito Juárez International Airport
## Mexico City, Mexico
### 7 May

THERESA BOYLE HAD NEVER USED COCAINE, BUT SHE COULD
understand how users, once tempted, could be attracted to
something so dangerous: she had the same weakness for
drug money. On more than a dozen occasions the petite
twenty-five-year-old beauty had carried, for no small sum,
a piece of luggage on board one of the American Airlines
flights between Mexico City and Dallas-Fort Worth on
which she worked as a flight attendant. She suspected that
the bags contained drugs, but she never looked. The men
who contacted her, usually while she was staying overnight
at the hotel near Benito Juárez International Airport in Mexico City, paid her to pick up a small piece of hand luggage
from one of the ground crew—after her own bags had been
through customs—and carry it on the plane as if it were
her own. She never had to touch the luggage after it was
on the plane; someone in the DFW ground crew recovered
the bag from the overhead compartment where she stowed
it.

Boyle was in it for the money, and that was it. She got
no secret thrill out of the illicit contacts, she did not try to
kid herself about what she was doing, and she never had
anything to say to the men she dealt with. To all appear-

ances she was what she purported to be: a sincere and clean-living young woman from a devout Irish Catholic family, a model worker, and an upright citizen. Her coworkers, who called her Mother Theresa more or less behind her back, never suspected her of any wrongdoing. But that was all a sham. Every job—called a carry—frightened her badly. Sometimes she became violently ill after it was over, when she was alone in Dallas with her money and her fears. But she hadn't yet learned how to say no to a great deal of cash.

Boyle was in the bathroom of her hotel room, brushing her teeth after eating lunch in the restaurant downstairs, when the phone rang. She spit out the toothpaste and checked her watch as she crossed the room; there were three hours until the weekday flight to Dallas–Fort Worth.

"Hello."

"Theresa Boyle?" a male voice said.

"Speaking." Theresa tried to remember if she'd given the room number to any of the pilots she'd met the night before. Not that they couldn't find her anyway. Her roommate came in, and Theresa smiled at her.

"I have a friend who tells me that you will carry a package for me," the man said.

Boyle dragged the phone into the bathroom, shutting the door on the cord and her roommate's hearing. "I don't know what you're talking about," she said.

"Yes. He said you would say that too, and that I was to respond by telling you that the package is for my mother, who is sick."

Theresa had dreamed up the little code-talk herself after reading a spy novel in which a handsome character named Jack something used an elaborate, preplanned conversation to identify his contacts. But the conversations on the hotel phone rarely delivered the kind of drama she hoped for, and she was never able, like the people in the stories, to enjoy spending the money. She was always teetering on the edge of hysteria.

*But there was always the money.*

"Go ahead," Theresa said.

"You will pick up two packages at the end of the tunnel,

from the operator," the voice said, referring to the person who drove the movable walkway that sheltered passengers as they entered an aircraft. "One of them—a small blue bag—will be ours. Put it in the port side overhead just behind first class seating. The other will be for you and will contain ten thousand American dollars."

Theresa did not answer at first. This was her standard rate, but lately she had thought about asking for more.

*After all,* she mused, *I am risking my job and my freedom. These people have the money to spare.*

"Are you there?" the voice demanded.

Her mouth was dusty dry, and she thought she could feel her chest expanding with each breath. She told herself that she had nothing to fear from these men, that she was only afraid of losing the business. But all of her worries churned in the faint hum of static on the line, and she backed down.

"That is acceptable," she said into the receiver.

"The operator will have the bags." There was a click at the other end, and the line went dead. She came out of the bathroom and met her roommate's inquisitive look.

"A passenger?" her roommate asked. Making dates with passengers was against company policy, though many of the women who worked the first class section did, in fact, *work* the first class section.

Theresa gave her a noncommittal shrug.

"I thought you'd be the last person," the other woman said, trailing off lest she say something about "Mother Theresa." "You're going to get yourself in a lot of trouble."

*I am going to get myself out of this business,* Theresa thought, smiling her act.

In spite of her misgivings, once Theresa decided to accept the luggage, she never looked back. Because there was so much at stake, she focused completely on becoming the ideal smuggler: cool and calculating, fully aware of everything going on around her. When she walked down the tunnel ahead of the passengers and other crew members, she saw a ground maintenance worker standing on the metal staircase that clung to the outside of the enclosed walkway. Theresa went to the small operator's window, smiled at him, and nodded. It took only a few seconds for the man to open the door and hand her a small nylon bag and a cheap zippered purse. Theresa did not look at either of the pieces, nor did she speak to the man. She ducked into the cabin of the Boeing 727 and placed her bags, along with the small purse, in the forward-most compartment for carry-on luggage. She stowed the nylon bag as she had been instructed. As she walked to the forward galley she began to count the hours she would have to live with the blue bag. Ten thousand dollars was a lot of money, but while she was carrying, Theresa was never convinced it was worth it.

Heinrich Wolf had paid handsomely for the information that led him to Theresa Boyle. Even so, the trail hadn't been that hard to pick up. He hired a private investigator in Mexico City to gather information about ongoing investigations of airport smuggling. The investigator used half of Wolf's ten thousand American dollars to get a few names from an old friend with the city police. Wolf fashioned and delivered a story about his being an investigative reporter for *Stern*, the German news magazine, but the investigator seemed not the least bit interested.

Wolf had used a name supplied by the Soviets to secure the device that was in the small nylon bag Theresa Boyle stowed in the overhead compartment. Wolf hoped eventually to lure the bomb builder, also German, to Mexico in order to guarantee access to what he needed.

In the bag three small barometers, set to measure the changes in cabin pressure over the flight path, were wired separately to an electronic ignition. Any two of the instruments could fail and the device would still work. The electronics were hidden in several tightly wrapped bundles, whose solid cores were put in plastic bags filled with talc, then the whole was finally wound in plastic sheeting and duct tape.

When the cabin doors were secured just before the plane began to taxi out to the runway, the flight engineer noted that the cabin pressure, measured in feet above sea level, was at seven thousand. Although this was two thousand feet higher than most aircraft maintain for passenger comfort, it was the norm for Mexico City, which sits in a mountain bowl of filthy air a mile above sea level. As American Flight 518 became airborne the engineer adjusted the cabin-pressure-rate knob to gradually lower the cabin pressure to five thousand feet, the standard for cruising. Among the bank of instruments he monitored at his station behind the copilot was the differential gauge, which measures the difference between inside and outside air pressures. The aircraft skin was made to operate safely with a maximum difference of 8.6 pounds per square inch, meaning that the air in the plane was exerting that much force outward. Double-sealed doors and hatches maintained the integrity of the cabin.

When Flight 518 was one hundred and fifty miles from its destination, Dallas approach—responsible for all air traffic in the area—contacted the pilot.

"American five-eighteen. this is Dallas-Fort Worth approach. You will begin your descent at one hundred and twelve miles."

"This is American five-eighteen, I understand begin descent at one hundred and twelve miles."

At one hundred and forty miles out, Theresa Boyle and the other attendants secured the carts from which they served drinks and generally readied the cabin for landing. The captain came on and announced, in Spanish and English, that the flight would arrive in the Dallas-Fort Worth Airport on time, at three twenty.

"Do you have plans for tonight?" one of the flight attendants, a handsome California native named Peter, asked Theresa. Peter was married but believed that there was nothing wrong with a little camaraderie among the crew. He had heard that this one, Boyle, was hopelessly straight, but he liked a challenge.

"I'll probably hang around the hotel," Theresa said.

"Maybe we could take a ride downtown," he persisted, sidling closer to her in the tight confines of the aft cabin. Then, more quietly, "I'll treat you to dinner."

He watched her face for some reaction. Just as she seemed about to answer, she pushed by him and hurried up the aisle.

"Cold fish," Peter thought, admiring her from behind.

Theresa had noticed that one of the other attendants was rearranging the baggage in the overhead bin where the blue nylon bag was nestled in a corner. "What's wrong?" she asked, surprised at the quiver in her voice.

"Somebody stuffed too many things in here," the man answered. "They always try to get away without checking their bags, and they make it inconvenient for everyone else." He pulled out a paper-wrapped parcel and tried to rearrange it for a better fit. He put the parcel on the floor and stuck his hand further inside.

"Let me help you," Theresa said. No one on the plane could connect her with the blue bag in the far corner of the overhead bin, but that did little to calm her. The steward was pulling back the lid she'd set on her fears.

"I should take a few more things out," the attendant said.

Boyle lifted the parcel from the floor and pressed it to her side. "You really don't have time," she said. "I'll just take this one to the back, where there's some room."

"That should work, I guess," the attendant agreed, finally shutting the door.

Theresa tugged at the bottom of her jacket and looked down on the seat below the bin. There was a boy of about six asleep in the aisle seat, his head resting comfortably on his mother's arm. The woman looked up at Theresa, who flashed her an attendant's smile before stepping off toward the tail of the aircraft.

Twenty feet from the bulkhead separating the first class and coach cabins, the flight engineer switched the cabin pressure controller from automatic to manual, setting the rate of descent at three hundred and fifty feet per minute. According to his plan, the inside pressure of the cabin would match the outside air pressure at Dallas when the attendants were ready to open the aircraft doors. During the descent the passengers, especially ones with head colds, would notice the falling pressure within the cabin, but most of the people on board would not be uncomfortable.

By the time Theresa returned to her seat, Peter had decided that Theresa Boyle was the most desirable woman on the plane. Her indifference made him want her more.

"So what about that dinner invitation?" he asked again as they lowered the crew seats.

She seemed not to hear him, but was transfixed by something further up the cabin.

"Is something wrong?" Peter asked, wondering if this was her brush-off.

"No," Theresa said, turning to him as if she'd just remembered he was there. She smiled at him, a barely noticeable upturn at the corners of her cupid lips, but she couldn't remember what he'd said. She was thinking about airport security and the fact that, in the States, there had been an increase in vigilance because of anti-American terrorist activity in Europe. She didn't want to get caught with one of the little packages of dope.

Eight and a half minutes after the flight engineer had started reducing the cabin pressure, the three barometers in the blue nylon bag registered two thousand feet of cabin pressure. The senior flight attendant was near the aft end of the plane, having checked to make sure that all passengers had their seat backs straight up, their trays locked, and their carry-on bags stowed under their seats. The attendant serving the first class passengers noticed the small boy sleeping in the bulkhead seat at the front of coach and smiled at the mother.

Theresa Boyle was in her crew seat, looking at her hands and wondering how she could get along without the extra money she made carrying the packages. Her plan was to move to Mexico and live like a queen once she had a hundred and fifty thousand dollars in the bank, and she was almost there. Just a few more trips.

Peter, sitting beside her and leaning close enough for her to smell his cologne, began to speak again.

\* \* \*

Two of the three barometers in the blue bag reached seventeen hundred feet at exactly the same time. When they did, an electronic firing device sent a charge over less than a foot of wire to an electric blasting cap stuffed into a fifteen-pound block of plastique. The cap detonated and started the sympathetic explosion of the main charge, which punched a seventeen-foot hole in the port side of the fuselage.

Three rows of seats on the port side of the plane were torn from their aluminum mounts in the floor panel and thrown out the gaping hole as the air in the cabin sought to fill the relative vacuum of space outside the plane, which was traveling at sixteen thousand feet and four hundred knots. Passengers in those seats were killed instantly as oxygen in the blood vessels of their brains suddenly expanded, like small hand grenades going off inside each head.

Passengers throughout the cabin lost hearing as eardrums burst with the sudden depressurization, and many of them, alarmed at the sight of their fellows bleeding from the ears, nose, and mouth, began to scream. Without the sense of hearing, their own screams seemed muffled inside their skulls.

The pilot, who knew immediately that they had been bombed, was surprised that they were still alive to hear the engineer shout that they had lost cabin pressure. While the copilot struggled to put on his oxygen mask, the pilot grabbed the controls to wrestle for control of a machine that was no longer airworthy. He pushed the nose of the aircraft down as far as possible and tried to level the plane, which had heeled to the left like a racing yacht on a strong starboard tack. He had a momentary flash that they might be able to make it; but that was because he could not see, from his seat, the damage in the back.

When Theresa Boyle was able to open her eyes, she knew what had happened and what she had done. Passengers throughout the cabin were fumbling with oxygen masks, trying to capture one from the tangle of plastic hoses that swung wildly from overhead. Up near the front of the plane, there was a wild intrusion of sunlight, and though she could feel the vibrations and see the open mouths, she heard nothing. She unbuckled her own lap belt, threw herself to the floor, and began to crawl forward along the aisle. She was there, on her hands and knees, her mind empty of all guilt, all fear, concentrating on reaching an elderly woman who was struggling with a mask, when the plane buckled and the weakened structure gave way, tearing the aircraft in two just forward of the wings.

The last thing the pilot saw, before the nose section hit the ground, was the dark shape of the fuselage, like a broken X, tumbling toward the earth.

"We've lost contact with American five-eighteen," the controller said to his supervisor. The young man did not sound concerned; he assumed that the problem was with the communications. It took him several moments to determine that all their systems were fully operational.

FOR THE CHIEF OF STAFF ONLY
SECRET
EYES ONLY

Department of the Army
Headquarters, United States Army Southern Command
Quarry Heights, Panama
11 May

MEMORANDUM FOR: Chief of Staff of the Army
                 The Pentagon
                 Washington DC 22332–0810

FROM: Commander
      U.S. Army Southern Command

RE: Investigation of Operation Sentinel Shooting
Incident

1. On 24 April, U.S. Army Captain MARK ISEN, 260–
11–5570, was involved in a shooting incident east of
Ciudad Mante, Mexico. This headquarters was directed by the Chief of Staff to conduct an investigation
into the shooting to determine what actions, if any,
should be taken against Captain Isen. Major Thomas
Kelly of this command was appointed to investigate
the incident. What follows is a summary of his report
and findings, as well as my recommendation.

2. Captain Isen is assigned to Operation Sentinel as
an adviser to a Mexican infantry unit. On 24 April at
approximately 0300, Captain Isen was participating in
an airmobile operation as part of his duties. The target
of this mission was a suspected drug smuggling operation on a remote airstrip east of Cuidad Mante. Two
American Blackhawk helicopters carried a reinforced
platoon of Mexican infantrymen to the site. The Mexicans were ambushed upon landing; both helicopters
and their crews were destroyed immediately by hand-
held surface-to-air missiles. Captain Isen, armed only

with his authorized side arm, was separated from the main body and was alone at the time of the shooting. According to his testimony, given to the investigating officer in a sworn statement on 30 April, Captain Isen was attempting to conceal himself in some underbrush when some of the ambushers began to search for him. He let them get to within fifteen feet before he opened fire with his pistol, killing two men.

3. Captain Isen is and was aware that the agreement governing the use of force by U.S. personnel in Mexico precludes any use except in self-defense under extreme circumstances. Since Captain Isen was alone at the time of the shooting, his actions must be judged solely on his own testimony. After visiting the site and hearing all the evidence, the investigating officer recommended that no action be taken against Captain Isen.

4. On 2 May, the Public Affairs Officer here fielded a request for information on this shooting. This request came from a correspondent with the *Los Angeles Times*. The correspondent indicated that he had spoken with several Mexican soldiers who were present at the ambush, and they credit Captain Isen with saving their patrol by "gunning down" the drug smugglers. The story filed by this same reporter has sparked a great deal of media interest in the case. Within the first seventy-two hours after publication of the story in the *Los Angeles Times*, the Operation Sentinel headquarters in Tampico received thirty-four calls from various news organizations in the United States. In accordance with Army policy, that headquarters referred all inquiries to the Public Affairs Officer here at Southern Command.

5. On 10 May, a representative from the office of Senator Matthew Stone (D-NY) presented himself at the Operation Sentinel headquarters in Tampico and demanded to see Captain Isen. The local commander pointed out that the man had not gone through the proper channels, and he sent the staffer away. He then

sent Captain Isen on an unplanned leave back in the United States.

6. Senator Stone's opposition to Operation Sentinel is well known and well publicized. However, he is only one of several dozen senators and members of Congress who would gladly make Captain Isen a scapegoat in order to focus public attention and increase public outcry for the end of this program. At any rate, offering any of these opponents this opportunity to scrutinize Army policy can do nothing good for the Army or for Mexican-American relations.

7. Although it may be true that Captain Isen acted in self-defense, it may also be true that he violated the clear guidance concerning the use of force. The fact that his is the only testimony available makes his case less than airtight. I believe it would be in the best interests of the United States Army, and in Captain Isen's best interests, to give him a formal letter of reprimand and relieve him of his duties with Operation Sentinel.

> M.B. Bartlee
> GEN, USA

Enclosure: MAJ Kelly's Report

*ED RUGGERO*

## President's Hospital Visit
## Not Stress Related, Aides Say

by O. Chorney
Special to *The Washington Post*

Washington, D.C., May 12—White House aides today flatly denied reports that the President's recent trip to Bethesda Naval Hospital was for treatment of a stress-related ulcer. The visit, they said, was for treatment of "a minor digestive problem." Nevertheless, the President's six-hour visit with his physician at Bethesda has fueled speculation that the chief executive's health has been adversely affected by recent events.

The bombing of an American Airlines flight en route from Mexico City to Dallas-Fort Worth, which resulted in the deaths of all sixty-seven people aboard, served to highlight the difficulties the administration is having in coming up with a coherent policy for dealing with the increasing violence being perpetrated by the Neu Deutschland Party, which has claimed responsibility for the bombing. The NDP, which has emerged only recently as a powerful anarchist group in Europe, has called for the complete withdrawal of the United States Navy from the Mediterranean.

In a telephone call to *The New York Times* the day after the bombing, a man identifying himself as a spokesman for the NDP said the violence would escalate in the coming weeks unless the U.S. president announced plans to withdraw American forces from Europe. It was the first time that an NDP communiqué had singled out the President for direct criticism. White House aides dismissed the significance of what they called a "slight shift in rhetoric."

In a statement read yesterday at the White House, the President reiterated the long-standing U.S. policy of not negotiating with terrorists.

Mexican authorities report that they are pursuing several promising leads as they investigate how the bomb got on the plane. A spokesman at the Justice Department said the Mexicans are "not eager" to accept American help.

To add to the President's troubles, a recent article in *The Los Angeles Times* claimed that a U.S. soldier serving with the controversial Operation Sentinel anti-drug campaign was responsible for the shooting death of at least one suspected drug smuggler.

These incidents, both connected with Mexico, have focused national attention on U.S. relations with that country and have raised a hue and cry in Congress and across the country. Opinions range from those of the most hard-line, who would like to see more force used in dealing with terrorists and drug smugglers alike, to those who believe that any U.S. involvement on foreign soil is dangerous. One man who has used the current administration crisis to gather attention to his own political aspirations is Senator Matthew Stone (D-NY).

In comments on Capitol Hill today, Senator Stone said that "the current administration has become complacent because their party has been in power for more than twelve years. Their policies are sloppy or nonexistent, and they have no plan for dealing with this—or any foreseeable crisis that does not call for a massive use of force."

In remarks later in the day, Congressman Edwin Dennis of California claimed that the army had interfered with the investigation of the shootings by an American GI in Mexico. "It seems clear to me," Dennis said in prepared remarks delivered before the House Subcommittee on Intelligence, "that the United States Army believes it owes its loyalty to the person of the President and to the President's policies. Do we need to raise the specter of a certain marine lieutenant colonel to remind the military that their actions are subject to the law?"

A recent call to the Pentagon regarding the shootings in Mexico turned up no new evidence, even though the alleged incident took place two weeks ago. One source said that an investigation was ongoing; another said that an investigation had been completed and was awaiting action by the army staff.

# 11

## Atlanta, Georgia
### 12 May

ADRIENNE ISEN LEANED FORWARD IN HER CHAIR TO TAKE another sip of coffee. She was worried that she might spill some of it on the front of her clothes, which she'd bought for this occasion. Adrienne had already been at the airport for two hours, an hour by her own design and another hour because Mark's plane was delayed.

She crossed her legs carefully, balancing the coffee off to the right, then smoothed out the front of her skirt. There was a man sitting across from her in the comfortable waiting area, not a bad-looking guy, Mark's age—thirty, maybe a year or two younger. Adrienne watched him for a while as he flipped through some typewritten sheets, then stuffed these in his briefcase. As he closed the case he noticed Adrienne watching him and smiled at her. She didn't smile back, but simply nodded her head the tiniest bit.

He took out a pocket calendar and played around with that awhile. Without really knowing why, Adrienne tried to see what he was writing. When he closed the book, he saw her watching him again.

"Are you afraid the plane won't get here?" he said.

Adrienne looked at him as if he were speaking a foreign language.

"Pardon?" she said.

"It looks like you're waiting for a plane, and, pardon me for noticing, but you seem nervous. Is it late?"

He didn't have a southern accent, Adrienne decided, although he could be one of those men who slid in and out of a moderate drawl depending on whom they were dealing with, putting it on for the Georgia crowd, taking it off for Chicago.

"I'm waiting for my *husband*," Adrienne said, not meaning to emphasize the word quite as much as she did.

"Yes, I gathered that," he said, inclining his head toward her hand, where she wore a plain wedding band unaccompanied by an engagement ring. "Is he on a business trip?"

Adrienne decided that this guy was a little too pushy for a casual conversation, and she considered getting up. But she was afraid that if she looked at the board again, Mark's plane would be delayed once more.

"Sort of. I mean, yes, he's on a business trip. He's coming back from Mexico," she said. The man across from her had pale blue eyes and looked very comfortable in his suit, as if he were made to wear one. Mark looked this comfortable only in shorts and a T-shirt. Or in uniform.

"Oh. Well, I hope he wasn't anywhere near all that nonsense out in the countryside. The Mexicans are taking their new drug war business pretty seriously, I guess."

"Uh-huh" was all Adrienne would offer. For some reason, she didn't want this stranger to know that Mark was coming from those battles. The man continued to talk, though he watched the people passing by the little seating area. Adrienne decided that he was probably just in need of some conversation. Besides, Mark would be here soon.

"I was reading in the *Journal* that, with all the help the U.S. is giving them, the Mexicans are doing a pretty good job of shutting down one or two of the big drug pipelines through their country."

"I think I saw that same article," Adrienne said, a trifle more friendly.

"I think we're throwing away a lot of money down there," he went on, believing that he had Adrienne interested. She was watching him intently now, and though he hadn't thought to make a pass at her, he did enjoy flirting a little bit. It made the time pass on these trips. And she was a beautiful woman. He wondered how long it would be before her husband's plane landed.

Adrienne was watching him, but she wasn't listening very closely. She was wondering how Mark would look in a business suit, how he would sit in a white shirt, in a tie. She tried to picture him with a leather briefcase, with his hair long enough to rest on his ears, but had trouble conjuring the image. She imagined him home at night, the two of them living in a house they owned, that wasn't on loan from the government or rented outside some army post. She especially liked the idea of his being home.

"I guess the program is worth a try, though. I mean, we have to do something about all that stuff coming into this country." He winked at her.

Adrienne was caught off guard. *What did he say when I wasn't listening?* "Pardon?" she said.

"I said it's probably worth it to try this . . . what did the paper call it? . . . the Second Mexican War, for a year or so. I mean, what have we got to lose? We've tried so many other things and they've failed. And I'll tell you, drugs are bad for business. Drives up medical costs for the big employers. Drives up taxes too, you know, to support all those programs. Rehab programs."

Adrienne uncrossed her legs and leaned forward. She unconsciously let her arm fall toward the floor, shaking loose the traditional Hawaiian bracelet Mark gave her at the end of their assignment to Schofield Barracks, Hawaii. The Hawaiian letters said *Kuuipo.* Sweetheart. Mark sometimes called her his steel sweetheart.

"We have a lot to lose down there in Mexico," Adrienne said. The man was watching a group of flight attendants walk by. Then he looked at Adrienne and smiled. He inched forward in his seat, thinking for an ignorant moment that she wanted to be closer to him.

"There are American soldiers down there," she said.

"Yeah, but those guys are in an advisory role. The Mexicans are doing the fighting," he said, smiling at her and running his fingers back through his fashionably long hair.

He liked a woman who glanced at the front page now and then, and he liked them with a little backbone.

"We have guys going out on all those missions, getting shot at and shooting back," Adrienne said. Out of the corner of her eye, she saw an older man just a few seats away lower his newspaper just enough to watch her over the top.

The businessman mistook her again, guessing that she was one of those peaceniks who couldn't ever see the need for using the military.

"Sure, sure, I know that," he said to Adrienne. "But that's what the army and those guys are for, after all."

Adrienne threw back her hair with one hand and pressed the other hand on her thigh.

*Well, that seemed to get a rise out of her,* the businessman thought. *I'll bet she's more beautiful when she's good and riled up.*

"Besides," he went on, still unaware, "now that we don't have the Russians or Iraqis to kick around anymore, those army guys need somebody to take their hostilities out on. It's probably good practice for them to beat up"—he lowered his voice just a bit—"some little brown men every once in a while. It'll keep those soldier boys occupied. We don't want all that frustration building 'til some crazy vet shoots up a shopping mall or something."

Adrienne's eyes narrowed as she straightened, both feet planted firmly on the floor. She drew her shoulders up and took a deep breath.

*She's got a great body too,* the man across from her thought as he watched her breasts swell in the tight fabric. *Now's the time to offer to buy her a drink.*

Adrienne found she could still control the volume of her voice, but not what she wanted to say. "You ignorant little fuckstick," she said crisply. The man across from her blinked his eyes. The old man who'd been watching over his newspaper lowered it completely.

"There are men down there getting killed so that you can keep down the costs of your medical plan." She felt her hands shaking, so she pressed them more firmly against her legs. When she stood up abruptly, the man across from her flinched. *He thought I was going to hit him.*

"And as for those crazy vets," she said, her voice even, venomous, "they'd all rather be back with their families and living the good life." She took a step toward him in the small space between the two couches, just to see if he'd move back in his seat. He did.

Adrienne tried to think of something else to say, but she was at a loss in the face of such monumental ignorance. She turned and walked away from the gate, and she noticed several people watching her.

"That's telling him, sister," someone said.

She turned to see a black man, in his fifties, giving her a thumbs-up sign and a wide smile. "Darn yuppies don't know that it's the vets who gave them all this stuff," the man said as she walked away, his voice fading.

Adrienne strode down the glistening corridor, followed by the sounds of her high heels striking the floor, wondering why she hadn't cried, wondering if she really believed that Mark would ever pass up the chance for this army brand of excitement just to stay home.

Adrienne didn't like the army or the army life, though she'd been at it for eight years, trying to strike a compromise with this prehistoric institution that demanded so much of her mate, and which her mate so obviously loved. She had an especially difficult time accepting Mark's decision to stay in the military after his combat experience. He had come back to her wounded, and she had secretly hoped that his love for the army had died of those wounds. She was disappointed.

Adrienne never did find satisfactory answers for all her objections to the military, but in the happy afterglow of having Mark back, she put her arguments aside.

Adrienne found the ad hoc community of the school at Fort Benning, where Mark had trained for Mexico, less friendly than what they had left at their last duty station. But after a few weeks Adrienne had made some friends and run into people she and Mark knew from previous assignments, and she put her disillusion aside for a while, pushed it back somewhere out of her daily concerns.

Once they decided that she would stay at Fort Benning while Mark was away, she found a position as a portfolio manager with a large insurance company whose office tower—the only such building in the city—sat amid a quiet residential neighborhood thick with old homes and old trees. The Columbus that existed beyond the strip joints, used car lots, and pawnshops that lined Fort Benning's north side turned out to be quite pleasant. She rented one half of a red brick duplex within walking distance of her office and settled in, but Mark suspected she was still fundamentally unhappy. He loved her as much as he ever had, but he lived with a nagging fear that she would lose her patience with the truce and along with it her ability to tolerate his profession and their life.

The confrontation in the lounge was still on Adrienne's mind as Mark's plane rolled up to the walkway, two and a half hours later than scheduled. Even as she watched the first people get off the plane, as she watched for his familiar face in the little stream of faces coming up out of the hallway, she knew that the final question would haunt his leave time. Would Mark ever pass up an opportunity to be where the action was? Would he trade his life in the army for a placid one in a business suit? Would he give it up if she asked him to?

She saw him finally, a glimpse of his eyes and forehead at the far end of the passageway, then he disappeared again behind the bulk of two large men. Then she saw that, yes, it was he, it was he, she was certain, though his face was sunburned, and he was wearing clothes she didn't recognize, and it looked as if . . . *Oh, God, his head's shaved again, or nearly so* . . . but it was he finally, after three months of his letters that she knew didn't tell the whole truth about the fighting, three months of sleeping alone in the small house in Columbus, three months of weekends as the fifth wheel when she went out with her friends, three months of going to the movies with women or to dinner alone.

It was Mark.

It was her husband. He dropped his bag where she stood against the wall, her tears coming now. He walked up to her slowly, in that calm deliberate manner he had, savoring the moment, and he took her in his arms, and she cried on his shoulder and laughed to have him back again. She marveled at how close he was now, though he had been thousands of miles and worlds away from her only yesterday, no doubt with men shooting at him. And now she held him.

"Hello, hello, hello," he said, over and over into her neck. Adrienne held him tightly, felt how thin he had become, found his ribs and bony arms and looked at his terrifically sunburned skin, the peeling on his nose and cheeks.

"Oh, Mark, you're so *burned,*" she said, stroking his neck, "and so skinny. What happened to you?" Adrienne thought she was gushing, but she didn't much care. "We've got two weeks to fill you out on some of this good ol' American food. I'm going to take care of you," she said.

"That's what I've been waiting to hear," Mark said, running his hand from her waist down the curve of her hip.

She cocked one elbow on his shoulder and dragged her nails across his lower back. "I've got some surprises for you too, soldier boy," she said with a leer.

"I hope so," he said. "I don't have any bags, so let's jump in the car and get out of here."

As they walked to the little train that would take them to the exit and the parking area, Adrienne watched her husband. She wrapped her arm in his and walked close enough to him that they were a bit off balance. She knew that she was acting like a schoolgirl, but that was just fine. She was glad to have him home, and as she slipped a finger into one of the belt loops on the back of his trousers, she wondered again if she could keep him home permanently, this time, or ever.

Adrienne looked great, better than he remembered, Mark had to admit. He was surprised, as he always was when he came out of the field, at how *clean* everyone was. The conditions he lived under in Mexico: returning to a base camp almost every night, showering almost every day, sleeping on a cot instead of on the ground, were a great deal better than he experienced on most field problems. But Adrienne reminded him that there were places where cleanliness was the norm. She didn't have dirt ground into the pores along the sides of her fingers, as he did. She didn't have a circle of grime just above the neckline of her shirt. She smelled wonderful, cool and fresh and clean all at once.

As he climbed into the car Mark became a bit self-conscious of his own appearance. Despite generous applications of sunscreen, the brutal sun in Mexico had played havoc with his fair skin. His arms were slashed and battered: there was a large purple bruise inside his right bicep that he had taken away from the most recent firefight, though he didn't remember how it got there. His hands were a maze of small cuts and scabs. These were normal fare for a field soldier, and Adrienne had seen him like this many times before. When he had been wounded, she had seen him worse off, lying flat on his stomach for days as the shrapnel wounds in his neck and back drained and healed. She had helped him limp around the hospital, then around home as he recovered from a near-crippling foot wound. But he had been almost proud of those scars. He had never said it aloud, but he thought of them as his own red badges of courage. There was something different about this time, though, and Mark Isen wasn't sure what it was. He pulled his short sleeve down across the bruise as far as he could.

"You look great, Adrienne," Mark said slowly.

"Thanks, babe. You look . . . well, you look tired." She tried not to make it sound like an admonition, but she wasn't sure how it came across.

"I'm okay," he said, looking out the window at the approaching Atlanta skyline, modern castles of silver and glass. He turned back to her and found her watching him. "Really, it hasn't been that bad," he went on, trying to make a joke about it. "I mean, it's hot as hell, and I've been sunburned for three straight months, but other than that I'm doing great."

"Uh-huh," Adrienne said suspiciously. "And I suppose you've been sitting around the supply tent or something down there, counting canteens and blankets, right?"

She still sounded playful, but Isen knew she was fishing

for information about what he'd kept secret from her. He wasn't giving.

"C'mon, Adrienne," Isen said, kidding her instead of answering her. He wanted to savor at least these first hours together before he thought about why he'd been hustled out of Mexico. He took her arm off the steering wheel and held it out full length, kissing the inside of her elbow, nibbling the skin there, sliding his lips up the pale skin of her bicep.

"Stop, that tickles," she said, but without pulling her arm away. He held her hand contentedly and looked out the window as the afternoon drew down against the sky. The lights of the suburbs sprawled for miles across the humid landscape in every direction. Suddenly he thought of the crews of the two Blackhawk helicopters that went down in the ambush. He wondered how many of the people out there on the Georgia landscape really understood—or cared about—the issues that were getting American GIs killed in Mexico and Colombia and elsewhere in South America. The troubles in Mexico—*his* troubles in Mexico—might merit a thirty-second slot on the national news, but people were always ready for the next news bite. The day-to-day sacrifices of the women and men in uniform—the separation from family, the dangerous training, the accidents that, even in peacetime, cost lives, got very little attention in the media.

Mark was silent as they drove into the hotel parking garage, and Adrienne thought it was in anticipation of being with her again. She was partially right.

They made love furiously the first time, just inside the door to the room, then on the bed, half on and half off, not fully undressed, struggling to overcome the distance that had worked its way between them. Adrienne was alarmed at the condition of Mark's body. They hadn't paused to close the curtains, so the slanting afternoon light poured straight into the room and lit the scars and bruises and burns across his thin frame. She wondered if he had been sick.

When they finished, Mark kissed her face and her hair,

got up from the bed, and went into the shower. He turned the water on very hot and let it run on him for a long time before he moved to unwrap the small cake of hotel soap.

Adrienne listened to him without moving, watching the sun trace red across the wall of the room. She let herself cry a little, partly because he was with her again, partly because of the hurts he had so obviously suffered and not told her about. And partly because he would go back again. In the bathroom, Mark sang in the clean, splashing water.

When he was done, he came out wrapped in one towel and rubbing his scalp with another.

"I'd forgotten what a real towel felt like, or a real shower, for that matter," he said. "All we have are those little canvas buckets with the watering spout thing on the bottom."

Adrienne turned to face him and patted the bed next to her. He pulled back the clean sheets and climbed in beside her.

"It's so cool here, so clean," he said at last.

She leaned over and kissed him, her hair falling down against his face in a fragrant curtain. They made love again, slowly this time, each drinking in the other's presence, outside of time.

They ordered from room service when they got hungry, and when the waiter brought the cart up, Adrienne stayed in bed, naked, with the sheet pulled up to her neck. The waiter, who looked as if he might be a college kid working at night, smiled at her unabashedly.

"I've always wanted to do that," Adrienne said when the boy had left.

"You hussy," Mark said, pulling the sheet away by tugging at it from the foot of the bed.

"Well, I'm not going to *stay* naked; I just thought it would be like the movies, people waiting on me hand and foot, while I hold you captive here as my sex slave." She slipped out of the sheets and came up behind him where he was investigating the dinner.

"Ouch! Your nails are sharp," he said, standing up quickly enough to loosen the towel he had on.

"Oh . . . big, tough soldier," Adrienne said, running to the bathroom laughing. "I'll be out in a second."

There was something enticing about it, Mark admitted to himself, something decadent about doing it in a fancy hotel room all afternoon. That was part of the attraction. Adrienne could always think of ways to spice things up, whether it was a business trip or their sex life, and Mark appreciated that. He was grateful, though too tired to come up with anything very original on his own.

He turned the light out and stood by the heavy drapes. The sun was gone from the western sky. There would be a moon, nearly full, chasing it, but they couldn't yet see it from their west-facing room.

*I wonder when we'll get around to it,* he thought at last. It was only a matter of time before he and Adrienne fought about his going back to Mexico.

The first time Mark went to war it was an accident of assignment. He just happened to be in that particular unit during that particular time. Mexico was different. He had sought this duty. He told himself that the service was about sacrifice, that his motives were selfless ones and had to do with containing the flow of drugs. But when he was with Adrienne, he couldn't deny the other side: he was doing this for himself too.

Mark Isen was no fool. He had seen the face of war up close, and so no longer believed in words like *glory,* no longer believed that it was an adventure. It was a bloody business with too much room for error that mangled and killed young men and robbed them of decades of life. He believed all this as strongly as he believed in anything, *saecula saeculorum.*

Yet there was an attraction.

The military was an odd profession in that people in uniform spent all their time preparing for an eventuality they hoped would never come. In fact, it was the stated mission of the army to *deter* war through preparedness. It was for this reason that many in the services felt that the army that came back from Europe following the collapse of the Iron Curtain was a victorious army: unbloodied, but every bit as successful in their mission as had been the soldiers who returned after VE Day. And the half of the U.S. military that had pounded the Iraqis into submission had sent a message to the rest of the world that America—in spite of its waning economic power and its staggering debt—was still the foremost military power in the world. And that statement—made by hundreds of thousands of men and women who endured heat and sand and loneliness, who fought the vicious lightning battle—might, by discouraging other aggressors, buy a few more years of a *Pax Americana*.

But there was something missing from the peacetime army, and soldiers were forever seeking challenges to prove themselves. Mark Isen had gone through the rigors of Ranger training as much to test his own mettle as for what he would learn. But for those who had never been in combat, there was something missing. Until he'd been to war, Isen felt as if he had not been fully validated as a soldier. He had shared this sentiment only once, with his closest friend in the military, after a half dozen beers in the officers' club bar at Schofield Barracks, Hawaii.

"It's not the kind of thing you say out loud, you know," he'd told Dale Barrow. Barrow, as a lieutenant, had been Isen's executive officer, the second in command of Isen's company. They became close friends after their shared experiences in combat.

"Nobody with half a brain wants war," Barrow had said, tracing the ring of condensation his beer bottle left on the bar. "But that's not the same as saying we won't rush to it if it comes."

"You'd think we'd know better," Isen said, "those of us who've been there."

"We do, but there's an attraction," Barrow said. "I never felt as . . . alive as I did then. Maybe it has something to do with being scared shitless."

"It's kind of like adultery," Isen said. "I mean, you know it's wrong and you know if you have a shred of decency you'll feel terrible when it's over. But the temptation is always there, like a dark secret."

Recalling that conversation now, as he watched the red-lined horizon from the clean hotel room, Mark knew that he'd been unfaithful to Adrienne. He'd volunteered to go to Mexico because he was looking for that exhilaration again. But the true face of war was so terrible that he didn't want to admit, even to himself, that he sought it out.

Adrienne came out of the bathroom.

"Why are all the lights off?" she said, switching on the lamp by the bed. She was dressed in a deep red gown that was tied together primly at the neck. She came up to him where he stood by the window. Now that the light was on behind him, Isen couldn't see out. He could only study his reflection in the glass. He watched the scene with keen interest: the beautiful woman came up behind the thin man and put her arms around his waist.

"What are you thinking about?" she asked.

He turned into her embrace.

They made their way to the hotel bar around eleven-thirty, both of them pleasantly exhausted but too wound up to sleep.

"You said on the phone you'd tell me why you were suddenly getting leave," Adrienne said after she'd climbed on the barstool Mark pulled out for her.

Isen had hoped to let this one go, at least until the next day. But there was no sense in delaying the inevitable.

"My superiors suggested I take a leave for a while, kind of disappear from the scene."

"Did something happen?" Adrienne asked.

Isen wondered if there was any way to avoid telling her all the details, then decided there wasn't.

"We got into a firefight a couple of weeks ago. I was in some brush, and there were some guys coming toward me. I thought one of them was going to step on me, so I shot him first."

He looked at Adrienne. He had never told her anything so explicit about what an infantryman does, about what he'd done or hadn't done, in all his experience. He expected she would ask if he'd killed the other man. She was staring directly into his eyes, looking as if he'd just told her he'd taken a lover. She didn't speak, so he went on.

"Anyway, that's technically against the rules of engagement for advisers. We're not supposed to shoot first. The Mexican lieutenant wanted to mention me in his dispatch, get me a medal or something, and I talked him out of it. A few days later some of the troops told the story to a reporter from the *Los Angeles Times,* and he wrote about trigger-happy American advisers and all the parallels with Vietnam. My boss sent me on leave to try to limit the damage. I guess there are reporters all over down there trying to talk to me some more."

"That was you?" Adrienne said, incredulous.

"You saw it?"

"I saw a piece about it on the *national* news," she said, emphasizing how widespread was his unwelcome fame. "At least they didn't use your name."

"Yeah, but this program is such a political football that some guys in the Pentagon thought that congressional opponents of the administration's policy might come after me to use me as a scapegoat. Try to embarrass the President by making it look like GIs down in Mexico are shooting smugglers."

Adrienne had begun to seethe. "Don't they know you were just protecting yourself?" she said at last. She was clearly angry at the same things that angered Mark, but he somehow knew he was going to be in the line of fire. This was one of the times when she was about to forget that they were on the same team.

"Let me get this straight," Adrienne said. "You acted to save your own life, and the Mexicans who were there think you're a hero, and now because some congressman has a hard-on for the army, they want you to lay low until this blows over?"

Over the years Isen had come to recognize several signals that his wife gave off, signals that portended an argument or a stony silence. She was using her clipped let-me-get-this-straight tone now, and Mark knew he should have kept quiet.

"Well, yes," Isen answered her. "Our orders say that we can fire when our lives are threatened. I was on the spot, and I didn't particularly want to wait to see if this guy was going to shoot first. But if you read about it in a dispatch, it might sound like I was shooting at the bad guys first. Attacking them, you know. Depends on how it was written.''

Adrienne put her elbows on the bar and covered her face with her hands. She took a deep breath, and Mark watched her shoulders rise. She pushed her hair back with both hands, and Isen suddenly felt as if he'd hurt her. Not because he'd told her, finally, about something that happened out in the bush, but because he was exposing himself to that kind of danger, while all she could do was worry.

"I can't believe you still want to go back," she said. It was not the remark he was expecting.

"I have to go back, Adrienne," he answered, missing the fact that she was talking about a larger issue.

"I know you *have* to go back *this* time, Mark. But when are you going to wake up and see that the army doesn't really care about you?" She pushed her hair back, paused, continued. "This tug-of-war with Congress is more important to the powers-that-be than what happens to some little captain," Adrienne said.

"Adrienne, those are real people making these decisions," Isen said. "My boss was looking out for me when he sent me up here. You make it sound like he's a movie bad guy."

"I'm not saying it's his fault, Mark. These guys make big decisions every day that get people—people like you— killed. Don't you think they learn to accept that?"

Isen didn't think so, and he almost said it. But then he remembered what it felt like to make decisions that would send other men to their deaths. His own experience in combat had taught him an awful truth. Even the best planned and executed military operations sustained casualties. Men died. Period. When a commander chose one platoon over another to lead an assault, he was making a choice that could get some of the men in that lead platoon wounded or perhaps killed. The decision didn't make the commander a bad person. The choices had to be made, and the leader who could accept that and move on to make the *best* plans and decisions was better off. So were his men.

But the director of Operation Sentinel wasn't a company commander. His decisions were harder to make and sometimes more costly in terms of human suffering. But his job was to make the calls. The particular call that affected Isen—American soldiers won't shoot first—was of course a political decision, a concession to Mexican sensibilities. Isen understood that, and in a rational world it even made sense to him.

But out in that darkness, with rounds coming down range, with dead men around and aircraft burning in a brilliant pyre—what made sense was instinct, and the instinct was self-preservation.

Isen twisted his stool to the bar and took a long pull at his drink. He wiped his lips with one finger and turned, smiling, to Adrienne, hoping to lighten things up a bit.

"He gets paid the big bucks to make the hard calls."

The attempt at humor didn't work, and Isen felt the point slipping away from him.

"He isn't making a decision about which goddamn uniform to wear, Mark. He's in some political mess now. He's playing a game where nobody knows what the rules are going to be next month, or next week. If some politician decides to go after this program—because you shot somebody or for whatever other reason—then all the work you've done will go right out the window."

Adrienne's face was flushed now, and she was leaning toward Mark, one foot hooked on the rung of her barstool.

"And what about those guys who got killed? What will their families feel when the politicians are on the news saying this whole thing was a mistake?"

Two men on the other side of the bar were staring at them. For a brief instant Mark wondered if she were going to start cursing like a sailor, as she sometimes did when she was really mad. *Then* they'd have something to stare at. Mark fixed the two men in his gaze until they turned away. He continued to stare at them, because he knew Adrienne was right.

Something had happened to the army, or at least to the army as he thought of it. The mission wasn't clear anymore. Mark had a sudden image of himself calling his boss.

*Am I going to war? If not, what the hell is this?* He wanted clear instructions. He wanted to be able to tell his wife that he wasn't risking his life for this week's political agenda, that it was a worthwhile cause. But when he looked up at her, at her beautiful breathlessness and anger, he knew that nothing he could ever say would convince her that there was something worth his death.

Adrienne was amazed at how much she loved this man who was so far from her in some things. She couldn't believe that logic couldn't reach him. She knew that Mark understood what she was saying, and she suspected that, fundamentally, he agreed with her. But he would go back again and again, as many times as they called. He knew something about it that she didn't know, something he could never tell her.

She wouldn't badger him or nag him. And she wouldn't leave him. Not this time at least.

She turned her stool to the bar and picked up her drink.

On the other side of the bar, the bartender noticed how quiet the couple had become. *They're probably married,* she thought to herself. *They're not even looking at each other.*

Mark Isen got the letter at home at the end of his first week of leave. It was postmarked Army Postal Service, Panama, and bore the return address of a Major Thomas Kelly. Isen recognized the name. Kelly had seemed like a nice enough guy, under the circumstances, and Isen never felt as if Kelly was out to get him. The major had even sent Isen a copy of his report—had probably taken a chance doing so. Isen dropped the other mail—mostly junk—on the couch and flopped down to read whatever Major Kelly had to say.

The letter was handwritten on white legal-pad paper.

*Dear Captain Isen,*

*You probably remember that I was the investigating officer from SOUTHCOM who looked into the shooting incident at Cuidad Mante. I finished my report right after I got back to Panama and sent it up the chain of command. I heard nothing about it, nothing that would indicate that the powers-that-be were going to do anything other than accept my recommendation (did you get the copy I sent you?) to drop the whole matter.*

*The other day I was talking to a guy who works in the CINC's office, and he mentioned that scuttlebutt up there was that the CINC contradicted my recommendation in the letter he attached to the report when he sent it to the Chief of Staff. All of this is second, third, and fourth hand, but I thought you should know. I was able to find out that some media people and some congressmen or senators or something were snooping around up at Tampico.*

*I wish I knew more to tell you, but I don't. I was already warned to stop asking questions about the CINC's personal correspondence with the Chief of Staff. I wanted to give you a heads-up so you won't get blindsided. Good luck.*

*Tom Kelly*

*PS. I submitted the report just like I said I would. I recommended no action against you.*

The strange thing was, Isen mused as he sat on the couch and looked out at the huge oak and maple trees that had attracted Adrienne to this neighborhood, the whole time he was reading the letter he was thinking about Kelly. This officer, who really didn't know him from Adam, had risked snooping around the SOUTHCOM headquarters so that he could give Isen a storm warning. He'd risked incurring the considerable wrath of a four-star general by prying into that general's communication with the Chief of Staff, knowing all the while that there was little Isen would be able to do to deflect whatever was coming.

Kelly had done his best to get to the bottom of what happened out at that ambush site, and he had conscientiously reported his findings to his superiors, because that was his mission, given and received in good faith. He had gone after the truth, and he didn't rest until he was satisfied that he had found it. And he had naively believed that that would be enough.

So had Isen.

What was it Cortizo had said? *With difficult questions, there are many truths.*

# 12

## Augusta, Georgia
### 25 May

AS HE WAITED FOR HIS FATHER TO COME HOME FROM WORK Mark Isen studied the various pieces of furniture that filled the small family room in his dad's house. The couch, only recently relegated to the second team, had been in the living room of the house at Fort Benning when Mark was a senior in high school. It was still in good shape because back then no one ever sat on it unless there was company. The dinette set came from a Killeen, Texas (junior high and Fort Hood), department store that was remarkable because it didn't charge usurious rates to soldiers. Isen could easily see the deep gouges in two of the legs: he and his mother (his father had been away at the time) had dropped that table off a trailer in a move from temporary housing to government quarters. There were prints of German castles (three tours with NATO) and a potted cactus his mother brought from their retirement tour at Fort Bliss.

But he could not find the collection of photographs and plaques and mementos that his father had always hung in whatever quarters they occupied. The old man jokingly referred to the testimony of his thirty-two years' service as his *I-love-me wall*. For some reason, it wasn't in this house.

Isen always felt, when he looked at the odd collection of

171

memorabilia, somewhat smug about his childhood. It seemed to him that the children of career soldiers (universally known as army brats) reacted to their tumbleweed lives in one of two ways. Some resented the constant uprooting: changing schools, leaving friends, every third year or less being the new kid at school. Others, and Mark Isen was one of these, loved the great adventure of moving to new states, new parts of the country. To his child's mind, a year or two was about as long a period of time as he could imagine, and a year or two at any one place seemed enough.

Isen used to think that moving around, living in all those different states, made the whole country his home. He counted himself lucky that he could be as much at home in Kansas as in Georgia or California. He had a renewed enthusiasm with each move, as if he were recharging his batteries.

But at some point he learned that those batteries, repeatedly called upon, lost their ability to hold a charge. The more you topped them off, the more quickly they'd run down. As he got older Isen began to doubt if he'd had homes in all those states. Instead of being a part of all of the states, perhaps he was part of none, floating along above the surface of Fort Riley and Fort Benning and Fort Irwin. And his wanderlust grew, so that after a while he was ready to move in two years, then at eighteen months he was tired of a place, then a year. Finally the restlessness threatened to close in on him, so that he could never feel settled.

His mother told him that the army was a family, and it was true that no matter where they went, the army provided certain constants: identical houses lined identical streets. The hospital and the schools and the churches were interchangeable, and frequently the neighbors from one post or another became the neighbors at a new posting.

Isen's father had retired as a sergeant major a few years earlier, a year after Isen's mother had died of cancer. Isen had been worried about the old man, puttering around a suddenly empty house with nothing but the ghosts of his wife and his years in uniform to keep him company. But lately he was glad he hadn't brought up his concerns. Isen's father had moved to central Georgia (*too many damn old people in Florida,* he'd confided to his son) and found work teaching shop to high school kids. Working with teenagers was not much different from working with young soldiers, and the elder Isen had always enjoyed that aspect of his profession. He was as happy as Isen could reasonably expect, and the son was happy for the chance to visit during this unexpected leave.

As he sat in his father's den (the old man had left the key under a rock in the tiny garden, as promised), Mark Isen watched the clock on the VCR and wondered what was in store for him after he hung up his uniform. His father had told him that he got home at 1607. The son might have thought the time hack odd had it come from anyone else. As it was, the elder Isen was simply in form.

"Hi, Dad," Isen said as his father walked in the door. He stood, chanced a glance at the clock—4:07.

"How're doing, son?" Sergeant Major (Retired) Allen Isen walked over and shook hands with his boy, formally, from a distance. Isen knew some of his friends hugged their fathers when they met, but he couldn't imagine doing that with "Top" Isen.

"How are they treating you, Mark?" his father asked. From this man of few words, Mark Isen knew the question was not rhetorical. His father was genuinely concerned. It suddenly occurred to him that he'd come here to tell his father what had happened to him in Mexico; but he wasn't ready yet. "Fair to middlin'," he said.

The older man went to a closet in the corner and put away his hat. Mark noticed creases along the legs of his blue work trousers.

"How're the school kids treating you?" Isen asked. He had a vague memory from junior high of a class full of young punks pestering a teacher—an old man to them at the time, but probably not much older than his own father was now.

"Good, good," he said. He considered his words. "I really like working with them, Mark." His father turned and eyed him suspiciously, as if he might not be able to

173

understand. "At the beginning of the year they want to give me a hard time, but I just lower the boom. There's very little any of these kids can do that I haven't seen some private do a hundred times before. You stayin' for dinner?"

"I thought we could go out and get something," Mark said.

"I got these leftover pork chops," the father said, peering into the small refrigerator. "If I don't eat them, they'll go bad. There's enough for you, you don't eat too much." He held out a glass bowl in which Isen could see dark discs.

"I think I'll pass, Dad. Maybe we can go out for a beer afterwards." Isen stood and walked around the small room while his father changed out of his sawdusty shirt.

They sat quietly as the old man ate his simple dinner of reheated chops, canned vegetables, and bread. Mark sat across from him at the tiny dinette table and drank a beer. They talked about the weather, about the ball games the old man had seen when he went to Florida to watch spring training. After the meal, Isen's father agreed to go out for one beer with his son. "Any more than that on a weeknight and I'm too tired the next day. Can't come dragging into school."

*Bad example for the troops,* Isen thought. There was something comforting about his father's predictability.

While the old man was in the shower, Mark washed out the beer bottle and put it in the recycling bin under the sink. He poked around the house a bit more, then called to his father in the shower.

"Dad, where're those framed citations I gave you for Christmas?" Isen asked.

There was a moment's hesitation. "Oh, I didn't get around to hanging them yet," he answered over the sound of running water. He came out a few minutes later, dressed in a clean pair of work pants just like the ones he'd taken off. Isen noticed that the hairs visible above the neckline of his T-shirt were gray.

"Well, where are they? I'll hang them up," the son said.

The Christmas before, Isen had had two of his father's citations, with accompanying medals, matted and framed, hoping that his father would hang them in the family room.

They had turned out beautifully: the Silver Star for bravery, the Purple Heart for wounds received in action on that same day in 1966 near An Loc, Vietnam. It had been quite a chore to get the originals out from under the old man. Isen had assumed his father was afraid the frame shop might lose them and had had to guarantee that he would see to the job personally.

"I don't think so, son," he answered, watching his hands go in and out of the folds of the towel.

*There's something more here than meets the eye,* Isen thought. He wished his mother were around; she was adept at interpreting the old man's signals.

"How come?" Isen asked.

"I just don't feel like looking at a bunch of army stuff anymore."

Mark Isen couldn't have been more surprised had his father confessed to being married again.

For as long as the son could remember, his father had lived, eaten, breathed the army. To the son's eyes, the old man had loved the service . . . not without complaint, to be sure, but steadily, solidly, like a marriage strengthened by its own record of constancy.

The old man saw something in his son's eyes, assumed that he'd hurt his son's feelings over the gift. He was no good at compromise, had very little social tact in situations like this. But he did know when something was wrong.

"I'm sorry, Mark. I really appreciate the gift, and they look real nice," the old man said. He went to the closet and got out a light jacket, started to put it on, then draped it over his arm. His son didn't answer, so he went on. His wife used to tell him that a little white lie every once in a while was okay if it saved someone a hurt.

"I'll probably drag all that stuff out in a month or two, hang the I-love-me crap. But right now I just didn't feel . . ." he screwed up his brow, thinking about what he wanted to say. Finally, it didn't sound any better. "I just didn't feel like looking at it."

They walked a half mile to a little bar and grill, Isen's father talking about the different kinds of flowers and plants that grew in his garden and along the street. As he listened to his father Isen wondered what had happened to change the old man's mind about the army. He'd heard that retirees sometimes got treated poorly at the military facilities where they went for the services, such as medical care, they were entitled to.

"Dad, do they treat you okay over at the hospital at Gordon?" Fort Gordon, the home of the army's Signal Corps, provided medical care to retirees in the area.

"No worse than anybody else," his father said.

"What does that mean?" Isen felt his voice go a bit angry. His father chuckled.

"I get to wait in line with all the other old people. Last week, no, two weeks ago I had to wait two hours for them to count out fifty pills for me."

"Why is it so bad?" Isen asked. He thought he knew the answer to that one. There were too many retirees to take care of with a staff that was designed to support the active-duty military community first.

His father looked at him. In the dusk, the old man's already inscrutable face was even harder to read. "It's because we don't count anymore," he said.

The son was still concentrating on some imagined slight by an inconsiderate doctor or pharmacist. "What? Who said that?" He could already imagine the righteous letter he would send to the hospital commander about how his war-hero father was being mistreated.

"Nobody told me that, Mark. It's just the way it is. We're a burden on the system."

"But medical care is part of your retirement package."

"So it is. And we get medical care. But nobody ever said it would be great medical care. I mean, it isn't cut-rate, but we're second-class citizens." He said it without a trace of remorse or self-pity, as if it were the most obvious thing in the world.

"That's hardly fair," Mark said.

The old man laughed. "Jesus, Mark, did I miss the announcement that life was going to be fair all of a sudden?"

They stopped on a corner and waited for two cars to pass. The neighborhood was filled with the smells of azaleas.

"Is this what gave you the attitude about the army?" Mark Isen asked.

"What are you talking about?"

"Is it because you're pissed off at the way you're treated that you don't want to hang all your plaques and stuff?"

"Look, Mark," the old man said, turning away from the street toward his son. "I may not be the brightest or most perceptive guy in the world, but when I was a private I noticed that retired people got shoved aside. It isn't personal; it's just the way it is. It's fine to expect individual people to act with kindness and fairness, but it's naive to expect a huge organization like the army to act that way. When I was a first sergeant, I made sure that the company commander paid attention to family stuff, because so many of the soldiers were married. But if I didn't do it, and the company commander didn't do it on his own, it might not get done. But those troops still had to soldier. It was good that we took care of their families, but we could have been SOBs and the troops wouldn't have had any recourse. You can't expect paybacks from the army in proportion to what you put into it. There's always somebody who'll screw you over in a heartbeat, and it doesn't matter if you're a combat veteran or a thirty-year man or the greatest soldier since Audie Murphy. You can give all you want, but the army cuts no deals."

Isen thought that this might well be the longest speech his father had ever given him about the army. He saw suddenly that he'd been wrong about his father. The old man's dedication to service had more than two dimensions, and this realistic attitude had probably always been there. And then Mark Isen thought about his own experience in Mexico, about how he'd worked hard, had really given of himself, and now he was on leave pending an investigation that could end his career. All because he didn't want to see if that young bandit was going to shoot him first.

Later, in the bar, Isen told his father everything about Operation Sentinel, about the drug interdiction mission the army seemed so anxious to take on, even about the shooting.

"No matter what comes of the investigation, Mark, I

know that you tried to do the right thing. You wouldn't have shot that kid if you saw another way out of it,'' the old man said.

Mark was sitting on the next barstool, and he wanted to put his hand on his father's arm, but the moment passed.

"As for this drug mission stuff,'' the old man went on, "I think that's a mistake. Soldiers aren't policemen. We shouldn't be dealing with civilians. That mission calls for microsurgery. Using the army is like using a Bowie knife.''

True to his word, his father didn't stay long, though Mark got him to drink a second beer. They walked back to the tiny house together, and his father made up the fold-out couch for him. Long after he could hear the even breathing of his father asleep in the next room, Mark Isen lay awake, wondering what other truths he'd missed.

His visit with his father convinced Mark Isen that he would be foolish to rely on the army to give him a fair deal in all cases. And this shooting incident was not something to be trifled with. First, there was the fact that four-star generals were sending letters back and forth talking about something he did. That kind of notoriety he could live without. Then there was the media attention on Mexico and the feeding frenzy the Democrats were trying to incite around the President. There were plenty of people around the country, most of them the President's political enemies, who would love to see a very public and very painful investigation into what the *Los Angeles Times* had called "the shooting of suspected drug smugglers by an American soldier.''

Somehow all the media attention on Mexico had melded the two problems. In a fundamental way, the problems— drugs and terrorism—were the same: they were both assaults on America's sense of security. Isen had no trouble keeping the two separate—it seemed to him just an unfortunate coincidence that the terrorists had chosen to operate out of the same country that the drug smugglers were using. But in the press and on television, everything had been lumped together and pinned on the President.

Isen had seen a political cartoon in *The Atlanta Journal* that showed a harried president struggling under the weight of a millstone around his neck. The stone was labeled *Mexico,* and on it danced two devilish caricatures: one was a little man with a bomb in his hand, the other an American soldier holding a smoking pistol.

*If they knew my name,* Isen thought to himself, *it'd be in that cartoon too.* Then he corrected himself. *When they find out my name . . .*

The first person he called was Spano, who was back at Bragg. Isen got him at home and explained the letter from Kelly.

"Has the army come out with formal charges?" Spano asked.

"No."

"Have they said you were getting a letter of reprimand?"

"Not yet," Isen said.

There was a pause at the other end. "Look, Mark, I know this sucks, especially the waiting around to see if the axe is going to fall. But until they make something out of it, there's little you can do. Technically, Kelly's report is the last word you have on it, and his recommendation was to drop everything, right?"

"Right," Isen said. But he felt no better. There *was* an axe above him, and the Chief of Staff could cut the string at any time.

"It's in the army's best interest to keep this under wraps, right? To say that they conducted, or they are conducting, an internal investigation. There's no reason they should want to throw you to the dogs."

Spano's phrase brought up an image of a front yard filled with TV cameras and lights, with obnoxious reporters shoving microphones and recorders in his face, hounding him everywhere.

"I guess I'm just afraid they might find out my name somehow. The media could really make life miserable for me and Adrienne."

"Can't you guys go away or something?" Spano offered.

"No, she didn't put in for a vacation because she wasn't expecting me home. She can hardly go in now and say 'I need some time so my husband and I can go hide out somewhere. He's the guy who shot the druggies down in Mexico.' I *was* thinking about trying to go off by myself somewhere, maybe keep Adrienne out of the spotlight, but the army told me to stay home in case they want to reach me. I had to get permission to go see my dad in Augusta."

"Shit, you might as well be under house arrest," Spano said.

"Yeah, I guess I am. I hate turning on the news anymore. All I see is friggin' Mexico this, Mexico that." He realized he was running on, so he stopped.

"I'm sorry for unloading all this on you," Isen said.

"Hey, no problem," Spano came back. "Have you called Cortizo to see if he knows anything about this from their end?"

"No. But I guess it couldn't hurt," Isen said. "Thanks for listening."

"If I come up with any bright ideas, I'll let you know," Spano said.

It took Isen several hours to get hold of Cortizo.

"Captain Isen," Cortizo said. "It is good to hear from you. How is your wife? Are you enjoying your leave?"

Cortizo seemed genuinely happy to hear from him, and Isen hated to drop the story on the lieutenant, but he needed to know what was going on down there as far as an investigation was concerned. Isen told him about the letter from Kelly, about the stories in the newspapers, and the national attention on Mexico. Cortizo listened, very concerned, interrupting a few times for clarification.

When Isen was finished, Cortizo said, "Perhaps I can find out something down here at the Operation Sentinel headquarters. At least we might know who is conducting further investigations. I can tell you if that politician sends more people down here."

"Thanks," Isen said. "That would help some."

"Captain Isen, you have done nothing wrong. I cannot believe your army would sacrifice you in a political fight over the President's policies. They have not charged you with anything yet, is that correct?"

It was the second time that question had come up that

day. Isen supposed he should draw some comfort from the answer, but he found none. "That's right," he said.

"What you need is something to give honor back to your name," Cortizo explained.

"How's that?"

"Stay in touch, Captain Isen. I'll let you know if something comes up," Cortizo said.

"I will."

When he'd thought of making the two phone calls, he had been comforted because it seemed as if he was taking some action. But Isen felt no better afterward, and he looked around and found that he was still alone.

# 13

## Fayetteville, North Carolina
### 28 May

MAJOR RAYMOND ANTHONY SPANO SAT AT HIS KITCHEN table, balancing his four-year-old daughter on his knee as they both tried to look at the same comic strip on the table in front of them.

"What's this one say, Daddy?"

Rebecca's small finger stabbed at the strip she wanted deciphered. Her father could see the trace of polish left from when the babysitter painted the little girl's nails two nights earlier, at Rebecca's request. Spano had no sooner launched into an explanation of the comic when she pointed to another, interrupting him in midsentence. "Read this one, Daddy."

"I haven't finished the first yet, baby." But Rebecca wasn't listening. She was looking out the bay window of the breakfast room at the family dog. The big Irish setter was frantically digging under the fence, throwing a red rooster tail of dirt up behind him.

"Rusty is tearing up the yard again," Rebecca said in a tattletale singsong.

Spano looked up at the pet he considered to be his wife's. "Yes, Rusty is tearing up the yard again, isn't he?" Ray Spano was determined that the stupid dog wasn't going to get to him today. He looked at the clock again, and for the fourth or fifth time that morning wondered where he would be if he were at work. He derived a perverse pleasure from constantly making such comparisons; they reminded him that he was off duty.

Spano had taken a three-day pass (which really consisted of only one day off, a Friday, in conjunction with a weekend) so that he could spend some time with his family. It was the first time he'd had off since returning from Mexico, and he wanted to catch up on their time together. His wife, Diane, and his son, Tommy, the sleepyheads in the family, were still in bed, taking advantage of the break from Rebecca's relentless morning personality. Spano and his daughter were always the early risers, which suited him just fine. He liked this unhurried time with his daughter.

Ray Spano was a happy man. The spring day stretched out before him, full of possibility. His daughter, whom he loved so much that it scared him, sat on his knee; his wife and son were safe and asleep upstairs. Spano had been reminded, when he saw those two Blackhawks go down in Mexico, that a soldier was never really far from the chance of violent death, and he now had the nagging pain in his calf muscle to recount the lesson for him every day. Consequently, he appreciated the genuine blessings he enjoyed.

Then the phone rang.

It was probably too early for one of Diane's friends to be calling, though it wasn't out of the question. Maybe it was the school. Tommy was staying out of class for the day so the family could spend time together. But then Spano realized that there was no one at the school yet to notice Tommy's absence.

The phone rang again. Spano surprised himself by actually entertaining the thought of not picking it up. But that passed. "Spano here," he said.

"Hello, Ray." It was Colonel Reeves, Spano's boss and the commander of E-1, the Delta Force's ground operations detachment. There would be no *good* reason why Reeves was calling.

"I'd like to talk to you, Ray."

That was it. That was all it took to let Spano know that

something was up with the Delta Force. Colonel Reeves was as good as his word when he told his subordinates that they needed their time off, that they needed to see their families whenever the group was back at Fort Bragg. Reeves was a classic work-hard, play-hard man, and he wouldn't interrupt Spano's day off without good reason.

"Fifteen minutes, sir."

Spano carried Rebecca up the stairs with him. "Let's be quiet so Mommy and Tommy can sleep, okay, sweetheart?"

"Can I wake Mommy up, Daddy?"

"In a few minutes."

Spano limped up the steps to the bathroom, brushed his teeth, and grabbed his rechargeable razor. He'd shave in the car. At least he didn't have to put on a uniform; Delta Force personnel adhered to what the army called relaxed grooming standards. In practice, this meant they wore civilian clothes (to blend in with the urban surroundings where they usually worked), and they could grow their hair longer than other soldiers. Spano had gotten a haircut before going to see Isen, but he hadn't had one since. His hairstyle would be conservative in most corporate boardrooms, but around Fort Bragg, home of the army's 82nd Airborne Division and the paratrooper "high and tight" haircut—skin on the sides and a small tuft of hair on the top—Spano stood out a bit. Sometimes when he was out in public at Fort Bragg or in Fayetteville, he caught some of the shaved heads looking at him askance, as if they were wondering what he did for a living. That, of course, was the idea.

Spano washed and dried his face, then pulled on a short-sleeve knit shirt. He found one of his sneakers in the bathroom and the other in Rebecca's room, where she'd slipped out of it after clunking around the hallway while he got ready. He sat on her bed and tied the laces, and when he looked up, Diane was standing there.

"You've got to go in?"

There was no anger in her voice, and for that Spano thanked his lucky stars again. In all the years of phone calls in the middle of the night, in all the years he had spent with regular tactical units, then with the always-on-call

Ranger battalions, she had rarely complained about the profession he had chosen, or what it cost her. She knew, when she walked down the aisle of West Point's Cadet Chapel to marry him, that Spano would always be a soldier. Bitching about it would have been a futile exercise. On the other hand, Diane was no superwoman, and she got into a blue funk whenever Ray had to be away at a particularly bad time, such as Christmas. But she didn't ask him to get out of the army. For his part, Spano had promised her that, after this tour with Delta, he would seek an assignment that allowed them a more normal family life.

"Yeah."

There was no sense in his saying, "I'll call you." Both of them knew that he might not be allowed to contact her once he entered the Delta compound. When they were given a mission, they immediately became incommunicado to prevent any security leaks. Nor was there any sense in her asking where he was going. If he knew, he wouldn't be able to tell her. It just happened that this time he didn't know. Finally there was no sense in her asking when he would be home. That question carried too much superstitious weight in the Delta Force community. The answer, always the same—*I'll be home as soon as I can*—was too close to *If I get home*.

Over the years, more than a few Delta Force members had left for work in the morning, expecting it to be a normal day: home by six, barbecue steaks on the grill, watch a movie with the kids, and make love in the warm evening of the North Carolina summer, only to come home in a box. The threat was always there. Diane handled it better than most.

"I'll tell Tommy that we'll do this family day another time."

She's the strong one, Spano thought. He hated telling his kids that they were going to be disappointed again. And though he suspected that the psychology of his telling them the bad news was better for their learning about honesty, he was at his weakest when they cried. He wasn't proud of it, but there it was.

Major Ray Spano kissed his wife good-bye and walked

through the garage to the driveway. When he backed the car out, he saw Diane watching through the window. He waved and smiled.

Major Ray Spano had fifteen years of army service under his belt, and he'd been separated from his family more times than he cared to think about. But he had never gotten used to it. He pursued the assignment with Delta Force as he did everything in the army—from his first meet as an army cross-country runner to the most recent challenge of the air force's Survival, Evasion, Resistance, and Escape (SERE) course. He went at everything full throttle. A top-notch company commander in the 3rd Ranger Battalion when that storied unit jumped into Panama, he sat out the war with Iraq because by that time he was a member of the special operations community and some mysterious *they* deemed it more important that he stay out of that fray. He'd worked hard to become a good operations officer, and he spent countless hours reading and studying to broaden his military education. He got what he wanted: Colonel Reeves trusted Spano more than any other major at Fort Bragg. But the reward had a double edge. He had become an integral part of a team that was not at war but was never completely at peace, either. Every time some half-crazed terrorist called in a threat, the Delta Force spent the next week on pins and needles, preparing for the most outlandish contingencies. The work was grueling, fast-paced, and intense. There was always some new contingency to plan for, there were always hot spots to watch and evaluate and worry over.

As Ray Spano drove through the quiet residential streets of Fayetteville toward some unspoken mission, he was painfully aware of two important facts: he loved his work, and his work was costing his family in ways that would not be apparent for years.

But he was all business now, had to be. He would drive onto the compound in a few minutes and be his other self, the cool operations officer, the strong right arm of the state, ready to go anywhere in the world to do the nation's bidding in the interests of what someone else, someone he would never meet, had defined as "a matter of national security." Spano necessarily trusted the men above him, though he knew they were capable of making mistakes that could cost him his life. Even so, it always took him a few minutes to adjust to being away from his everyday life, not just physically removed, but intellectually removed enough that he could do his job without worrying what might happen to Diane and the kids. He owed that much to the team members who expected his undivided attention in the mission planning he did. It got harder with each call-up, with every year that passed, and Ray Spano had wondered, during the long hours of more than one night, if he was losing his edge.

Spano made his way to the planning cell and found Colonel Reeves seated at the briefing room conference table. Large military maps, held down by plastic coffee cups, papered the table. Reeves turned when Spano came in.

"Come on over and sit down, Ray."

Spano took the chair next to Reeves. The Colonel was always in a jovial mood when there was something going down that needed Delta Force attention. The maps on the table, Spano noticed, were of Mexico. *Now the shit hits the fan*, Spano thought.

"They finally decided they had enough to call us in on this one, Ray," Reeves said to Spano.

The ops officer opened his black binder and prepared to take notes.

"You know this plane that went down between Mexico City and Dallas-Fort Worth?"

"Yessir," Spano said. "We're talking about the NDP, right?"

"Yeah, the same group of nuts who killed those sailors and that lady and her kids in Germany." Reeves was agitated, talking fast. He clenched his trademark unlit cigar between his teeth, rolling it back and forth distractedly between sentences.

"The Mexican police think they have a line on how they got the bomb on the plane. A cop in Mexico City was asking around about airline smugglers just before this thing went down. When the investigators questioned him, he clammed up, but his wife told the cops that her husband had a friend who was a private investigator in the city. When a couple of detectives went to ask about this sudden interest in airline smugglers, the guy—the private eye—had disappeared. Turned up a day later in the trunk of his own car in another part of the city," Reeves said.

"Any hard evidence that makes them think this guy was connected with the NDP?" Spano asked.

"The private eye's secretary said that the stiff met with a tall European guy a day or two before the bombing. It's all circumstantial, of course, but it certainly seems an unlikely coincidence. Anyway—we've got nothing else."

"Do we know where this European is?"

"We have no freakin' idea," Reeves said, pulling one of the maps toward him. "We know where he was last seen, but he's had plenty of time to move since then. He could be just about anywhere by now." Reeves folded his hands over the map and lowered his face for a few seconds as if reading fine print. Then he looked up at Spano. "Not only that, but we don't even have a possible ID. This Neu Deutschland Party is an offshoot of a group the German police, specifically, the BKA, thought was defunct. They have a list of suspected members still in Germany, and they're watching those people to see if any of them make a move for Mexico or the U.S. But the list is old, and the Germans don't have a lot of confidence in it. Basically, we got squat."

Spano wrote "Mexico" on the blank notebook page on his lap. He had hoped, when he'd returned after being wounded, that he'd seen the last of that country. In his after-action report, Spano had recommended—in language as strong as he thought he could get away with—that the special ops community stay out of Mexico. In spite of the meager increases in support for operations such as Cortizo's, in general the Mexicans didn't want American help, and there was very little that could be done to overcome a stumbling block like that.

"Then there's the political heat to contend with, and the heat is on in a big way. People in this country are pissed off and want something done. So far, the NDP has made good on every threat, and everybody—especially the President—knows that.''

Spano looked up. "So what's the plan, sir?"

Reeves let out a breath and pushed the map away. "The Mexicans have asked for our help on this. The FBI and the CIA, not to mention the German police, are all in on this investigation—what a jug fuck that must be. But we're going to be the strike force, whenever it comes to that. The Mexicans just don't have the experience in antiterrorism stuff. I'd like to send you down there today, because the Germans just passed word that some men identified as possible NDP operatives are coming from Europe today. If this tip pays off, they'll have you there as an adviser."

Spano was thinking to himself, *If nothing turns up, I get to sit on my ass for a month or two and watch Mexican detective work. Then, if we're not careful, one of these rabid politicians will have a field day with us just like they're having with Mark Isen.*

Something clicked when he thought of Isen. "Can I request some help, sir?" Spano said.

"What did you have in mind?" Reeves asked.

"One of the things I learned in Mexico was how much I don't know about Mexico. But the guy I followed around down there is back here in the States, and I happen to know he's just marking time right now. If it's possible, I'd like to have him go with me."

Reeves looked curious. "Is he from special ops?"

"No, sir. He's a straight-leg grunt." Straight-leg was the unflattering term applied to infantrymen who walked—as opposed to riding or parachuting—to battle. "He got into some trouble because he shot first in a firefight with some smugglers, and he's cooling his heels right now."

"I read something about that," Reeves said. "Is he a hothead?"

"No, sir. As a matter of fact, he's very levelheaded," Spano said.

"Could be that the President's opponents are trying to make some political hay by hanging this guy," Reeves said.

Spano didn't answer. Reeves chewed the inside of his lip

for a moment. He liked to give subordinates what they needed for a mission.

"If you'd like to have an area expert on the ground, I'll call Washington. Doesn't hurt to ask," Reeves said. "You'd better take some civvies, since you'll be working with the police."

Spano, like all other Delta personnel, kept several bags packed and stored at the compound. One of these held civilian clothes, but he wasn't sure he had the right kind of street clothes to blend in in Mexico. Somehow, the thought of going home again and seeing the kids for only as long as it took him to pack a few things seemed worse than just leaving without returning. His whirlwind presence in the house for a half hour or so would only disturb the calm, would certainly confuse Rebecca, his youngest. There was no way to know when he would be home again, but as much as he wanted to see them, he decided he'd better stay away.

# 14

## Mexico City, Mexico
### 30 May

RAY SPANO GAVE ISEN FORTY-EIGHT HOURS TO GET USED TO
the idea of being yanked off leave to return to Mexico.
Spano hadn't thought the delay would be a problem, but
now it looked as if Isen might miss the whole reason for
their coming to Mexico at all.

Spano sat on a bench tucked in the miserly shade offered
by some trees along the curb. He'd been there almost an
hour, and the combination of the heat and the city's thin,
polluted air conspired to make him nauseated. Twenty feet
away, two Mexican police officers in plainclothes stood
drinking Pepsi-Cola from bottles. Although his escorts
hadn't briefed him fully, Spano expected to witness, in the
next hour or two, a strike by a police squad against the
suspected hiding place of several members of the Neu
Deutschland Party.

The Mexican authorities had been alerted by German officials that three suspected NDP members had made plans
to travel to Mexico on the twenty-eighth. The Mexicans
were waiting for them when they arrived, on three different
flights, in Mexico City. The police tailed the men closely
but hadn't wanted to close in on them until the chief investigator thought they might have a chance to bag the other

individuals who were probably already operating in Mexico, as well as the stash of explosives and whatever other weapons they'd carried with them. But the political pressure was too much—there would be no more waiting. Now the three Germans were assembled in this pitiful stretch of town, west of the central part of the city, where one of them had rented a room.

Spano had tried to remind the police that these men were not your common, garden-variety criminals; they had the potential to be very violent, as they had already proven, and they were probably well armed. The senior investigator seemed unimpressed. In any case, he told his American guest, the patrolmen were armed. Spano had tried to press the point, but the chief detective was suddenly unable to follow Spano's English.

As Spano brooded about how stupid it was to be down here when no one would listen to him—the same situation he'd found Isen in back in April—he thought about how he might approach the target house. Then he spotted a Mexican police officer walking toward him on the other side of the street. Mark Isen was with the policeman.

"I thought you were going to miss the party," Spano said. He didn't stand; he barely looked up.

Isen caught the cue to play low-key. He simply sat on the bench next to Spano and looked out across the same dusty street. "I can't understand why you can't schedule these things in more convenient locations," he said. When he looked over, Spano had a slight grin.

During their weeks together in and around Tampico, Spano hadn't been one for joking, and Isen had written him off as another example of a West Point-trained prig. Now it was fairly obvious to Isen that Spano thought pretty highly of him—another previously undisclosed fact. So Isen was prepared to concede that there might be other facets to Ray Spano that he didn't fully appreciate. *Maybe I was the one who was distracted,* Isen thought.

"I can hardly believe you got me out of the States, much less back into Mexico," Isen said.

"We only do the big missions, and we get what we want," Spano said melodramatically. He looked at Isen.

"Seriously, it took a call to the Chief of Staff's office, but we wanted you here . . . I wanted you here. You have experience dealing with the people, and, unlike a lot of other so-called experts I could have asked for, you don't have your head up your ass."

"Thanks," Isen said, a bit embarrassed. "What, exactly, am I supposed to do?"

"Just watch," Spano said. "I think you're about to see a police raid on that house over there." He glanced only briefly at the narrow three-story wood frame building across the street and down about seventy-five meters.

"Who do they think is in there?" Isen asked.

"The German police were watching all the people they thought were members of the NDP. When three of them made arrangements to come to Mexico, the Germans let the Federales here know."

"And they followed the three here?"

"Not exactly. They came in separately, so the Mexicans tailed them around the city for a while, hoping to find out where they kept their equipment: weapons, explosives, so on."

"Did they find anything?"

"No. But the three men at least decided to get together. They went into that house—there's an apartment up on the top floor—last night and haven't come out yet."

"So why do they have you sitting over here?" Isen asked.

Spano was angry with the turn of events, but he didn't know his pique was showing.

"More to the point, what the hell am I doing getting involved in this terrorist shit?" Isen asked.

"I asked for you," Spano said. "As an area expert."

"And a way to pull my chestnuts out of the fire?"

Spano looked over at Isen, but before he could answer, he spotted two of the plainclothes detectives he'd seen earlier making their way down the opposite side of the street.

"I think it's show time," Spano said.

The two Americans watched as the officers entered the front door of the building.

"What do you think?" Isen asked.

"I hope they're going in to look around. Those two, however tough they are, shouldn't be going in to confront three armed men, even with the element of surprise."

"How would you do this?" Isen asked.

"First of all, I'd get these civilians off the street." Spano indicated, with a nod of his head, several old women and a young couple who were near the house. The young couple were leaning against a car just a few meters past the entrance to the building.

Spano continued. "Then I'd go in and look around only if I couldn't find someone who could brief me on the floor plan. Otherwise you take a chance of alerting the targets."

*Interesting choice of words,* Isen thought. *Targets.*

"Anyways, I'd at least wait until it got dark, and if I could, I'd wait until the middle of the night, say, zero three hundred. That way, there's a much better chance of catching them with their guard down. And whenever I went in, it would be in force, violent. If the job needed two guys, I'd take four, if it needed four, I'd take eight."

"So why didn't they listen to you? I heard from Colonel Reeves that they were all excited to have an American Delta Force adviser."

"The federal government was excited, but these local guys think I'm out of line. It's as if they have something to prove to the feds, and the only way they can do it is to pull this off without any of the things the federals provided."

"Sounds like the kind of crap I went through with their army," Isen said. "Except that here, those kinds of games can get innocent people killed."

"You got that right," Spano agreed.

The first sound reminded Isen of popcorn popping on a stove in the next room. An airy, ineffectual sound.

"This is it," Spano said. "I can't believe they sent two guys in there to start a gunfight."

Isen kept his eyes trained on the house across the way. There were at least several weapons involved now. Along the street, Mexican policemen were suddenly running toward the house, pistols drawn. Several had shotguns.

Then someone shouted in Spanish from inside the building. The officers on the street gradually halted, as if held up by something they all discovered at the same time.

More yelling in Spanish.

Suddenly, at the door, one of the two police officers who'd gone in a few moments earlier. Except that he was being held from behind by someone; the Mexican's arms were pinned behind his back. He was young, twenty or twenty-five, and the small dark face above his white shirt was a study in terror, in suddenly glimpsed mortality. Isen caught a flash of gunmetal pressed tight against the side of the detective's head, then he could make out a man, not much bigger than the Mexican, who was holding the hostage, and for the moment at least, the initiative.

Spano moved quickly off the bench and into the questionable shelter of a doorway. Isen followed, and the two men tried to squeeze into a space barely big enough to hide one of them.

"A good sniper could take that guy down from here. He'd never fucking flinch," Spano said.

His voice seemed transformed, somehow, but when Isen looked at his face, close now, he had the same flat expression. Except for the eyes. There was something new there: bloodlust, revenge, hate. Whatever it was, Isen was glad it wasn't directed at him. Spano had palmed his weapon and now held it lightly in his hand. Isen, still wary of Mexican rules, had no pistol.

It didn't look to Isen as if the terrorist had much of a chance. Police cars blocked both ends of the street. Behind these crouched officers armed with everything from pistols to automatic rifles; they all looked eager to fire.

"Bring me a car," the cornered man shouted in English. Isen could see that he was about thirty-five and sported a thin beard. There were no doubt Mexicans in the area who could speak English, but none of them offered a comment.

"I SAID BRING ME A CAR," the young man shouted again, his voice strained in fear. He pulled on the police officer, and the man staggered back a bit, forced to lean some of his weight on his enemy.

"He's keeping the cop off balance," Spano offered. "This guy knows what he's doing."

"Except it doesn't look like he's going to get out of this one," Isen said.

The terrorist lowered his pistol, and Isen thought for a moment that he was going to drop it. But then he reached around the policeman's leg and shot his hostage in the foot. There was a little smoke, and that popping sound, then the officer went down like a dropped doll. The terrorist crouched low behind his victim, so that the snipers still didn't have a clear shot past the police officer, whose face was contorted in pain. There was a low whining sound, as from a dog, and Isen could see the officer's face twisted grotesquely. There was something surreal about watching it from this close, unable to do anything to help.

"Head shot," Spano said.

"What?" Isen asked.

"The sniper has to get him with a head shot. Otherwise you take a chance of only wounding him. He might get another round off and kill the hostage."

Spano's voice was calm, as if he were discussing the best way to winch a car out of a ditch. Isen found himself staring at Spano's face, which was only inches away in the tight confines of their shelter.

The sniper fired prematurely, before he set up his shot, and it plucked the terrorist's side. Isen thought he saw a spray of red where the bullet exited the lower back. The man curled up on himself in pain, but he never let go of the weapon. Isen just had time to think that Spano had been right about the head shot when the German brought the pistol up to the policeman's head. He did not even hesitate, just pressed the gun to the back of the man's head and pulled the trigger. The officer's face slammed down onto the pavement, and the sniper fired again at the terrorist. This time, he got the head shot.

Down the street, police officers rushed the building where the fighting had started. Spano stood immediately and moved out into the open. Isen took a few tentative steps to follow, but something didn't seem right. When he looked down the street to his left, he saw several police officers with their weapons trained on the Americans.

"Hold up," Isen said quickly. Spano looked up and noticed the firing squad. He put both his hands into the air. *"Americano,"* he said. One of the officers signaled for them to stop, and they did.

"What a fucking abortion," Spano said through the corner of his mouth. He didn't take his eyes off the police officer still watching them, although the Mexican had lowered his weapon. "They sent those guys in there to get slaughtered."

"Maybe they don't have the resources," Isen said. "You know, to train antiterrorist guys or a SWAT team or something like that."

"That's only part of it," Spano said. "There's too much politics involved. The local guys don't want to cooperate with the federal guys, and there's no mechanism in place to define jurisdiction on this type of thing. So nobody knows what anybody else is supposed to do. If you add a couple of headstrong local police or state administrators to the pot, you've got a real goat-screw on your hands."

They paused as some Mexican patrolmen carried out four bodies wrapped in sheets and blankets. Spano was clearly angry, and Isen thought it had to do with the unnecessary deaths of the two officers sent into the building first. But he got madder still as they moved away, once it became clear that the Mexicans weren't going to let their so-called advisers near the crime scene.

Finally, Isen had to ask. "This isn't all that great a working relationship, is it?"

Spano seemed surprised by the comment. "What? Yeah . . . You're right about that. But I'm also pissed off about what this is going to mean for us."

"Who's us?"

"If it turns out that this raid didn't get all of these NDP characters, there's more of a chance that the Mexicans will ask for, and we'll send in, the Delta Force."

"What makes you think that?" Isen said. "Isn't it just as likely that they'll just be more cautious, use more firepower?"

He and Spano were walking back to Spano's car, which was parked about a half mile from the site of the raid. The two men were soaked through with sweat before they'd covered half the distance.

"That's a possibility, I guess. But this thing has national attention. Both presidents are going to hear about this . . . today." Spano wiped the bridge of his nose with one hand, then put on a pair of aviator sunglasses. "There's too much involved, too many people have been killed. So everybody's going to want to send in the big guns, and that's us. But these local guys will hamstring us just like they did you guys in Sentinel, and if things are fucked up, we'll get blamed."

Isen dropped his eyes and watched the tops of his shoes for a few steps before asking the question that was on his mind. "Is that what you were really down here for, to lay out missions for the Delta Force?"

Spano, who was massaging the wounded muscle in his calf, looked away. There had been no reason for Isen to know his real mission on his first trip to Mexico, and he suspected that Isen would understand the need for secrecy. But there was still something vaguely dishonest—on his part—about it. He hadn't lied to Isen, but he had misled him. And what made it worse was that Isen had opened up to him, about his concerns for Operation Sentinel, about what he thought was going to happen to the army, about his own feelings of betrayal. Now Spano felt like one of the betrayers. The betrayal had a face.

"That's not exactly it," Spano began, looking up. They were only a few yards from the car; Spano stopped and moved under a canopy that shaded a sidewalk stand. The odor of fried food was strong under the canvas, but they had to get out of the sun.

"I wasn't there to drum up business, if that's what you're thinking. I was there to see if there is a role for Delta in drug interdiction."

"Obviously somebody thinks there's a role for special operations down here," Isen said.

"I suppose so, otherwise they wouldn't have thought to test it out. The U.S.-Mexican border is a fucking sieve, and it doesn't take a genius to see that our next war is going to be here chasing bandits, like Black Jack Pershing going after Pancho Villa."

Isen looked unsettled. Spano shifted his weight from one foot to the other before speaking again. "Look, Mark, this kind of antiterrorist mission"—he gestured over his shoulder—"is what we train for. But in my report I said that I thought bringing Delta Force in on the drug stuff would be idiotic. I even went so far as to say that involving regular army folks—like you and Sergeant Worden—was lunacy as well. This drug mission is not what we're supposed to be doing. I suspect you joined the army to be a soldier, not a detective or a G-man."

Isen thought about Spano watching the terrorist and hostage. *Head shot,* he'd said.

"But you know what I found out, Mark? It really doesn't matter what you and I think, and we can write freakin' reports until hell freezes over. The good citizens are sick and tired of the druggies and the bombers, and the President and Congress are willing to do anything to keep those voters happy. And if that means sacrificing the army that you and I and Sergeant Worden and Colonel Reeves and all the poor dumb fuckers like us have built up over the last twenty years, so be it."

The smaller man started to say something, paused, then laughed quietly to himself.

"What's so funny?" Spano said.

"Look at us, standing around in sweaty civilian clothes under a canvas fly in the middle of no-fucking-where, Mexico, talking like somebody is going to ask us what we think about this mess." He looked over at Spano and suddenly felt sorry for him. Spano had committed his career to the shadowy world of fighting terrorists, people like the three NDP thugs the Mexicans had just fought. And all his work was slipping into the same abyss that Isen saw: a hollow army of confused soldiers going through people's garages, trampling civil rights, burning villages in South American jungles. He thought about the kid he'd shot when Cortizo's men had been ambushed. A kid, not even old enough to be a clever enemy. But there was nothing to do except go on.

"I guess we'd better figure out how we're going to catch the rest of these NDP goons," Spano said. "This thing is out of hand, and I have a feeling we're all about to be dragged in."

# 15

## Mexico City, Mexico
### 1 June

WHEN THERE WAS NO SIGN OF THE THREE MEN WHO WERE TO join him by the first of June, Wolf went underground for a while, hiding out in the teeming expanse of Mexico City. He had no idea how much the authorities knew but was still fairly confident that his quick rise in the NDP meant that they didn't have a dossier on him. Nevertheless, he didn't want to go around looking for the missing men, as that would entail showing himself around Mexico City, perhaps drawing attention to himself. He was angry that he would have to continue to work alone, handling the money and material and coordination by himself, at least for a while longer. His detailed plan called for sharp timing, but there was little he could do. He sent word back to Europe for more help, but decided to delay, for another week, plans for his next move. That should give him time to come up with a way to get the job done by himself until help arrived.

During one of the afternoons he spent in the bar of a Mexico City hotel, Wolf met a Mexican Army officer who was in the city to brief some government officials on the American antidrug air interdiction missions along the border. Like soldiers everywhere, the man spent a good deal of time fighting boredom. Plied with a few drinks Wolf contributed, the major had proved more than willing to talk about his work.

"The Americans rely always on technology," the major said to Wolf. Apparently he thought that Wolf, a European, shared the same stereotypes of the gringos from the north.

"I wish I had one percent of what they spent to bring their equipment down here to set up their radar net."

"They are always throwing away money," Wolf agreed. He'd told the officer that he was an engineer, in the city on business.

The Mexican turned his shot glass—his second in ten minutes—upside down over his open mouth. He'd unbuttoned his uniform blouse, so that his large Adam's apple wiggled up and down as he swallowed the whiskey. He put the glass on the bar, and Wolf raised a finger to the bartender.

"Thanks." The officer belched.

"At any rate, I am glad they are stopping some of the flow of drugs," Wolf said. "I know I would worry about my own children being brought up in a society so troubled by the problems the Americans have."

The major turned a sour look to Wolf.

"Their problem is that they have too much money," he sneered. Wolf half-expected him to say something about the German standard of living, but he didn't. "They don't know how good they have it."

Wolf wasn't sure how to respond to this, so he kept silent.

"But they are being beaten again, smug as they are," the major said. He leaned toward Wolf, full of whiskey and camaraderie built on what he thought was a shared dislike of Americans.

"They are being beaten again by the most primitive methods."

"How's that?" Wolf asked, smiling. He turned toward the bartender and ordered himself another soda, then reached down the bar for a bowl of little red nuts. He didn't want to seem so interested that he frightened the major into silence.

"You have read, perhaps, of their experiences in Vietnam?" the major asked.

"A little," Wolf said.

"The Americans thought they could shut off the flow of supplies from North Vietnam by bombing all the little jungle trails." The army officer, by now a good way through his third neat whiskey in less than twenty minutes, was bleary-eyed. He moved his hand over the bar, palm down, making little sounds of explosions as he opened and closed his fist. "Boom, boom, boom," he said. "Bombed the shit out of a bunch of jungle."

Wolf smiled.

"But the North Vietnamese carried enough stuff on their backs to keep the war going."

He appeared to be finished, or at least at some impasse. Wolf wondered if that was all he was going to hear about the defeat of the Americans at the border.

The major raised his empty glass to the bartender, giving Wolf an inquisitive look.

"Certainly, have another," Wolf said. "This is all on my company's tab anyway."

The bartender returned with the bottle and splashed some of the liquid into the glass. The bottle bore an expensive label, but judging by the bartender's looks, Wolf doubted that the major was sampling the original contents. The officer put the glass to his lips delicately, then, in one sweep of his hand, he tilted the whole thing into his throat. Wolf figured he'd better work quickly.

"The smugglers have a trail they use?" he asked.

The major narrowed his eyes at Wolf, and Wolf could almost sense the fuzzy mind trying to divine just why this German would want to know this piece of information. But apparently no alarm bells went off, and the major continued.

"No, no. That's not what I meant." He wiped the back of his hand across his mouth, then looked up and down the bar. Wolf thought he was looking to see who might overhear them.

"You ever buy any women with your company's money?" he said.

Wolf was listening intently to every word, but he was still taken aback. "What?"

"You ever buy any women with your company's money? There's some here that even take credit cards. Did you know that?" His speech was slipping, and his head was lower to the bar than it had been a few moments before, Wolf noticed.

*It may be time to give up on this one,* Wolf thought. But then he might still strike a deal with the man; a woman, bought with Wolf's money, in exchange for some information. Such a trade would be overt; there would be no mistaking Wolf's intention after he made such a proposal. He was weighing the possible danger—the authorities might already be looking for him—against the value of what he might learn, when the army officer obliged him.

"They're carrying everything on their backs," he said into his glass.

"What's that?" Wolf asked.

"I said the smugglers are hiring people to carry the stuff over the border on their backs." He looked up at Wolf, wanting more liquor, but Wolf wasn't ready to give in yet. Sensing this, the Mexican went on.

"It's not so hard, really. There are lots of people who make the crossing on foot. Sometimes they pay a guide to get them into Texas. Now the smugglers are hiring these people, who are usually seeking work in the United States, to carry drugs across. The promise is that they can start their life in America with some good American dollars."

Wolf leaned his elbows on the bar and stared at his reflection, just above the rows of bottles, in the mirror behind the bar. He signaled the bartender for another drink for his informer, then watched the reflection of his own smile.

The Mexican officer's story prompted a change in plans for Wolf, drawing him north to the flat coastal plain of Tamaulipas State. He knew that many of the northbound shipments of drugs coming up the peninsula from South America by air touched down here. From Tamaulipas north, the amount of surveillance increased dramatically, and it was heaviest along the border between the United

States and Mexico. So it was here, on the plains beside the blue gulf, that the smugglers started to break down their shipments for transport. And it was here that Wolf was to meet some of those Mexicans who, wanting nothing more than a chance to work hard and earn a good wage, would carry his weapons across the border for him.

Originally he had planned to ship the weapons north with the other contraband, hidden in truckloads of fruits and vegetables or in the stuffing of cheap furniture. But the risk involved increased dramatically after the spate of bombings. Bulk freight, long a favorite of smugglers, was now being scrutinized more thoroughly by customs, as was the mail. Air freight would be nearly impossible. This left only those methods that did not pretend to be legitimate.

His Soviet benefactor approved the use of funds to move the material overland. Wolf opened another bank account in Tampico and passed the wiring instructions to the Soviets. In that conversation, he left out the exact details of what he intended to do. The contact pressed him for information, but Wolf pleaded that the telephone lines weren't secure. Afterward, he wondered how long a leash they would allow him, and he even considered contacting them again with more details so they wouldn't be tempted to cut off funds. But when the money he asked for appeared in his account, he forgot about trying to keep them happy and concentrated on the task at hand.

# 16

## Tampico, Mexico
### 4 June

WOLF WIPED THE NECK OF THE BEER BOTTLE WITH A WHITE handkerchief he had taken from his pocket. *Probably still dirty,* he said to himself. The fat waitress had brought him a glass, but he was sure she'd carried it with one finger stuck inside. He made her take the first bottle of beer back because she hadn't opened it at the table in front of him as he'd instructed her.

Wolf liked many things about Mexico, but the whole country seemed designed to torment fastidious people such as himself. He found Tampico particularly loathsome, with its polluted lake and the fetid stench of the Rio Pánuco, and everywhere the nauseating signature of the oil refineries. But the city was an important transportation center on the northern part of Mexico's gulf coast, and for that reason Wolf was staying.

It had taken him three days to establish contact with one of the "guides" who worked north of Tampico ferrying contraband into the United States on the backs of illegal aliens. He had chosen a public place for the first meeting, thinking a crowd might provide him some guarantee of safety. But as he looked around the seedy cantina, he wondered if any of the locals there would even report the murder of a foreigner by another Mexican.

It was ten minutes past two when he looked at his watch for what seemed like the fourth or fifth time in as many minutes. His contact, known to him only by the code name Diablo, was late. Wolf swept his gaze over the room again, noticed a few restless teenagers, an old man who sat chain smoking at the plank bar. He was watching the Mexican teens when the young men took notice—all at the same instant—of someone at the door. Wolf turned in his chair and was just as surprised to see a woman enter the room.

She was about five-eight, too tall for a Mexican, especially a Mexican woman. She wore men's jeans and workshirt and rough cowboy boots. Her hair was trapped in a dark bandanna, and beneath that her dirty face drew to a point at her chin from a wide forehead. She went straight to the bar and spoke to the bartender without looking at anyone in the room.

Wolf found himself wondering what she would look like in women's clothing. The rough life in Mexico aged women quickly, and he thought it a shame. *So many of the young ones are beautiful,* he thought. He had been too busy since his arrival in Mexico to indulge himself in that regard, and he decided, even looking at the woman in men's clothes, that his chaste period would have to end soon.

The woman left the bar and a few moments later two men came in. One of them, large, dangerous-looking, backed up to the bar, where he stood watching the one foreigner. The other one came directly to Wolf.

"I am Diablo," he said without preamble.

Wolf was unsure of the etiquette here, but he knew that appearances were very important to these people, so he thought it might help to show some respect, even mock respect. He stood.

"Please, sit down," he said to the Mexican, motioning to the other chair at the table. *Diablo,* Wolf thought to himself, *is a pretty big name for one so young.*

The man before him was no more than twenty or twenty-one. He also was tall for a Mexican, with a long face and deep-set, hungry eyes. He had a scarf tied around his neck, not for decoration, but as if he'd just ridden a motorcycle. There was a suggestion of danger about him, and he looked like the kind of man who enjoyed violence.

"You are looking for help," Diablo said in uncertain English.

"And I come to you," Wolf finished. "I have some things I would like to move into the United States." The Mexican didn't respond, so Wolf continued after what he thought was a reasonable pause. "Small things that don't weigh much . . . they might easily be carried . . ."

The Mexican interrupted him. "I decide how things are moved," he said.

Wolf merely inclined his head. The impertinence angered him, but he was willing to let the young Mexican play his hand.

Diablo went on. "How much material are we talking about?"

"Two or three trips, five or six loads of twenty-five pounds each time."

"Why not one trip?" the Mexican asked curtly.

Wolf was about to say something about the fact that he was paying for the trip, but he caught himself. *If I offend his adolescent machismo, it might take days to find another carrier.*

As Wolf thought about his answer the woman who'd been at the bar earlier came up to the table and put a shot glass in front of each of the men. At close range, Wolf saw a great deal more. She didn't look Mexican. The hair at the edges of her scarf was light, her eyes green or blue. She was also young, eighteen or nineteen perhaps, and quite beautiful. The men's clothes, even the dirt could not hide delicate, very feminine features. She'd been doing outdoor work, he guessed, because her hands were rough—but her forearms, just visible beneath the pushed-back sleeves of the workshirt, were evenly tanned, hairless, smooth. Wolf looked at her arms, tried to divine the shape of her breasts beneath the loose shirt. Then he felt Diablo's eyes upon him.

The young man had clearly caught Wolf's study, and there was something welling up behind the Mexican's eyes.

*Now you've done it,* Wolf thought. *You got caught coveting his woman. Now the little prick will probably want to fight you or some such nonsense.*

If it wasn't for the fact that he needed to move his material within a few days, Wolf might have found the incident amusing. As it was, he had to lower his eyes to keep from betraying what he was thinking. He found himself looking at the shot glass, and he saw how Diablo might regain face.

"What is this?" Wolf asked, holding the tiny glass delicately between his thumb and index finger. Over the rim of the glass, Diablo looked at him incredulously. For a moment, he seemed to forget the girl, who was standing slightly behind him.

"It is tequila," the Mexican said.

"It is for a toast to business," the girl added. Diablo threw her an acid glance, and she turned and walked to the bar, but not before her eyes met Wolf's for a brief second.

*There is something there,* Wolf thought.

Diablo turned back around and glared at Wolf, but before he could say anything further, Wolf raised the glass. "Prosit," he said.

The Mexican raised his glass slowly, and Wolf put his own to his lips, tipped his head back, and poured the tequila in.

Wolf shot forward in his chair, spit the tequila onto the table and began to gag. His eyes filled with tears, and he grabbed at his mouth. The Mexicans, at first shocked, began to smile. Then Diablo burst out laughing and even pointed at the German. Over at the bar, the big man who'd come in with Diablo was also laughing, and even a few other patrons were smiling by this time. But the young Mexican sitting across from Wolf was near hysterics. He might have been genuinely amused, and he might have been grateful to have something to take his mind off the fact that the European had looked longingly at his woman. Whatever it was, it took the edge off the moment.

Wolf feigned distress, and after a few moments the woman brought him a warm beer, handing it over without looking at him directly. Wolf was careful about where his eyes roamed, and he squeezed them shut as he lifted the bottle to his lips.

"That was some drink," he choked. "I guess I'm just not used to that strong stuff."

"I thought Germans knew how to drink," the Mexican said.

"So did I," Wolf answered, chancing a smile.

The Mexican, smug again, turned to the man at the bar, and the two of them shared another laugh. *I played you easily enough,* Wolf said to himself as he eyed the young smuggler across from him. He could see, out of the corner of his eye, that the woman at the bar was looking away. *And I will play her as well.*

The next day Wolf drove out to the northern edge of town and parked along the side of the road as he'd been instructed. They must have been watching him from somewhere, he thought later, because they came up very quickly.

This time it was Diablo, another bulky bodyguard type, and the woman. Wolf did not get out of his car until they had pulled up behind him and were out of their own pickup. He watched in the mirror as Diablo and the other man got out and approached his car, stopping at the rear to rap on the trunk.

"Let's go. I haven't got all day," the young Mexican said.

Wolf thought about the automatic pistol under the seat and about how much pleasure it would be to shoot the young punk and just leave him out in the sun. Instead, he yanked on the door handle, got out of the car, and walked around to the back wordlessly. He didn't chance a look into the Mexican's car until Diablo and his helper were bent deep into the trunk of his car, looking at the plastic-wrapped packages there. The woman was sitting in the front seat, looking straight ahead, her face purpled with bruises.

Diablo was talking to him. "You may pick these up in Texas in four days' time."

Wolf paid half the money due for the service and arranged to drop the rest of the payment in Tampico in ten days. That would give him enough time to ensure he'd gotten his money's worth. If it went well, there were two more shipments to be made. When he left the Mexicans on the side of the road, he headed back to the cantina where he'd met with Diablo and started asking questions about the woman.

# 17

## Fort Hood, Texas
### *10 June*

WOLF WAS ALMOST DISAPPOINTED THAT GETTING ONTO FORT
Hood, the largest U.S. military base in the United States,
wasn't a bit harder. During the war with Iraq the American military had been apprehensive about terrorist activity and had made access to military posts difficult. But
when the threat failed to materialize, security grew lax.
His own actions in Germany had caused another bit of
stiffening up, but he had guessed—correctly, as it turned
out—that the largest military bases, with thousands of civilian workers streaming in every morning, would have a less
rigorous security system than a smaller installation. It simply wasn't feasible to check all the cars coming on to Fort
Hood.

The logistics were straightforward. Wolf had given shipping instructions to Diablo, who paid an American woman
in Laredo to carry the parcels to a shipping company and
send them to Austin. Wolf flew to Austin from Brownsville, using one of the three passports provided by the
Soviets. He rented a car on a credit card that matched
his passport, recovered the package, and drove north
through Texas.

When he arrived in Killeen, the little town whose existence depended on the post, Wolf called the Fort Hood Public Affairs Office and explained that he was a German historian doing some research on the beginnings of the American army's armored forces. The clerk was friendly and overly familiar, even for an American, and she promised Wolf a hearty Texas welcome, whatever that was. He set up an appointment for two o'clock in the afternoon, two days hence, and asked for directions to the post museum.

The following day he rose early and spent some time coloring his hair with dye from a theater makeup kit, adding a touch of gray to the sides. He dressed in dark blue slacks and a sport coat, then armed himself with some things he thought a historian might carry: notebooks, a few extra pens, and two books on the United States Army that he'd bought in the local bookstore. He drove his rental car directly to the information center, where a Military Police officer gave him a map of the sprawling post. He was prepared to give her the name of the public affairs officer he was supposed to meet the following day, but she didn't ask. She smiled at him brightly, and he returned the favor.

Wolf drove to the central part of the post in the stream of civilian traffic headed to work. Even without the map, he was able to identify the sprawling silver mass that was III Corps headquarters. He had first seen it on a television special in Germany about American units returning from duty in the Gulf War. It was decidedly modern, three wings radiating like a star from a center atrium, in stark contrast to the other drab government buildings at the edge of the yellow plains. Wolf chose it for his destination because he thought it would be easy to find, and he was right. He parked his rented car in one of the visitors' parking slots, retrieved a large leather case from the trunk, and blended into the crowd streaming into the main doors. The workers here, like office workers everywhere, made their way glumly to their tasks, and no one took notice of him. Once inside the building, he located the men's latrine on the first floor. He noted the time on his watch, then waited only thirty seconds before picking up his case and making his way out of the building.

Just inside the door there was a large easel supporting a cork bulletin board, which was turned so as to be visible to people leaving the building. At the top of the board was a banner of two-inch high letters that read SECURITY.

Wolf slowed, wanted to stop, but forced himself to keep moving when he saw NDP in the headlines of one of the newspaper clippings on the board. The message behind the display was a call for increased vigilance. Wolf found one headline near the top almost amusing: *Americans Brace for Next Threat, Attack.*

*Yes, indeed,* Wolf thought.

The dry run was finished. He went back to his motel room and watched television for an hour. He took two meals in a fast food restaurant right next door, passing the time in between reading the books on the army and the magazines in the room, most of which extolled the virtues of Texas. At ten PM Wolf drove back to Fort Hood and the parking lot outside the headquarters building. As he expected, the cleaning crews were inside, and he could see them through the big windows, sweeping, vacuuming, emptying trash. Twenty minutes later he was back in his motel, pleasantly tired and satisfied that the building was cleaned at night. Although he probably could have slept, he sat up until eleven-thirty, mentally rehearsing the sequence of events for the next day. When he turned the lights out, he thought of the rough-dressed girl who'd been with Diablo.

The next morning he was up at five, pacing the room. He was nervous, but knew that some concern was healthy, even safe. The original plan had called for him to have a partner in Texas with him, but the disappearance of the first three men from Germany had left him only two options: do it alone or delay even more than the week he'd allowed himself. He couldn't imagine tampering any further with his carefully worked out timetable, so he was in Killeen by himself. From the window of the cheap motel, he watched a red sun roll up from the horizon, and he caught himself wishing for the early spring light and cool mornings of Germany.

At six he colored his hair, but he was still far ahead of schedule. By seven he was sleepy again, but he was afraid that lying on the pillow might smear the gray coloring or make it uneven. He stayed awake, drinking the awful instant coffee the motel provided, until lunchtime. By then he was so glad to get out of that room that he forgot how nervous he was. He packed his leather case in the trunk and drove to Fort Hood, where he sat for a few moments in the parking lot by III Corps headquarters, watching the lunchtime crowd come and go. Most of the soldiers who came out either carried bags of athletic gear or were already dressed for running. Civilian workers paraded into the building carrying sacks of fast food.

Wolf studied his hands on the wheel of the car, ten and two.

*Everything is going according to plan,* he told himself. *And this step will go well too.*

But his breathing was fast and shallow, and he could feel his shirt pasted to his spine. All around him, people near the end of their lunch hour were hurrying to the building. Wolf blew a long breath from a parched mouth, got out of the car and removed the case from the trunk. He hadn't walked five steps when someone called to him.

"Excuse me, sir."

Wolf turned to see a military policeman walking behind the cars parked an aisle away. He tried to swallow, but there was nothing there.

The police officer was on the small side, with a bit of a paunch visible even beneath the loose-draped camouflage uniform. A long billy club bounced against the side of his left leg, a nine-millimeter pistol decorated his right side.

Wolf called up a smile, tried to speak, but his lips seemed stuck together. *No, they could not have found me so quickly.*

He put the case down close to a parked car. It wasn't clear that the MP, whose view was blocked by cars, had seen it. "Yes?"

The MP was beside Wolf's car now, and Wolf reminded

himself that his own pistol was inside under the passenger seat and not visible. Unless it had slipped forward when he stopped. Unless the MP asked to look inside.

Wolf stepped forward; he suddenly had a tremendous urge to urinate. He would have to retrieve the case eventually; the evidence inside was too incriminating to leave behind.

The MP, now at the back of Wolf's car, put both hands on the trunk lid and pushed down. There was a small click.

"Yep," the soldier said. "I thought you left your trunk open. I could see it from back over there."

Wolf found his voice. "Thank you," he said. "That was very kind of you."

The MP passed, happy with his good deed. Wolf picked up his case and walked into the building without noticing anyone else. In the men's latrine he put the case down and hurried to the urinal for relief. That done, he splashed cool water on his face. Within a minute he'd calmed down enough to notice that he was the only one in the room.

There were two stainless-steel frames built into the wall, paper towel dispensers with attached trashcans. Wolf bent over to look under the stalls, then hefted the large case onto one of the sinks. He dialed the combination quickly, folded back the two flaps, and pulled out one of the motel's towels. There were two packages under the towel. He put the smaller package into the bottom of the trashcan on the right, the larger package in the can on the left. He pulled a few paper towels from the dispenser, taking pains to cover completely the large brown paper parcel.

On the way out, he bumped into a soldier coming in.

" 'Scuse me," the soldier said.

"No problem," Wolf said, smiling.

Two hours later, Heinrich Wolf landed at the sprawling Dallas-Fort Worth Airport aboard an American Eagle flight from Killeen. He bought a newspaper from a vending machine and, after checking the masthead on page two for the number, placed a call from a phone booth to the newsroom of *The Dallas Morning News*. He would rather have made the call a week in advance, to give them time to simmer in their worry, but the fact that he was working alone necessitated some changes. Then it occurred to him that this way might be even more diabolical.

At three twenty-five, a nervous city reporter took the message that the Neu Deutschland Party was tired of waiting for the U.S. government to concede. The next blow in the escalating war against the American military establishment would be struck soon. After that, the pace of the war would quicken even further.

At three forty-five there was an explosion in the men's latrine on the first floor of headquarters of the U.S. Army's III Corps at Fort Hood. There were no immediate injuries, and the blast did little damage to the building. The building's occupants evacuated in an orderly fashion, congratulating themselves all the while for the calm they maintained in the face of this attack. It took only ten minutes for the first news cameras to arrive on the scene to conduct interviews among the workers, who were told to go on home for the rest of the day. The camera crew then moved just inside the foyer of the impressive building—up to the yellow tape put in place by the Military Police—to get some shots of the visible damage. The media attention was a catalyst for the bustle, and more than a few soldiers took the opportunity to pass in front of the camera lens. Outside, another news crew had to be content with shots of the building's exterior, as the Military Police didn't want the lobby inside to become too crowded. Nevertheless, there were two dozen people in the vicinity of the latrine when the second, much larger bomb went off.

Heinrich Wolf, waiting in the airport lounge for his flight to Mexico City, saw a few minutes of live coverage from Fort Hood on the cable news. Apparently there had been a camera crew located just outside the building when the second blast occurred. There was some incredible footage of the front of the building, huge sheets of glass buckling as if struck with a giant hammer, and some grisly shots of people trying to get out of the wreckage. Wolf was riveted by the image of a body—he couldn't tell if it was male or female—visible only from the waist down. The uniformed legs were splayed, the feet turned at awkward angles, pointing to the ground. Then they were calling his flight, final boarding call, and Wolf turned away from the screen and the carnage and the newly drawn battle lines, to hurry to his flight.

# 18

## Columbus, Georgia
### 11 June

ONE OF THE INTERESTING PHENOMENA THAT WENT WITH being married to someone in the army, Adrienne had once told Mark, was that civilians seemed to believe that military spouses had some sort of direct news link to the Pentagon. All during the war with Iraq, Adrienne's co-workers constantly asked what she thought was going to happen in the desert: how long it would last, how many troops it would take, what the casualties would be like—as if she knew more than the average educated person who watched television news and read the papers. Mark had told her, cynically she thought, that the public liked to believe there was a plan somewhere, in somebody's head. Then he told her not to let the truth out.

The first person she ran into when she got off the elevator at work asked her all those kinds of telltale questions.

Annie Stearns worked in the tax-planning department with Adrienne. She was lately a blonde and was mildly famous in the company for her ability to clear a room with nothing more than the sound of her voice, which was high, breathy, and marked with a nerve-shattering twang. "Looks like we got another situation on our hands," Annie said. Her "hands" seemed to have a couple of extra letters in it. *Hayynds*.

"What's that?" Adrienne asked. The morning paper was tucked under her arm. She'd taken longer than usual with her shower and hadn't got to read it at home.

"Those terrorists have obviously moved to Mexico."

*Here we go,* Adrienne thought. She pulled the newspaper from under her arm, then decided she didn't want to stand and talk to Annie while she read it. Instead, she continued to move toward her office.

"I'll bet we wind up sending more soldiers down there," Annie said to Adrienne's back. "I don't see why the army can't get this mess straightened out. If they can win a whole war in a hundred hours, why can't they stop a few sneaky smugglers and some crazy terrorists?"

Adrienne wasn't listening. She dropped her handbag just inside the door of her small office, sat down in one of the chairs facing her desk, and opened the paper.

The thick headline ran the entire width of the page. *Terrorist Bombing at Fort Hood, Texas*. She looked up and out the window onto the tops of the trees that stretched toward the river in the distance, and she suddenly wondered if Mark had been called away for this. In the first few paragraphs of the story, she learned that the Neu Deutschland Party, the same people responsible for the recent spate of bombings, had claimed responsibility in a phone call made just before the explosion.

"Adrienne, didn't you say Mark had gone back to Mexico?" Annie had followed her into her office, though not far enough that Adrienne could see her without turning around.

"Yes." Annie already knew too much, Adrienne decided.

"So, are we close to catching these guys?" Annie asked, walking behind Adrienne's desk.

"I don't know, Annie." The worst thing she could do, Adrienne had learned over a few years, was to fuel the idea that she knew more about what was going on than anyone else. For her part, she didn't think that Mark was tracking down these Germans. That seemed like a job for some police organization, not for a field soldier. He had mentioned working with some Delta Force people, but that had been out in the field, and so probably meant they were still chasing drug smugglers. *No, he's relatively safe*, she told herself. *He's probably sitting somewhere in Mexico wishing he were tracking down these people, because that's where the action is.*

Adrienne lowered her head and pretended to read, but Annie was not discouraged.

"I think they should just seal up that border down there, then we wouldn't have these problems with all these illegal aliens and such," Annie sniffed.

Adrienne wanted to ask her how she proposed to seal thousands of miles of border but didn't want to extend the conversation.

"All they'd have to do is move a bunch of these army guys down there, let 'em ride around in their tanks and shoot up anybody trying to come across. I guaran-damntee you it wouldn't take long for the message to get out that people shouldn't try to sneak across the border."

When Adrienne didn't answer, Annie pulled at the bottom of her blouse. "Well, I guess I have some work to do." She stepped off for the door. "I hope you hear from Mark real soon, now," she said.

At lunchtime Adrienne walked the two blocks home to check her answering machine. There was no reason to expect that Mark had called—long distance phone service from Mexico was fairly unreliable—and she tried not to get her hopes up. Still, there was an uncomfortable twinge of disappointment when she saw the little zero in the window on the machine.

She wished she knew when to worry. There were probably only minutes out of the months he was away when he was actually in mortal danger, but Adrienne wanted to share the fear with her husband, her best friend. But that was impossible, and she was constantly aware of how ignorant of the whole mess she was at all times.

She fixed herself a microwave lunch and sat down in front of the television on the little sun porch at the rear of the house. The news, as she expected, was dominated by the story of the bombing in Texas. Although authorities

221

were releasing few details, it was clear to the media that the explosions had been staggered to catch emergency workers, bomb-squad people, and military police officers at the scene. In the footage taken by the crew that happened to be outside the building, a soldier ran from the building, streaming blood from bright slashes on his arms and face. Another clip, taken later on, panned across three bodies covered in white cloth, waiting on the glass-strewn sidewalk.

Adrienne's lunch grew cold in front of her. She suddenly saw how foolish she'd been, just a few hours ago, to believe that Mark could not be involved with this. Once she allowed herself to think about it, she had no trouble imagining another scenario: he had been called away from leave because they had expected something like this was going to be staged from Mexico. She felt cold, and she rubbed her hands along her arms.

It was starting again. When Mark was away at war, she had found it absolute torture to be at home, unable to do anything to affect what was going on. She had never felt so powerless as she had during those days, pretending to go on with her life as if nothing were wrong. At least then the attention of the nation had been focused on the war and on the soldiers. Now she was alone. Most of the nation had no idea that she and a few hundred other families were going through the same hell, playing out the game as if everything were normal, trying not to wonder, every hour, if something terrible was happening. And all this was the norm in army life: when Mark came home, someone else would take his place, and so it would go on. There were always families separated, in peace and war, but America noticed it only during war. This was the truism that so angered Adrienne. Her husband was putting his life on the line as surely as he had when he led his company into the combat that had riveted the nation, yet now no one knew, no one cared. All she could do, she realized as she looked at the clock on the stove, was go back to work. Adrienne Isen sat on the little sun porch of her rented house, alone with her worries, unsure of what dangers her husband was facing, wondering what had happened to the uncomplicated life she had wanted when she married Mark Isen, soldier.

She worked the rest of the day in a mild fog. No one bothered her. She went running when she got home after work, then fixed herself a large glass of ice water and settled on the floor of the sun room to watch the local edition of the evening news. The first report was from nearby Fort Benning, which was being turned into a fortress. On the screen, Military Police blocked the interstate that ran onto the post, while behind them, large flatbed trucks were delivering the concrete barriers used to divide highways under construction. These, apparently, were to be used to make some sort of baffle for traffic, a maze that drivers would be able to negotiate only by slowing down. Adrienne had seen this during the war with Iraq, when the MPs, pulling double shifts, were obliged to watch all the cars coming on post. Roads on the southeast side of the post, which opened up to the roads from central Georgia, were thick with patrol vehicles. A carload of Canadian tourists on their way to the Gulf took a wrong turn and wound up outside a basic training barracks. The shaken civilians told an interviewer from the news that they had been held at gunpoint by some equally jumpy MPs.

The network news was worse. A man had been arrested at the San Francisco Airport for striking a ticket agent who wouldn't refund the customer's ticket money. The attacker claimed that it was no longer safe to fly, and the airlines should acknowledge that fact. In New York the police bomb squad received two hundred and thirty-one calls during the first twenty-four hours after the bombing in Texas. Although all of the suspect package, suitcase, and bag calls turned out to be harmless, the police were obliged to respond to every call. Traffic in Manhattan came to a two-and-a-half-hour standstill because emergency vehicles and office workers from evacuated buildings were clogging the streets. Several groups were already planning marches on Washington to force the government to do something. And in one man-on-the-street interview that Adrienne found troubling, a straight-faced Chicago businessman told the reporter he didn't see why we didn't just "go in there with the army and kick some butt." Adrienne wondered where "there" was and whose butt was to be kicked.

Halfway through the program, Adrienne turned off the set and looked outside as she drank her water. The woman who lived in the other half of the duplex, a forty-five-year-old substitute schoolteacher named Julie, was unloading a suitcase from her car in the yard they shared. Adrienne went to the screen door.

"Julie, I thought you were going to visit your mother up in Charlotte," Adrienne called.

"I don't expect I will for a while," Julie said dreamily. Adrienne thought Julie was an airhead. She had once driven all the way to Wynnton Elementary School wearing her bedroom slippers with her dress.

Julie put the suitcase down at the bottom step to fish in her handbag for the keys. "Some people at the airport talked me out of going," she said. "I think just about everybody who was supposed to be on this flight canceled, except for a few soldiers who were going home on leave."

"Why?" Adrienne asked.

Julie looked up at her, her large glasses reflecting so much of the sky that her eyes were invisible. "You haven't heard about all these bombings?" Julie asked.

"Well, of course I have," Adrienne said. "Is that why people are canceling?"

"I guess so," Julie said. "I sure don't want a bunch of Mexicans blowing up my plane." She was still looking for her keys, then noticed that they were dangling from her little finger. "Here they are."

"The terrorists are *German,*" Adrienne said.

Julie was on her own step now, twenty feet away. "That plane was from Mexico, wasn't it? The one that crashed on the way to Dallas?"

"Yes," Adrienne explained. "But the group claiming responsibility was German. The same people who killed that woman and her babies over in Germany a few weeks ago. They also shot some servicemen over there."

Julie put her suitcase down on the step, holding it pressed up to the door with one knee. She didn't try to unlock the door. "Lord a mercy," she said. "It's just plain craziness."

They stood that way for an awkward moment, unsure of what to do next.

"Adrienne," Julie said, "would you like to come over for a nice glass of lemonade? I was about to make up a pitcher, and I'll be done by the time you're showered."

Adrienne wondered if Julie was hinting that she needed to bathe. Julie was one of those southern women who thought exercise was something for high school football players, and she might have thought it odd that Adrienne liked activities that involved sweating. Then Adrienne felt ashamed; Julie was completely harmless and didn't have a mean bone in her body. Before she knew what she was doing, Adrienne accepted the invitation.

"Good," Julie said, smiling. "I'll see you in a few minutes."

Adrienne smiled back, but groaned once she was inside her own house. It wasn't that she had anything else to do; she probably would have spent the evening curled up with a book. It was just that she had nothing in common with Julie. She went into the bathroom and peeled off her running shorts and T-shirt, wondering what she and Julie might talk about while they had lemonade.

"I'd rather have a margarita," Adrienne said out loud as she twisted the knobs in the shower. "I wonder how quickly one can politely drink a glass of lemonade?"

Fifteen minutes later Adrienne was standing in Julie's kitchen, which was a negative of her own floor plan, everything reversed. Julie was bending over, reaching into a cabinet under the sink for a glass pitcher. Adrienne scanned the room. Clean, clean.

"So you said there were lots of people canceling flights today?" Adrienne asked.

"The ticket agent told me they had two planes take off today with only two or three people on board," Julie said, straightening. She held a flowered pitcher in one hand, and she used the other to push her glasses back up her nose. "And she told me that it was like that in Atlanta too. Lots of folks just up and decided they didn't need to travel as badly as they thought they did."

"I guess I can understand their concerns," Adrienne said. "But it isn't as if we can just stop everything, all business, all travel, everything. That would be caving in to these terrorists in the worst way."

Adrienne wasn't sure if Julie was listening. The schoolteacher poured lemonade from a squeezer into the pitcher, smiling her inscrutable all-purpose smile. "I suppose," she said. When she'd filled the pitcher with ice, she put it and two glasses on a tray. "Why don't we go sit out front?"

"Fine," Adrienne said.

"You take this and I'll get two chairs."

Adrienne carried the tray through the dining room toward the front of the house, while Julie got two straight-backed dining-room chairs, carrying them by their ladder-backs. Adrienne had never been in Julie's house before, and she slowed down a bit to inspect the photographs on the mantelpiece. A few of them showed the same little girl caught in various poses from toddler to her teens. There were several shots of the girl with a younger-looking Julie.

"That's my daughter," Julie said. "Samantha."

"I didn't know you had a daughter," Adrienne said. She immediately regretted the remark: suppose something bad had happened?

"She lives in California," Julie said, bypassing Adrienne with her load of chairs. No further explanation seemed to be forthcoming.

"She's very pretty," Adrienne said to Julie's back. She suddenly wanted to be out of the room, and she moved toward the front door again. She was stopped short by a photograph, at the very end of the mantel, of a man in uniform. He was a lieutenant, though Adrienne couldn't tell, in the black-and-white photo, if the bar was gold or silver, the difference between a second and a first lieutenant. He wore the shoulder patch of the Special Forces and a Combat Infantryman's Badge above a single row of ribbons. He wasn't smiling, and his hair was cut very short, but he was handsome nonetheless.

Adrienne joined Julie out on the wide porch. The two of

them sat down with the tray on the flagstones beneath them. Adrienne felt very awkward sitting in the straight, hard chairs way up in the middle of the otherwise empty porch.

"That last picture in there is of my husband," Julie said suddenly.

It was obvious, Adrienne figured, that since there was a daughter, there had been a man. But she never would have guessed that her mousy neighbor had been married to a soldier, much less a Green Beret. Adrienne sipped from her glass; it seemed as if Julie wanted to say more. But the two of them sat there for a few moments, quietly watching the sun trace patterns on the sidewalk through the branches of the trees.

"His name was Michael," Julie said, her voice lower. "He was killed in Vietnam."

"I'm sorry," Adrienne offered. She didn't know what else to say.

Julie turned to her and smiled, and some part of her childlike self came back from somewhere.

"Oh, it was a long time ago." She sipped from the glass, then wiped at her pants leg where the condensation had moistened the fabric.

"Sometimes I can't remember what his voice sounded like," Julie said. She looked over at Adrienne. "Isn't that terrible?"

"It's been a long time," Adrienne said, more uncomfortable than ever. She wanted to leave, but she wanted to stay, to see what would happen next.

"Twenty-five years. Can you believe that? More than half my life." She hesitated, looked at Adrienne as if noticing her for the first time. "I'm sorry. I didn't mean to be so morbid, especially with your husband down there in Mexico."

"It's okay," Adrienne said, not at all convinced that it was okay. "I think he's pretty safe."

Julie went on. "I wanted to talk to someone because I see it all happening again."

"What's happening?" Adrienne asked, a bit afraid of the answer.

"All these people talking about how easy it would be for us to go down there to South America and straighten things out." Julie's voice was clear now, insistent. "As if the very fact that we're Americans will make everything work out."

She looked out to the street as a car drove by.

"In 1964, Michael and I were in college, and he told me he wanted to go to Vietnam. Course, he had to get a map and show me where Vietnam was—nobody knew back then—and explain what was going on there." She looked at Adrienne and gave her a tiny smile. "We were planning to marry after I graduated, and of course I was worried about him going off like that." She looked back down at her hands, both of them wrapped around the lemonade glass.

"He told me that nobody over there could stand up to the U.S. Army, that he was hoping that they wouldn't just run away when they heard there were Americans coming, so that he wouldn't miss his chance to fight. So we got married during my junior year. I was twenty."

Adrienne felt a sudden rush of sympathy. Julie wasn't an airhead; she'd had her spirit crushed by something too big for her to understand, and she had never recovered.

"Anyways, I see the same thing happening nowadays, and I wanted to let you know that somebody does understand what you're going through." She reached out and took Adrienne's hand.

Adrienne felt something well up inside her, and she was surprised to find it was anger.

"This is not Vietnam," Adrienne said. She was afraid she might hurt Julie's feelings, but she couldn't remain silent. "I don't see us going to war like that again."

Julie held her hand. Up close, Adrienne noticed, she didn't look as helpless.

"Oh, I'm not talking about a war," Julie said. "It really doesn't matter much anyways."

"What doesn't matter?" Adrienne asked.

Julie was looking at her closely now. "Do you think it made me feel any different that my husband was killed in a war? What does circumstance have to do with it? My husband died. All the rest of what they want to tell you is just so much . . . so much . . ."

*Bullshit,* Adrienne thought.

"Oh, I'm sorry for bothering you," Julie said meekly, beginning to cry. "I'm sorry I told you all this. You must think I'm just awful, just an awful person to upset you like this. I had no right to intrude on your privacy." She was her old self now, fluttering, humble, uncertain. "But sometimes I lie awake at night worrying about your husband, and then I have these confusing dreams, and I wake up in a panic and think it's Michael."

She sniffled a bit, wiping at her face on her sleeve without letting go of Adrienne's hand. They sat there for a while, then it was suddenly dark, and they went, side by side, into their empty houses.

That night, Adrienne Isen dreamed that she was Julie, and she dreamed that waking up to an empty bed was the norm, that there would be no husband beside her, no husband ever again.

When she woke, she was already crying. She got out of bed and walked into the living room, where the light from a street lamp outside plaited shadows on the floor. In the kitchen she turned on the kettle, and the little blue light warmed her a bit. She found the tea bags, and a mug in the drainer without turning on the light. *This is my home,* she told herself, trying to let the concrete world around her force away doubts about what she couldn't see.

While her tea steeped, she thought about Mark, wondered what he was doing at this same moment. She knew that he kept no schedule to speak of, often he would be up for days at a time. Once, at Schofield Barracks, he had gone for a week doing something called reverse cycle training, where he and his soldiers trained in darkness and slept during the day.

She dunked her tea bag up and down, up and down in the cup. When the tea was ready, she went into the dining room, where she kept a small desk, and got a tablet and an envelope. She turned on the dining room light, rubbed her eyes against the sudden brightness, and sat down to write to Mark.

> *Dear Mark,*
> *I have a confession to make. When you were home a few weeks ago I harbored a secret hope within me that this bad experience with the army and all this stuff in Mexico would be the last straw. I hoped that you would give it up, finally, and come find the life I want us to have. I keep seeing things on the news about Mexico, so I guess it may still come to pass—the pressure is certainly on the President. But now I hope you don't get a raw deal. I want you to leave the service, but I don't want you to be forced out because I know how much the army means to you and I wouldn't want you to leave under those circumstances.*

Adrienne sat back in her seat, sipped at her tea, and read what she'd written so far. Yes, that was all true. She had wished those things, and now she felt bad that she'd wished them.

But if she realized that she had been trying to force something on Mark that he didn't want, she also knew that his being in the army was doing the same thing to her: he was forcing her to live a life she didn't want, this life of waking up alone and wondering when he was going to come back.

She leaned back over the paper.

> *Usually when you are away, I never trust my feelings, because they're so mixed up with missing you. But tonight I feel remarkably clearheaded. I have come to see that the things we want may be incompatible. You may choose to submit to the army's whims—going where they want to send you, doing all those things that make you happy—but I do not choose this life. When you make choices in the army, you are not making them just for yourself. Everything in this life-style is so drastic—the separations, the dangers, the fears— that you cannot make a choice that doesn't affect me.*

*Your decision to stay in uniform subjects me to all sorts of things.*

As she wrote it occurred to Adrienne that she was writing a "Dear John" letter, but she found she could not stop.

*Frankly, I don't see why your desires should carry more weight than mine.*

She looked down at what she had written, thinking about Mark as she read. But she did not think of Mark as he was now, she thought of him as he was when they met, as he was when they married. He had always wanted the same thing, and he had always been painfully truthful with her about his dedication to the army.

"Of course, people change, and I might change too," he'd told her a few nights before they became engaged. "But I wouldn't be honest with you if I didn't tell you that right now, as far as I can see, I want to make the army a career. And it's a tough career for a family."

She had held him then, thinking it was wonderful to have a man who knew what he wanted, and she wanted him then. And now the pain came because after all she was the one who had deluded herself. Mark had grown up around the army; he knew all along that it would be like this. She was the one who chose to believe she could have it both ways, and it took her this many years to find out otherwise. She felt she'd let him down because she hadn't been as honest about what she wanted and what she could live with.

And now, to try to make everything even with a letter seemed cruel. But she continued to write, trying to find in her pen what it was she thought, trying to find in her heart and on paper the right words to say what she felt. She read the last line again.

*Frankly, I don't see why your desires should carry more weight than mine.*

*That's it, isn't it?* she thought. *That's the whole problem.*
That was the line she had to live with and the line he was
going to have to live with. If they were to be married, they
were to be equals.

*I can't ask you to give up the army any more than
I can ask you to change your personality. I understand
that soldiering is not what you do, it's what you are.*
*I am asking you to cut me some slack as far as the
kind of assignments you take. There are lots of jobs
that don't always take you away and send you in
harm's way.*

She liked that last line. It was poetic, and true. There
were plenty of jobs in the army that Mark could hold for
a few years—just time for the two of them to take a
breather. *We'll look for one of those jobs,* she told
herself.

Adrienne felt sleepy again, so she drained her tea and
folded the letter into the pocket of her bathrobe. Something
about putting it all down on paper so that she could consider it in the morning put her mind at ease. She was done
worrying and back asleep a few minutes after leaving the
table.

For the next few days, Adrienne carried the letter around
in her purse like a stone. She knew it was there, nagging
her to do something, but she couldn't bring herself to send
it to Mark. She delayed and procrastinated until she
thought maybe she ought to write it over again. She didn't
doubt that she was right, but she was wary of sending it to
him while he was away. He counted on her letters for support, and she didn't want to pull it all out from under him.

Then she thought of another approach. While she was
reading *The Army Times,* it occurred to her that she might
present Mark with a fait accompli.

In the back pages there was a small advertisement that
read in part, "Seeking Professors of History." Below that
was the logo of the United States Military Academy. This
particular ad was searching for someone with a doctorate

in history to join the permanent faculty. But Adrienne knew that the academic departments up there also took on instructors for the rotating faculty, officers who earned master's degrees on the army's time and then served a three- or four-year stint on the faculty.

One evening after work, not long after she wrote her letter, Adrienne went to the public library and found the college catalogue for West Point. It was filled with all sorts of drivel and propaganda aimed at the high school kids who were its primary audience, but there was enough of substance there to intrigue her. If nothing else, the school was physically impressive: fortresslike granite buildings clinging to the mountains of the Hudson highlands. The pictures taken from a distance might have been of a castle town on the Rhine, Adrienne thought.

*There are worse places,* she thought. Then she wondered if she was being influenced by the pictures the same way the high school kids would be.

*Well, the look might not be the most important thing going,* she thought, *but it isn't a crime to want to live someplace pretty.*

Yes, that seemed in keeping with her new attitude. *Compromise means I get some of the things I want too.*

A phone call to nearby Fort Benning got her the number of Mark's assignment officer in Washington. She tried to get through a dozen times with no luck. When she called back to Benning to make sure she had the right number, the officer she spoke with set her straight.

"Oh, that's not unusual. Those poor guys have to answer all kinds of questions all day long, got people calling them up from all over the world, asking for every kind of assignment available. Best thing to do, ma'am, is call early in the morning, six-thirty, seven."

"Thank you," Adrienne said. "I will."

"And make sure you get the name of the person you speak to."

It still took her several tries, but Adrienne got through to one of the captain's assignments officers the following morning. For someone who spent all day listening to officers' demands about their next assignments, she thought the guy was very pleasant. She told him that her husband was in the field in Mexico—true—and had asked her to make some inquiries—not exactly true. He explained to her that West Point chose its instructors from among those officers who had successfully completed a command, who had a strong record in the army, and who had the academic credentials to get into a good graduate school.

"Would my husband have to go to graduate school at night?"

"No, not at all. As a matter of fact, that's one of the good deals. We send these guys to school, pay their tuition. They continue to draw their salaries, and they devote all their time to being full-time students."

Adrienne considered that for a moment. This didn't sound like the army she'd come to know. "What's the catch?"

"Well, your husband would incur an additional service obligation. Three years for every one he spends in school. But if he's committed to a career in the army, that's not much of a problem."

"No, that won't be a problem," Adrienne said. *The problem will be getting Mark to slow down enough to take what he'll see as a desk job.*

Adrienne mulled it over for a while, finally deciding that it would be better to pursue this than to send Mark the letter she had in her purse. Doing all the preliminary work before she brought it up to him would accomplish two things: he wouldn't be able to drag his feet if the date for an interview were already set, and the fact that she'd gone through with it would underscore how serious she was.

In the next week she talked to the departments of history and English up at West Point. The people she spoke with were helpful and pleasant, and Adrienne allowed herself to think that was because they were all happy with their work. She filled out some paperwork on Mark's behalf ("He's almost incommunicado," she told one woman on the phone) and even went back to the library to look at the catalogue again. A week after she wrote the first letter to Mark—the one she never sent—she told those two departments that, yes, they would be up to have an interview whenever Mark got out of Mexico.

*The next step,* Adrienne thought, *is the hard sell.* She tried not to think of it in terms of an ultimatum—you take this assignment or we're in serious trouble—but she guessed it was significant that she didn't throw away the Dear John letter. Adrienne bided her time and worried about her husband, but she was content because the compromise she'd discovered would answer some of their difficulties.

## Public Tilts Toward
## Withdrawal

by K. Goodlynnd
*The Des Moines Register*

Des Moines, June 11—The President's policies concerning the status of United States forces in Europe suffered a setback today when the Gallup organization released the results of a nationwide poll showing that many Americans favor a pullback from Europe. Recent calls by the Neu Deutschland Party, a German terrorist organization, for the withdrawal of the American navy from the Mediterranean have prompted a unified response from administration officials. Throughout the recent rash of bombings and demands by the NDP that America get out of European waters, the President has maintained that the United States does not negotiate with terrorists. The White House has also pointed out that the full resources of the FBI and the CIA are at work in cooperation with Mexican and German authorities to apprehend the persons responsible for the terrorist attacks.

It seems, however, that attitudes in America are changing. On Capitol Hill today, a group of Democratic congressmen, recently returned from visiting their constituencies, announced that the people have had enough. Representative Pauline Connist (D-CA) told reporters that "the President has painted himself into a corner on this one. Pulling the navy out would save billions of dollars on a still-swollen defense budget, and would pass the responsibility for defending Europe over to the Europeans. It's a good decision we should have reached ourselves."

Congressman H. Weldon Hynes (D-OH), who had been a vocal supporter of the President until the bombing of an American airliner en route from Mexico to Texas, said that the United States shouldn't have to stick with an outdated policy (maintaining a naval presence in the Mediterranean) simply because "that's the way it has always been."

"We should bring these ships home," Hynes said. "It makes sense economically and militarily. But instead of saying, 'We need to do everything we can to bring these people to justice,' the President has drawn a line and said, 'We can't bring these ships home.' So now the most sensible course of action is blocked because the terrorists demand that course, and we can't do what the terrorists want. That makes no sense to me. We have given up the initiative."

Hynes continued: "The President is saying, on the one hand, that we must not allow terrorists to dictate policy. But that is exactly what is happening. Because of this inflexible rule, the NDP can force us to keep our ships in the Mediterranean simply by demanding that we get out. We should have decided years ago, on our own, to bring the fleet home. The fact that that is what the terrorists want is merely coincidental. At the same time, we should do everything in our considerable power to bring to justice the murderers responsible for this tragedy."

Republican leaders, many of whom would normally rush to defend their popular president, were somewhat hesitant today to square off against what appears to be a shift in public opinion. Senator Charles Shelley (R-MI) said that public opinion is "not always a reliable barometer, in the short term, of what is best for the country. Sometimes the President must make the hard, unpopular choices."

While the politicians decide where to stand on this issue, Americans are moving. Twelve hundred people turned out last night, in a light drizzle, for a candlelight vigil in downtown Des Moines. Organizers say that a rally planned for next weekend is expected to draw five thousand.

# 19

## near Tampico, Mexico
### 12 June

LIEUTENANT MANUEL SIMON JESUS CORTIZO KNEW THAT most people thought he was a prig, and that generally didn't bother him. He had learned his formal manners from his mother, who had insisted he know how to act in polite company because, she told him, "you are destined to be in the ruling class." The unlikelihood of this prediction coming true did not occur to him until he was thirteen or fourteen years old, when he saw that he would not have the education it took to rise to that class. By that time, his mother's manners were already a part of him.

His schoolmates described him as stiff, a word he found odd, since he figured that if he were literally "stiff," he would be uncomfortable. But for the most part, he was very comfortable with himself. Except when he was upset and did not know how to express his feelings. Captain Mark Isen's call from the United States at the beginning of the month had affected him that way.

Cortizo was not naive, and he was not surprised that an organization as big as the United States Army would be willing to ruin the career of one officer—a fine officer, but, for all that, only one man—in order to protect itself and one of its programs from the kind of public lashing that the

THE COMMON DEFENSE

American media so enjoyed orchestrating. But Cortizo's worldly attitude did nothing to make him feel better about what was happening to his friend.

Isen called him again when he got back to Tampico, this time with Major Spano and the special operations people. Cortizo was happy to hear from him, but disappointed that Isen would not be coming back to Operation Sentinel. Isen did not want to talk about his situation on the phone, so Cortizo agreed to meet him for dinner.

"At first it didn't make much sense to me either," Isen said. "According to the U.S. Army, I'm too dangerous to be riding around the countryside with you guys—as a matter of fact, I was told to stay completely away from any Operation Sentinel business—yet they let me in here with these other people, who are more trigger-happy than anybody I've seen lately."

Isen had picked up—from Spano, Cortizo guessed—the habit of referring to the Delta Force as anything but "The Delta Force." Instead, his speech was filled with lots of "these people," and "our friends," and "Spano's team."

"I guess it shows how much they're concentrating on this terrorism thing. Major Spano thought it'd be good to have me along. Next thing I know, here I am."

Cortizo nodded.

"Major Spano kind of rescued me. When I called him, I told him I was concerned about hanging around at home doing nothing. It seemed to me more likely that the press would find out my name and start hounding me there." As he talked Isen slid his beer bottle distractedly across the table top, watching the patterns the condensation made.

"I think the Operation Sentinel people were glad to get me off their books," he said.

"So you still have heard nothing about what is going to happen to you?" Cortizo asked.

"Nothing official."

Cortizo studied his fingertips for a moment. "Remember when you told me the motto from your infantry school? *Don't do nothing.*"

Isen smiled. "Well, it's kind of an unofficial motto, but it works."

"Doesn't that apply here?" Cortizo asked.

"I wish it did, but the army seems perfectly content to do nothing. I hope they're just waiting for things to blow over."

"No, I mean does it apply to you? Isn't there something you could be doing?" Cortizo asked.

"Not that I can think of," Isen said. He answered right away, but Cortizo could tell he was mulling it over.

"Did you have something in mind?" Isen asked.

"Nothing specific," Cortizo said. "I was just thinking that if you came up with something that could help with this terrorist thing, wouldn't that help you?"

"I suppose it would, but I doubt if I'll be working much on this. In spite of the pressure, I'm kind of decoration around here. Spano justified getting me here because I'm a so-called area expert." He smirked at the term. "Hell, I don't even speak Spanish."

Isen drank his beer, seemingly content with that answer. But Cortizo wasn't going to let it rest.

"How are they pursuing the investigation?"

"What do you mean?"

"Where are they looking for information?" Cortizo said.

"Well, the aviation people are trying to find out how the bomb got on the plane. If they've developed any leads from the Fort Hood bombing or the three guys they shot in Tampico, they're keeping quiet about it. The feds are investigating whatever leads the German police gave them, you know, about people coming into Mexico, or into the U.S. And that's another angle, they're watching the airports and ports for people traveling from Europe, material being brought in from Europe, stuff being brought into the U.S. from Mexico."

Cortizo nodded. "Suppose the material is already here? Let's say that these people stockpiled all the material they would need, knowing that scrutiny would increase once the attacks started."

"Okay," Isen said, warming to the mental game. "The

next step then would be getting it into the United States. Unless it's already there."

"If it's already in the United States, we have a different problem," Cortizo said. "Let's assume, for the moment, that the material is in Mexico. How would they move it north?"

"That's the whole problem . . ." Isen almost said "with this country," but caught himself. "That's the whole problem. There are lots of ways to move stuff and few ways to find out where it is."

"Perhaps, but let's look at it logically. Either they use existing means or they make up their own," Cortizo said. He was holding up his fingers, and he ticked them off as he spoke. "The air route is becoming less and less reliable, thanks to our efforts."

"It isn't shut off yet," Isen countered.

"No, but it is not the safest anymore," Cortizo answered.

"If they take it overland there are hundreds of small-time operators who could do it," Isen said.

"And it would be in the best interests of the terrorists to choose a small operation. Many people will turn their heads away from drug-smuggling—in part because it's so prevalent—but something like this would attract attention."

"Are you saying the smugglers would get scruples over this?" Isen asked.

"No, but if it got around that there was a lot of interest in this, there would be a lot more blackmail. That kind of stuff is easier to control if you only have to pay off a few people—or threaten a few."

Isen finished his beer, held up two fingers to the bar maid.

"Okay. Let's assume he goes with a small operation. Doesn't that make it harder to track?"

"Well," Cortizo said, "I've been thinking about this. The smallest operations, the ones that involve the fewest people on either side of the border, are those that smuggle people."

"People?"

"The guides, the ones who will take you over the desert into Texas for a few hundred dollars."

Isen thought about it for a moment. "That way they could avoid all the sophisticated aircraft and radar and such. Just walk." He looked away for a moment as the woman delivered the beers and took some of his money from the table. Then he leaned over toward Cortizo. "They would carry the material on their backs?"

Cortizo nodded. "A few years ago, this was not an uncommon way to smuggle drugs. But it is not cost-effective. A man can only carry a few pounds across the desert. And if they die, the material is often lost out there."

"Okay," Isen said. "Let's say, for argument's sake, that we have this all figured out. That we took all the right turns in our assumptions. Where does that leave us?"

"I'm not sure yet," Cortizo said. "Give me some time."

But Cortizo knew exactly what he was going to do. The next morning he left for Ciudad Victoria, a grueling drive of about a hundred and fifty miles from Tampico. He arrived in the late afternoon and was met by one of his cousins. Cortizo did not spend a great deal of time with members of his family from his father's side. A good number of them, like this cousin, earned their livelihoods by questionable means. He was on good terms with all of his relatives, because like many Mexicans, he believed strongly in the family. But it was unusual for him to call on one of these people, and so this cousin, an older man named Zacata, expected the visit to be a business affair.

"Good day, cousin," a sweating Cortizo said as he found Zacata in the café where the man spent most of his day.

"And to you," Zacata said. "Why don't you have something to wash away the road dust?"

Cortizo didn't notice any signal, but in a moment a waiter appeared with a cold beer for Cortizo and a glass of milk for Zacata's ulcers.

"How are you doing?" Cortizo said, indicating the milk.

"Oh, I have good days and bad," Zacata said. "How are you? Are you staying safe?"

THE COMMON DEFENSE

Cortizo laughed. "I am all right." He looked around at the other people in the room and understood why his cousin had made no direct reference to the fact that Cortizo chased down and shot smugglers. The people here looked like the kind Cortizo chased.

"What can I do for you?" Zacata asked.

"I have a friend who is in trouble," Cortizo said. "He had some goods he was going to ship north, but some people stole these things from him. He believes they are shipping the material north on the backs of peasants who are paying for guides to help them cross."

When Cortizo looked up, Zacata was smiling at him.

"You don't expect me to believe that my little cousin has gone bad, do you?" He reached over and patted Cortizo gently on the cheek. "You? Involved with people who smuggle drugs across the border?" He laughed again. "You wouldn't be looking for information to help you . . . in your work, would you?"

It had occurred to Cortizo that this might happen. His reputation as a straight arrow was legendary in his family. Aunts and women cousins held him up to the small children, the ones not yet corrupted, as an example to be emulated.

"I am sorry, cousin. You are right, of course, I am not friends with those type of people. But I am certainly not trying to use you; I need your help." Cortizo paused. Zacata stared at him, still smiling.

"Unfortunately I work for such a man."

"Your boss in the army is a smuggler?" Zacata laughed out loud. "And he wound up with you for a subordinate? He is an unlucky man indeed."

"He doesn't know that I know. A gang of Europeans, Germans, I think, stole some of his goods. He put me on the case—that is what we do, chase smugglers—and has been hounding me to come up with a solution. It was only by accident that I found out that we are tracking material that belongs to him."

Cortizo took a nervous pull at his beer, kept his eyes on the table. "He says I am incompetent, and that if I don't

243

find out where this stuff is, he will relieve me and see that I get a bad report in my file."

"You want me to kill him?" Zacata asked straight-faced.

Cortizo felt his eyes widen. "No, no, not that at all." He almost chuckled at the turn the conversation had taken. A moment ago he had been afraid that his trip was wasted, that Zacata would refuse to help him. Now this.

"All I need to know is who is carrying this material for Europeans."

"Coke?"

"Yes. But they may have explosives and some other weapons too."

"What makes you think it will come through here?" Zacata asked.

*Good question,* Cortizo thought. *What is the answer?* He couldn't think of another convenient lie, so he told the truth.

"I am hoping it comes through here, because you are the only one I know who can help me."

"Your boss is very dirty if he is smuggling weapons," Zacata said.

"He is a jackass," Cortizo said solemnly.

Zacata picked up his glass and carefully drank the milk all at once.

"I will help you, cousin," he said. "If this material goes north anywhere on this side of the country, I will find out. Do you want me to seize it for you?"

"No," Cortizo said. "It will look better if I capture it."

"Fine. But you ought to let me help you more."

The lieutenant stood up. "How?"

"You ought to let me kill your boss," Zacata said.

Cortizo laughed, thinking that it was a joke. Zacata, who did not share Cortizo's opinion that army majors were safe from assassination by criminals, just smiled.

Zacata called him two days later.

"I have found what you need, cousin," he said.

"That was very quick," Cortizo said, genuinely impressed.

"Well, that was the good news. The bad news is that

this shipment is already out in the bush, or it will be in the next twenty-four hours."

"What do you know about locations? Anything that will help me?"

"I do have one piece of information that should be useful, that is, if you use it correctly."

"I am desperate," Cortizo said, trying to put emotion into his voice.

"These people work out of Tampico, and I have the name of a man who should know what is going on," Zacata said. "I have a man standing by who can talk to him."

"No, no," Cortizo said. "I must do as much as possible myself."

"This one may not cooperate," Zacata chuckled. "You are probably not good at hiding the fact that you're with the law."

"Nevertheless . . ." Cortizo said.

"As you wish," Zacata said. "It turns out that this one is also unhappy with his boss—just like you—and may be bought off."

"I am listening," Cortizo said.

The information Zacata gave him had demanded immediate attention, and Cortizo wasn't that ready. He had intended to approach Isen and explain what he was about, but because he wasn't sure Zacata would come through for him, he had delayed. Now, when he did call, Isen was not in Tampico; he had gone to Brownsville with Spano for a day or two.

Cortizo was not afraid to contact the smugglers himself. But he figured that, if something should happen to him, it would look as if he were doing something illegal. It would not do to ask any of his subordinates; they would have helped out of affection for Isen, but Cortizo didn't want them to know he was bending the rules. Instead, he called Worden, who had been transferred to the Operation Sentinel headquarters in Tampico. The big American NCO had been extremely frustrated after the ambush because they were able to strike back only at the little guys they caught on the ground. He had complained bitterly to his superiors that that program needed to be more aggressive. His superiors had responded to his rage by sticking him behind a desk, where his anger smoldered. Once Worden heard that Cortizo was out to help Isen get out of a jam, the American NCO was in.

The plan was for Cortizo, posing as the owner of the goods just shipped north, to approach the man Zacata had identified and offer him a bribe for more information. Worden's function was to be in the area in case things went wrong and Cortizo needed help getting out.

It was easier than Cortizo expected to find the man: he spent most evenings in a bar down by the smelly waterfront, where his job for the organization was to handle shipments as they came across the piers. Cortizo spent an hour at the bar before he asked for the man by name.

If the bartender thought there was anything suspicious going on, his face didn't show it. He pointed to a corner table where an immensely fat man sat wedged between the table and the wall.

Surprised, Cortizo asked the bartender again. "That is Fuentes?"

"The very one."

Cortizo bought two bottles of beer and walked over to the table, not exactly sure how to proceed. He had a sense of Zacata's bluntness, an attitude of nonchalance about his business.

"I would like to talk to you about some business, my friend," Cortizo said. He began to sit down, but Fuentes interrupted him.

"I don't know you."

Stopped halfway, Cortizo had time to think that he wished Worden could do this. Worden was a born actor, but he was also obviously an American, and that always aroused suspicions.

"That is the point here, isn't it?" Cortizo said. He pushed one of the beers to Fuentes. The big man picked up the bottle and tilted it back over his mouth, draining half of it without a pause.

"What is it you need?"

Cortizo put both arms on the table. He tried to slouch

forward, thinking that the pose would make him look surly, but it didn't work. He was still sitting straight. "I had some goods taken from me, and I think the thieves shipped them north overland. I am trying to find out who is dealing with these Europeans."

Fuentes tossed back the other half of the beer, belched appreciatively, wiped his mouth. "I don't know what you're talking about."

"I am willing to pay for the information," Cortizo said.

"Go fuck yourself, *Federale*."

*Now what?* Cortizo thought. He had, of course, expected the man to resist telling him everything right away, but he didn't expect to be pegged immediately. *Maybe he's bluffing.*

"Go fuck yourself, big man," Cortizo said. "I am being friendly about this now, and I am even willing to negotiate a price. But rest assured that I will leave here with the information I need."

Fuentes sized him up for a few seconds longer. Cortizo thought his speech had been pretty good.

"I may know something," Fuentes said. "But we cannot talk here." He pushed back from the table, or rather, he pushed the table away from his bulk.

Cortizo had a moment of doubt as he stood. *I'll wager that people conduct business in this place all the time.* But he dismissed it as his own nervousness, and he stood up and headed for the door.

"This way," Fuentes said, pointing to the back.

Cortizo followed him into a small hallway that appeared to lead outside. Fuentes stopped, presumably to open the door. When Cortizo came up behind him, Fuentes lifted one big arm and smashed the elbow backward into Cortizo's nose.

The lieutenant let out a gasp as he reeled backward, arms pinwheeling. In a flash, he realized that there was a closed door behind him, and that the huge Fuentes could kill him in this tiny space in a matter of seconds.

When his back hit the wall, Cortizo bent over at the waist and charged forward, ramming his forehead into Fuentes's enormous stomach. Cortizo stumbled backward again, thinking that he'd had no effect on the giant. But when he looked up, he realized he had at least stopped Fuentes's forward motion. Without hesitating, he charged forward again.

Cortizo felt something pop in his neck as he hit his target. But the big man lost his footing and crashed through the flimsy door and out into the dark lot behind the bar. Cortizo had one hand on his neck, the other on his bloody nose as he hollered for Worden and kicked at the figure in front of him. Still, Fuentes was able to get up to his knees, and he caught one of Cortizo's legs. He twisted the foot viciously, throwing Cortizo down. Now the monster was above him, and he appeared to be grinning as he made ready to fall on the little lieutenant.

Fuentes's head, moving toward him one instant, suddenly snapped sideways as Worden kicked him in the jaw. Cortizo scrambled away on all fours but was still able to watch Worden deliver several more kicks to Fuentes's midsection and back. Cortizo wiped his eyes and tasted blood in his mouth. He sat down and held his neck. In a few seconds, Worden was standing over Fuentes, his eyes wide with excitement. Fuentes's huge bulk heaved with every breath, like a stabbed fish.

"So, did he tell you anything?" Worden asked. He didn't take his eyes off Fuentes.

"Not yet," Cortizo mumbled.

The big man was down and in pain, but he was not unconscious. It was obvious that they had to do something quickly; since they were not police officers they could hardly say they were arresting Fuentes. Cortizo was still on the ground, holding his face and neck, when the first curious patron came out the back door. Worden looked up, surprised, when the light above the door suddenly came on, illuminating Fuentes.

"GET THE FUCK OUT OF HERE," Worden snapped at the gawker. When the man didn't move fast enough, Worden stepped forward, ready to dish out another beating. The man retreated inside, dousing the light as he went.

Cortizo watched Worden, wondering if the American was feigning his rabid stance.

"He didn't tell you anything?" Worden asked again. His voice was high, edgy, and Cortizo decided that Worden was not completely in control.

"No."

"You think he knows something?" Worden pressed, looking down as if he might start kicking the man again.

"Yes," Cortizo said. His nose bled more when he talked, so he leaned his head back. "Otherwise, I don't think he would have tried to beat me."

On the ground, the big man stirred and moaned, slipping his hand down to his groin, where Worden had delivered a debilitating kick.

"If we're going to get anything out of him, we're going to have to take him somewhere, fast," Worden said.

Cortizo had not anticipated this. He had no place to take the man, and no desire to try to move him. Besides that, it would be kidnapping. And while Fuentes hardly seemed the type to complain to the police, Cortizo did not want to violate the law. He lowered his head so that he could see, out of one eye only, Worden standing in front of him.

"We're either in it all the way or not at all," Worden said.

Cortizo was unsure. Fuentes was scum and had just tried to beat him, if not kill him. On the other hand, Cortizo had no right to do what Worden suggested, and of course Worden had no business being involved at all. In a flash Cortizo thought about all the men he'd worked for who'd disregarded the rule of law, all the men for whom expediency was the most important consideration in pursuing results.

"We cannot kidnap him," Cortizo said.

"WHAT?" Worden was incredulous and angry, and his voice rose and fell in amazement at Cortizo's decision. "He just tried to *beat the shit* out of you in there. He's a fucking *scumbag smuggler,* the same guys who shot up your patrol and those two helicopters. Don't you *remember* that?"

"We don't know for certain that he was in on that," Cortizo said. He tried to sound authoritative, but the broken nose made his voice nasal, and because his head was tilted all the way back he had no volume. "We cannot take the law into our own hands."

Now Worden was enraged.

"The law! The law!" He threw his hands up, slapped them down to his sides. "Are you talking about the same fucking law that said we couldn't carry rifles? The one that said we couldn't defend ourselves when people are fucking shooting at us?"

Worden stepped over to Fuentes and delivered a swift kick to the man's back. "The fucking politicians make up the laws," he shouted, waving his arms around the empty alley. "Do you see any politicians down here hanging their asses out?"

"Of course the politicians make up the laws," Cortizo said. He had lowered his head, and he could feel blood running into his mouth, but he kept his eyes fixed on Worden. "But just because you don't like the politicians doesn't make the laws invalid. You still can't make rules up as you go along."

"They don't give a *fuck* about us," Worden yelled.

He was standing over Fuentes again, and Cortizo thought he might start kicking once more. The lieutenant got up and moved over to straddle the smuggler's feet. It wouldn't take much for Worden, who was a giant next to Cortizo, to knock the Mexican out of the way, but Cortizo was banking that Worden wouldn't go that far.

"They don't give a fuck, and they send us down here to see if they like this approach or that approach while they debate what's going on. And as long as we're only dying in twos and threes, they don't care."

Cortizo could feel Worden's spittle on his face.

"This isn't Iraq, with droves of reporters following every GI around. Hardly anybody back home knows we're down here, and most of the ones who do think we're wrong."

He squared off with Cortizo, both men straddling Fuentes, who let out a low moan every few seconds.

"Now, we're close to winning one, and you want to split hairs?"

Cortizo did not respond. He wondered how his idea had gotten so out of hand, wondered what he was going to do with Fuentes, who had probably heard everything they were talking about. He looked down and was surprised to see the big man looking up at him. Worden looked down too.

"You awake, motherfucker?" Worden said. In a flash he pulled a pistol from behind his back. He dropped to his knees by the smuggler's head and placed the muzzle of the pistol flat up against the pallid forehead.

"Where is the shipment we are looking for?" Worden said in Spanish.

Fuentes's face did not move. He had closed his eyes when he saw the gun and had not opened them.

"I don't think he understands you," Cortizo tried.

Worden looked up at Cortizo. "Then you ask him."

Cortizo drew a shallow breath. "No."

Worden snorted in disgust. When he looked down, Fuentes's eyes were open. Worden lifted the pistol up about a foot and snapped the butt of the weapon down on Fuentes's nose. There was a cracking sound and the softer sound of flesh giving way, but the smuggler barely moved. Worden repeated the question in Spanish.

At the same time Cortizo had decided he would fight Worden for the pistol, Fuentes spoke.

"Stop." It was barely intelligible, and as he spoke blood and air bubbled through the center of his shattered face.

"They left from Ciudad Victoria last night. Tonight they will be in Nuevo Laredo, and tomorrow they will try the border fifteen miles northwest of there."

Worden looked up at Cortizo and smiled. "See, all you need to do is ask."

He brought the pistol up again, down again on the same spot. Fuentes was so far gone in pain that he didn't even try to turn his head.

"If you're lying," Worden said, "my friend here will come back and kill you."

With that, the American got up and stuck the pistol back in the waistband of his pants. He walked away in the darkness without looking at Cortizo.

The Mexican lieutenant went back to the wall of the building and leaned there until the dizziness passed. He had gotten the information he wanted, but the trade was more than he'd anticipated.

# 20

## Tampico, Mexico
### *15 June*

ISEN WAS SITTING AT A FIELD TABLE WRITING A LETTER TO Adrienne when the call came in.

"Captain Isen?"

"Speaking," Isen said. "That you, Sergeant Worden?"

"Yessir," Worden said. "You finished fucking off over there? Ready to come back to work yet?" Worden asked.

*Same old Worden,* Isen thought. And yet there was something in the voice.

"Nah. I think they're about to make me the commander-in-chief or field marshal or something, so I'm going to stick around, see how it turns out," Isen said.

"You would," Worden said. "Listen, sir, Lieutenant Cortizo called and told me to give you this information."

Worden told him what they'd learned from Fuentes, embellishing Cortizo's part and leaving out his own interrogating.

"Why did he want me to have this?" Isen asked. As he talked he turned to the map posted on the wall and put his finger on Tampico, then traced it north to Laredo, Texas.

"He said you two had a conversation about this matter, and he thought the information could help you," Worden answered.

"Ciudad Victoria, Nuevo Laredo," Isen said, mangling the pronunciation. "I got it." He listened intently for a few minutes without further comment, looking away from the map only long enough to scratch a few notes, in his indecipherable hand, on the pad by the phone. Then he hung up.

*Someday I'll have to ask Cortizo how he came by this,* Isen thought.

He went into action immediately, sending a runner for Spano and calling Colonel Reeves—who was en route from Washington to Brownsville—and their point of contact in the Mexican Federal Justice Police. He and Spano didn't have to wait long for their instructions, which Reeves called from the air to Spano.

"Looks like the Mexicans are going to invite us in on this one," Spano said.

"That's good, isn't it?" Isen said. "I mean, doesn't that mean they trust you more?"

"Maybe," Spano said. "But they told Colonel Reeves that it's because they think the bad guys may have chemicals."

Isen faltered for a moment. "Chemical weapons? Like gas?"

Spano was smiling. "Yeah. But the information about the possible shipments comes from a U.S. source."

"What the hell is so amusing about that?"

" 'Cause I wouldn't be surprised if Colonel Reeves or some other gringo told them they were facing chemical agents, just so they'd call us and we'd get a chance to do things right."

"I'm not sure I follow," Isen admitted.

"The Mexicans have no hard evidence that there are chemicals involved. But the U.S. intelligence community passed them word about some shipments that might have been made out of Libya through Cuba."

"Why would we make up something like that?" Isen said.

"Because we know the Mexicans don't have the capability to handle chemicals; so it's a sure thing they'd call us. There's a lot of political pressure at home right now to get these NDP bastards, yet we have to be invited by the host government before we can operate in another country."

Isen, who didn't think of himself as naive, was amazed nevertheless. "So we made this thing up?"

"I don't know that for sure," Spano said, studying the map closely. He turned and grinned. "But that would be my guess."

"So where do we go from here?"

"Colonel Reeves will be in Brownsville, Texas, this afternoon." He stabbed the map with his finger, indicating Brownsville, which hung at the very tip of the lower end of Texas like an afterthought. "And he'll have two teams down there a few hours after that. What we have to do," he said, "is get our butts up north and make contact with the Federale in charge of the investigation. You and I will do the initial recon, then we'll go out with the team and get the bad guys."

Spano picked up the paper he'd been writing on and shoved it in his pocket. "I sure make it sound easy, don't I?"

By the time Isen had picked up his weapon and field gear, Spano had talked to the flight detachment at the nearby headquarters for Operation Sentinel, and they sent over the on-call Blackhawk helicopter. Two and a half hours after they received the phone call from Colonel Reeves, Isen and Spano were near Ciudad Victoria, listening to a briefing by the chief investigator for the Mexican Federal Judicial Police. The headman—short, dark, thickset—chain-smoked as he talked. He rattled off a few sentences in Spanish, then another officer interpreted for the Americans. Isen and Spano turned to each man as he spoke in turn, with occasional glances at a badly drawn sketch map spread on the hood of a car.

"The local police in Nuevo Laredo have evidence of some walkers coming through," the Mexican said. "They have people out on the ground now. We were going to send out a helicopter, but the inspector here said we should let you decide when to do that, since this was going to be your chase. He said there are not many places they could hide out there, and that you will be able to find them with your . . ." The man hesitated, searching for the right word. "Your heat-looking sights."

"Our thermal sights," Isen offered.

Spano chewed his lip, then looked up and smiled at the inspector. "Please excuse us."

Spano took Isen by the arm and the two men walked until they were thirty feet away.

"Do you think it's them?" Isen asked, meaning the NDP.

"Yeah, and the Mexicans seem to think so too." Spano paused, considering the problem. "They either have a lot of confidence in us and our equipment," Spano said, "or they're really scared to get close to these people. I'm not sure which it is."

"Does it really matter?" Isen asked. "Regardless of the shenanigans that have gone on up to this point, the fact remains that your team still has to go in and get them."

Spano nodded slowly. "And we'd better do it right the first time. Colonel Reeves doesn't like fuck-ups, and he especially doesn't like fuck-ups in front of other people."

After studying the situation and questioning a Mexican officer who had experience trailing overland smugglers, Spano came up with a tentative plan. According to the Mexicans, there were a limited number of routes the band could travel on foot after leaving their daytime bivouac. Spano was sure that a helicopter with thermal-sensing equipment could cover enough ground to locate them within a couple of hours. Once they had pinpointed the target, they would use three helicopters: two with assault teams and one as a command-and-control platform, with Colonel Reeves and Spano on board.

Isen was surprised when, a few hours later, Colonel Reeves invited him to fly in the command helicopter.

"I can't promise that you'll see anything, but since Ray has dragged you halfway across the countryside already, I can hardly leave you stranded out here. Besides, you can carry a rifle and pull security for me while I jabber on the radio."

"Sounds good, sir," Isen said. "Can I make a suggestion?"

Spano was standing nearby. It was almost dark now and

difficult to see faces in the gloom, but it was easy to tell that Spano was mildly surprised. Apparently he hadn't expected Isen to suggest anything new after they'd collaborated on the plan.

"This just occurred to me as I was thinking about the Mexicans," Isen explained. "I think you ought to ask the chief investigator to come along, also."

"But they're out of this," Spano said.

"It's still their country," Isen said. It sounded a bit harsh, but Isen was getting tired of the Ugly American syndrome. "I mean, it's bad enough we come in here and take over. He was put in a tough spot by the federal government—having to explain to the locals around here why the Federales couldn't handle this. He's bound to be pissed off by now. If there's nothing classified that he shouldn't see, it wouldn't hurt to invite him along."

"Sounds like a decent idea to me," Reeves said. "What do you think, Ray?"

"As long as he doesn't get in the way," Spano said. "I suppose it makes sense to watch out for their sensibilities."

While the teams loaded their equipment onto the helicopters, also borrowed from Operation Sentinel, Isen sought out the chief investigator. He didn't go into a lot of detail about why he thought the man might want to go on the mission; he simply offered the invitation. The Mexican turned it down just as quickly. A few minutes later Isen brought the news back to Reeves and the little command group.

"Where's the cop?" Reeves asked.

"He didn't want to come along," Isen said. "I guess they're not real keen on this chemical warfare stuff."

"Neither am I," Reeves confessed.

When the Colonel moved off to talk to the two teams, Spano approached Isen in the dark.

"Did you know they'd turn us down?" he asked.

"I kind of figured it," Isen answered truthfully.

"So why bother? Why bother the colonel?"

Isen was getting a little tired of explaining things he considered obvious. "I bothered the colonel because they

256

might have said yes," he said, speaking slowly. "I asked them in the first place because it is very important for them to save face. Our asking makes him more important in the eyes of his subordinates."

"Even though he turned it down?"

"That was just common sense," Isen offered. "They really don't train for this chemical warfare stuff."

Spano tried to study Isen's face in the dark. "Pretty clever maneuvering," he said.

"You asked me to be an adviser, so I'm advising," Isen answered.

The two men heard helicopter engines start up again just after it got good and dark. The reconnaissance bird would go out first, the others would remain on call. Isen was surprised to see Ray Spano light up a cigarette.

"I didn't know you smoked," Isen said.

"Only when I'm sending guys out on a plan I made." He shook his head, as if he couldn't quite believe that himself. He was holding the cigarette cupped in one hand. "Hell, I don't get this nervous when *I'm* going. Just when I send other people."

"I know what you mean," Isen said. He remembered a lieutenant who'd joined his company just before they went into combat, a youngster with the makings of a good infantry leader. Isen sent him on the patrol on which he was killed. Isen had never doubted that the patrol was necessary, but he had wondered, more than once, if he could have said something to the lieutenant, given him some warning or word of advice that would have made a difference. *Old war stories,* Isen thought.

Ray Spano got through six cigarettes while the surveillance chopper searched the routes he and the Mexicans had plotted for it. The EH-60 Blackhawk, an electronics-laden version of the army's standard utility helicopter, was equipped for electronic intelligence gathering. But it made two passes over each of the corridors—wide, flat valleys running north and south—where the smugglers were likely to be traveling, all without finding a thing. Isen spent the whole time computing how far a group of men on foot might have gone in twenty-four hours. Colonel Reeves was at the point of calling off the air search when the radio in the command chopper—which was still on the ground—came alive.

"Juliet four-seven, this is Tango three-three." The copilot's voice vibrated with the thrumming blades.

"This is Juliet four-seven," Spano said into the handset.

"We still have nothing in the valleys you wanted us to search, four-seven. But we have spotted what we think might be a campfire in a parallel valley, maybe fifteen miles to the east."

Spano held the handset without answering and looked over at Isen and Reeves. The colonel spoke first.

"They're not soldiers. Maybe the concept of light discipline has never occurred to them."

Isen thought it would be an incredible stroke of luck. Soldiers from any army would have known that campfires give away positions at night.

Spano keyed the handset again. "Gimme a fix, three-three."

There were several moments of silence while the intell operators on the aircraft pinpointed the fire. They read their own position—accurate to within ten meters—from a digital display linked to a satellite that pinpointed objects on earth. Then they turned a laser range finder on the suspected target and squeezed off a burst of invisible light. With these three pieces of information: their own position, the distance, and direction to the target, they were able to plot, with great accuracy, the location of the campfire. All within forty-five seconds.

Spano marked the spot on the U.S.-issue maps Reeves had brought along. "Do we go now, sir?" he asked.

"If it isn't them we might scare away the real bandits with all the noise,' Isen offered.

"Tell the surveillance chopper to keep at it in case they find something while we're moving. We're going to go on this one," Reeves said.

Spano made the calls, then briefed the air crews on the mission while Reeves talked to the two team leaders one last time, stressing the importance of capturing one or more of the smugglers alive. A few minutes later Isen could see, in the dim lights from the helicopter cabins, the sixteen Delta Force soldiers climb aboard the other two birds.

While they were in the air, Spano showed Isen the target location on his map. The campfire seemed to be near the center of a small valley. Only about six hundred meters separated the two ridges that ran along either side. The helicopters would deposit the troops just over the crest on the two ridges, out of sight of the valley floor, one on each side. One of the teams would move into the low ground north of the target, then turn south and advance along the valley floor. The other team would approach the target directly. Any firing would cross at right angles in the vicinity of the campfire.

Isen wasn't sure where Reeves was going to set down, and he couldn't make himself heard above the engines to ask Spano, but he figured he'd find out soon enough. He tried to pick out forms on the surface of the dark earth, but there was little visible. A few minutes into the flight, the crew turned off all lights, and Isen, like everyone else on board, slipped night-vision goggles over his face. When he pulled them down and saw everyone else with the ungainly contraptions, he had a sudden vision of the crews of the two Blackhawks destroyed in the ambush of Cortizo's men. He tried to push the images of the blackened helicopters from his mind, but it was hopeless. He licked dry lips, wondered what Adrienne was doing.

Isen felt the bird slow, a gentle swinging of the aircraft belly, then saw one of the other aircraft alongside their own. When the earth came into view at the bottom of his field of vision—everything in green through the goggles— he figured that Reeves was landing alongside one of his teams. Isen followed the colonel and Spano, who still moved gingerly on his wounded leg, out of the chopper, lowering his head instinctively as the aircraft took off again. When he looked up, he saw a couple of shadowy figures moving quickly over the edge of a rise in front of them.

"Let's go," Reeves said after giving his teams a few moments' head start.

\* \* \*

The smugglers, who had been asleep around the camp-fire, were all on their feet as soon as they heard the approaching helicopters. Several of the load carriers, the men who were paying to be led to the United States, broke and ran down the valley to the south—the way they had come. Only a few of them got away before the guides turned their weapons on the rest of the group and forced them to pick up the heavy bundles, including the ones abandoned by the runaways. This group was headed north in the shallow valley when the first of Delta's helicopters landed. The leader of the group, a twenty-eight-year-old Colombian who'd been making this run for a year, heard one of the choppers land to his left front, and he suspected that the soldiers might try to cut them off in the valley. But he had outrun Mexican patrols twice in the last five months, and so thought he and his group could make it past before the soldiers, who moved slowly because they were afraid to fight, could cut them off.

The Delta Force soldiers hustled, bounding down into the valley one section at a time while the other section covered them. The eight men, coming from the north, were in position across the neck of the valley less than thirty seconds before the first of the smugglers walked into their sights.

One of the Americans shouted first. "Halt."

The Mexican who was in the lead was advancing with his weapon, a sawed-off Remington shotgun, held at his hip. When he heard the call from the darkness directly in front of him, he pulled the trigger.

From the top of the little rise, Isen could see the whole thing clearly. The Mexicans, nearly blind in the moonless dark, were moving along the floor of the valley, walking upright directly at the line of U.S. soldiers. All the Americans, equipped with night-vision devices, could see the valley as if in daylight. It was like watching a showdown between a blind man and a gunslinger.

To their credit, the Delta team shot only those smugglers who were armed and shooting. All of this was fairly easy to determine, using the scopes. The rest dropped to their knees or huddled on the ground. There wasn't a lot of shooting, a dozen or so very accurate shots from rifles and assault guns. There was even a moment of quiet before the soldiers started shouting instructions to the remaining men, telling them to get down on the ground, arms and legs spread wide apart. The terrified Mexicans, who still could not see anything but the wall of blackness, did as they were told.

"Pretty clean," Spano said beside him.

"Can't go much smoother than that," Isen said. The three men stood and began to walk down into the valley. Off to the left, team members were searching the men on the ground. Because of the boxy night-vision headsets, the men on their feet looked like two-legged bugs moving around the prostrate figures.

One of the team members jogged up to Reeves.

"GODDAMN," Reeves swore. "The only guys we caught alive weren't armed."

Isen, who was standing next to the colonel, was puzzled. "Sir?"

"That means we probably killed all the people who might have told us anything worthwhile," Reeves answered more calmly. He was ready to move on to the next problem. "Go over and see what they dropped," he told Isen and Spano. "I'm going to have the chopper relay the message to higher that we made our strike."

Spano and Isen walked over to where they could make out some bulky packages on the ground.

"Be careful," Isen told Spano as the ops officer turned over a knapsack. "They may be booby-trapped."

Spano pulled off his goggles and put on his protective mask and rubber gloves, then unhooked the straps on the canvas bag. He put his hands inside, then looked up at Isen without pulling them out.

"What is it?" Isen asked.

Spano didn't answer but pulled out two small metal cannisters wrapped in a foam-rubber sheet. One end of

261

each bottle was wrapped in duct tape that might have covered some sort of valve.

Spano turned a tiny penlight on the bottles. "Holy shit," he said, his voice muffled by the thick mask. He looked even more bug-eyed behind the wide eyepieces and black rubber. He looked up at Isen, who still hadn't donned his own mask.

"I guess I'm at least as safe as the guys who carried the stuff," Isen said.

Spano looked around at the prisoners a few feet away, then pulled his own mask up off his face.

"I guess I was wrong about us bullshitting the Mexicans," Spano said. "That is, if this stuff is real."

"At least we caught them," Isen said.

"Yeah, but I wonder if this was the only shipment," Spano said.

Thirty minutes after they'd landed, the Delta Force teams, their new prisoners, the contraband, and the dead all flew off in the same three helicopters. The plan was to turn the bad guys back over to the Mexicans, who would pursue the investigation. But Reeves had already determined that the initial contact had killed the four smugglers outright. There were no Europeans in the group, and their prisoners were merely laborers who knew nothing about the origins of the shipment. The Americans got a break when the ambush was successful, but they weren't much further along in catching any NDP members.

When they left the aircraft again at Ciudad Victoria, Isen commented to Spano, "I guess this means we have to assume the worst."

"You mean that they're still out there operating?" Spano asked. "You betcha."

"And that they have other chemical weapons."

"The White House will draw that conclusion from Colonel Reeves's report. I'm sure the pucker factor will go up for the guys checking the border, but they'll have to keep that one under wraps. Can you imagine what the public would do if word got out that these NDP characters have chemical weapons?"

**Headquarters
Department of the Army
Special Operations Command
Fort Bragg, North Carolina**
17 June

Memorandum for the Chairman of the Joint Chiefs of Staff

Reference: Raid by Delta Force personnel on suspected terrorists near Nuevo Laredo, Mexico, 170120 June.

1. Interrogation of prisoners after the raid indicated that the initial report was correct: all of the smugglers who were running the operation to carry contraband into the United States were killed in the firefight with U.S. personnel. The men captured alive had all paid to be led across the border into the United States, where they planned to seek work. They were pressed into service as bearers for the smugglers.

2. The chemical agent found in small metal cannisters was GB, a nerve agent originally manufactured in the Soviet Union and now made by the Libyans and Iraqis.

3. Because we do not know if the captured material was the entire stockpile of chemical agents in Mexico, we must assume that the NDP still has a chemical capability. The Mexican Army is not well trained in chemical warfare, nor do they have a special weapons and tactics capability to handle such a contingency. Therefore, although the presence of American forces is politically sensitive within Mexico, I believe it is likely that the Mexican government will ask for U.S. assistance in capturing other NDP members.

4. The Delta Force is the best unit for this job. They have already established themselves in Mexico and are

working closely with the Mexican Federal Judicial Police.

5. I anticipate a growing movement in Congress to remove all U.S. forces from Mexico. We should resist that influence because the Mexicans will need us, and because we have the best tools available to stop the Neu Deutschland Party.

E. A. Gorham
Major General, USA

# 21

## Tampico, Mexico
### *16 June*

WOLF LAY LOW IN MEXICO CITY FOR A FEW DAYS BEFORE
returning to Tampico by air. He took a cab from the airport
to the hotel where he kept a room. There he checked the
messages for Herr Denning, who was registered as a Dutch
businessman, an engineer who specialized in fittings for the
transfer of bulk oil. As he expected, there were three separate messages about people coming to Mexico to meet him.
There were no times or dates for the meetings, but each of
the callers had left word of plans to call upon Herr Denning
soon, possibly in the next three or four days. Wolf was
convinced that the police had somehow gotten the first
three men who were supposed to have joined him in Mexico. He didn't much care about the fate of the three, what
really bothered him was that he couldn't do a damage assessment. What did the authorities now know about him
and his plans? His solitary work had also been more difficult than he had expected.

But now that he was satisfied that he would have enough
help to do the next task he'd outlined for himself, Wolf
turned to his next problem. Before leaving Europe, he had
agreed to contact his Soviet sponsor before executing each
stage of his plan. Now that he was in North America, not

only was making the contact more difficult, but the requirement seemed particularly intrusive, as well. If it wasn't for the fact that he needed their money, Wolf would gladly have left the Soviets out of the picture.

After showering and changing into clean clothes, Wolf rode another cab down to the docks, where a week earlier he'd spotted a cantina that advertised, on a faded sign in the window, *Teléfono Internacional*. As he expected, he had to wait in line behind a couple of sailors who were riding the coasters up from South America. But Wolf didn't mind the wait; it was well worth the inconvenience to be in the kind of place where people considered it rude—dangerous, even—to notice someone else's face.

After two tries, the international operator was able to get him the number he wanted, which was in Berlin. At the other end of the line an answering machine clicked on, and a roughly accented voice, struggling to speak German, began: "You have reached . . ." then trailed off. After a pause of a few seconds, another voice, just as awkward in the unfamiliar tongue, read a number different from the one Wolf had dialed. He made a note on a slip of paper, broke the connection, and dialed the operator again, giving the new city and the number the machine had given him. On the second ring, a human voice answered.

"This is the United States," Wolf said. He was told to wait.

A long minute later, another voice came on the line. "What is it?"

"I am ready to proceed with the next step."

"Yes?"

"I have chosen a spot that is not near where the other commotion has been, and I plan on escalating the . . . weaponry," Wolf said.

"All of your parcels arrived intact, then, I assume."

"I have had no trouble with the material or the money, but I have no one here to help."

There was a pause at the other end and a muffled sound, as if someone were talking with a hand over the mouthpiece.

"Didn't you know that the authorities have detained some of your friends?"

*Damn.* "I guessed as much," Wolf said. "How did they know?"

"The police in your country have been watching them."

Wolf held his breath, swallowed. It was entirely possible that the voice he was talking to belonged to a police officer as well. Who could say how much they had infiltrated his scheme?

"No matter, more help will be here any day." He suddenly wanted to be off the phone. "I need the money."

"And you shall have it," the voice said. Another pause while Wolf sweated. "Ensure that you continue to contact us as you proceed."

"Yes . . . yes, I will," Wolf said.

The line went dead, and Wolf put the receiver down quickly, as if holding it were enough to tie him to the voice on the other end. He had been expecting the investigation to get closer to him, had planned for ways to avoid his pursuers. What he hadn't planned for was the fear that now rose from deep inside him. It was possible that the authorities in Europe had established his identity and the Mexican police were even now looking for him, perhaps with a photo in hand.

Wolf left the booth and walked to the bar across a floor sticky with spilled drink. One or two of the patrons looked at him, then looked away.

It would take two or three days to get the money and get ready to leave again, back to the United States. *I need a place to lie low,* he thought. He considered simply checking into another hotel in the area, since he would have to be around to check on the messages from the new men who would soon arrive in Mexico. But of course, the police would check the hotels thoroughly. He wondered if the operation was slipping away from him, wondered if he would even be able to tell when he was losing control.

*Calm down,* he told himself, shaking his head to clear it. *You have just pulled off a successful bombing; you still have the Americans on the run, and every day more of their politicians call for a compromise.*

But the monologue did him little good. The fact remained that he was alone, far away from anyone on whom he could rely. In Germany, he knew how to watch the police; here, he had no way of knowing if they were closing in on him. In his moment of fear, he did what always worked for him. He took comfort in his plan, which was still on schedule after all, and he relied on his strong points. He looked up at the cracked mirror behind the bar and watched himself for a moment. Inspired, he straightened his shoulders, brushed his thick hair back with two hands, and smiled at the reflection.

Wolf had been right about the woman; she was not Mexican. The owner of the café where he'd met Diablo told Wolf about her after some money changed hands.

"She's an American," the old man said. "Spoiled rich girl who ran away from her parents and now has no money to go home." He eyed Wolf in between sentences, but the German's face remained a mask.

"You like her, I can find out where she lives." Another pause. "You like her?" This time he accompanied the question with a universal gesture, forefinger in circled finger and thumb.

"I want to know where I can find her," Wolf said.

The old man grinned lasciviously. "She stays at Diablo's place, near here, though he is gone much of the time. I can find out if he is away now, if you want." The old man cocked his head, as if Wolf could miss the fact that he expected to be paid.

"Do that," Wolf said, sliding some folded notes across the bar.

"If Diablo finds out, he will kill you."

"Let me worry about that," Wolf said. "Of course, if he finds out from you, I will kill you."

Wolf had his answer in a few hours. The old man seemed much less amused when Wolf returned for the information, perhaps because of the death threat hanging over him. Still, he took the money. He gave Wolf the directions without looking directly at the European, and he was extremely anxious to get Wolf out of the bar as soon as their business was concluded.

Diablo kept a room in a soot-stained block of buildings near the refinery, down by the port. The smells of the industrial plants were almost unbearable here, but still Wolf watched the door for an hour before he approached. The girl answered his knock, and Wolf smiled as if surprised to see her there.

"I am looking for Diablo," he told her.

"He is not here," she said, looking beyond him to the empty street.

She was definitely an American, with some variation of that distinct southern accent that Germans found so fascinating in American movies. The wariness she showed when she answered the door waned a bit as she took in her visitor, and Wolf turned his head slightly, posing in the doorway.

"When do you expect him back?" he asked.

"Not for a few days." She leaned on the door as she said this, relaxing a bit. She was no more than eighteen, Wolf decided, with light brown hair, almost blond, and green eyes. They hesitated for a few seconds, each sizing the other up.

*This one is a hell-raiser,* Wolf thought, *and will be fun and useful.*

He smiled at her, and she returned it, unabashed, and threw her hair back in what she probably thought was a womanly gesture, but was merely obvious.

Wolf gambled, anxious to cut to the chase. "Are you going to ask me in?"

She didn't answer but merely stepped out of the doorway, letting him close the door behind him.

"Aren't you afraid that Diablo will come here and find you?" she said teasingly.

"Not if you aren't," Wolf answered.

She walked to a tiny refrigerator and pulled out two bottles of beer, opening both and offering Wolf one without asking.

"What made you think I'd let you in?" she asked, coming closer, pressing the mouth of the bottle up to parted lips.

"The way you looked at me in the bar the other day."

She walked toward him, then passed by to lock the door from the inside. "Well, I have been kind of bored lately," she said, turning around. She drank from the bottle and wiped a few errant drops of beer off of her mouth with the back of her hand and wrist.

Wolf came to her and kissed her, hard and full on the mouth. She kissed back, standing her ground as he pressed against her, feeling the swells and hollow places through the slightly damp fabric of her cotton shift. Her lips and throat were salty, and damp tendrils of hair hung down her neck where he mouthed the column. She pushed him back toward a bed in the corner, where she faced him and sat down on the edge, the upper half of her dress now in folds around her waist. She put her arms around him and pulled his middle toward her, tugging at his pants, kissing his stomach, then taking him greedily, hungrily in her mouth until he groaned and she fell back on the bed, licking her lips with a lusty grin, raising her buttocks so that he could pull her dress free.

Wolf made small noises in his throat and performed as athletically as ever, while in his mind a calm voice said, *Yes, this will do nicely.*

They made love twice on that first day before he found out her name—Karen Charles—and learned that she was, as the bartender had said, a spoiled rich American girl who'd run away and now was afraid to go back home. At first she told him she was twenty-one, and though Wolf didn't believe her, he didn't press the point. It was during that first night, when she remembered that Diablo would come back in a few days, that she grew fearful and told him what he thought was the truth. They had traded their considerable skills in the dusky and humid bed, each trying to outperform the other, all without mixing anything more intimate than what their bodies offered up. Afterward, spent, some of her hardness melted away.

"I'm eighteen," she said into his neck.

Wolf opened his eyes to the darkness; he had been expecting a time of confession. He was thinking, *Where did she learn these tricks at this age?* But he said, "How did you get yourself into such a mess so early in your life?"

The woman of an hour earlier became a girl next to him. He could see only part of her face in the stingy light reflected through the window.

"I ran away from my parents while they were on vacation down here in Mexico. I was pissed off because they wouldn't let me wait a year before starting college."

There was a tinge of whining in her voice, and Wolf couldn't help but think, *This is where the teenager shows through.*

"All I wanted to do was bum around for a while, but they said I had to go right away." She sat up on the bed next to Wolf and stared at him, as if afraid that he wasn't paying attention.

"I was in this shithole"—she moved an arm around, and he assumed she meant Tampico—"when I ran out of money."

Wolf was still, but when she paused, he put his hand on her leg to let her know he was listening. That gesture, which she interpreted as human warmth, cracked her hard exterior, and suddenly she was crying, a little at first, then with greater force, until her shoulders were convulsed with sobs and her long hair shook in front of her face like a curtain. It occurred to Wolf that she probably hadn't told this story to Diablo.

Wolf sat up and took her in his arms. "There, there," he said. He didn't feel safe here, and now that he'd had her he was ready to leave. He sat staring at the dark spot on the bedside table where his watch should be. Then she held him at arm's length and spoke again.

"Will you help me get home?" She was breathless from the crying, and she began to lose control again. "I don't need all that much money. I thought he would give it to me but he just keeps me here as his whore and now I'm afraid he will find out about us and will beat me again, please help me get out of here . . ."

Wolf pulled her to him again and held her. "All right," he said, "all right, I can help you get out of here." And as he spoke he realized he could see the face of his watch as the room filled with the dawn.

He stayed with the girl for three days, leaving only to check at the bank for the funds that were to be wired in, and to check at his hotel for messages from the new arrivals.

They came in ones and twos, until there were ten of them, from Germany and Ireland, France and Italy. Wolf sent them out as soon as he gave them instructions, believing it was better to have them dispersed, even though that meant his direct control was compromised. He gave them instructions to phone Herr Denning and leave a phone number he could call at prearranged times.

Some of this new group had been around the old NDP, even before Wolf arrived on the scene. But it took the excitement of a new campaign to bring them out of their torpor. Others had agreed to join him because of his success so far, and though he was enjoying the fallout from the name he was making for himself among the disaffected political anarchists in Europe, he was not entirely pleased with the crop of recruits. Wolf picked the best of the lot, a thirty-three-year-old Berliner named Becht, to be his second in command. He divided the remainder into three groups. The most reliable pair would go to the United States, specifically to northern Virginia and the Washington metropolitan area. One of these men, the German who'd manufactured the device that brought down the flight out of Mexico City, would continue to manufacture and distribute the devices Wolf would use in his campaign. It occurred to Wolf that he might send one of the other men—the Irishman or Frenchman—along since the authorities were looking for Germans. But the bomb-maker was a sullen man, and he did not get on well with any of the foreigners. Wolf sent along another German.

The least reliable group would stay closer to him so that he could keep an eye on them. The middle group he sent north in Mexico to open more avenues for shipping material overland. He had nothing much for them to do there, but he didn't worry too much. None of them seemed of the intellectual caliber that required constant stimulation. Then there were the two who came together: they were openly affectionate with one another, so Wolf sent them north, away from him.

Once he had his teams dispersed, he felt as if he had more of a foothold on the continent. With the additional manpower, he could go ahead with his plan. He wouldn't have admitted it, even to himself, but simply having the other people around made the danger feel less acute. He listened to himself as he briefed Becht on the situation and found comfort in the confidence he heard in his own voice: the Americans were rattled, footage of various bombings played again and again all the time on American television, so that the public could hardly escape it. Politicians from both parties were openly expressing dissatisfaction with the administration's policies. Wolf even found it amusing to read that the President was having difficulties in Mexico due to the presence there of unwelcome American troops. He was annoyed that he could not, as yet, account for all of the shipments of explosives but told himself it was a mere inconvenience.

"They will need only a few more shoves," Wolf told Becht, "and the one big one I have planned, before they capitulate."

Becht, who was a perceptive man, saw the strain evident in Wolf's eyes and wondered if Wolf would have the strength to push hard enough.

# 22

## Tampa, Florida
### 19 June

WOLF FLEW TO SOUTH AMERICA FROM MEXICO, THEN TOOK
an evening flight from Bogotá to Miami, then on to Tampa
in time to have dinner at the airport hotel, where he enjoyed a grilled swordfish steak and a bottle of a white California wine. *I suppose one could get used to American
wine after a while,* he told himself as the waiter poured the
last from the bottle.

When he registered, he mentioned to the clerk that he
was expecting a delivery in the morning, a package with
some things he needed for a conference two days hence.

"And I wonder if you could tell me, is it possible to jog
here on the beach? I'd like to get some exercise after all
these hours on the plane, and I thought that since I'm so
close, why not take advantage of the seaside?"

"Well, the beach is not all that close," the clerk said,
producing a map from under the counter. "That is, if you
want to run on the Gulf. You could park along the causeway here and run alongside the bay. That's a pretty
stretch," she said, her *pretty* coming out *purty*. She pointed
to a straight line of highway that looked, on the map, like
a long bridge spanning Old Tampa Bay and leading toward
Clearwater and the Gulf of Mexico.

"Where is the beach where all the people will go swimming?" Wolf asked. "The people I am doing business with here told me not to miss it."

The clerk, who looked about fifty, smiled. "They must have been talking about all the thong bathing suits."

Wolf returned her smile. "Perhaps," he said shyly.

"That would be here, along Clearwater Beach." She pointed to a narrow island that lined the edge of the Gulf. "But you need to get moving early. Traffic gets pretty heavy around ten or eleven, and then it's really tough to get out there, much less park. The beach will be jammed by twelve and will stay that way most of the afternoon. Then all the roads headed back this way will look like parking lots."

Wolf studied the map. There appeared to be only two ways off the island: a bridge back to the mainland and another connecting it to the coastal island to the south.

"I believe I will stay on this causeway, then. I do not wish to get stuck in traffic." He smiled mischievously at the woman. "Besides, the bathing suits on American beaches are rather tame compared to what you might see in Europe."

"Well, then," the woman said, chuckling deep in her big chest, "a body must get an eyeful over there."

Wolf bought four different metropolitan newspapers at the hotel newsstand and carried them up to his room. As he expected, the papers were full of speculation about the NDP's next move, a frenzy of reporting fueled by his calling, three days earlier, a Chicago television station with another threat. The papers dutifully reported that the caller had said the next strike would be within a week, and that the pace of the attacks would soon increase. But two of the papers descended into a hairsplitting discussion over whether that meant within six days or seven days of the call.

Wolf imagined the tens of thousands of readers fascinated by the NDP's ferocious plan, and seeing his handiwork, he almost wished he could publicly take credit for it. Once, when he was a teenager, he'd had an affair with an older, married woman, the wife of the Wolf family's landlord. The energetic teen made love to her almost every day throughout one winter, and in the spring she came out into the sunshine sporting a new hairstyle and clothes a great deal less dowdy than those she wore in the fall. When Wolf realized that he was responsible for her new outlook, he wanted to tell someone. But of course, he could not.

Reading the stories of his new exercise of power, he felt the same way. He wanted to tell someone, but of course, he could not.

The next morning Wolf rose at seven, called for coffee and rolls in his room, and took his time getting ready. He oiled himself with a strong sun-block lotion, dressed casually in shorts and a pullover shirt, then put bathing trunks and a hotel towel into a small canvas bag he'd brought in his suitcase. He put his Mexican money and his airline ticket in a plastic bag, which he hung from the inside edge of the toilet tank. He scanned the room again, then took the elevator down and called for his car. When he left the hotel, the big clock in the lobby said nine-fifteen.

The Tampa Airport was surprisingly easy to get out of, considering its size, and in no time at all Wolf was spinning west on Florida 60. The little overpasses were substitute hills on this flat landscape, and Wolf got to see a little bit of the hazy spread of Tampa to the east. There were palm trees all along the roadway, many of them with boards holding them up, as if they'd been planted recently. Within minutes he was on the Courtney Campbell Parkway, and he saw that the hotel clerk had been right in her assessment: it was a real pretty stretch. There was a width of green and a narrow belt of sand on either side of the divided four lanes. Campers and recreational vehicles sat at angles to the water line every few hundred meters, and there were already plenty of fishermen standing in the shallow water.

He followed the same route all the way out to the little bridge that finally connected the island to the mainland. The west-running road ended quickly, and he found a parking spot along the street two blocks east of the beach. He locked the car and made his way toward the sound and smell of the water.

The beach was already beginning to fill up. Off to the

right Wolf could see a concrete jetty, bristling with fishermen's lines at the end and, along the rest of its length, with bicyclists walking their bikes out for a glimpse of the water. Wolf took off his shoes and headed off to the south. He walked at least a mile before turning to head back, taking note of where the families seemed to congregate, what parts of the beach belonged to old people and what to the college-age crowd. At one point he looked up to find that he was behind a beautifully sculpted couple wearing matching black thong bathing suits. They strolled ahead of him, stretching their leg muscles and shaking loose with each step some of the tiny particles of sand that adhered to the cheeks of their buttocks. Wolf enjoyed watching the man and woman enjoy the reactions of people who noticed them; he figured that their appearance represented an investment of a dozen or so hours a week at the gym and thought that perhaps they deserved their moment.

Wolf spread his towel on the sand in front of the Holiday Inn, where he bought a soda from the beachside bar. Two college girls on a blanket next to his flirted with him a bit, leaning up on their elbows to talk as they lay on their stomachs. The straps of their bikini tops were unhooked, and they seemed to enjoy the attention paid them by the handsome European. Wolf knew he should ignore them—he did not want to be remembered by anyone—but he couldn't fight his libido. He smiled and made small talk and agreed to watch their towels and shoes and radio for them while they went swimming. When they stood in front of him, leaning over to brush the sand from their oiled legs, he thought about the young American girl back in Tampico.

Wolf took off his shirt and passed the time talking to the girls and watching the people until his stomach told him it was lunchtime. When he stood, he took his time folding his towel, confident that the sunburned young women next to him couldn't see behind his dark glasses, couldn't tell that he was counting the people who were within an imaginary circle a hundred meters across.

When he got back to the hotel, the desk was holding a package for him, just delivered by express parcel service from Washington, D.C. He thanked the clerk and carried the box, the size of a deep briefcase, up to his room. He left it unopened as he showered and changed into long pants and a short-sleeved white shirt that was cool against his hot skin.

Once dressed, he took out a pocketknife and carefully slit the plastic sealing one end of the box. Then he pulled the flap loose and removed another, smaller package, which was wrapped in bubble plastic. He unwound the bubble wrap, carefully turning the package over in his hand. Inside was a radio cassette player and a small stainless-steel thermos. Out of curiosity, he pushed the *play* button on the top of the machine. It didn't give.

Wolf put the player on the floor behind the thick curtain at the window, then set the metal bottle inside the toilet tank with his other things. He left the hotel again, driving east this time. He found what he wanted on one of the main north-south streets. The Americans called them drugstores, or sometimes pharmacies, but Wolf thought that a misnomer. This one, for instance, carried everything from beer to beach chairs, greeting cards to eyeglasses. Wolf selected a bright yellow beach towel, a hard plastic cooler, a six-pack of soda, and two cassette tapes, all of which he paid for in cash. He put his purchases in the trunk of the rental car, then drove north away from the city. He ate alone, spent some time in the bar, turned down at least one interesting offer from a woman whose tan lines showed she usually wore a wedding ring, and was in bed by eleven to watch the local news.

At the top of the hour, the anchor said that they would show footage of remarks the President made at the White House. Wolf sat up in bed, feeling a twinge in the pit of his stomach, a nervous rumbling. He sat very erect, placed his hands on his knees, and concentrated on the glowing tube in front of him. There were no other lights on in the room. The news from Washington led the program, and Wolf watched until suddenly, he was there, as clear and as close as if he were in the room with Wolf. Wolf sucked in his breath and waited for the other man to speak. The American president stood behind a podium in the Rose Garden with an awkward, frozen smile, his eyes pinning Wolf to the chair.

"You look terrible," Wolf said to the screen. The sound of his own voice in the quiet room startled him a bit.

The President seemed to be responding to questions. He began, "Yes, it's true that our country faces several crises. From the outside, terrorist groups assault American citizens in their peaceful hometowns, while from within, certain segments of the population and even some elected officials seem bent on creating another crisis."

Wolf was surprised at the bluntness of the President's statement. He was willing to name his enemies, it seemed, within and without his own government.

"Over the past weeks, American citizens both at home and abroad have come under attack. The aim of this campaign is to force the withdrawal of the American navy from the Mediterranean Sea. This campaign of terror began with the murder of a young mother and her twin babies, and two soldiers in Germany. Then three young American sailors were shot to death in cold blood. The list of victims grew and eventually included soldiers and civilians at Fort Hood, Texas, and on board commercial airliners. The persons responsible for these crimes exaggerated reports of nuclear accidents aboard navy ships so as to drive a wedge between our country and our allies in Europe."

Wolf was barely breathing; he watched the President carefully. The American hesitated but did not seem unsure. He was gathering himself. The President licked his lips and looked up at the camera from his notes.

"Rest assured that the United States government, in concert with our allies, is doing everything possible to bring these murderers to justice."

Wolf sat still in the chair, pressing his hands to his thighs.

"Unfortunately, there are people inside and outside government who do not support our policy of refusing to negotiate with terrorists. These naysayers would have us believe that all we have to do is give in on this one request to withdraw the navy—a move they claim makes fiscal sense—and the terrorists will leave us alone."

The President put the papers flat on the podium and shifted his weight. Wolf felt his own shoulders tense.

"Let me assure you that nothing could be further from the truth. If we let terrorists believe that they can dictate policy to the United States of America simply because they have no moral compunction against murder, then we open the floodgates for untold tragedies."

"Well said, well said," Wolf blurted out, hitting his thigh with a closed fist.

The President went on earnestly. "We will not let a small group of murderers dictate our foreign policy. And though I respect the right of every citizen to disagree with the government, I need support in this effort. A divided citizenry will only encourage the terrorists to continue their attacks on Americans and on peaceful people around the world."

Wolf sat back in his chair. He had not expected the President to be so blunt in his assessment of what Wolf was trying to do. Despite his comment about the freedom of dissent, it was clear that the President did not want dissent. As Wolf expected, the politicians interviewed immediately afterward homed in on this point with a vengeance. One politician, a heavy-faced congressman, was particularly vehement in his objections. He claimed that the President was merely trying to divert attention from the administration's failure to accomplish anything in the investigation.

Wolf couldn't listen to the whining a moment longer. He reached across the space separating him from the television and pushed the power knob. The screen went blank, plunging the room into darkness. Wolf was alone with the flickering memory of the President's face still before his eyes.

*All of these others matter not a whit*, Wolf thought. "We are the principal adversaries," he told the screen. "And you are becoming a worthy opponent, Mr. President," Wolf said to the darkness. "A worthy opponent indeed."

He stood and walked to the window, where he pushed back the heavy curtains. Below the hotel, a few cars and trucks crawled along the street, pushing tiny circles of light ahead of them. Wolf looked out on the city and wondered who, asleep in bed tonight, would come near him on the beach.

The next day, Wolf checked out of the hotel before eating a big breakfast in the restaurant. He drove back over the causeway and found a parking spot on the same street he'd been on yesterday. He left his cooler and radio cassette player in the car and walked on the beach until almost eleven o'clock. By that time he was hungry again and so bought a hot dog at a little lunch counter on a side street by the Holiday Inn. After he'd eaten, he went back to his car and took the cooler, with the metal thermos inside; the cassette player and the bright yellow beach towel from the trunk. He made his way back to the beach and gladly dropped his things near where he'd been the day before. He looked around hopefully for the two young girls, but they weren't in sight.

*Probably sunburned,* he thought. He wrapped the tape player and the steel bottle in the white towel he'd brought from the hotel and sat the bundle next to the cooler. He balled up his shirt and used it as a pillow as he lay on his back, rehearsing the next few hours in his mind. He kept himself from checking his watch by sheer force of will. When he thought enough time had passed, he sat up and did a quick count of the people around him.

Immediately in front of him, a young couple was taking turns applying lotion to one another's already tanned backs. To their right, three young men with short haircuts guilelessly ogled the women walking by. One of them wore military identification tags—the GIs in Europe called them dog tags—which gave them away as soldiers. To Wolf's immediate left, a young couple sat on either side of a baby, who was asleep under his own little canvas canopy, while behind him, more college-age men and women exchanged compliments, phone numbers, and wildly exaggerated stories about their nights. There were at least twenty-five, perhaps as many as forty people within a circle of a hundred meters.

Wolf checked his watch and found that he had gone past the time he'd planned to leave, though only by three minutes. He slipped his hand under the white towel that covered the metal bottle and radio cassette player and turned the selector dial on the player all the way to the left until he heard a click. Then he put on his shirt and picked up his shoes. The young mother on the next blanket looked his way.

"Would you mind keeping an eye on my stuff while I go for a walk?" Wolf asked.

"Not at all," she said, smiling. Her husband, who was facing away from Wolf, leaned back on his elbow to see whom his wife was talking to. He nodded to Wolf, then looked back at the water.

"Thank you," Wolf said to the woman, who was still holding eye contact. He winked at her; she winked back.

Wolf stood and faced the water.

"Hey there."

A woman's voice, behind him. He turned to see one of the young women who'd been next to him the day before.

"Hello," he said, calling up a look of pleasant surprise. "Nice to see you again." The girl had been sunburned, Wolf noticed, though that didn't keep her from wearing another revealing suit today. He glanced appreciatively at her sunburn.

"Looks like you got a little sun yesterday," he said. He overcame the desire to look at his watch. *I must be five minutes behind by now,* he thought.

She brought her hands up to her flat belly and pressed the oiled flesh there with her fingertips. When she took her hands away there were little white marks where her fingers had been. "I guess I did." She looked up to find Wolf staring at her again.

"You like my suit?" she asked.

"Very much." He smiled again but was thinking of his watch and the white towel a few feet away. "I was just going for a walk. You want to come?"

"Sure," she said happily. She dropped her bag on his beach towel. "My name's Wendy," she said, offering her hand.

"I'm Dietrich," Wolf said, taking her small hand in his.

"You're not from here, are you?" she said. Then she

brought her hand up to her mouth. "Oh, that didn't sound very good, did it? I didn't mean anything . . . it's just that you have a slight accent."

"I'm Dutch," Wolf said. "I'm here on business." He steered her out to the water, then paused when he thought the couple watching his stuff wasn't looking.

"Why don't we go up and get a drink?" he asked, pointing to the beach bar at the hotel.

"Sounds great."

Wendy talked the whole way to the hotel, but fortunately her narrative didn't require a response. As they moved away from Wolf's towel, he felt more in control of things and confident that he could give the slip to this forward American girl.

"So I decided to take last semester off," Wendy was saying as they reached the wooden staircase that led to the bar. "I'll graduate this December."

Wolf saw a sign above a door that led into the lower floors of the big hotel. *Men's Locker Room, Stairs to Lobby.*

It was all working perfectly well after all. He felt relieved, strangely so, since he hadn't been conscious of real fear.

"I have to stop in here," Wolf said, motioning to where men in bathing suits were going in and out.

"Okay. I'll wait here," Wendy said.

*She really does have a pretty smile,* Wolf thought giddily. He was elated that it was going to work. He turned toward the hall, then spun around quickly and kissed her. As he did he slid his hand down the back of her bathing suit bottom. She started, and that moved her closer. Then he backed off before she could react, chuckling to himself as he walked through the locker room, up the stairs, and out the door to the street, where his car waited. He laughed all the way back to the airport, where he had allowed himself forty-five minutes to turn in the rental car and clean up in the rest room before his flight to Miami. He would connect there with a flight to Panama and would be back in Tampico in twenty-four hours. He had enjoyed playing with the young American girl at the beach, and as he drove he thought about another American girl, and the sweetness of temptation, and he wondered if Diablo had returned yet.

The radio cassette player that Wolf left in the care of the young mother on the blanket next to his contained a pound of Semtex, a plastic explosive manufactured in Eastern Europe and sold throughout the world to legitimate users and terrorist states alike. The blast from the exploding radio cassette player killed a half dozen people in the area immediately around where Wolf had been sitting. The force of the blast also shattered the metal bottle that had been under the towel with the recorder. The pressurized cannister contained several pounds of the nerve gas. The explosion caused an immediate overpressurization of the air in a rough circle around the blast, and this forced air spread the gas quickly, pushing it out in a balloon shape at least a hundred meters in diameter. Those people in the immediate vicinity who weren't killed by the blast were by no means fortunate, for in less than thirty seconds thirty-two people had inhaled a tiny but fatal dose of the gas. Some of them died quickly as the gas cut the signals between the brain and muscle—including heart and diaphragm. Others managed to stagger away, bleeding from the concussion, only to die on the hot sand closer to the hotel where Wendy, Wolf's jilted companion, stood on the balcony near the bar.

On his first drive around the airport a day earlier, Wolf had noticed the signs for rental car return, which appeared to be in the parking garage that was conveniently located next to the terminal. What he failed to notice was that his rental car company, which had a satellite office outside the airport, had no parking spaces for turn-in at the lot. Wolf learned this from the parking attendant.

"I'm sorry, sir, you'll have to take your car to the lot located right outside the airport." The clerk was a middle-aged man who seemed mildly retarded. For some reason, Wolf found this infuriated him. He was not about to let his plan be thrown off by some dim-witted American valet.

"You mean where I picked it up?" Wolf asked. The attendant nodded.

"I don't have time to drive all the way back there," Wolf said. *Friendly but firm,* he counseled himself.

But apparently the valet had encountered this situation before, and his instructions were clear. "I'm sorry, sir, but you can't leave that rental car here. You'll have to take it . . ."

"I know, I know," Wolf interrupted. "But listen to me. I cannot miss my plane because of this car."

The man seemed puzzled for a moment, as if he wanted to help Wolf but couldn't imagine how. Trained to give but one answer, he reverted to form. "I'm sorry, sir . . ."

Wolf was sitting in the car, which was at the entrance to the tiny lot where other companies' rental cars could be returned. He had remained calm but was very much aware that his timetable was slipping away from him. First Wendy, then the traffic, now this. He glanced in his mirror, as if the police were behind him already. *And they will be,* he thought. His mounting fear conspired to strangle him, push him off his tracks. It was beginning to be too much for him. In a second he was out of the car and approaching the valet menacingly.

"I am leaving this damn car HERE," Wolf hadn't intended to shout but found the release good. "Do you understand me?"

Whimpering, the lot attendant raised his hands, convinced that Wolf meant to strike him.

Then there was a thunder close by.

"WHAT THE FUCK DO YOU THINK YOU'RE DOING MAN?" Wolf stopped and turned to his right. An enormous black man, dressed in the same uniform as the lot attendant, was striding toward him. He seemed to be about nine feet tall, and he swung huge, coal-black arms as he moved over the ground. Wolf couldn't have been more startled if the man had risen out of the ground. *Time to retreat,* he thought.

"I'm sorry," Wolf said, smiling, backing away. "I didn't mean to frighten him; it's just that we had a misunderstanding about . . ."

"THERE AIN'T GONNA BE NO MISUNDERSTANDING WHEN I BUST YOUR FUCKIN' HEAD LIKE A MELON!"

The man was screaming now and only a few yards away. Wolf could see that he was enraged, and that there was no sense trying to placate him. Wolf reached inside the open door of the car, grabbed his bag, abandoned his dignity, and ran as fast as he could for the terminal. He covered about fifty meters before he dared to look back to where the black man was comforting his friend and still shouting at Wolf.

"I'm gonna break your scrawny white neck you ever mess with my man again like that, you hear me, motherfucker? You hear me?"

Wolf's mistake was being noticed.

At first Wendy was too shocked to be angry at the European who'd slipped his hand down her bathing suit bottom. But it was so obvious that he'd done it to shock her that she began to feel as if she should be angry with him. She waited outside the rest room door, trying to imagine a way to tell him off without driving him away—in spite of her good looks, it had been a pretty boring break. She hoped he'd apologize first.

But then he never came out, and she went upstairs, bought a beer, and leaned on the railing overlooking the beach. She was there when the bomb went off, and she was still there when a half dozen police officers passed through the crowd, asking the patrons if they'd seen any suspicious persons. Wendy watched one particularly good-looking young officer make his way toward her on the deck, and though her mental image of a "suspicious person" had been formed by newspaper pictures of Arab terrorists, when the police officer finally got to her, she surprised herself by telling him about the jerk-off European who'd fondled her.

A half hour later, she was sitting with the cute officer in the lobby of the hotel when the patrolman's supervisor came in to talk to her.

"You said he was European. Do you know what nationality?" the detective asked.

"I forget. Dutch, German maybe," Wendy said.

# THE COMMON DEFENSE

At the Tampa Airport, the black parking lot attendant called for a tow truck to remove the car abandoned in the driveway. He told his boss all about how some asshole foreigner had been bothering Billy, the mentally handicapped valet. He left out the part about threatening to break the customer's head.

The police started checking at the airport fairly quickly, and when they did, they found that the description of the European man who'd fondled the college girl matched the description of the man who'd abandoned his rental car. The clerk at the car rental agency was able to tell them that the car was contracted to an F. Zeitler. Checks at the ticket counters for that name turned up nothing, and by the time the police got copies of an artist's rendering, based on Wendy's description, around to all the counters, the clerks had changed shifts. The young lady who would, late the next day, identify the man in the picture as the passenger Dietrich Denning was in a St. Petersburg bar when Herr Denning got off the plane in Panama and booked a flight to Mexico City under the name Johann Hagen.

287

# 23

## Tampico, Mexico
### 22 June

MARK ISEN WAS SIMPLY ASTOUNDED BY THE NEWS FROM THE
United States.

"Can you believe this? On a beach, for God's sakes."

Isen was reading a copy of *The New York Times* that
one of the advisers had brought with him the day before
from a U.S. airport. He was addressing Sergeant Worden,
whom Isen had just caught up with at their Operation Sentinel headquarters in Tampico.

"I read where there were some babies around when the
bomb went off," Worden said. He was lying on his cot,
the heel of one boot perched on the toe of the other. "This
is really going to change things, Cap'n."

"You bet," Isen said, still reading. He stopped and
looked up when he realized Worden was looking at him.
"How's that?"

"This is the way the Great American Public is going to
see it," Worden said, sitting up with elbows on knees. "It
was bad when the terrorists were attacking GIs and civilians overseas. Then it was worse when American civilians
who were traveling out of the country got killed. But Joe
Six-pack could always say, 'Well, they knew traveling was
dangerous.' Then the bad guys came into the U.S., right

into the sacred backyard.'' Worden shook his head, smiling to himself as if someone had just revealed to him the NDP's whole game plan, and he'd learned his predictions were right. ''Then, just when we thought it couldn't get any worse, those NDP motherfuckers upped the ante one more time. See, at Fort Hood it was mostly military people getting whacked. Now every person who's ever been on a beach feels threatened.''

Isen nodded in agreement. ''They've shaken things up, that's for sure. There have been a couple of big protests already, in Washington and New York. Adrienne wrote and told me how haggard the President looks on TV. People are fed up with us getting pushed around. The public doesn't want to be calm about these escalations, that's for sure.''

''Not only that,'' Worden added, ''but anybody in Congress who isn't brain dead will be pounding the table, yelling that something better be done, 'cause the folks back home in the voting booths are not happy these days.''

Isen folded the paper and put it on the field table nearby. ''I think the country has gotten spoiled—we always want a quick victory, you know? Send in a couple of paratroopers and maybe some tanks, tie a few yellow ribbons, and right away the public thinks the hard part's been done.'' He was becoming angry again, because of everything that had happened, because of the inevitability of what was coming. ''You know what I think is going to happen now?''

''What?''

''All of these agencies, the FBI, CIA, will be under a lot of pressure to do something. Delta Force, at the business end of things, will have to make things happen when they get the call.'' He snapped his fingers. ''Just like that, no time for consideration.''

''Maybe the pressure from the top will shake something loose,'' Worden said.

''Could be,'' Isen said. ''Or it could force them to act prematurely, do something stupid.''

Worden chewed his lip. Just as he was about to speak, the telephone rang. The two men looked at it, then looked at each other.

"If that's Major Spano, you're a friggin psychic, Cap'n," Worden said.

Isen laughed, picked up the phone. "Isen here."

"Mark, this is Ray Spano. We'd like you to come over here and sit in on our meeting."

The connection was bad, so Isen pressed the receiver up to his ear, held a palm to the other ear. As he did so, he smiled at Worden, mouthed *Spano*.

"Sure, I can do that," Isen said into the mouthpiece. "I'll be there as soon as I can."

Spano had set up a temporary headquarters in a rented Tampico storefront. Since Colonel Reeves had no idea where in Mexico they might have to strike, it seemed logical to have a fairly central location. Spano and several communications people manned the cell full-time, while the teams returned to Brownsville, Texas, just north of the border, so as to be as unobtrusive as possible.

Colonel Reeves, who was logging a tremendous amount of air time as he coordinated Delta's efforts, was there when Isen arrived. There were two other Americans in the room—from Delta, Isen assumed, though they could have been from the embassy—and two Mexicans, Federal Judicial Police.

"Well, I didn't think this could get much worse, but I was wrong," Colonel Reeves said by way of introduction. He was clearly running out of patience. "The White House is throwing a fit, so is Congress. We have all sorts of people who think they can come down here and get this thing straightened out in a hurry."

The Mexicans looked angry, Isen thought. Reeves continued.

"But I told them they were wasting their time because we already have an investigative team on site, made up of people who know what the hell's going on around here."

The Mexican investigators were barely mollified. *Good move, Colonel,* Isen thought. As if he didn't have enough to worry about already, Reeves had to stroke the Mexicans as well.

"Here's what we have from Europe." Reeves turned in

his seat and one of the Americans Isen didn't know took over.

"The Germans are using computers to examine wire transfers of funds from German banks to Mexican banks for the last year. There might be something there—these people had to transfer funds somehow. They are also pursuing known members of the NDP. They've also determined that more of these suspected NDP guys have left Europe, but they haven't been tracked here to Mexico. Mexican customs officials are checking records at entry points. One problem is that the NDP seems to have been revamped, from within, and the authority to spend money and give orders centralized. That means there's less of a trail to follow."

He paused, cleared his throat, flipped over a couple of sheets on his legal pad.

"That's probably why we have no ID yet on this guy, the one wanted for questioning in the Florida bombing." He held up a drawing of a man of indeterminate age whose most distinguishing feature was thick, dark hair that swept back in waves from a handsome face. "He could be somebody new to the organization, or even an outsider hired for this job. The Germans have copies of the drawing and are trying to get a make on this guy from the known NDP types."

"We were able to track a man who fit this description," Reeves continued, "from Tampa to Miami and on to Panama, then back to Mexico City. The FBI found out this guy stayed at the Tampa Airport hotel for two nights before the bombing, and he received a package there. Checks of the shipping company's records show that the package was sent from northern Virginia. They're working on that area for clues."

"What about the pattern of the attacks?" one of the Mexicans asked. "What about his . . . what do you call it? His MO?"

"He's been yanking us around quite a bit, making threats anywhere from two to three weeks early to a few hours before."

"And now?" the Mexican asked. His English was almost flawless.

"And now, no call," Reeves interrupted. "Although he did say, in his last message, that the pace of the war would quicken. And we *know* he'll strike again."

One of the Mexicans, older by a few years than his partner, studied his fingers as he spoke. "We will examine the larger pattern of his past actions. That may give us an idea about where he will strike next."

"That would be great, Inspector," Reeves said.

Isen pulled a credit-card-size pocket calendar from his wallet and looked at the date. When he first joined Operation Sentinel, he had marked off the number of weeks he had left in Mexico. Now he looked into the weeks ahead. He had a feeling that there was an answer there.

"Sir," Isen said.

"What is it, Mark?" Reeves asked.

"Maybe we should also be looking ahead. I mean, if we look at his history, that might create a pattern, but we also might get a clue if we look for what *opportunities* there are for him in the near future."

"This one is a detective?" the younger Mexican asked. Even though Isen was in civilian clothes, it was fairly obvious that he was a soldier. Reeves didn't acknowledge the slight.

"No, he's one of our guys from down the street at Operation Sentinel." Then he turned to Isen. "You mean we identify targets of opportunity and try to predict which ones he might hit?" The shift to the single pronoun *he* was subtle, but the sketch of the man in Tampa had at last given the NDP a face.

"Something like that," Isen answered.

"That's worth looking at," Spano said. "But there are an awful lot of targets out there, and no real pattern to the timing of his threats."

"There is a pattern of sorts," Isen ventured.

"What is that?" the older Mexican asked. His partner was looking out the window distractedly.

"Well, of course there's the clear escalation: big body counts, more civilian deaths, more damaging weapons. But there's something else too. He seems to be varying the timing of his attacks with regard to the threats—some before, some after, to keep us off balance psychologically.''

"That almost goes without saying," Spano said.

Isen ignored the comment and pressed on. "But suppose that *is* the pattern—maybe he's looking for the psychological kill.''

Everyone in the room was looking at him.

"Remember how the Tet offensive in '68 rocked everybody back on the home front because of the impact of seeing Vietcong guerrillas inside the U.S. Embassy? That was a psychological offensive. Suppose the NDP is that shrewd? What targets would they pick?''

Isen paused. A few seconds later, the Mexicans looked at him as if to say *Well?*

"I don't have an answer to that last one yet," Isen said. He looked down at the calendar in his hand. *But I know it's here someplace, and I have a feeling it's going to be bad.*

"That is a possibility," the Federale said. "But a theory is only so useful." He turned to Reeves. "You will keep us informed of developments?''

"Certainly, sir," Reeves said.

The Mexicans left after exchanging a few halfhearted handshakes.

"Nothing like trying to work a friendly crowd," Spano said.

"You could cut the tension in here with a knife," Reeves said.

Isen was ignorant of developments in the investigation, but he knew enough about Mexican resentment to know that the Delta Force wasn't getting all the cooperation Reeves wanted. But there was more to it than that.

"I think," Reeves said, standing and stretching his arms above his head, "that our Mexican friends might just need a little shaking up themselves, something to let them know we're serious.''

"How's that, sir?" Spano asked.

"Everybody involved knows how bad this is—there are kids getting killed here—babies. But the sense of urgency just leads to more frantic chasing around and not necessarily to more cooperation or more efficient work. The Mexican problem probably stems from the rivalries between the state police agencies and the Federales." Reeves was staring out the window now, looking at nothing in the distance. "If we just had some way to demonstrate how serious we are."

Isen chanced a glance at Spano, but the operations officer was sitting stone-faced, eyes on the colonel.

"But, until we get an opportunity to move, we pretty much have to wait for the investigation to turn up something else," Reeves said. He was back in the room now, grinning at the four men sitting around the table. "I'm headed back to Brownsville, then to D.C. I'll be running back and forth for a while," he announced.

"Okay, sir," Spano said. "I'll be in touch the whole time."

"Right. Mark, call me if you come up with an answer to that puzzle you proposed," Reeves said.

"I will, sir."

Reeves left the room, and the other two Americans trailed him on his way out.

"What the hell was he talking about there?" Isen demanded of Spano when they were alone.

"What do you mean?" Spano said. He was not looking at Isen.

"What kind of demonstration is he talking about?"

Spano picked up some papers left behind from the meeting and took them over to a metal can in the corner, where he tore them into tiny pieces. He was deliberate, methodical, careful about what he was going to say.

"Look, Mark," Spano said. "Reeves thinks a lot of you. As a matter of fact, you're the first outsider I've ever seen him allow into any of our meetings or briefings." He paused a moment to let that sink in. "But you have to understand that we do things differently."

Apparently there was no elaboration forthcoming, so Isen was forced to draw his own conclusions.

"You don't really think that the answer to everything is

more force, do you?'' He realized he was making a terrific assumption, but he didn't know enough to think otherwise.

"Did it look to you like these Mexicans were interested in helping us out?" Spano said. He stood before Isen, hands on hips.

"Did it ever occur to you that they hate having us down here, telling them what to do? We've been shoving our way of doing things down their throats for years, and it hasn't gotten them a thing. They're sick of Americans.''

Spano had looked as though he was ready for a confrontation, but he suddenly relaxed and sat down heavily in one of the metal folding chairs. "Colonel Reeves is under a lot of pressure to get this thing solved quickly,'' he said. "And that pressure starts at the White House.''

"I know," Isen said. "I just wonder at all we're capable of in the name of expediency.''

The two men sat in silence. Spano thought about the tremendous weapon they had in the Delta Force and the fact that they couldn't bring it to bear. Mark Isen thought about being the Ugly American, and he thought about the dark-haired man, who was probably somewhere under the same Mexican sky, planning his next move. Isen couldn't help believing he'd crossed the dark-haired man's tracks.

## ED RUGGERO

### Opposing Groups Clash Near White House
Associated Press

Washington, D.C., June 22—In a scene reminiscent of the Gulf War, marchers and countermarchers clashed today in Lafayette Park just outside the White House grounds. Police made at least a dozen arrests on both sides as tempers flared in what is surely one of the most frustrating scenarios in modern American politics.

The march began peacefully at about ten-thirty when a group of two hundred, mostly college students and suburban residents from surrounding northern Virginia communities, gathered at the park to protest the ineffective government response to the rash of attacks against American citizens. Some of the marchers carried placards with large pictures of the victims of the bombing, a few days earlier, at Clearwater Beach, Florida, while others carried pictures of passengers who died in the bombing of American 518 out of Mexico City. One marcher, whose sign reflected the confusing welter of competing concerns, proclaimed himself to be "Antinuke, antibombing, and just plain scared."

"What do we have to lose if we pull out of Europe?" asked the march organizer. "The President's intransigence is costing American lives."

Counterprotesters, some carrying signs with pictures of Saddam Hussein and bearing the legend *Just Say No to Terrorism,* joined members of the park's regular lunchtime crowd as they began to heckle the marchers around noon. One counterprotestor was arrested and charged with assault after tearing up a sign and punching several people who tried to intervene. The man, who identified himself as a veteran of the Gulf War, shouted from the back of the police cruiser, "I didn't spend eight months in the desert so these people could cave in to every nut with a gun or a bomb."

White House spokespersons had no comment on the clash, although the President was in the Oval Office at the time, and uniformed White House security personnel have increased the size of their patrols on the grounds of the executive mansion.

# 24

## Tampico, Mexico
### 23 June

WOLF STOOD LEANING AGAINST THE OUTSIDE WALL OF THE cantina, waiting for the public phone beside him to ring. Down below him, just at the foot of the gentle hill, the Gulf spun eastward in shiny metallic stillness, looking every bit as hot as the land under the glowering sun. To his right sat the dirty apparatus of the port, industrial driftwood at the water's edge. But out beyond that, somewhere over the horizon where one could no longer see the land, he knew the water would be beautiful.

He'd let his mind wander to the landscape because he was trying to forget the morning. He had been surprised, as he took breakfast at an outdoor table, to see one of the men he'd sent north, one of the ones he wanted away from him for a time. This one, Erich Jager, a heavyset fortyish man with a childlike face and, Wolf believed, a child's understanding of the world, fancied himself a trusted subordinate, Wolf's lieutenant. Wolf had entrusted him with the money to establish a base up north only because he believed Jager didn't have the imagination to steal the money and flee the country.

Jager had sat down without being invited.

"We are bored up there," he announced.

Wolf simply looked up at him. "We are not running operations with the goal of keeping you happy."

"But you cannot expect us to sit around forever," Jager said.

As much as he hated to, Wolf choked back the urge to curse this man. There was nothing to be gained from losing Jager or those other men.

"Of course not. And I will brief you shortly on your first missions," Wolf lied.

"You said that before," Jager replied.

*This one is smarter than I gave him credit for,* Wolf thought.

"We want to strike against the Americans here in Tampico."

Wolf nearly choked on his coffee. By the time he regained control, he could feel that his face was red and puffy with anger.

"First of all, you cannot strike the Americans ahead of schedule; that would only alert them to our presence. Second, if we act here we will have no place to hide out."

"That's what our base is for," Jager whined.

Wolf had ignored the comment. He knew what it would take to get Jager off his back and out of Tampico, but he was loath to trust the man with anything important, and he didn't care how bored they were, as long as they were ready when he needed them. Still, he could easily get rid of him. He leaned forward and lowered his voice. "Besides, this will all be over in two weeks."

Jager's eyes lit up; he was thrilled to be privy to the information. "We are going to make them howl, yes?"

"Yes," Wolf had said. "A final battle."

After that revelation it had taken Wolf only a few minutes to get rid of the suddenly eager Jager. As he watched the fat man's wide figure retreat Wolf had wished he could do it all himself.

Now, warmed by the sun, waiting for the phone to ring, he thought again of the American girl, the one trapped here in Tampico. They were pleasant thoughts, and they stirred him now as they did on the flights back to Mexico City, except that here, in the hot stillness, his mental picture of the firm-fleshed young girl was even more alluring. He chuckled to himself, laughing at how quickly he forgot that she was just a teenager—there was little for them to talk about, after all, and that had annoyed him quite a bit those first two days. But talking was not what she did best.

The ringing of the public phone interrupted his reverie.

"Yes," he answered.

"Congratulations," a voice on the other end said. "You have been very lucky and have enjoyed another remarkable success."

Wolf was about to say that it was due to his planning and execution, not to luck, but instead he found himself wondering why this was a new voice on the phone. None of his contacts even had code names, and he was never sure from one time to the next, if the numbers he called were in the same location. *As long as they send the money,* Wolf thought.

"It is unfortunate that they have a description," the voice said.

Wolf was sure he'd heard something else. "What?"

"There are drawings of a suspect being circulated through American newspapers. It is an unfortunate but not insurmountable problem."

But Wolf heard nothing. His mind was racing over the hours he'd spent in Florida, in Panama. He recounted all the aliases, all the hotel registration forms and airline tickets. There was the incident with the car rental workers, but he thought them too incompetent to report him. Then it came to him: the girl on the beach.

He had gotten sloppy and, in a moment of exhilaration, had made the mistake of fondling her. He should never have flirted with her in the first place. She had probably become angry—American women, even the flirtatious ones, were very sensitive about these things. And, of course the police would have questioned everyone around the explosion. *I should have left her to watch the cooler and tape player.*

"Are you still there?" the voice asked.

"What? Yes, I am still here," Wolf was muttering now. For a moment, he expected a tongue-lashing.

"It is nothing compared to the success. They have no information other than the drawing. And you can certainly change your looks."

Wolf brought his hand up to his temple, to the wave of thick hair. He was quite vain about it, but obviously it would have to go. "Yes," he said. His head spun. He was trying to stay one or two moves ahead of the people on the other end of the line and, at the same time, assess the damage that he might have done by being identified. There was no telling if the authorities had his name, if they'd traced his flights . . . the voice was still droning.

". . . and although you've done well on your own to this point, we feel that this step is necessary."

"What?" Wolf said into the receiver. He wanted to hang up, to call back the next day and start all over again at the point in the story where no one knew his face.

"I said that we think you need some help on this next project," the voice said.

"I have my own help," Wolf answered. He had ten men in Mexico and the U.S. now, spread out along the network, all doing his bidding.

"We want you to accept more," the voice said. There was no attempt at persuasion, it was a statement. "You will call again on the day after tomorrow from Mexico City. At that time we will let you know the location and the time. Your contact will bring the required capital."

There was a pause, and Wolf strained to hear breathing on the other end, some confirmation that there was a human being there. But the line was dead quiet.

"Do you understand?" the voice asked, startling Wolf.

"Yes. I am to call in two days time from Mexico City. Is that where the meeting will be?"

"Yes," the voice said.

"I understand."

As soon as he was off the phone, Wolf hurried to the airport, where he was able to buy three American newspapers. Two of them did have an artist's drawing that was unmistakably he. The forehead was too wide and the chin a little more pointed than the real thing, but the drawing captured his eyes. Perfectly. He felt as if someone had just pointed to him on the street and shouted, "There is the murderer!"

The story of the bombing dominated all three editions. The authorities had correctly identified the nerve agent he'd used, as well as the explosive. One paper had small photos of some of the victims, and he recognized a photo, several years old, of the woman he'd asked to watch his tape player, the young mother who'd winked at him.

Wolf went back to the car he'd had one of his men buy, stuffed the papers under the driver's seat, and sat down. He pulled on sunglasses and studied his face in the mirror. The scalp would be very pale. If he tried to tan too quickly he would get a sunburn, and that would be as noticeable as the white skin. Even with the drastic change in his hair, it would not be safe to go back to the United States. He had come back to Mexico for what he hoped would be the last time, only to check on Diablo and the shipment of the remaining chemical weapons. Now he was trapped. Here.

He slapped his hand on the hot steering wheel. One sloppy day—among all that he'd spent pursuing his goals— one error, and they'd closed in by that much.

It occurred to him that they might even have had the description while he was still traveling. They might have checked the manifests for . . . his name. *They would have found out his alias because he'd abandoned the car at the airport.*

There was a rumbling of nausea deep within his stomach, all the way down to the top of his groin. Wolf felt control slipping away from him, little pieces at first. The pace of events was suddenly outdistancing his plan; he could not act quickly enough to stay on top of things.

Wolf bought a cap and some rough shears in a small general store. In the public rest room of a bus station, he used the shears to cut off his hair. Once he got close to the scalp, he lathered his head with soap and began scraping away at the remaining hair with a razor. His scalp was very sensitive, and Wolf cursed his carelessness in Tampa.

He was finished in thirty minutes, and the activity actually calmed him. He washed the hair from the sink and kicked at that which had fallen to the floor, spreading it out among the considerable grime there. He shook out his shirt, then put on the cap and checked himself in the mirror.

"I wonder if the Soviets will recognize me," he said to himself. He smiled at his reflection, but the grin had lost something.

Two days later Wolf flew to Mexico City and made the call as he'd been instructed. The contact—yet another voice—told him to be at the northeast corner of Alameda Park at one o'clock. There he was to sit on the first available bench facing Avenida Hidalgo, the street running along the north side.

Wolf parked his rented car and walked around the area, looking for other people who might be European. There were plenty of people around: couples kissing on the benches, groups taking photos of the statues of saints and the tiny fountains scattered around the park. He had been worried that the park would be empty; now he was nervous because there were so many people that he didn't think he would be able to spot the Soviets before they saw him.

When the last bench opened up, he sat down, but then an older Mexican couple sat down next to him. Wolf glowered at them, but they did not move. He got up, exasperated, considered offering them money to move. He paced along the curb by the street and checked his watch continuously. He bought some refried beans from a vendor who was cooking on top of a metal sheet suspended over a fifty-gallon drum, but when he sat down his stomach turned on him.

*This is ridiculous,* he thought. *They are courting my favor; I have given them more success than they even imagined was possible.*

But the litany did little good, and as the seconds on his watch ticked toward one, Wolf felt ill.

He saw the Soviet with the case first.

The man who was apparently the contact carried a briefcase that looked to be about thirty years old. He was no more than five and a half feet tall and at least forty pounds overweight. Wolf felt better just looking at the man, who did not appear to be much of a threat. *They sent an accountant to deliver the money,* he thought.

"I trust your trip was uneventful," the man said in crude German as he sat with Wolf.

Wolf, still paranoid, wondered if the man was fishing for information. *Surely they could trace the calls if they wanted,* he thought. Then, *Perhaps not without the help of the Mexicans.*

"I came only from Toluca," Wolf said, naming a city just west of Mexico City.

"And you have changed your hair," the Soviet said.

*This is one of the voices on the phone.* "Yes," Wolf said. "I believe you have something for me?"

"Yes," the Soviet replied. "I have instructions for you."

*Arrogant bastard,* Wolf thought. He looked at the man beside him, and the Soviet grinned at him. His teeth were very bad, his breath worse.

"But we cannot conduct business here," the Soviet said. "It is too hot, and we have too much to talk about. I know a place on Tacuba, right near here, where we can go."

As he spoke he looked around, but it was not casual—he was looking for *something.*

*He wants to make sure I've come alone,* Wolf thought.

"This is a public place?"

The Soviet looked at him curiously. "Herr Wolf, your operation has done very well. You have nothing to fear from us. We believe you are on the verge of success."

Wolf stood and began to walk beside the fat man along Avenida Hidalgo, which became Tacuba a little way east of the park. Intrigued, pleased, Wolf pressed the point.

"What makes you say that?" he asked, trying to mask the eagerness in his voice. He watched the Soviet instead of watching the street.

"Our sources indicate that their president's health is failing. He will soon be hospitalized for bleeding ulcers." The Soviet belched unexpectedly, making no effort to cover his mouth. Wolf gave him more room.

"If the Vice-President takes over, we will have won a

great propaganda victory. What is more, the President's opponents in Congress are gathering momentum. They have only yesterday called for a debate in the Senate—or House, I cannot keep them straight—about whether or not they should pull more troops and ships out of Europe.''

"That is excellent,'' Wolf said, suddenly buoyant. The worries of a few minutes earlier seemed embarrassing now. "Excellent, indeed.''

In spite of the setbacks, in spite of the fact that they had drawings of him and had captured some of his material and men, everything was still moving forward. All of those things were minor disturbances; his grand plan, so carefully drawn, still inched forward toward his goal.

*I will bring down their pride,* Wolf thought.

The little fat man walked slowly, wheezing in the heat and the thickly polluted Mexico City air. Wolf felt like running.

"Yes, you have shaken their complacency,'' the Soviet said.

Just then an attractive young Mexican woman walking in the other direction dropped a package near Wolf. The German, always conscious of feminine beauty, was about to bend over and try to capture the fruit rolling on the sidewalk for her. For some reason he would never understand, Wolf looked at the Soviet before he stooped, and he caught the man nodding. He looked up to see two light-skinned men in cheap Soviet clothing coming toward them, about fifty feet away.

Wolf quickly turned to the fat man, who was already trying to get away. He shoved the Soviet forward, sending him sprawling on the hot pavement. Wolf tried to leap over him, but the man began to stand, and so Wolf became entangled, falling down on top of the scrambling Soviet, tearing the skin from his knees and the palm of one hand. The small automatic Wolf had tucked under his shirt clattered away from him in the fall. Wolf kicked at the man's face as he climbed to a crouch and grabbed the handle of the briefcase the Soviet contact had been carrying.

The two men were running now, pumping their arms, big automatic pistols moving up and down, up and down in their hands. Wolf ran for the car, knowing that if they chased him, they would get there before he could drive away. He chanced a look over his shoulder as he ran. Incredibly, one of the two men had stopped to help the fat one. Wolf ran another ten yards, letting the one still after him gain, worrying that the Soviet would shoot him in the back rather than try to tackle him. When he heard the footsteps near him, he spun around, swinging the briefcase full force and catching his pursuer on the side of the head with the sharp edge of the case.

The man collapsed even as he continued moving forward, so that he splattered to a stop at Wolf's feet. For a second or two, Wolf was transfixed: the case had sprung and showered blank white paper over the sidewalk.

*There is no money.*

Wolf did not bother to look for the other man chasing him. He made it to the car and was in it with the motor running before he had another thought. *They were setting me up to kill me.*

A mile from the park he had to stop and vomit out the open door. For a few moments while he was sick, Wolf wanted to give it all up. He was being pursued from all sides now, and he wasn't sure if he had enough funds to continue. He had less than trustworthy help in Mexico, slightly more reliable people in the United States.

But he forced the fear into some crammed-full corner of his brain. *No, they want me to give up,* he thought. *But they will still pursue me. There is nothing to do but go on.*

He took small comfort in the rationalization, and if he had been able to look at himself from a distance, he would have been hard-pressed to say that he was running to— rather than from—his own plan.

Rather than risk being seen in the airport, Wolf stole the rental car and drove back to Tampico. He came up on the city in the late afternoon and rolled north off the hill, toward the port and Karen's tiny room. He was in a daze, having driven the two hundred miles over rough roads without stopping for water or food. When he found the building again, he drove past it and abandoned the car with the keys in the ignition, knowing it would be gone within the hour. He took out his small bag and the newspapers, and carried the bundle under his arm as he walked back along the street. He approached the door without the slightest notion of what he might say to Diablo if the Mexican had returned.

No one was home.

Wolf broke a small pane of glass in the window next to the door and cut himself when he thrust his arm in to unlock the door. Once inside, he drank two warm beers in quick succession to steady himself. In an hour, he had calmed down enough to go on and do something. He washed in the grimy sink, then traded his sweaty shirt for a relatively clean one he found on a chair. He sat down on the bed—its squeak familiar to him—and began reading the papers.

As he read he grew confident that the police didn't have anything more than the drawing and perhaps a description of his accent. Not that they'd release a lot of details to the press. Calmer now, he noticed that he was hungry. He lowered the paper and looked around the dirty room. He doubted that he'd find anything there safe to eat, so he continued to read.

There was an article about the restructuring of the American military presence in Europe. Wolf read with interest, looking between the lines for some indication that they were getting ready to concede something to his campaign. He knew that a sector of the American public was already calling for further reductions in NATO, not a capitulation to his demands, per se, but close enough. But there was nothing in this article, which included remarks from a typically arrogant American general in Europe.

*They need to be humbled,* Wolf thought. He had always found American smugness loathsome, but since their stunning success in the desert, they had become even more insufferable. And even though their defeat was close and readily imaginable, he couldn't bear to read any further, though he scanned the rest of the column.

Then something caught his attention.

The American general mentioned something about a change in Soviet budgetary policy—an increase in spending over levels of the last few years. Although the amount the

Soviets were spending on their military was minuscule compared to what it had been at the height of the Cold War, the American officer thought it significant that they had reversed the downward trend.

"We believe that the Soviet military, the army in particular, has won some battle in its struggle to regain prominence in the Soviet Union. If this is the case," the general was quoted as saying, "we must be even more vigilant."

Wolf lowered the paper and thought about the sudden change in plans—the one that had required him to meet with a Soviet and had almost cost him his life.

*They were using me to pressure the U.S. and its allies while they sought a bigger military budget,* Wolf thought. *I was a mere backup plan. Now that the military has regained some status, they are no doubt anxious that their involvement in this business be hidden.*

He scanned the article again, looking for some other clue as to what the Soviets were doing, something that might disprove his theory. But there was nothing. The Soviets did not need him anymore, and they were anxious that their sponsoring terrorism should remain secret. That's why they tried to kill him.

Now he would have to go ahead without them. There would be no money to pay the Mexican, Diablo, but Wolf could get around that. He would not be able to use the passports the Soviets had given him. It was unlikely that they would give the names to the Mexicans or Americans—that would be far too suspicious; but they could watch the airports. They might even be more aggressive, come looking for him.

He could still succeed. The American president was under fire from all sides, his health was failing him, and Wolf was about to land the final blow. But when he thought about the park, Wolf was chilled by the thought of how close he had come to dying. It was pure luck that he had escaped, but he resisted the idea, trying to surface from his subconscious, that his luck might run out someday. Wolf sat back amid the rumpled and sweat-smelling sheets, the small room growing closer.

\* \* \*

The American girl showed up first; Wolf went outside to meet her when he heard her approach. She studied his new, clean-shaven head for a few moments before deciding it was he.

"What are you doing here? And what the hell did you do to your head?" she asked. She was obviously frightened, but just as obviously glad to see him. She looked quickly around to see if anyone was watching, then came up to him and squeezed his hand. "Let's go upstairs."

"I've already been up there," Wolf said, smiling woodenly. "I broke the window, and I didn't want you to get scared when you saw the glass—or the shiny head."

"Have you seen him around?" she asked, jogging up the outdoor stairway.

"Diablo?"

"Yes. He was supposed to be back a few days ago. He's late." She opened the door and went in; glass crunched underfoot.

"No, I haven't. Don't worry about him," Wolf said, putting his arms out for her. He had forgotten that she was freshly beautiful in spite of the hard months she'd spent in Mexico. She was wearing a loose-fitting man's shirt, unbuttoned almost halfway, and there was a light sheen of perspiration on her throat. Having her near calmed him—not because he felt safe or even comfortable with her, but because he knew more than she did about what was going on and what was going to happen. With Karen Charles he had some control, and that helped him back into character.

She pushed him away. "Don't tell me not to worry," she said, suddenly angry. "Not unless you're going to take me away from here."

"I told you that I would take care of you," Wolf said, his voice barely even.

"Yeah, then you left me. What if he'd come back then and found out you'd been here?" She had been carrying a mesh bag of groceries; when she put the bag on the table, cans and fruit rolled out. She kicked at them as they hit the floor.

"I want to get out of here today, *now*," she said, her voice sharp. But when she turned again to look at him, there was something there that quieted her. With his butchered hair and scowl he was a far cry from the handsome European she'd singled out in the cantina and seduced the first time she was alone with him. She wasn't quite sure what signal he was sending, but it was unsteady, and so she took the only course open to the weak, she gave in.

"I'm sorry I lost my temper," she said, wiping at her eyes with the back of one hand. "I've just been very afraid here, that's all."

Wolf moved closer and pushed her hair back off of her face, pulling the ends a bit, just enough to make her tilt her head back. There was violence just below the blue pools that were his eyes.

"Take this off," he said, pulling at the collar of her shirt.

She obliged, pulling the shirt from her shorts and unbuttoning it. Wolf watched while she did what he bade, and the feeling of lost control suddenly seemed far away.

Afterward, Wolf watched, half asleep, as she moved languidly about the room. It registered in his mind gone suddenly limp that she was naked, and that pleased him, for she had a wonderful body. Slowly it came to him, as if from a distance, that she was looking at one of the newspapers. He sat up then, but it was clear from her face that she had seen the pictures.

Wolf moved slowly, smiling at her as he approached. "That was wonderful," he said as he slipped around behind her and massaged her tense shoulders. "Better than I remembered, even."

She was a big girl, and she began fighting him as soon as she felt his fingers tense around her throat, his long fingers searching to crush her windpipe. But he was angry at the men who tried to kill him, and he took that out on her. The months of being beaten down in this hot and unfriendly place had sapped much of her strength and her spirit, and her pitiful blows fell only on his shoulders and arms.

Alone again in Diablo's apartment, Wolf had a chance to think about the necessary alterations to his plan. Two things drove the need for change. First, Wolf couldn't return to the United States. No doubt the drawing that had been in the papers was posted in every airport and in every police station in the United States. Second, he needed to assert his control over the events that were about to unfold. He did not want to leave anything to chance. The last week had rattled him, and he wanted to do something that would allow him to grab the reins again.

There were two men in the United States waiting to receive the package Diablo had sent, which contained the chemical agent, the only other material they needed. They were supposed to wait for Wolf to come and supervise the next mission, but that was now out of the question. He would send Becht, with instructions, in his place. But he had no intention of relinquishing control, especially when he was in Mexico and the important work was being done in the United States. Neither the two men already in the United States, nor the third man he would send, had to know the final target until Wolf chose to tell them. He would dispatch them, then contact them, at a prearranged time and place, with their final instructions just hours before the attack was to take place. The rest of the group, frustrated as they were, would continue to lie low in Mexico.

Although the plan did not allow much room for adjustment—the three men would not know what to do if Wolf failed to get in contact with them—it did allow him to maintain control. And they could always use the resources, safely stashed in the United States, to fight another day.

If the attack was successful, especially if the American president relented, he would return to Europe and take advantage of his celebrity to pull together the political activists still adrift there. With that kind of manpower, he could raise more money by selling protection to smugglers and drug traffickers. The close calls of the last weeks had convinced him that he could not pursue political objectives indefinitely; the law of averages would catch up at some point and he could wind up dead. But he could imagine himself in South America or the South Pacific, resting on a nice stash of money.

Wolf and his dreams sat on the floor by the door. The lowering dusk soon blocked his view of the dirty room and the dead American girl.

As it turned out, Wolf had to wait only a few hours for Diablo. By that time it was after dark, and when Wolf heard footsteps on the stairs, he stood to one side of the door. The young Mexican was apparently motivated by some of the same urges that had brought Wolf back here, because he did not bother to check the door before he came in.

Wolf put the pistol against the man's head as soon as he was inside.

"Do not move," Wolf said. He pressed the cold muzzle up to the base of the Mexican's skull for emphasis. "Are you alone?"

"Yes," Diablo said. "How did you find this place?"

"It is my business to know," Wolf said. The room was still dark, and Wolf could feel the Mexican wanting to turn around. "Did the last shipment go well?"

There was a second's hesitation, as if Diablo was debating whether he should admit that his usefulness had ended. Wolf pushed the pistol forward, curious to see if the Mexican would own up to his failure.

"Yes. Everything has gone well," he lied. "I saw to the last shipment myself yesterday in Laredo, Texas. Your package should arrive today or tomorrow." In fact, Diablo knew that one of three shipments had been intercepted, but he didn't think this was the time to bring it up.

"I will call," Wolf said, "and check." The promise to do something in the future implied that there would be a future and had the effect he wanted. The Mexican seemed to relax a bit.

Then Wolf turned on the overhead light. The girl was still in the chair, bent over its back, hair trailing almost to the floor. Her throat was bruised purple, her nakedness ghastly in the yellow light from the single bulb. Diablo let out a little gasp—very unprofessional, Wolf thought—before he turned around.

"Why?" he asked.

"She knew too much," Wolf answered. "But I'll say this for her, she was a good fuck."

He waited a second or two, just until he could see the hatred well up, before he pulled the trigger.

Wolf wrapped the woman's body in the bedspread, then put a plastic bag over the man's bloody head and shoulders. He planned on staying in the apartment until he could work out the details of his adjusted plan, and he would have to get the bodies out first. He hefted the woman on one shoulder, turned out the light, and peered through the window. There was nothing moving on the street below.

He let himself out and walked carefully down the stairs. *I will have to be especially careful with the other body,* Wolf thought. *It will be heavier.*

He was on the bottom step when he heard a voice nearby.

"Diablo?"

Wolf was startled, and he hesitated for a deadly second, long enough, apparently, for whoever was out there to decide that the dark figure on the stairs wasn't Diablo.

The muzzle flashes, incredibly bright in the darkness, all but blinded Wolf. He felt the slugs thumping into the body on his shoulder, and he went down to his knees, still holding the corpse. There was a car a few meters away, and he slipped from under the bloody package and skidded off to its shelter. His pulse thundered in his ears, and his legs melted with fear. Incredibly, someone stood behind another car parked nearby and walked toward where Wolf had dumped the girl's body. Apparently the ambusher thought the corpse was Wolf.

Wolf crawled to the front end of the car to get the angle on the shooter, but before Wolf could fire, whoever it was realized that the target had gotten away. The big figure headed right for the car Wolf was crouched behind. Wolf almost didn't get his pistol up fast enough. The shooter was only three feet away when Wolf fired, and the light from his pistol lit up the big target. The man went down heavily with the first shot, but Wolf kept firing, pumping rounds into the body, working out his fear.

He stopped shooting when he heard a low groaning, which he found was coming from inside him. He was more frightened than he would have thought possible, but the fear did not turn to a focused anger. He was rabid with panic, and he kicked at the body after emptying his weapon.

Wolf sat on the ground. The dead man was Diablo's bodyguard, the one he'd brought with him at that first meeting. The Mexican had lied when he said he was alone.

*He lied, and this one almost killed me.* Wolf writhed in frustration and kicked at the body from his sitting position, pumping his legs in anger and hatred and fear. He had been in personal danger twice in thirty-six hours, and it nearly pushed him over the edge.

Tampico had suddenly become dangerous, and though Wolf was sure that it was merely another unfortunate coincidence that the bodyguard had been outside, it gave the lie to the feeling of invincibility he'd brought with him to Mexico. He had felt, until the incident with the Soviets in Mexico City, that he had all but reached the end of his plan.

*Perhaps I should move now to one of the outlying areas where I can be surrounded by my men.*

The first curious onlooker emerged from an adjacent apartment minutes after the last shots were fired. Wolf tucked his head down in his shoulders and shuffled quickly away, feeling much smaller than he had when he returned to Mexico.

**Police Department**
City of Tampico
Tamaulipas State

June 26

From: The Office of the Chief
To: The Office of the Mayor
Memorandum: Illegal activities of American Personnel

We have confirmed our initial report that at least one and possibly two Americans were involved in an assault against TOMASINO FUENTES on 14 June.

Although Fuentes is reluctant to cooperate with our investigation, I believe that we can prevail upon him by offering him immunity from prosecution on an outstanding complaint against him: specifically, a charge of sexual assault by the mother of a fourteen-year-old girl supposedly raped by Fuentes.

Fuentes is a Mexican citizen. In spite of his questionable activities, his testimony may prove useful in sending a signal to the Americans that we do not want them here and will not tolerate their unlawful behavior. I recommend we pursue this course of action aggressively.

J.A.X. Moruza
Chief of Police

# 25

## Tampico, Mexico
### 28 June

MARK ISEN WAS SITTING OUTSIDE THE COMMUNICATIONS center of Delta's forward headquarters when one of the Operation Sentinel people came in.

"Hey, Captain Isen," the soldier said. His name was Meyers or Meier, Isen couldn't remember which, and like the rest of the people manning the fort over there, he was wearing civilian clothes—and thus no name tags.

"Howdy," Isen said. "What brings you over here?"

"That guy you work with, Major Spano, isn't he from Fort Bragg?" Meier or Meyers asked. He was agitated, and his eyes swept back and forth across the small room.

"Mm-hmm."

"We got a call a little while ago that there was a bombing there, maybe a school. I came over to tell him . . . he got kids?"

"Yeah," Isen said, sitting bolt upright. "That's all you know?"

"Yessir. And that's not official. One of our guys was on the phone to somebody back in the States and heard this. We didn't have time to check it out yet."

"Thanks," Isen said as he hurried from the room. He

found Spano making himself a cup of coffee in a little space fitted out for a break area.

"Hey, Mark, what's up?"

Isen suddenly wished he had checked out the validity of the rumor. He was about to drop a bomb on Spano, and he didn't even know if what he was saying was true.

"Ray, I just heard from one of the Sentinel guys that there's an unconfirmed report of a bombing at Fort Bragg."

"At Bragg?"

"Maybe at a school," Isen said.

Spano reached out to put his coffee cup on the table and missed completely; the cup crashed to the floor. "Oh, God." He squeezed past Isen and made for the commo shop, his long legs eating the distance in a hurry.

"You know anything about a bombing at Bragg?" he demanded of the on-duty operator.

"No, sir," the soldier said. "I can have you through in a minute, though."

Isen caught up then, only to watch helplessly as Spano agonized. He knew that the Spanos had two children, one of whom, a little boy, was in third grade at the post school.

The operator punched a series of codes into a rather ordinary looking telephone that was connected to a satellite dish on the roof of the building. Sometimes the satellite link went down in between the quarter-hour checks. This was one of those times—no connection on the first try.

"Oh, shit—has it already been down today?" Spano asked. "Maybe they've been trying to reach us."

"No, we made all our checks on time," the commo man said. It must have been clear to him that Spano was in pain, but to his credit, Isen thought, he realized the best thing to do was to remain calm and do his job. He tried again to raise Delta Communications at Bragg.

Nothing.

Spano walked from one side of the room to the other. He pulled on each long finger with the other hand and blinked rapidly, fighting for control. "Did the guy from Sentinel know anything else?"

Isen shook his head, wishing there were something he could say. "No."

"I'm getting through, sir," the operator said. In a calm voice that made Isen think of pilots and air-traffic controllers, the operator asked for information concerning an incident at the post school. Isen thought to correct him—the message had been about a bombing—and was about to speak when the answer came back over the loudspeaker.

"Yes, we have some sort of information on that. Wait."

Spano slumped into a chair. "Oh, Jesus," he said, pressing his fists up to his eyes. "Oh, Jesus, don't let it be true, Jesus, please."

Isen, oddly embarrassed at so much emotion, stared at the back of the operator's head.

"Ask them about a bombing," Isen said.

The operator relayed the question and got another "Wait."

There was a government-issue clock above the operator's console, and Isen watched the second hand spin around while Spano murmured behind him. It went around five times before they had a response, so that when it came over the speaker, it startled them all.

"Yes, something did happen over at the school today. The duty officer wants to get the full report before we release any information. He's working on that now."

"What the hell does that mean?" Spano asked, his voice rising for the first time.

"They have to be accurate," Isen said, trying to sound comforting. "It would be terrible to give out bad information, especially if there are . . ." He almost said "casualties"; he caught himself, but it didn't matter. Spano looked at him and knew what he meant.

"Let's step outside and let this guy do his job," Isen said, trying to take Spano by the arm. "We'll be right out here when the word comes in. Don't let them forget to give us a prompt answer," Isen said to the operator, as much for Spano's benefit as for the commo specialist's.

They were out there for five minutes before Spano spoke.

"If they did something to my kid, I won't rest until all of those bastards are dead," Spano said. "And I don't give a fuck about the rules."

He took out wallet photos of his children, showed them

to Isen, who was at a complete loss for what to say or do. The little boy was a smaller version of Spano: same hair, same eyes and grin.

The two men paced together and separately, and Isen could feel his partner pass from anger to fear as the minutes ticked by. Spano was carrying the little photos in his big hand, and as he looked at them he seemed to unravel a bit. The change was gradual—but it was steady, like a glass vessel filling with dirty water.

Isen kept thinking about an incident some years back when strong winds knocked down a cafeteria wall in a New York grammar school, sending tons of brick and steel falling onto the tiny bodies of first, second, and third graders. Though he had no children of his own, the sheer faith-shaking injustice of that incident had rattled him so much that he thought he could imagine what Spano was going through now. The more he thought about it, the more frightened and angry he became. Beside him, Spano was struggling.

"You know, I left home last time without really being able to say good-bye to them," he said. "They only know me as the guy who comes breezing in and then leaves without telling them why." As he walked his foot caught the leg of a metal chair. He tried to pull away, but the chair moved with him. He grabbed the back with both hands, slamming it to the floor again and again until the legs bent. When he put it down, he thrust his hands into his pockets.

"My daughter is only four. If something happened to her brother, she wouldn't even remember him when she got older." He put the pictures in his pocket. "If something happened to me, they'd both forget me by the time they were eighteen."

"No, they wouldn't," Isen said.

"My little girl would." He turned to Isen. "You remember things from when you were four?" When Isen didn't answer, Spano said to no one in particular, "This is some kind of life we have."

The two men continued to pace for the rest of the thirty-five minutes it took Fort Bragg to come back on the air.

They heard the static of transmission inside the adjacent room. Isen's impulse was to go in, and he took a step, but Spano remained fixed to the spot. He was afraid to hear the news.

In a few moments the commo specialist came out to them. "There was a bus accident this morning," he said. "No fatalities, a couple of kids injured, none seriously."

"No bombs?" Spano asked, his voice shaking.

"No bombs. It was just a minor traffic accident."

"Thank you," Spano told the commo man. "Thanks very much."

"No sweat, sir. I'll get a phone link to your house so you can check in with your wife."

"That would be great, thanks," Spano said.

In another minute they were alone. Isen couldn't tell whether Spano wanted him to stay or not.

"They're winning," Spano said at last.

"What's that?" Isen asked.

"The terrorists. The fucking NDP. They're winning. They got us scared to go out at night, for Christ's sake." He looked over at Isen, and Isen noticed the big face had been softened by the emotional roller coaster he'd been riding over the last hour. "They got us so we see a bogeyman behind every tree."

"Nothing happened," Isen said.

"But it was possible, and I believed it." Spano was staring somewhere off in the distance. "They proved in Florida that they can get anyone they want. We're all vulnerable."

Isen had nothing to say. He felt as if the truth of what Spano said vindicated the work they were doing with Delta. There had to be someone capable of stopping these people. But they'd been working hard on this case, so were the Mexicans, so were the FBI and the State Department and the Germans, and so far no one had been able to stop this little group of determined men.

"We've felt safe for so long that we don't know how to deal with being afraid," Spano said.

Mark Isen and Ray Spano sat in adjacent metal folding

chairs, elbows on knees, identical portraits of sad concern. Nothing, after all, had happened at Fort Bragg, but the possibilities had frightened them into the realization that in this war, as in no war since the middle of the nineteenth century, American civilians at home were more vulnerable than their soldiers in the so-called combat zone.

# THE COMMON DEFENSE

## Arab-American Beaten in Wake of Recent Terrorist Scare

by M. Howze
*The Raleigh News and Observer*

Fayetteville, June 29—An Arab-American taxicab driver, a resident of this country for sixteen years, was severely beaten by a crowd in Fayetteville yesterday in the wake of a false report that a terrorist's bombs had caused an accident on a school bus. Police report that a crowd of six or seven men, diners at a local restaurant, set upon the driver after hearing an unconfirmed report that terrorists had struck a school bus on nearby Fort Bragg. One of the men who is under arrest said, "We lashed out at the nearest foreigner we could lay our hands on." Police have arrested four other men and are pursuing additional suspects.

Police Chief Buck Henry said that the case highlights the incredible tension the community feels as more and more Americans become victims of terrorist attacks. He made his remarks at a news conference hours after the incident. "The fact that the victim was from a completely different ethnic group than the suspected members of the NDP, the fact that there was no bombing on Fort Bragg or anywhere else, the fact that these normally law-abiding citizens struck out violently at a completely innocent man, all point to the frustration the nation feels as we face mounting attacks by foreign subversives."

An ACLU spokesman in Raleigh announced an investigation by that organization, while the National Congress of Arab-American Businessmen said that the incident was just the latest example of how Arabs are persecuted for the crimes of others.

In Washington, Senator Matthew Stone, a vocal critic of administration antiterrorism policies, said that America is becoming desperate. "We live in fear for our lives and the lives of our children, while the White House simply repeats its obviously outdated and ineffective position, like a chant prescribed by some witch doctor."

# 26

## Tampico, Mexico
### *Wednesday, 30 June*
### *0620*

MARK ISEN LISTENED TO THE SOUND OF COFFEE BREWING
and reminded himself that it was important to be thankful
for the little things. The accommodations at the temporary
headquarters Spano had established in Tampico weren't luxurious, but Isen was able to shower every day, and it had
been weeks since he'd spent a night on the ground. Spano's
latest addition to the creature comforts of his four-man staff
was a coffee maker, delivered by one of the couriers from
Fort Bragg.

Still, the work could be boring. Spano had left the previous evening to talk with the Mexico City Police about coor-
dinating more transportation assets for the Americans. On
his way out he had complained that he was spending more
of his time trying to keep things moving rather than actually
pursuing the investigation. Isen still thought that the way
his fellow Americans approached the Mexicans was the
cause of those problems. Spano wasn't as bad as some, but
Isen had met a few in Operation Sentinel and in the Delta
Force whose unspoken message to the Mexicans was:
*We're here to straighten out the mess you've made of
things.*

Isen poured his coffee but hadn't even taken the first sip

when someone began pounding at the door. He walked past the commo room, where the on-duty operator was making his quarter-hour commo check with Bragg, to the door of the little storefront they'd rented.

"I'm coming, I'm coming," Isen said over the banging.

There were three Tampico police officers standing outside. When Isen opened the door, the one closest to him—a wormy-looking young man in an ill-fitting uniform—pushed past and entered the building.

"What are you doing?" Isen said. He thought to grab the officer by the arm to keep him from seeing inside the commo room, but in a second he realized that these men probably wouldn't even know they were looking at classified equipment and wouldn't know what to tell anyone about what they'd seen.

"You are Isen?" another officer said.

Isen turned. This one appeared to be a supervisor—there were red tabs on the points of his collar. "Yes, I'm Captain Isen. Would you mind telling me what your man is doing entering here? We have an agreement with your chief of police as well as with the Federal Judicial Police . . ."

He was still talking when the officer whipped out a piece of paper and began reading in Spanish. He paused after looking at Isen, who obviously wasn't following, then went back to the beginning and translated.

"Your agreements are void because members of the U.S. contingent here have engaged in illegal activities, specifically, kidnapping and assault."

Down the hall behind him, Isen could hear the off-duty commo operators telling the police officer who'd entered, "Get the hell out of here, Mac. You ain't supposed to be in here, this is a restricted area."

*There we go again, making friends,* Isen thought. "I have no idea what you're talking about," Isen told the red tabs.

"You are to come with me to the police headquarters."

Isen assumed that they wanted him because he was the only officer in the place at the time, and he thought that this might be a time to show some of the bluster that Mexicans admired on occasion. "You can't yank me out of here," he said. "I'm protected under a status of forces agreement between our governments." But even as he acted Isen was already worried about his past sins coming back to haunt him. There wasn't a day that went by that he didn't think, *It all might end today.* All it would take is a letter from the Chief of Staff, a decision from somewhere on high to make an example of him. He had managed to lie low in Mexico, thanks to Spano, but he suddenly saw how a second strike—such as being arrested—could send his career spinning into oblivion.

The officer had anticipated this. "You will see, if you look at that agreement, that soldiers accused of crimes are subject to detainment for questioning."

A light went on for Isen. "You're accusing *me* of a crime?"

"Yes," the policeman said. But there was some hesitation there, as if the police officer didn't quite believe it himself but was just trying to carry out his orders. Isen pressed his momentary advantage.

"I will go with you to the police headquarters on the condition that you remove your men from this building and that you don't interfere with our work here."

"I am to shut down this building."

*I was afraid of that,* Isen thought. *Think fast. I've got to get word out about what's going down here.*

"If we go off the air," Isen said, "a mobile reaction force has orders to come down here to see if we've been shut down by terrorists. There'll be all kinds of helicopters and armed men running around your town. That will be hard to explain to the federal authorities."

It was a bald-faced lie, but it seemed to gain a foothold. The police officer chewed the ends of his mustache.

"Your men may stay here, but they may not leave the premises," he said.

"Let me get my stuff," Isen said, spinning around before the Mexican could ask what stuff a fully dressed man needed. When Isen reached the other Mexican police officer, who was squared off with two of the commo men in the tiny space outside their shop, Isen pointed back over his shoulder with his thumb. "Your boss wants you outside," he told the Mexican. When the young man hesitated,

Isen wondered if he understood English. He made his voice more emphatic and pointed again. "Get moving. He wants you *now*."

It worked. The policeman traded sneers with the Delta Force commo men and hurried down the hall.

"I'd like to kick that little motherfucker's ass," one of the men said.

"Listen carefully," Isen said, all business now. "Get a message to Colonel Reeves or Major Spano and tell them the locals are trying to shut down our operation here. Tell them that the Mexicans have taken me to the police station here to question me about some kidnapping they claim I was in on."

"Got it, sir," the senior man said. "You want one of us to go with you down there?"

"What for?" Isen asked.

"Well, I don't want to alarm you, but you wouldn't be the first person in this country who disappeared in police custody."

The thought hadn't even crossed Isen's mind. Although he knew the local police officials loathed the Americans and their presence, he doubted that they would go so far as to murder an American officer. *Still* . . .

"If I'm not back by . . ." Isen looked at his watch, "sixteen hundred, call for me. Then send somebody down once reinforcements arrive here. You've got to keep the net up here, that's the most important thing right now."

"You got it, sir."

When he went outside, the Mexicans were waiting for him in a jeep. Isen climbed in the back next to the skinny officer who'd pushed past him in the building, stepping on the policeman's foot in the bargain.

"Sorry," he said.

They drove past the little row of stores that were the newest buildings on the street. But instead of turning north toward the center of town and the police station, they turned south and east, toward the Gulf.

"Where are we going?" Isen asked. He noticed then that all three of the policemen were armed and that there was a shotgun on the floor up front, between the front seats.

The butt of the weapon rested near his feet. He got no answer to his question, so he leaned forward to speak directly into the leader's ear.

"Where are you taking me? Isn't the police station the other way?"

Red tabs didn't answer him or even turn around. When Isen sat back up, the scrawny one was smiling.

"Fuckyoubuddy," Isen said quickly. He turned his attention to the problem of getting away. The jeep was moving at about twenty-five now on one of the wider streets on the south side, too fast to dive to the ground. He could hardly take on all three of them, not without shooting them, and that would never do. Isen nudged the butt of the shotgun with his foot. It was not strapped down. But the policeman next to him said something in Spanish and red tabs picked up the weapon and put it across his lap. He turned partway in his seat and shook his head disgustedly.

Just as Isen considered backhanding the wormy one to send him off the rear of the jeep, they made a turn that looked familiar to him.

"Are we going to Operation Sentinel headquarters?" he asked.

Red tabs turned around completely. "Of course we are. Where did you think we were going?" He said something in Spanish to the other two, apparently translating the little joke, and the three of them had a good laugh about it.

They stopped short of this other headquarters building, and red tabs got out and walked. He returned a few minutes later, climbed back in and gave directions to the driver. A few blocks away they approached an outdoor café that Isen knew Worden favored; the big American NCO was sitting by himself at a table under the awning. Once again, red tabs got out thirty meters or so away from the café and walked over. He approached Worden, gestured at Isen in the jeep, and apparently convinced Worden to come along.

"Hey, sir," the NCO said as he climbed in the jeep.

"What did he tell you?" Isen demanded.

Red tabs turned around. "Be quiet, you two."

"Fuck you, pal," Isen said.

Worden's face changed visibly. "He said we were all going to go look at some evidence about the NDP."

"He gave me some story about an assault," Isen said. "But since they brought you along, my guess is that this has something to do with when we worked together." As Isen put the pieces together, he became more despondent. "I hope this isn't more about that friggin' ambush and shooting." He thought he'd put the events of that night behind him.

Worden was staring straight ahead. "I don't think it is, sir."

Red tabs put Worden and Isen in a room on the second floor of the blocklike Tampico police headquarters. He left the door open, but there were bars on the windows. Seconds after they were in the room, they were joined by a moon-faced detective in a stained white shirt.

"You are Captain Isen?" the detective said to Worden.

"No, I'm Isen. This is Sergeant Worden," Isen said.

"I am Detective Herndez. Do you know why you're here?"

"No," Isen answered right away.

Herndez fixed Worden with a stare.

"No," Worden said.

"On fifteen June, you men were involved in the kidnapping of a local resident by the name of Tomasino Fuentes." He looked up, as if expecting the two Americans to admit their crime. "You deny this?"

"Of course we deny it," Isen said. "I don't know what the hell you're talking about."

"Captain Isen, you are involved in the investigations in pursuit of the German terrorists your government says are operating out of Mexico."

"What the hell does that crack mean?" Isen said, abandoning any pretense of civility. He was angry. "They *are* operating in Mexico," he said. "We captured some of their material." He was angry, and he knew it showed in his voice, but he was beyond caring. "Where is this bullshit coming from?"

Now it was Herndez's turn to be angry. He slapped his

notes on the table between them. "You are accused of a very serious crime here, and *I* am asking the questions. It will be best if you cooperate with me."

Isen sat back in his chair. He was quiet, but he gave up nothing.

"Fuentes has given us a statement saying that he was kidnapped from a bar near the waterfront by two men who accused him of being involved with smuggling and then beat him." Herndez looked up; the Americans sat stone-faced.

"He identified the two of you after observing your respective headquarters."

"He's lying," Isen said.

"Why would he come to us and give us such a statement?" Herndez asked. "He stands to gain nothing from this."

*You probably put him up to it to get rid of us,* Isen thought.

"I must tell you," Herndez went on, "that the chief of police here is outraged at this attack on a Mexican civilian. Pending the outcome of this inquiry, he has ordered both of the American operations in Tampico closed."

"What inquiry?" Isen said. "All you have done is make accusations against us, with no evidence other than the word of a smuggler."

"Señor Fuentes is not the suspect here, my friend," Herndez said. "You are." Satisfied with that answer, the detective went on. "He will be here later today to make a formal accusation against you."

"You must let us contact our headquarters," Isen said. "And the American Consulate."

Herndez smiled at them. "Until Fuentes makes his statement here today, there is no formal accusation. At that time you will be afforded those opportunities."

"Then we are free to go?" Isen asked.

"No, no, no. You are our guests until then." Herndez stood, angry that Isen insisted on pointing out the inconsistencies in the police position. "We want to make sure you are here when we need you."

When he left, he pulled the door shut behind him but didn't lock it.

"Isn't that a Catch-22," Isen said. "Where the hell do they get this stuff?"

Worden was uncharacteristically silent at the table, his hands folded before him. "Sir."

Isen was pacing back and forth in front of the door. "What?"

Worden was staring at his fingers. "I've got something to tell you." He looked up at Isen as he spoke. "And you're not going to like it."

Worden told Isen about the source of the information that led to the first successful strike against the NDP's assets, leaving out the parts about his confrontation with Cortizo and the beating he gave Fuentes. Isen listened impassively until Worden was finished.

"Frankly, I'm not at all surprised that you went along with this—I'm just as frustrated as you are at the snail's pace of this operation," Isen said. But that was the only bone he was going to throw Worden. He came closer to where Worden was sitting and leaned both palms on the table. "But you're certainly sharp enough to realize that you can't play fast and loose with the law in a country that doesn't even want us around to begin with."

Worden continued to look at his hands. He was a loose cannon, sometimes, but he was genuinely interested in doing a good job.

"I guess I just got fed up with having to do everything by the book when that doesn't work."

"Sergeant Worden, what we accomplish down here is no more important than how we accomplish it," Isen said. But even as he spoke, he wondered if that was always true.

"I apologize, sir," Worden said. "I fucked up. But doesn't it seem odd that with all the crime going down in Tampico, the police zero in on us?"

"Yes. And it burns my ass that we volunteered for this operation and we're getting more flak from the Mexicans than anybody else. But we have to be smarter than that."

He moved away from the table to look out the barred,

glassless window. "We know they're out to shut us down," Isen said, "and I think we just gave them a good excuse."

"*I* gave them a good excuse," Worden said dejectedly.

"Maybe we can get Lieutenant Cortizo to get us out of this," Isen said.

"And implicate himself?" Worden said sarcastically. "I doubt it, sir. If the locals are really after us they probably would just ignore Cortizo. He might even be in on it."

Isen was inclined to disagree, but he was more intrigued by Worden's apparent hostile attitude. He attributed it to their being detained. Finally he decided an argument with Worden would be pointless.

It had been two hours since he'd left the Delta Force headquarters, and Isen wondered if the commo guys had found either Reeves or Spano, wondered what either of those two men would be able to do from a distance. He hadn't known Worden was going to be involved, and so didn't tell the commo men to get in touch with Worden's superiors at Operation Sentinel. There was little chance that the commander over there, a lieutenant-colonel, would even know that someone needed his help. Since Worden had just finished all-night duty when the Mexicans picked him up, his colleagues would assume he was sleeping; it would be hours before the Americans realized he was missing. Isen thought about simply walking out of the police station, but since learning that the Mexicans did have something on Worden, he thought that would only make things worse.

At 0900, the ball was definitely in Herndez's court.

Jack Worden spent the next hour worrying about what Mexican jails must be like for Americans. When he was a private serving in Hawaii, another soldier in his company had been convicted of beating a local man. The military turned the soldier over to the civil authorities, and after his conviction, the soldier went to the county jail, which was easily ten times worse than the military prisons. Worden had visited the man and had a distinct memory of an overcrowded, smelly jail where the threat of violence against prisoners—by other prisoners and by guards—was as thick as the humid tropical air. If American jails were like that on the inside, Mexican jails must be like descending through the circles of hell.

At eleven o'clock Herndez returned. He was alone.

"Señor Fuentes is here, and he has spoken to the chief," the Mexican detective said. "He says he will identify his assailants and will help us press charges." He smiled at them. "This afternoon, we will close down your American outposts in Tampico." Herndez left the room and returned a few minutes later with the huge Fuentes in tow.

Several things were immediately clear to Jack Worden. The first was that he had beaten Fuentes worse than he remembered, so badly in fact, that Isen would probably be able to figure out the score. The man's nose was completely misshapen, and it was only on seeing it that Worden remembered the anger, remembered smashing Fuentes's face with the butt of the pistol. The second thing Worden noticed was that Fuentes recognized him immediately, even though he couldn't have gotten a good look at the American in the dark alley. Finally, Worden determined that Tomasino Fuentes was here against his will. He moved like a pouting child as he followed Herndez into the room, and he had to be told twice to sit down. Once inside the room, the smuggler did not look at Isen or Worden; instead he scowled at the detective. Worden wondered what they'd threatened him with to get him to confront the Americans.

Herndez placed a small tape recorder on the table between the men and pressed the buttons to record. He recited the date and the place, as well as the names of those present, which he read from his notes. Worden was able to follow most of the Spanish.

"This statement made by Tomasino Fuentes will be used to determine if a crime has been committed against a Mexican citizen." He pushed the recorder closer to Fuentes.

"Tell me again what happened on the evening of fifteen June," Herndez said.

"A man came up to me, I was sitting at my regular table, and started asking me questions about smuggling. I told him I didn't know what he was talking about, but he kept bothering me. I tried to leave, but he followed me. Then another guy came out in the alley and they beat me."

"This man who came up to you inside, did you get a good look at him?" Herndez asked.

"Yes." Fuentes still had not looked up from the table.

"Is he in this room?"

Fuentes looked at the detective, then back at his hands. "No."

"What did you say?"

"He is not here," Fuentes said.

Worden wasn't sure, but he thought there was a trace of fear, or maybe annoyance, in the Mexican's voice.

Herndez poked the tape recorder, shutting it off. "Out in the hallway," he said to Fuentes. The detective picked up the recorder and stomped out of the room. They went a good distance down the hall, but Worden could still hear the two of them going at it in Spanish outside.

"That the guy?" Isen asked.

"Yes."

"What was all that about?"

"Fuentes said a guy came up to him in a bar and started asking questions about smuggling," Worden explained. "Then Fuentes said that neither of us was that guy."

"And that's what pissed Herndez off," Isen offered. "No telling what the police threatened him with before they brought him in here," Isen said. "He looks scared to me."

"You think so too?" Worden asked.

Even though he knew full well that what he'd done to Fuentes was dead wrong, Jack Worden was not one to roll over and wait for things to happen to him. He believed that there was a way out of this mess, and something told him it lay in the fact that Fuentes was not completely willing to cooperate with the police.

They came back a moment later. Herndez pulled out Fuentes's chair and slammed it on the floor before taking his own seat. Worden watched Fuentes, but the Mexican never looked up.

"Shit," Herndez said, standing again; he had left the recorder in the hall. He stood up abruptly, knocking his

332

chair over behind him. While he was out in the hall, Worden made his move.

"Fuentes," he said.

The Mexican looked up, and Worden held out his hand, forefinger and thumb extended in a child's play version of a pistol.

"Bang," he said.

Isen couldn't believe it. Worden's antics had gotten them both in more trouble than he cared to think about, and now *this* desperate move, right under the nose of the detective. He felt like smacking Worden on the side of the head.

Herndez was back in the room in ten seconds. He slapped the recorder down on the table and got it going again.

"You say the man who approached you in the bar is not here. What about the one who beat you in the alley?"

There was a long fearful moment of waiting for Fuentes to answer. "I did not get a good look at him," Fuentes said at last. "It was dark."

Herndez looked like someone had hit him in the gut. He reached across the table and smashed Fuentes on the ear with a balled-up fist. Then he grabbed a handful of the fat man's hair and twisted it until Fuentes fell out of his chair. When the smuggler was on the floor, Herndez kicked at him until he moved toward the door. No one in the room said anything. The two Americans watched in amazement as the detective beat his witness and the testimony against the servicemen crawled away.

When he reached the door, Herndez turned back to them. "Don't you two think you're going anywhere," he seethed. "This is not over yet."

When they were alone, Worden smacked the table with his hand. "*Hot damn!* Did you see that? Ha, we beat them at their game." He was ecstatic.

But Isen was far from relieved. "When are you going to stop these fucking games?" he demanded, his voice barely controlled. "Don't you know we've got one foot in a Mexican jail cell?"

Worden was a bit cowed. "But they have no testimony," he protested.

*He honestly thinks it's all over,* Isen thought.

"They'll make up whatever they want, especially if he told them once before that you were the one." He struggled to control his voice. *No sense yelling out all the evidence they need.*

Herndez left Isen and Worden isolated for another hour. Then he came in and told them that Fuentes had made a credible statement placing both of them at the café on the day he was beaten up. The detective left and returned again shortly after that, claiming that Fuentes's statement was unimportant, that they had found another person who was involved and who would testify against them. He seemed no more confident of the second statement than he was of the first; the difference was that Isen and Worden both knew there was such a person.

When Herndez left, Worden spoke first.

"Do you think Cortizo has turned on us . . . on me?"

"No," Isen said. But he wasn't sure himself. "Herndez is probably trying to bluff us."

"But how would they even know Cortizo was involved unless he told them?"

"The same way they got a make on you, I guess. Somebody at the bar, somebody in the street."

Worden thought about whom he'd seen that night. He remembered no one in particular, but whereas he might forget seeing one Mexican among many, it wouldn't be unusual for a Mexican to remember a six-foot-five-inch American with red hair.

"How long before we hear something from Reeves or Spano?" Worden asked.

"No telling. I hope the message got through," Isen answered. "Thing is, I think you and I can get out of this mess, but unless we come up with something, this is going to throw a real monkey wrench into the NDP investigation and into Operation Sentinel."

"So I blew it for everybody," Worden said.

Isen looked over. He felt sorry for Worden, but the

NCO's actions—well-meaning but misguided—had gotten them into this. And his comment was probably true.

"Maybe, maybe not," he said.

A Mexican police officer brought them some food just after noon. Isen ate greedily, while Worden, who'd been up all night, slept fitfully in the hard chair.

Lieutenant Cortizo walked in the door at half past twelve.

Worden snorted. "I told you it was him."

Isen ignored his NCO. "How are you?" he said to Cortizo.

"I have been better," Cortizo answered glumly. "How long have they had you here?"

"Since about seven o'clock this morning," Isen said. He wanted to hear Cortizo's side of the story that Worden had told him, but he thought it might be better to let Cortizo bring it up.

"Did you tell him everything?" Cortizo said to Worden.

"I told him it was your idea," Worden said crisply.

"Did you tell him about the beating, about how you wanted to kidnap Fuentes?" Cortizo said, his voice rising. "Did you tell him about breaking his nose with the pistol? About threatening his life?" Cortizo stood away from the table; Isen had never seen him this angry.

Worden leaned way back in his chair, apparently determined to egg Cortizo on by remaining calm.

"No, and I didn't tell him how you changed your mind once you realized we were playing hardball. How you suddenly wanted out of it, started talking about the goddamned laws, and . . ."

"That's enough, you two," Isen said. "It's obvious that you both pulled a major league fuck-up here." He could see Cortizo recoil—he had never criticized the Mexican lieutenant so directly, but it had to be done. "But instead of calling one another names, why don't we try to figure out what we can do about getting ourselves out of this," Isen said.

Cortizo came back to the table and sat down heavily. "That is not the problem, Captain Isen," he said, with a little more of his usual decorum. "The police here have no desire to detain you, and they will probably let you go in a few hours."

"Then why did they bring us here and go through all this bullshit?" Isen asked, still angry.

"You can be sure this was not Fuentes's idea; he wouldn't want the police involved. No doubt they were offering him something in exchange for testimony against you," Cortizo said.

"But I wasn't even involved," Isen protested.

"They are not pursuing truth," Cortizo answered. "They merely want an excuse to shut down the two headquarters here."

"They're serious about that?" Isen said.

"They won't be able to make that stick," Worden interjected. "We have the federal government behind us."

"They don't have to make it last long," Cortizo answered. "If they succeed in shutting you down for a few hours with even a shred of reasonable pretext, if they learn, for instance, of your troubles with the U.S. Army, they will have won a major battle. The local governments have been resisting all along the American presence, which was forced on them by the federals. I'm sure you noticed that the army has been less than fully cooperative."

"You got that fucking A right," Worden said.

Isen silenced him with a cold look. "But what do they hope to accomplish?" Isen asked.

"If Tampico can stand up to federal and American pressure, these officials believe that other local governments will resist actively also."

Isen thought that what Cortizo described sounded too organized to be the result of disparate communities acting independently.

"Is the army behind this?" he asked.

Cortizo looked away for a second, then looked back. "No," he said. Then, in a lower voice, "I don't know."

"Well, goddamn, if we let them get away with shutting our headquarters down, even for a little while," Isen said, "then not only will the whole antidrug operation get thrown off course, but this terrorist hunt might also slow down nationwide, right?"

Cortizo simply nodded. That's what this was all about, after all.

"Look," Isen said carefully, "I know your army resents Americans coming in here, pretending to know how to do everything. But isn't it true that if we get pulled out of this it will allow the NDP several more weeks of freedom while your government tries to get the investigation back to the point it is now?"

Cortizo looked as if he'd been slapped.

"So that has been your attitude all along?" he said. "You've been telling me how difficult it is to be an adviser, and how Americans must learn that they don't know everything. You even told me that you understood when I said your people look at things with American eyes." Angry as he was, he still spoke in measured tones, the palms of his hands pressed flat on the table.

"But all along you think also that you are the only ones with the answers, the only ones capable of capturing these people."

Isen felt the point slipping away from him, and he sensed a light going out in Cortizo's eyes.

"No, that is not it at all. You are oversimplifying it. I am saying that the investigation has progressed to the point where it would be a major setback to change the players. These people"—he gestured around him at the walls—"want to disrupt our work because of politics, but right now stopping the NDP is the most important thing, certainly more so than their political agendas."

"And what then?" Cortizo said. "If your people are in on the capture, we will not hear the end of how the Americans came and straightened everything out."

Isen felt as if he'd drawn the battle lines wrong. He was trying to get Cortizo to accept that his country couldn't handle the investigation alone. Such an admission was all but impossible for a man who'd staked his reputation on the professionalism of his soldiers.

"What do they have on you?" Isen asked, determined to try another tack.

Cortizo sighed. He was no more anxious than Isen to argue. "They have placed me in the bar that night," Cortizo said. "They want me to say that you two, or one of you, was there with me and beat the fat man."

"So just tell them they're wrong," Worden interrupted.

Cortizo looked at the NCO, then shook his head. He turned to Isen. "Sergeant Worden wanted to kidnap Fuentes. I said we must follow the laws or we are no better than the smugglers." He was speaking almost in slow motion, weighed down by untold sadness. "When I said no to the kidnapping, he beat the man."

But Isen's mind was already beyond the messy particulars of what happened when Cortizo and Worden had visited Fuentes; he was considering the trouble about to be stirred up when the Mexicans shut down the headquarters in Tampico. The work they'd done to this point might be lost forever.

"If you turn him in," Isen said, "we are going to lose a lot of the work we did together."

Cortizo looked at the man who'd become his mentor; Isen had not asked him to lie, but he was clearly asking for something short of the truth.

"You would have me lie, Captain Isen? Isn't that the kind of behavior you Americans are so quick to criticize in us?"

He looked at Isen, then Worden. Neither had anything to say.

"How can you keep both those thoughts in one heart, Captain Isen?"

Cortizo stood up slowly, pulling himself to his full height. "We took the law into our own hands, and that was wrong," Cortizo said. "It was wrong when I thought of it; it was wrong when we did it. I cannot let what we did go unpunished."

Cortizo saluted and waited for Isen to return it. Then he left the room.

"Why did you let him get away with that shit, sir?" Worden asked. He was by no means resigned to accepting what the Mexicans were about to dish out.

"I can't force him to go against his conscience," Isen

338

said. He felt remarkably calm, even though he was sure that all the work he had done for the past months was about to be derailed because Cortizo had a conscience. At first he felt sorry for himself and the other Americans who had volunteered to serve in Mexico, then he felt sorry for Cortizo, who would always have this same difficulty: trying to reconcile his search for the right thing—the truth—with the fact that he lived in this imperfect world. In that, Isen saw something of himself in Cortizo.

"I hope his conscience keeps him company when we're in jail," Worden said.

They spent another hour in the room, waiting for the bad news. Finally Herndez stuck his head in the door. "You two may leave now," he said. He might have been talking to someone who'd been waiting for ten minutes.

"You mind telling me what's going on?" Isen said.

Herndez walked away, Isen in pursuit.

"I think we should get out of here, sir," a relieved Worden said.

"Hold on a second," Isen said to Herndez's retreating back. "We've been in this room all day—DO YOU HEAR ME?" he yelled.

Herndez turned slowly.

"You owe us an explanation," Isen said.

"Get your stooge Cortizo to tell you about it," Herndez said. "The chief chose to accept his version of the story."

"What do you mean 'his' version?" Isen asked.

Herndez leaned forward; Isen could smell his breath.

"He said he beat Fuentes, and that it was all his idea."

Isen's face may have betrayed what he was thinking, but there was little Herndez could do with the unguarded reactions of Americans. When the detective walked away, Worden came up beside Isen, who stood with his mouth open.

"How 'bout that shit? I guess he wasn't such a straight shooter after all," Worden said.

"He *was*," Isen said. "He was until we dragged him around a while."

## President Says Independence Day Celebrations
## Must Go On

by David Browne
Special to *The New York Times*

Washington, D.C., June 30—In comments made during a Rose Garden ceremony today, the President said that Fourth of July celebrations must go on in spite of the threat of terrorist activity.

"We are taking extraordinary measures," the President said, "to ensure the safety of our people by tracking down and bringing to justice the perpetrators of these crimes against humanity. Terrorists prey on our fears. To cancel the observance of the very holiday meant to celebrate freedom would be to capitulate completely."

Presidential aides said that the chief executive, who usually spends the holiday at his vacation home with his family, will either stay in the capital for the ceremonies here or travel to New York City, where he has been invited by that city's mayor to "stand tall for freedom" at the public celebration.

A White House spokesperson, when questioned about the President's health, said that the chief executive and his physician are of one mind on this: the President will not curtail his public appearances. In spite of these assurances, the strain of the current situation was visible on the President, who delivered his remarks in what was, at times, a barely audible monotone.

Although the President's critics have been quick to pounce on nearly every White House announcement pertaining to the terrorist crisis, voices of dissent against the President's call for Independence Day celebrations have been silent. Even Senator Matthew Stone (D-NY), one of the President's biggest detractors throughout the course of the current problems, has conceded that the symbolic importance of the Fourth of July is worth some degree of risk. "But it is doubtful,"

Stone added in comments from his Capitol Hill office, "that the administration is taking adequate steps to keep the country safe."

Senator Stone will be attending the fireworks celebration in Washington, where National Park Service Police and District of Columbia Police are already rehearsing the operations that will, in the words of one police spokesman, "make you safer here in D.C. than home in your own bed." A spokesperson for the FBI's Special Task Force on Terrorism said that, while a Fourth of July celebration in a place like New York might appear to be a lucrative target, the pattern thus far suggests that the bombers will look for something unexpected. "Each one has been a surprise," Special Agent Carolyn Greinder said. "If there is another strike, it will probably be in some unexpected quarter as well."

When the spate of attacks started, the FBI put together a task force to work on the NDP bombings. So far, the Bureau will admit only that the crime lab has been able to identify the explosives and chemical agent used. One congressional source close to the investigation said that the FBI's efforts have been hampered by the fact that most of the terrorist activities have originated outside the United States.

*The Washington Post* yesterday published a report claiming that the CIA is involved with the investigation going on in Mexico. But spokesmen at the Agency's Langley, Virginia, headquarters, as well as Mexican spokesmen at that country's embassy, both deny the report.

# 27

## Alexandria, Virginia
*Thursday, 1 July*
*0845*

PATROLMAN BLAKE TERRY WAS HAVING DIFFICULTY STAY-
ing awake. He had been up a good deal of the night with
some sort of stomach bug, and although that seemed to
have passed, he was dog-tired. The morning sun coming in
flat over the already sticky landscape didn't help any, and
the cruiser's air conditioner was making small headway
against the rising temperatures. *Gonna be a hot one today,*
Terry thought.

There was a Donut Delite shop just off Duke Street
where he could stop, get a cup of coffee, and escape for a
few minutes the crunch of morning traffic. Terry rationalized his idleness by planning to sit facing the windows that
made up the front of the small building, so that he could
keep an eye on the street as he drank his coffee.

He pulled his cruiser into the shop's parking area, but
thought twice about cramming it into the tiny front lot.
Instead, he moved it around to the side, where there was
room to park it facing the exit, in case he got a call and
had to leave in a hurry.

"Morning, Chief," the old man behind the counter said
as Terry walked in. The elderly clerk played this game with

everyone. All military people of any rank were "General" or "Field Marshal," all police officers were "Chief."

"Morning," Terry answered with a smile that belied how he felt. "How's it going?"

"Fine, just fine."

Terry walked around to the portion of the counter that faced the street. He selected a stool, pulled a napkin from the dispenser, and cleaned off the top of the seat. Sitting down, he extracted another napkin and wiped the counter in front of him and for a foot in either direction, just in case he put his elbows up. No sense soiling a clean uniform at the start of the day. When he was settled, the old man stood in front of him. Terry had come in for coffee, but was now tempted by the smell of doughnuts in the shop. It occurred to him that perhaps he ought not to eat a doughnut, but he rationalized that a man had to have his minor vices.

"What do you have that isn't too messy?" Terry asked.

"How about a whole wheat?"

Terry liked the sound of that. Healthy, almost. "Sounds good. Let me have a coffee too."

While he ate his doughnut, Terry read a newspaper that someone had left on the counter. When he was finished, he wiped the corners of his mouth carefully, then folded the napkin and placed it beside his coffee cup. He lifted the cup and surveyed the small room over its rim. Two young women by the takeout counter were supervising a clerk as he filled a box with a dozen doughnuts. Most of the crowd that stopped on the way into work had long since gone. There were a few people, like Terry, on a coffee break, most of them drivers or delivery people of some sort who had the luxury of stopping whenever they wanted. Terry watched the two young women leave. One of them smiled at him through the glass window, and he smiled back.

They were no sooner out of the parking slot when a brand-new sedan pulled in, a rental car, Terry judged from the looks of it, with Virginia plates. Two men got out of the car and looked around, then came inside. One of the pair, tall, thin, with a neatly trimmed beard, fortyish, checked his watch as they sat down at the counter across from Terry. His partner, almost as tall but younger and a good deal heavier, in a stocky, athletic sort of way, saw Terry first.

Many people believe that police officers have some sort of sixth sense that tells them when a person is a criminal. Terry thought this himself when he was still in training. But in his five years on the force he had come to realize that it was more elementary than that. Guilty people, or people who didn't like cops, merely reacted visibly when they saw a police officer watching.

The heavy man tensed when he spotted the police officer. He was startled by the uniform, but he forced a smile. Terry smiled back, then decided to order a second cup of coffee.

It was already in front of him before he thought that decaf might have been easier on his stomach; he sipped it anyway, wondering why he had decided to stay. The men across from him were dressed almost identically in jeans, button-down dress shirts, and loafers. Because the counter didn't reach the floor, he could also see that neither wore socks. The heavy one had a bracelet of some sort—it looked like a leather thong from where Terry sat.

*They aren't dressed for the heat,* Terry thought. But they weren't dressed for work, either, not without socks.

The clerk approached them from behind the counter.

"Coffee?" he asked. The two men simply nodded.

Terry could feel the second cup of coffee working against him now, an unsettled feeling deep in a stomach not yet recovered from last night. Down in his stomach, clear down to the tops of his legs, he sat on an uncomfortable excitement.

The two men said nothing to each other, though the tall one checked his watch twice in five minutes. Terry watched a few more cars fill up the parking lot. When a large American sedan pulled in and found all the spaces full, the driver took the car around to the side of the building where Terry's cruiser was parked. Another piece of the puzzle fell into place.

*They didn't see my car when they pulled in. That explains the reaction—they weren't expecting a policeman.*

Terry's stomach turned over, and he had to straighten up in his seat and lower his head to keep from belching out loud. The shop was noisier now; there were at least ten people in line. Even with little chance that Terry would overhear them, the two men did not speak to each other.

They were dark, though they didn't look Hispanic. Still, Terry expected to hear them say something in Spanish. The classic profile around big cities was two or three men traveling in expensive rental cars up the interstate highways of the east coast, carrying shipments of drugs to the bloated cities. Terry had read a recent article about the New Jersey State Police who, on one stretch of the southernmost portion of the New Jersey Turnpike, regularly hauled in hundreds of suspects fitting that description.

Two of the clerks disappeared into the back, leaving only one out front. A few of the customers started to complain loudly. One of the men across from Terry leaned over and said something to his partner, but it was lost in the noise. By this time Terry could feel his pulse hammering. He braced his hands on the counter in front of him, flexing his shoulders so that newly formed beads of sweat could run down his back between his shoulder blades.

*There's nothing about those two to cause alarm,* he told himself. *This feeling is from the coffee.*

Still, he wanted to get to his car and look at his notes from the morning roll call, see what new suspects were out there on the street. He got up unsteadily, swimming against a strong current. He made his way around the counter and behind the two men, and then suddenly the nausea left him.

The two men said nothing. Both of them had their heads down, studying their coffee mugs as the police officer walked behind them. Terry touched the second one on the shoulder.

"You guys need directions or anything?" he asked.

He felt the man stiffen a bit under his touch, but the face that swiveled around in the seat was smiling. The man forced a wider grin, and his expression became even more artificial. He said nothing.

"I said, do you two need any directions or anything?" Terry insisted. He was leaning over the man now, the taller one, and he noticed that their clothes were not clean, and they had not bathed in a while. He wondered where they'd driven from.

The tall man opened his mouth and said, in almost a whisper, "No." He added, as an afterthought, "Thank you."

Terry straightened, glanced at one, then the other, and turned toward the door.

There was an accent there, all right. It wasn't Hispanic, but Terry hadn't heard enough to guess what it was. He mentally checked off the morning's roll call briefing, all the daily information police officers are given before they hit the streets. But there was nothing. Then yesterday's. He was out the door before he remembered what was bothering him.

*The accent was German, just like those terrorists.*

Even as he considered it, Terry wondered if he was guilty of a gross generalization. That would never do. He prided himself on his knowledge of and adherence to procedure. He did things by the book, first, last, always.

The police officer continued to walk. His insides were swirling, and the question of the man's accent and the sudden thoughts of the holiday traffic—he had to work on the fourth and the fifth—all contributed to his discomfort. *Oh, God, the traffic.*

Now he *knew* that he was going to throw up, but he forced himself to keep walking to the corner of the building, around the side and to his cruiser. He had nothing on the men inside, nothing that justified his suspicion. The sickening feeling he had in his stomach came, he was sure, from the coffee. But he kept thinking of those thousands out on the grassy slopes below the Washington monument.

A terrorist's dream.

He suddenly wanted a backup, though he had no justification for approaching the men. He wrenched the door open, ducked in, and grabbed the radio handset.

There was traffic on the air. He waited to key the microphone, listening to his breathing, shallow and fast. He set one foot on the frame of the car door and turned back to the front of the shop.

The two men were getting in their car.

At this point some of his colleagues would have looked for any reason to detain the two men, anything to give the hunch a chance to play out. But Terry believed in the law, and the book, and procedures. He squeezed the push-to-talk switch, but the other transmission—something about a broken down police cruiser—was still going on. He could not reach anyone. *Loosen up*, his partner had once told him. *You'll be a better cop.* While the radio chattered and he wondered how he might answer a harassment charge, Terry made a decision. He flipped the mike to the seat and walked around the open door, reaching down as he did so to unbutton the strap that held his revolver in the holster.

"Hold on please, gentlemen," Terry said. Even as he spoke, he was wondering what he was going to ask them about. They had done nothing wrong in the restaurant. He had observed no traffic violation, however small, when they drove in.

"What is it, Officer?" the tall one said.

The accent again. *Vat iz it, Offizer?*

"May I see the rental agreement on your car, please?" Terry said. *Buy time, man, buy time to think.*

"Certainly," the tall one said. They must have realized there was no point in trying to hide their nationality any longer. He spoke sharply to his partner, two quick phrases in German. The younger man opened the car door, reached into the glove compartment, and produced a couple of sheets of paper. He handed them to Terry, then made as if to sit in the car.

"Please stay outside the car," Terry said.

The younger man shot a glance at his partner.

"As a matter of fact," Terry said, "I'd like you to both move around to the front of the vehicle please. Stand in front of the hood here." He pointed to the sidewalk directly in front of the car's shiny plastic grill.

The tall man spoke again. "Is there anything wrong, Officer?"

Terry was seriously nauseated now, and he could feel

the sweat up on his temples, under his chin. He wanted to
go behind the building where he could stick his finger down
his throat and get rid of the coffee that was working on his
stomach. *I should've done that before I stopped these
clowns,* he thought.

"I . . . uh, I just wanted to check your rental
agreement," Terry said, aware of how lame it sounded. *I
could get creamed for harassment here.* He hoped the two
weren't diplomats out slumming in the suburbs. Suddenly
he felt the urge to cough, and he fought it, knowing that
the contents of his stomach would follow. Terry put his fist
up to his mouth, felt his cheeks swell. The younger man,
standing only three feet away, saw what was coming and
slid back.

Terry lurched away, took three steps around the side of
the building before he lost control. He vomited in the parking lot, felt the hot fluid splatter on his trousers. He knew
that he was in full view of the big plate-glass window on
the side of the building, and he guessed that half a dozen
people could see him clearly. He took a few more steps so
that he was behind the cruiser, heaved again, then wiped
his mouth with his handkerchief. As fast as it had come
on, it was gone.

*God, I hate to throw up in public.*

Terry straightened just in time to see the two Germans
back out of their parking space. He had their rental
agreement in his hand.

"This is unit Alpha Five in pursuit of a late model sedan,
light blue, license . . ."

Terry had just gotten his car in gear and was spinning
the steering wheel when a panel truck turned into the narrow parking lot right in front of the Germans. The rental
car smashed head on into the van, which had tried to turn
away at the last second.

But Terry had already jammed the accelerator, and his
cruiser swung around the sharp corner and plowed into the
back of the rental car. One of the men, who'd been slumped
forward against the dash, was whipped back by the impact.
Terry couldn't see the driver.

He barked his location into the mike as he pushed open

the door, feeling strangely clumsy. A terrible white flash of pain split his leg when his foot touched the ground, and he fell behind the open door, his leg doubled up underneath him. He looked down, but it didn't look broken.

Terry could see, under the door of his cruiser, the rental car's driver's side door open and the driver get out. The police officer grabbed a handhold and pulled himself to his feet, his badly sprained leg dead weight beneath him.

The tall German had staggered clear of the wreck and was leaning on another parked car. Two men got out of the van and started walking toward the German.

"STAND BACK," Terry shouted.

The two men, construction workers by the look of them, hesitated.

"POLICE. GET BACK IN YOUR VEHICLE," Terry yelled. He felt the exertion clear down his leg. He watched the construction workers make it back to the van and didn't notice the tall German bend over. The man pulled something from alongside his leg and stood quickly.

Terry saw the winking light of the small caliber handgun a split second before he heard the muffled report. For some reason, the fact that the man's weapon had a silencer seemed especially ominous—*a serious shooter here*—as if the fact that he was shooting at Terry wasn't alarming enough.

Terry brought his pistol up, but the German stepped to one side, knowing that the police officer wouldn't fire when civilians were behind the target. Several slugs banged into the side of the police car, and Terry heard the pop of the rolled-down window shattering inside the door. The German turned away from Terry and began to run. When he was even with the van, he fell forward over a leg that suddenly appeared from behind the van's open door.

Terry stood up and hobbled forward, his pistol trained on the German. But the two construction workers had thrown themselves on the man even before he hit the ground, and they were sitting on him—one on his torso, one squarely on his head—before Terry got within three feet. The German had dropped the gun, and one of the vigilantes had kicked it under the van.

"The other sonofabitch don't look like he's going to be much trouble, Officer," one of the men said.

Terry guessed that the speaker, who was sitting on the prisoner's head, tipped the scales at about two hundred and forty pounds. Not much of a chance that the suspect was going to get up.

Terry lowered his pistol into the rental car, but the other German hadn't stirred. Terry slapped handcuffs on the man on the ground.

"Thanks, guys," he said. His stomach was still doing flips. "He knew I couldn't shoot with all these people around."

"Well, we just wanted to show our appreciation for your restraint," one of the workmen said. The two of them laughed loudly at this, nervous now that they had a feel for what they'd done.

Terry hustled around to the passenger door of the sedan and pulled it open against the loud squeal of bent hinges. He checked the pulse on the throat of the younger man. Slow but strong enough. He lowered this one gently onto the seat, watching closely for signs of broken bones, especially the neck. He pulled the man's arms in front of him and slipped a plastic restraint over the wrists. It would be enough to hold him if he woke up before the backup arrived. As he eased out of the car, Terry heard the agitated wail of a siren.

He walked slowly to where the rear of the sedan and his cruiser were married in a flowering of twisted metal. His ankle was beginning to hurt acutely now, and he put his hand on the side of the rental car to steady himself.

The front of the patrol car didn't seem too badly damaged after all, certainly not as badly as the rental car. The trunk of the sedan was sprung, so Terry pushed down on it with the flat of his hand. It didn't move. He put his fingers inside one exposed flange and, resting his weight gingerly on both legs, pulled upward. The trunk lid snapped up quickly, and the police officer almost lost his balance. There was another stabbing pain in his leg as he tried to use both feet to keep his balance. When the shards cleared from his vision, he saw what looked like a footlocker or steamer trunk in the back of the rental car. There was a hasp, but it was unsecured. He couldn't get behind the car because his own cruiser was there, so Terry leaned well into the trunk and released the catches on the lid.

The open footlocker appeared to be full of gray foam, but on closer inspection Terry realized it was a lid of sorts, cut to fit exactly the inside dimensions of the footlocker. He pinched one corner and lifted the top rectangle of foam. There was more gray foam underneath, with four deep cavities, each about a foot in length and six or eight inches across, cut out of the material. Terry reached into one of the cavities and felt a smooth, cold metal cylinder. He thrust his hand under the device, being careful not to disturb it too much, and felt a long plastic cylinder that was taped to the metal bottle.

He was like that, balancing himself on one foot as he bent over at an awkward angle, the upper portion of his body completely inside the trunk of the car, his hands thrust deep into the foam and pinned under this device, when it occurred to him that it was a bomb.

He held his breath and stared down at the cold metal. Slowly, he began to slide his hands free.

"What do you have there?"

There was another police officer beside him, one of the cops from the first backup.

Terry breathed. "Call the bomb squad."

"*Shit*," the officer said as he pivoted and raced back to his own squad car.

Terry wondered if this device was like the one that went off in Florida, with nerve gas built into it. He knew, from the lectures they'd had in the academy by the bomb guys, that anything that can be carried around in the trunk of a car can probably withstand some handling. Terry didn't think the device would go off; it was the metal cylinder that frightened him, and he stared at it as if it were a living enemy, some unpredictable animal that sensed his fear and was ready to strike.

When he got his hands clear of the cavity he breathed again. He considered that he could have smashed the cylinders in the crash, and he felt a cold fear brush by him, as if he were standing too close to a highway, cars whizzing by just inches away. Terry shook his head to clear it, licked his lips with a dusty tongue, and leaned against the side of the car. On the road to his front, rubberneckers had slowed traffic almost to a half. A moment later he looked over his shoulder at the edge of the black metal cylinder visible in the first cavity. He leaned back into the trunk and stuck his hand into the next hole in the foam.

It was empty.

So was the next, and the next. The Germans had delivered three of four packages.

There was a groaning in the back of his throat, and all around him the people moved on the highways of the unsuspecting city.

# 28

## The White House
### Thursday, 1 July
### 2330

THE WHITE HOUSE SITUATION ROOM SITS OFF OF AN UNIM-
pressive hallway one floor below the more famous rooms
of the west wing. The little hall ends at a short flight of
stairs. Downstairs and to the left is the entrance to the staff
dining room, a short-order window for those staffers whose
rank doesn't earn them a table in the seating area, and a
closet where the kitchen staff stores supplies. To the right,
across from the kitchen entrance, is a wooden door with a
small brass sign that White House security will not even
allow to be photographed.

Colonel Tommy Reeves hurried across the small street
from the Old Executive Office Building, his plastic security
tag bouncing against his chest. The guards at the desk just
beyond the side entrance scrutinized his pass, his identification card, and one of their own lists before they let him
enter.

"Thanks," he said to the white-shirted guards, who were
members of the uniformed division of the Secret Service.
The young men nodded.

Reeves shifted his burden of papers from one hand to
the other as he walked. The hall was lined with an odd
combination of decorations: valuable sculptures of Ameri-

can historical figures—Nathan Hale stood on a side table, his hands and feet already bound for hanging—side by side with large, showy color photographs of White House activities: the President and his family, the President jogging, the President fishing, the family out on the south lawn for the Easter egg hunt or a charity dinner.

Reeves had been in the White House once before, on a tour given to some members of the Delta Force hierarchy by the National Security Agency. This time, there was a great deal more pressure. Reeves was sure that he'd been summoned only because he happened to be in the D.C. area; the Chief of Staff of the army—who was upstairs meeting with the President—ordered Reeves to come by just in case the chief executive wanted a firsthand account of what Delta could do in Mexico. The chief, General Michael Abbott, had told Reeves about the bomb found earlier that day in Alexandria and shared with him the frightening speculation about the next target.

Reeves knocked on the magnetically sealed door to the Situation Room and was photographed by the automatic camera that peered through the panel. After he'd identified himself and the staffer inside was satisfied, the door opened, revealing the small room manned by the shift crew. Someone was always on duty here.

A woman approached him, hand extended. "Colonel Reeves?"

"Yes."

"I'm Moira Behan. General Abbott asked me to give you a rundown on what's going on upstairs, just so you'll be up to speed if you go up there."

"That sounds like a good idea," Reeves said.

"Follow me, please." Moira Behan led Reeves out of the entrance area.

The Situation Room was not a single space but a series of connected rooms. It had come about after the Cuban Missile Crisis, when President Kennedy found that there was no central clearing point for the mind-numbing amounts of information that flowed into the White House from intelligence activities around the globe. Managed by the National Security Council, the Sit Room was manned by professional intelligence officers from military and civilian agencies. Behan was on the support staff, the people who sorted through incoming materials and generally kept an eye on world events. She had one office across the street and a computer console here in the bank of half a dozen stretched under the windows on the outside wall. The computer systems were linked, via secure lines, with government intelligence agencies: the CIA, the National Security Agency, and the various intelligence services of the armed forces. There were small televisions at the end where the duty staff sat, and these were almost always tuned in to CNN, which watched the world and didn't cost the government anything extra.

Hollywood would have made such a room fifty feet long with twenty-foot ceilings, with ranks of colonels and majors manning multicolored telephones and watching radar screens. The real thing was not all that physically impressive. The L-shaped room wrapped around the presidential conference room and was furnished with moderately up-scale office equipment. The room was impressive for its quiet sense of power, and Reeves felt that the people in here were in touch with the whole world.

Moira Behan headed for the conference room. Reeves remembered being surprised, on his first visit, at how unassuming this room was.

"Small room. Keeps the straphangers down to a minimum," his host had explained.

Behan pulled up a chair along the wall of the conference room. Reeves sat two seats down from her. Behan looked to be around thirty years old, and though she was dressed in a fairly severe suit, no jewelry, and little makeup, she was attractive. Reeves wondered if she was a military intelligence officer or a civilian analyst.

"You know that we believe the next target is the Fourth of July celebration here in the capital?"

"Yes," Reeves answered.

"The men captured today had already delivered three bombs. We don't know if there are any other teams out there or not, so there may be more than three devices planted in the city. The FBI crime lab says the one we found them with had the same type of nerve gas that was used on that beach in Florida. We think they might use it at the fireworks celebration or something like that."

Reeves whistled through his teeth. "Whew."

"Exactly. General Abbott has been on the phone for the last hour with the commander of the Eighteenth Airborne Corps at Fort Bragg. Abbott and the corps commander have been discussing plans for bringing several thousand soldiers to the capital to help with the orderly evacuation of the city in the event that the President decides on that option."

Reeves felt his mouth open involuntarily. "He's thinking about evacuating the city?"

Behan settled in her seat. She had been completely calm, almost detached, while telling Reeves about the bombs and the fireworks. Now Reeves's reaction seemed to affect her too. "The President is between a rock and a hard place." She looked around, as if there might be someone listening in this room, one of the most secure rooms in the nation.

"He's been telling people all along that we can't stop our daily business. We have to go on living in spite of these terrorist attacks. Now, if he calls off the Fourth of July celebration in the nation's capital—which, by the way, he's not sure he can do—he'll be backtracking on everything he's said all along."

"What about the risk to the public?"

"The President is very much aware of that. They're discussing several options up there, I believe. Your people are one of those. Evacuating the city is another. Canceling the Fourth of July is another, although there's no guarantee that the people would go away."

"Jesus," Reeves said.

Behan nodded, and the two of them waited for the men upstairs to come to a decision.

General Abbott came down half an hour later. "Good to see you again, Tommy," Abbott said. He turned to Behan. "Thanks for filling him in. You can go now."

"Yes, sir," Behan said.

Abbott took off his uniform blouse and hung it over the

back of one of the chairs. The chief had been a wrestler in college, and though he stood just under five seven, his athletic build made him look taller. He wore his hair, as Reeves did, close cut.

"Well, here's where we stand," he said. He pulled a chair out from the table and wheeled it closer to where Reeves had been sitting. "The District police, the National Park Service Police, and soldiers from the Old Guard are looking for these bombs in trashcans, under benches, wherever one might be hidden. But we're after the proverbial needle in a haystack. We don't know shit about where the things are, and the two guys we nabbed aren't cooperating. In fact, they haven't even given their names." He paused, looked at his watch. "But the German Embassy here has offered to question the suspects on the grounds of the embassy." It didn't take a genius to see what the Germans were offering.

"Sounds like the Germans are most anxious to see this case resolved, sir," Reeves said.

"You got that right. This stuff started in their country, and their police have been unable to come up with much of anything." Abbot rubbed his face with both hands. The men upstairs were under unimaginable pressure.

"They did come up with a name, finally," Abbott said. He got up quickly and went to the door that led to the staff workspace.

"Moira, can you get me that packet the Germans dropped off?"

Behan appeared a moment later with a manila envelope. Reeves was fairly certain now that she was army, since she was obviously the one Abbott leaned on when he needed something.

Abbott dumped the contents of the envelope on the conference table. There were several grainy photographs that looked like enlargements. A few of the others were better-focused, surveillance shots. They all showed the same man: he was tall, judging by the blowup from the group shot, and very handsome. A dark beard framed his square face, and he had an engaging smile. In one of the photos he appeared to be embracing a woman at an outdoor café.

"His name is Heinrich Wolf," Abbott said. He was holding a typed paper that had been in the envelope. "Thirty-one, well-educated, a loner by all accounts. He disappeared from Germany about two months ago. Shortly after that, two of his former colleagues were murdered. The German police think it was a power play by Wolf."

Reeves was studying the pictures. "The composite sketch by the police in Tampa showed a guy with no beard."

"He probably changes to suit his needs," Abbott said. "Now you know what he looks like with and without the beard."

"All we have to do is find him," Reeves said.

"Well, we might get some help on that matter," Abbott said. He looked at his watch again. "Let's hope so, we're talking hours now."

"Until the fireworks, sir?"

"No. We have to get the troops moving if we want to have them in place by Saturday afternoon. The President still hasn't decided what he's going to do. There's talk upstairs of letting the fireworks go on. If that happens, the President will be out there with the public, mixing it up. The Secret Service guys are going nuts."

Abbott pushed the papers toward Reeves. "You take these. You're going to need them." Then he fixed Reeves with a powerful stare. "If we find out something tonight, we're going to have to move fast. If we have to call off the Fourth of July, it's going to hurt the country—no matter how much we cry safety, a lot of the people will see the President knuckling under to terrorists when he's been saying all along to stand up. But he won't risk innocent lives."

Abbott breathed deeply, flexed his shoulders. "And if we have to bring the troops in, that will be a major goat-screw. First of all, it will look like we're invading the city. But moving all those civilians? Forget it, folks are going to get hurt, there's going to be looting, all kinds of things, none of it good."

Reeves knew what was coming next, and he spoke first. "If we get a chance, sir, we'll take care of this."

"I hope so," Abbott said. "You're the last best hope we have."

An hour after he left the White House, Reeves was in the backseat of an air force fighter rocketing down the runway at Andrews Air Force Base.

"Here we go, Colonel," the pilot said cheerily as the sleek aircraft nosed into the darkness.

"I don't know who you are or why it's so damned important for you to be in Texas by first light," the aviator continued in what Reeves guessed was a North Carolina drawl. "But you came to the right man."

"Well, then, that's something that's gone right today," Reeves said.

Three hours later, the first troopers of the 82nd Airborne Division's 2nd Brigade filed past the open tailgates of five-ton army trucks parked adjacent to the green-ramp holding area at Pope Air Force Base. They were already puzzled by the load of ammunition they'd drawn: less than twenty rounds of small-arms ammo per man, with no hand grenades or machine-gun ammunition. The grenadiers, who carried M203 forty-millimeter grenade launchers, were issued tear gas rounds. As each man walked into the circle of light at the truck's tailgate a soldier from the division's chemical company handed him a foil-wrapped chemical protective suit and three sets of inserts for his protective mask.

The prospect of entering a chemical environment was something that could shake even the most hardened troopers; but in spite of how assiduously the paratroopers questioned the soldiers issuing the suits, no one seemed to know where they were going. And that was the most frightening part.

The two men captured by Officer Terry of the Alexandria Police were delivered to the German Embassy just after two o'clock in the morning. Waiting for them there were an intelligence officer and two assistants who had been briefed—in person—by the ambassador and who understood that Germany would not tolerate any more acts of terrorism from its citizens. The three men also understood that time was critical.

The assistants took the two handcuffed men to adjoining rooms in the basement of the large building. They sat the younger of the two suspects in a chair and began to question him, all within earshot of the older man in the other room. The game went as expected: the officer asked a few questions, the youth offered no answers.

"Well, I don't have time to fuck with you two, my friend," the officer said loudly. He walked to a table shaded in the dark recesses of the room and picked up a stun gun, an electronic device that delivers a debilitating but non-lethal electric shock through a pair of contacts on its face. The officer had read about a case years ago in which a New York City police officer had gone to jail for allegedly using a stun gun to coax a confession from a recalcitrant prisoner.

When he raised the black box and pointed it at the man's chest, the tired, confused youth obliged him by yelling out, loud enough for his accomplice in the next room to hear, "NO!"

As the officer pressed the electric contacts to the prisoner's skin, one of his assistants fired an automatic pistol into a sand-filled drum that had been wrestled downstairs earlier in the day.

The prisoner jerked free of the chair and fell to the floor with a convincing thud. The two men grabbed the unconscious man by the legs, and together they dragged the dead weight past the open door of the room in which the other man sat. The officer then took the pistol from the table, stuck it in his waistband, and entered the room where the older German was ready to talk.

# THE COMMON DEFENSE

## Politicians Sidetrack Economic Growth

editorial from the Tampico *Voice*

Some politicians in this town, anxious to make a name for themselves, have forgotten—once again—about those people who live on the very edge of starvation. These politicians and civil servants, eager to discredit the Americans, forget that the poor of Mexico and Tamaulipas State will be greatly helped by the new economic aid America is providing. Instead, these power hungry local figures dream up charges against innocent men, interfere with important investigations, and generally make a nuisance of themselves.

Local police recently tried to shut down the headquarters of two United States Army operations in Tampico. The chief of police claimed that two Americans were involved in the beating of a local citizen and detained them for questioning; however, the *Voice* has learned that the citizen involved is a known criminal with a long record.

Nevertheless, on these trumped-up charges, the police stormed into the American headquarters and arrested two soldiers, then detained these soldiers all day without filing any charges. This kind of roughshod justice can only increase the hostility between our people and the Americans, who are here, after all, to help keep us from becoming another Colombia, ruled by drug merchants. One has to wonder if the police and politicians would like to see more drug money available in our fair state, more money for bribing local officials, more money to line the purses of those in power, while the common people suffer in poverty.

The Americans are here at the request of our government, and they deserve protection under our laws. And if law does not reign supreme, then we may as well invite those South American drug lords to come in and take over.

# 29

**Brownsville, Texas**
*Friday, 2 July*
*0515*

COLONEL REEVES HAD JUST LANDED IN BROWNSVILLE AND
made his way back to headquarters when the call came
from the White House. He took it at the duty desk, where
his commo section had set up two secure lines, scribbling
notes on a legal pad as he talked into the receiver pressed
between his ear and shoulder.

Reeves had moved three of his teams into the Texas
Army National Guard Armory on Porter Street shortly after
the first air assault they'd conducted in Mexico. The idea
was for the Americans to spend as little time as possible
in Mexico, since their presence there was a sore point. The
men from Fort Bragg had taken over the building, temporar-
ily displacing a mechanized infantry company of the Texas
National Guard. None of the guardsmen knew what was
going on; they were simply told to stay away, and they did.

"We'll check out whatever's there, sir," Reeves said,
"and I'll have the team up and ready to move, waiting on
your call." He put the phone back in its cradle and told
the NCO standing next to him, "Go get Spano, and tell the
rest of the team to can the PT this morning. We're getting
ready to rock and roll."

Reeves had called Spano before leaving the White

House, ordering the major to fly to Brownsville. Reeves wanted to brief Spano in person on the situation, and he found it easier to work face to face with his chief planner. Now, with what he had learned from Abbott's call, Reeves was glad he'd had the ops officer travel during the night.

By the time Ray Spano joined him, Reeves was studying a map of Monterrey, Mexico's third largest city, which sits in the eastern Sierra Madre mountains two hundred miles almost due west of Brownsville. Because Monterrey is an important hub for legitimate transportation, there were Operation Sentinel teams there who worked in northern Mexico. Spano had talked to most of the Sentinel teams, gathering whatever intelligence on the areas they could provide.

"What do you know about this place, Ray?" Reeves asked his operations officer.

"Monterrey? Haven't been out there myself, sir, but I know the Sentinel people have a team on the ground."

Reeves turned away from the map. "Yesterday the police in Alexandria, Virginia, caught two German guys with a bomb of some sort," Reeves said. "It looks like they already dropped off at least three bombs before they got caught—and the FBI thinks somebody is going to use them on the Fourth of July celebrations in Washington." He ran his hands over his hair. "These bombs are made to spread more nerve agent."

"Holy shit," Spano said quietly.

Reeves turned to an office table in the middle of the floor; on it he placed the only map they had of the city. The map showed no buildings, only blocks, and its information was dated 1965.

"Oh, and we found out who we're looking for," Reeves said. He dumped the contents of the manila envelope on the table, and Spano picked up one of the photos to study.

"His name's Wolf," Reeves said. "Anyway, one of these German guys spilled his guts. Says they gave the bombs to a third guy to place. But we got a phone number that is supposed to be a safe house or something."

"How dated is that information?" Spano asked.

"A few weeks ago, at least. But he says that Wolf didn't like to be alone and may be nearby."

"So we get to scope it out?" Spano said as he bent over the table.

"For a few hours," Reeves said.

Spano looked up. "Sir? We have forty-eight, or thirty-six, at least," he said, glancing at his watch.

"Negative." Reeves straightened and looked into Spano's eyes. "The President was going to order the city evacuated tonight . . . he was even going to bring in the Eighty-Second to help with the evacuation. But he's decided to put it off until Saturday to give us a chance to get Wolf."

"Do any of the other agencies working on this have a firmer idea of where this guy might be?" Spano asked.

"We're coming at him from lots of different directions, but no one is—as of this morning, anyway—as close as we are," Reeves said.

"And we are going to go in—when?—tonight?"

Reeves nodded. "Yes." He scratched his head and bent back over the maps. "I hope we have time to do this right."

"I hope Wolf is where this guy says he is," Spano said.

Colonel Reeves had more information before he left the Brownsville Armory. The two men in Monterrey, both Regular Army soldiers assigned to Operation Sentinel and detailed to Reeves for this operation, had found the building that the German informant claimed was Wolf's headquarters in Mexico. The Mexican police were able to determine that the building, a two-story block structure with a flat roof and a garage on the first floor, had recently been rented out. The owner had no idea who the renters were, but they were not Mexicans or Americans, and they had paid cash.

"Keep your eye on it," Reeves radioed the two men in Monterrey. "We'll be there in a couple of hours."

\* \* \*

The two soldiers watching the building spent the long hot morning sitting in a car a few hundred meters away, taking turns peering through binoculars for the man identified, in the drawing sent down after the Florida bombing, as Heinrich Wolf. They'd spotted no one who looked like Wolf by the time Reeves, dressed in jeans, huarache sandals, and sporting a baseball cap and a growth of beard, walked up beside the car.

"I'm Reeves," he said into the open window.

The two men inside were soaked through with sweat. There was no shade around and not a hint of breeze.

"We haven't seen the big guy, sir," the soldier in the driver's seat said. "But we have seen a couple of others coming and going."

The soldier in the passenger seat had a green army memo book on his lap. He flipped it open and began to read.

"We got here at zero nine oh five. At zero nine five zero a white male, five ten, a hundred and seventy pounds, left building. Returned fifteen minutes later carrying what looked like two bags of groceries. Two more men arrived at ten thirty driving a blue van. Different guys. They left on foot at ten forty five and returned a half hour later." He closed the book and bent over so that he could see Reeves, who was standing by the driver's window. "As far as we know, there's at least three men inside; none of them appear to be Mexican."

"See any weapons?" Reeves asked.

"Nothing, sir," the driver said.

"Okay. You guys go back to your command post and take a break. Some of my men are already there, monitoring the radio in case we get any traffic."

When the two men drove off, Reeves walked back down the dusty street and around the corner of a nearby building to where he'd left Spano.

"What's it look like, sir?"

"Looks like shit, Ray," Reeves said. "Nobody has seen Wolf. That building may have three guys in it, but it's big enough for forty. There isn't a lick of cover anywhere around it, so there's going to be no crawling up to a window to see what's going on. And any minute now, I expect that the President will be on the phone asking us why we haven't moved yet." Reeves took off his cap and wiped his forehead with a red handkerchief he pulled from a back pocket.

"You think they'll want us to go in even if we haven't spotted Wolf?" Spano asked.

"This is the only game in town," Reeves said. "The President doesn't have time to wait; and besides, if Wolf isn't in there, the people who are might have a better idea of where he is. It doesn't really matter one way or the other, since we don't know where the hell he is." Reeves looked down at the ground and spit between the toes of his sandals.

"I want you to go ahead and alert the teams that we'll hit this place after dark if we get the word. I'm going to walk around here for a while and come up with a plan to assault this place."

By 1500 hours, Spano had faxed copies of Wolf's photo to all Operation Sentinel teams and to the Mexicans. He conferred with the Federal Judicial Police, but there was no sign of Wolf anywhere else, no new leads. By 1600 hours, Reeves and Spano had discussed the assault plan the colonel had come up with, and by 1800 hours, all the soldiers on the team that would perform the raid had been briefed and were conducting rehearsals.

Reeves squatted alongside the back wall of a warehouse and watched a four-man section rehearse the choreography for clearing rooms in a building. One of his men came to find him.

"Sir, we think we spotted Wolf."

Reeves trotted the quarter mile to where one section had set up an observation post on the second floor of a deserted building. A couple of video cameras were trained on the target structure, which squatted at the end of a small street, and two small television screens glowed dimly on the floor. This videotape setup gave them the capability of seeing the pictures immediately, something they couldn't do with conventional photographs.

"Run it back," the NCO said as he and Reeves entered the room.

The other soldier punched a few buttons on the recorder, clouding the screen with fuzzy lines. Reeves couldn't see at first as his eyes adjusted to the gloom after the painfully bright sunlight outdoors. Gradually, things took shape, and then he could see the building appear on a screen. A light blue car, too clean to be from the area, pulled up to the building; one of the two men inside got out and walked toward the door as the car drove away.

"That's him," the sergeant said.

"That's Wolf?" Reeves asked.

The camera operator stopped the image on the screen and fiddled with some knobs on a console hooked to the television. The image on the screen grew larger.

"I think he got a haircut, sir," the NCO said.

Reeves wasn't sure. There was no one else in the frame by which to judge how tall the man was, and the best angle offered only a profile of the face. In the enlargement, the edges of the profile were hazy.

"Not exactly a positive ID," Reeves said. The sergeant didn't answer but merely shrugged his shoulders when Reeves looked up at him. He was trying to do the best job he could.

"Still, it does look like the guy in the pictures," Reeves offered.

Spano walked in at the moment, rubbing his eyes. "I hear you got a picture of Wolf," he said.

"We got a picture of somebody," Reeves countered.

"It *is* a little rough," Spano said, leaning over so that he could be closer to the tiny screen. He stood and took down one of the pictures of Wolf that was tacked to the wall. Holding it up next to the monitor, he said, "Looks like a pretty good match to me."

He straightened and followed Reeves as the commander walked to the side of the room.

"What do you think, sir?" Spano asked.

Reeves thought that the pressure they were under—everyone on the team knew that they were going to make it or break it in the next twenty-four hours—might well be creating a mirage. "I think I'd better call the White House," he said. On his way out the door, he thanked the two soldiers on the surveillance team. "Keep a sharp eye, and call me if you see that guy again; especially if you get a good shot."

For as long as he'd been with the Delta Force, Reeves was always amazed at the communications that were available to him on their operations. He and Spano left the building where the cameras were set up and walked a few meters down the road to a parked van. In the back, the commo section had established a secure satellite link with the White House. In a moment Reeves was on the line with the Situation Room, marveling at the clarity of the connection. He might have been talking to them on the phone from another part of Washington.

General Abbott must have been close by. He came on the line in less than a minute.

"The President is in a meeting upstairs," Abbott said brusquely. "What have you got?"

"We have a possible ID on Wolf," Reeves said, knowing that the way he worded his report could well influence what his instructions would be.

"How good is 'possible'?" Abbott wanted to know.

Reeves sucked in his breath, hesitated for a moment. He was being asked to quantify something that defied objectivity.

"About fifty percent, sir," he said at last.

"Any word from the Mexicans on other possibilities?" Abbott asked.

Reeves shook his head as he answered. "Nothing."

"I'll go to the President with this," Abbott said. "But be ready. I think he's going to say 'go ahead,' but he has to call the Mexican president first," Abbott reminded himself and Reeves.

When Reeves didn't answer, Abbott pressed him. "You don't sound too sure about this, Tommy. Is it just because you'd like to have more time?"

"No, sir," Reeves answered. "I mean, I don't think we

need any more time to prep the mission. I wish we had time to make sure that Wolf is in there. But we might get some good information from whoever is in there."

"I understand," Abbott said. "But you know that the President is in a hurt box up here."

Reeves looked at his watch. In thirty-six hours, the first of the thousands of tourists expected in the capital to celebrate Independence Day would be converging on the city. The lawns below the Washington Monument would be packed with people waiting to see the fireworks.

"Yes, sir," Reeves said. "I guess we have to go."

Moonset was at 0237 hours.

At 0230 Reeves received the call from the White House. The President, backed into a corner, told Reeves to execute the raid.

At 0240 the Colonel keyed the radio handset he was holding, setting in motion a chain of events that would probably result in the deaths of several people in the next few minutes. Reeves had long ago accepted that death was an integral part of what he'd chosen to do with his life. But he had never reconciled that acceptance with the responsibility of sending other men to die.

The eight men from Team Two who were to make the assault began to crawl toward the barely visible building, using for cover a small depression in the ground that might, at one time, have been the bed of a small drainage ditch. The soil was dry and dusty, and the men got bits of grass in their mouths and eyes as they crawled, facedown, the first few meters of the two-hundred-meter gap between them and their goal.

The windows on the first floor of the building were small rectangles at least ten feet off the ground. There was a garage door on one end of the ground floor and a screen door next to it. The garage door was closed, but as far as the observation team—Reeves, Spano, and three snipers— could see, the people inside had closed the screen door but left open the heavier wooden door inside that. They had apparently decided that the security risk was not worth being shut up in the sweltering building. The assault team would enter through that door. Reeves could see, through his night-vision glasses, the small black lumps that were his men making their way up to the building. There was almost no cover around the structure, and if it had been possible for Reeves to hold his breath the whole time it took his men to crawl that far, he would have done it. He wiped his brow with the back of his hand, smearing black face paint.

Thirty minutes later the men were almost halfway to the building. From his vantage point off to the side of the squat rectangle, Reeves could see both the front and the back. His men were approaching from the rear, to Reeves's right. His scope gave him an almost daylight view of everything that was going on. Now that the team was closer, he could pick out the bulky night-vision goggles the men wore; he could even see the stubby weapons, mostly Uzi submachine guns that clung to the dark man-shapes. The only sound was his own breathing. Then he saw, clear as day, a man walk out the front door.

*"Freeze,"* Reeves said into the mouthpiece of his transmitter.

The men behind the building, all of whom could hear him through their own headsets, responded instantly.

"There's someone out front," Reeves said. "Let's wait a minute and see what he's going to do."

Beside him, Spano inched closer. "The sniper can nail him if he sees us," he said.

There were two primary snipers, one dedicated to the back of the building, one to the front, and their job was to take out anybody who tried to get away once the shooting started. The third rifleman was a backup. Their rifles were outfitted with a targeting device called AIM, a little box mounted in line with the weapon that sent out a bullet-straight beam of infrared light—visible to the sniper through his goggles—whenever the shooter pushed a button. The sniper simply adjusted the strike of the light beam until he was satisfied, then pulled the trigger.

"Stand by," Reeves said. "Let's see what he does."

He could tell, thanks to the quality of his night-vision

device, that the man was naked. Even in the heat, even for a European—he assumed this one was also German—this struck Reeves as odd. The figure walked some distance out in front of the building and urinated on the ground. Finished, he walked back to the front wall but did not go back inside. He leaned back against the wall and cocked one foot under him, the sole flat on the blocks.

"What the hell is he doing?" Spano whispered.

"Do we have him?" Reeves asked.

Spano walked the several feet to where one of his snipers lay, rifle propped on a sandbag, baseball cap turned backward on his head. In a moment, he was back by Reeves.

"We got him, sir. We can take him out any time you say." Spano thought of the snipers as a precaution; after all, as far as they knew no one in the building had done anything criminal. But he began to wonder how Reeves looked at it. Did the fact that the order was passed directly from the President justify, in Reeves's mind, extreme action? Spano adjusted his combination earphone and mouthpiece so that he could talk to the sniper. Satisfied that it worked, he looked at Reeves. He wanted to make sure he heard every instruction clearly.

"Let's give him another minute or two," Reeves said.

A moment later another man came out through the door. This one was also naked, but he did not venture away from the building to relieve himself.

"I ain't believing this," Reeves said under his breath.

Spano stood close to him. "What is it, sir? What's going on?" He was trying to focus his goggles, which weren't working properly.

Reeves glanced behind the building, where his men were still crouched in the shallow depression, waiting for the word to move again. They could hear everything he said, but they wouldn't respond unless it was absolutely necessary. There was no noise.

He looked again to the front of the building, where the two men confirmed his suspicion.

*"They're fucking making out,"* Spano said, louder than he should have.

"I can see that," Reeves answered. "The question is, what are they going to do next?"

The two figures weren't as distinct up close to the wall of the building, but Reeves could see movement there.

"Twenty years in the army, at the pinnacle of my career," Reeves said, "and I'm out here sweating my balls off watching two queers get it on."

"You want us to rush them, sir?" Spano asked.

Before Reeves could answer, the clear sound of a laugh came at them across the quiet night, and the two figures broke free of the gloom by the wall and went back inside the building. The soldiers could hear their giggling clearly.

Reeves waited ten minutes after explaining to the men on the ground what was going on. "There's at least two of them might be awake in there," he said, "so be careful."

The assault team moved again. When they reached the side of the building, they shimmied up the wall until they were standing, then they went inside, two at a time. Reeves felt even more isolated from his men.

Sergeant First Class Carl Blair was the first man in the door. He stepped gingerly inside and flattened against the wall to his right. The gray-green image presented by his night-vision goggles showed that the whole of the first floor was a garage. Straight ahead, he could see a midsize American car backed up against the wall. Both of the side walls were lined with workbenches, and all of these appeared to be covered with trash—bits of paper, metal, and wood left behind by the previous tenants. Off to his left, a wooden staircase climbed the open space up to the second floor. There was a small landing, three feet to a side, suspended above the cars below. Blair paused for only a few seconds to survey the room, which seemed empty, before he took his left hand off the stock of his weapon to signal the men behind him.

In a moment, Blair had three more men inside the room, and another four poised to enter. One soldier stayed by the door, one at the foot of the rickety staircase. Blair and a third soldier began to climb.

Because he was afraid the stair would creak, and because he wanted to hear everything that was going on, Blair tugged his headset off his ears. He took an extraordinary amount of time to mount each step, testing daintily with the ball of his foot. But it was paying off; so far the stairs were quiet.

He was six steps off the floor when he heard something else.

It was coming from the car.

Looking down from several feet off the floor, Blair could see into the backseat, where the two men Reeves had spotted earlier were at it again.

Blair gave the signal to freeze, but even as he did so, one of the men inside the car sat up and stared right at Blair. The American sergeant was sure that they made eye contact, and it took him a few seconds to realize that this was an illusion. There was no light within the garage, so the man in the car couldn't possibly see him. All Blair had to do was to remain still and wait for them to go back to doing what they were doing.

Unfortunately, they were finished. One of the men opened the car door and, in the timid glow of the courtesy light, spotted the soldiers. Blair's man at the foot of the stairs covered the distance in three steps and brought the stock of his weapon up and across the man's face. There was no sound except the crunch of steel against soft flesh. The other soldier moved quickly, but Blair knew that there was no way to keep the other man in the car from crying out. Turning his attention back to the staircase, he bolted toward the top.

He was within a few feet of the door when the man in the car below screamed a warning. Blair reached the small landing and took a split second to gain his footing before launching his two hundred pounds into the door, already thinking he would have to shoot whomever he saw in there before they had a chance to shoot back.

The door didn't budge.

Blair careened off the wooden door and almost lost his

footing on the painted wooden boards of the landing. The soldier who'd followed him up the stairs tossed him an axe. Blair grabbed the handle in both hands and turned to the door.

The shotgun blasts—two in quick succession—caught Sergeant Blair full in the chest just as he stepped forward to punish the door again. He was protected by his Kevlar vest, but the force of the impact knocked him backward, the heels of his boots dragging across the board landing while the top of him tumbled out into space above the car parked on the ground floor. Only his head and shoulders cleared the far edge of the sedan's roof, and the force of the fall snapped his neck and killed him instantly.

The door opened from within, and the soldier who'd been behind Blair opened fire with his automatic weapon, but he was crouched on the stairs and so fired high. Most of his slugs peppered the ceiling of the darkened room. He saw a hand flash out past the protecting edge of the doorjamb, then two small shadows tumbled away from the hand and over the heads of the soldiers now rushing up the steps. The grenades exploded behind and below the four men struggling to get up the stairs, the hot shrapnel tearing into the unprotected backs of their legs and buttocks.

The stairway was too narrow for the soldiers inside the building to bring their firepower to bear—the men in the back couldn't get to the front on the tiny passageway. The officer in charge of the raid, who was directly behind the top man on the stairs, pressed his hand against his earphone and gave the code word for the alternate plan.

"It's a botch on the inside," Colonel Reeves said to his second team. "Go on up."

The second team of eight men poised outside the building tossed four grappling hooks onto the roof. Two of the hooks caught and supported the men who scrambled up the knotted lines. They reached the level of the second-floor windows in less than thirty seconds, just in time for someone on the inside to shoot out a window near one of the climbers. The Delta Force soldier, straining to get out of the line of fire, slipped from the rope and fell to the ground.

But the other soldier managed to hold on long enough to toss two stun grenades into the building through the shattered glass.

On the inside, the soldiers held up at the bottleneck of the stairs rushed into the room while the blast was still shaking the building.

# 30

**Tampico, Mexico**
*Saturday, 3 July*
*0330*

HEINRICH WOLF WOKE WITH A START.

He looked around the room, which was dimly lit by the pitiful street lamp outside the hotel. Everything seemed to be in order. His clothes were spread neatly on the chair beside the window, his nylon bag barely visible, folded on top of the rickety dresser. He stuck his hand under the pillow and felt the reassuring steel coolness of the nine-millimeter automatic. He drew in a breath, let it out.

Wolf swung his feet over the edge of the bed and scuffed over to the washstand. He didn't have to turn on a light to know what his face would look like in the cracked and peeling mirror. The strain of the last few weeks—he'd hidden in five different towns in the last ten days—had begun to tell on him also, and he was trying to ready himself for the intensification of the manhunt that was sure to follow his actions in the next few days. Wolf was so avid for control over all things that he refused even to consider the possibility that he was afraid. But it was always worse in the darkness. In the daytime he felt confident, alert; he was even enjoying the thrill of avoiding the Mexican Federal Judicial Police. The consequences of getting caught—by the

Mexicans or the Soviets—were unthinkable, and in the day-time he could avoid thinking about them.

But the night was a different story. When he woke in his sweaty bed in the cheap hotel in Tampico, in a room rented by one of the men he'd sent north, all things were frightening, and he could not imagine how he had hoped to avoid capture. In the darkness, he seemed always at the edge of despair, and it was easy to imagine all sorts of terrible endings. He heard the footfalls of policemen outside his windows and doors, and no matter how many times he checked and found the streets empty, no matter how many times he told himself that it was a dream, that his normal rational defenses were down because he was sleeping, he could not shake the tremors. In the darkness, alone on his chaste cot, he was a small man dreaming impossibly big dreams.

Wolf splashed some water on his face, ran his wet fingers across his teeth, then rubbed face and chest with the hotel's dirty towel. He heard people talking on the street outside, and he crept to the window.

Two nights earlier he had discovered a whore servicing a man right on the street below his window. The woman knelt on the filthy sidewalk, the man leaning against a lightpost, his hands grasping the pole behind his head. The man had been moving his hips, made visible in the pale light by the shirttails flapping free of his pants.

Wolf had watched, straining his eyes to see in the darkness, completely aghast at the public nature of the spectacle. Of course, there was no one else on the street in the middle of the night, except for a few other whores, and they weren't about to pass judgment. For all its sordidness, the scene had an appeal. Here were two people completely oblivious to the world: they didn't care who saw them or what anyone thought. Wolf almost wished he could walk up to this woman afterward, almost wished he could take her in the open, in the hot air. But he remained in his room, watching through the dirty window, and he knew that there was no going back. Even if he made it through this ordeal, he would spend the rest of his life a hunted man.

Now he heard voices again, and Wolf crept to the window, trying to deny the delicious anticipation he felt. But when he pressed his face to the screen, there was no one in sight. He could hear the tail end of a conversation—a woman's voice—as someone walked with her around the nearby corner. There was nothing else on the street but a single car.

Then Wolf saw the men.

There were two of them in the front seat, though one appeared to be slumped forward, probably sleeping. The other one, behind the steering wheel, was sitting upright and facing Wolf's hotel.

*They know where I am!*

In his nearly three-month rampage, this was as close as any investigator or law enforcement officer had gotten to Wolf. And he found the close-in threat unnerving; there was that same feeling he'd had in the shootout outside Diablo's apartment, the same nauseated feeling he'd had when the Soviets had tried to do him in, the slide into bubbling chaos, the loss of control.

*Get a grip on yourself,* he thought. *There are only two of them, and if they were sure of their target, they would not be watching, they would have already arrested me.*

He was calmed by the reassuring measure of his own logic, and he began to immerse himself in the challenge of figuring out his next move. He checked his watch. The ceremonies in Washington would start in less than thirty hours. In twelve hours he would telephone Becht in suburban Virginia, and Becht would be able to carry out the attack. In eighteen hours he would be free of the burden of holding together the whole operation. If the strike in Washington was successful, he would simply abandon the rest of the men he'd brought to Mexico—they were only part of his backup plans.

Getting out of Mexico would be tricky; he stayed in the country only out of fear of being caught trying to leave. But he had hope that the chaos following his triumph would make his escape possible. Then he would slip out of Mexico and await the political repercussions of the slaughter. The American president would be broken by this last straw, and

Wolf planned to watch it from the comfort of a German city. But he could not stay in this hotel another hour.

He dressed quickly and threw his few things into the nylon bag, which he slung over his shoulder. He pulled back the action on the automatic pistol until he could see the dull gleam of a shell in the chamber. Three more magazines went into the pockets of his trousers, the pistol into the waistband of his pants in the small of his back. He glanced again at the street scene. The two men had not moved.

*I can't believe they sent only two policemen,* Wolf thought. *I have killed hundreds of people, and tomorrow I will kill hundreds more. What fools they are.*

He checked the room one more time, then let himself out into the hallway. He stole down a back staircase and out a door that led to a dirty trash lot behind the hotel, on the side opposite from the car. An alley ran parallel to the back of the hotel, emptying onto side streets at either end. By the time he reached the alley, his fear had overtaken him. He stopped at the corner of the building. To the right was a series of darkened streets, anonymity, escape. To the left he could see the poorly lit street and the parked car.

The sleeping man was still in the car, but Wolf couldn't see the other one, and he suddenly wondered if the man was watching him.

He reached up and felt the heft of the pistol pressing cold and awkward against his lower back. There, close to him, swelled the sickly surge of excitement and regret that he felt when he watched the woman and the man under the lightpost. The same feeling of isolation. *They want to destroy me.*

Wolf turned and hurried along the back side of the hotel. From there he could move directly away from the two men, keeping the darkened building between them. He stepped into the dull circle of light behind the hotel exit and immediately saw his mistake. The missing policeman had walked around from the other side and was now on the bottom step of the staircase Wolf had just descended.

Wolf pulled the pistol from his waistband, raising it even as he slumped against the building for cover. The man on the step was not as quick to react; he was only pulling his weapon free when Wolf's shot hit him in the chest. He fell backward, snapping the rotted railing, his pistol clattering to the ground.

Wolf raced back around to the front of the building and made it to the corner just as the other cop was getting out of the car. There was very little light to pick out the target, but the officer, disoriented from his sleep, didn't think to use the cover the building provided. He ran in a straight line for the corner of the hotel, right across the open area of the street. Wolf held the pistol in front of him until the muzzle was across the man's chest. The report startled him. The man went down but was still trying to move, still trying to reach the cover of the wall. Wolf stepped out into the street, took careful aim, and shot the man three more times.

Sick with the sudden stench of powder and blood, Wolf looked around the street, which was still empty, then moved closer to the corpse. Even in the poor light of the streetlamp, Wolf could see that these men were not Mexican federal police, not even Mexican. For a flashing, frightening moment, he wondered if he'd made a mistake. Perhaps these men hadn't been after him. But who would they have been watching? He turned away from the body and the smell of hot blood and walked back to the corner of the hotel.

*No, they were policemen,* he assured himself. *And if they weren't Mexicans, they must have been Americans.*

## THE COMMON DEFENSE

### Arrest of Two Foreigners Fuels Speculation on Spread of Terrorism

by John Myles
Special to *The Washington Post*

Alexandria, VA, July 2—Alexandria Police acknowledged yesterday's arrest of two men it would identify only as "foreign nationals," fueling speculation that the men might be part of the terrorist Neu Deutschland Party.

Although police spokespersons refused to give details or identify the officer involved, *The Washington Post* has learned that the patrolman was assisted by two civilians. These men, who asked to remain anonymous, were involved in the three-vehicle crash, in the parking lot of a local doughnut shop, that led to the arrest. The two men apprehended were trying to outrun a police car in the small parking area when the two workmen turned into the lot, blocking escape.

"Next thing we know, there's a guy shooting at this cop, then running past us," one of the men said. "So I just stuck my foot out and tripped the guy."

Other witnesses report that the two civilians then overpowered the armed suspect until the officer cuffed the man. The other suspect was apparently knocked unconscious in the collision. The police quickly cordoned off the area, then called the bomb disposal unit. No information has been released as to why the bomb squad was called.

The Neu Deutschland Party has already claimed responsibility for several terrorist acts within the United States, including the bombing of a military installation at Fort Hood, Texas, and the bombing of a public beach in Florida.

A District of Columbia Police spokesperson said the department is taking special precautions for the upcoming Fourth of July celebration in the city. "But these precautions are the result of the earlier attacks against American civilians and are not the result of arrests in nearby Alexandria." The spokesperson went on to say that the department expects "normal" sized crowds in the city. "We are not going to discourage people from coming. Americans have a right to celebrate Independence Day," she said.

The White House is expected to announce today whether the President will travel to New York City or stay in Washington for the holiday. A White House spokesperson noted, "Either city is safe."

# 31

## Tampico, Mexico
### Saturday, 3 July
### 0745

MARK ISEN AND STAFF SERGEANT JACK WORDEN WERE BOTH
awake, monitoring the radio setup Spano had left in their
care. Worden had just finished copying a message Spano
had sent to all Operation Sentinel posts.

"Here it is, sir," Worden said as he handed his notes to
Isen. "And it ain't pretty."

The Delta Force had, without the permission of the Mexican government and with only a nod from the U.S. Army,
recruited the assistance of all American military personnel
in the country. For Isen, who had expected it, the shift
was not all that surprising. But he could imagine that, for
all the other American soldiers in Mexico who'd gone from
soldier to antinarcotics fighter to detective—the change was
abrupt. At least Isen got to work with Worden again; for
all his faults, the NCO was a good man.

Isen read. *Strike against suspected terrorist location in
Monterrey captured five suspects but failed to turn up Heinrich Wolf or evidence of his whereabouts. Wolf must be
apprehended or stopped in the next twelve to eighteen
hours. Make every effort to check all possible leads in your
sector. Use of deadly force authorized.*

"I wonder what happened to the gig up in Monterrey?" Worden asked.

"No telling," Isen replied. "But whatever it was obviously didn't do the trick."

There was a burst of static-laden Spanish from one of Worden's procurements, a police-band scanner for which he had bribed a local official in hard U.S. currency.

"I figure it might help to know what the local police are up to," Worden had said. "There's no guarantee that the locals would share information on a sighting. They might want all the credit for themselves."

Isen didn't think this likely, but the scanner was a good idea nonetheless, and Worden's Spanish was good enough to interpret the transmissions.

"So what are they saying?" Isen asked.

"There's been a double homicide on a street in a seedy district about seven or eight blocks from here," Worden said, pointing to a local map they'd tacked on the wall.

"Another couple of druggies murder one another?" Isen asked.

"Nope." Worden leaned toward the speaker, and Isen quieted. "They were white, pale skinned even, at least according to the guy making the initial report."

"Americans?" Isen asked.

"He's not saying." Worden shrugged, then looked over at Isen. "I'm not sure how it could be connected, but you have to admit that there are a lot of people involved in this thing—American and Mexican agencies both. Lots of guns on the street."

Isen sat for a few moments and listened to the radio traffic. His command of the language was improving daily, but he was still a long way from being able to interpret the police jargon he heard on the scanner. Most of what he heard fell on uncomprehending ears. In his idleness, Isen turned the problem over in his mind.

If he had learned anything from his experience with Operation Sentinel, it was that the arms of the government do not always work in tandem. One branch of his own government had sent him to Mexico, and someone in another branch had wanted to ruin him to show that the program in Mexico was a bad idea. And he suspected that it was all to satisfy some political agenda.

*So who else would the President send down here to look for Wolf without telling Reeves?* Isen wondered. Perhaps the CIA was in Mexico, or maybe someone out of the embassy had been sent to check out a lead. If they were amateurs from the embassy, that would explain how they'd gotten caught flat-footed by the shooter.

"I think I'm going to go over there and have a look," Isen said. He held a piece of paper in front of Worden. "Is this what you got for the address?" Isen asked, waiting for Worden to check his translation of the simple directions.

"Yessir," Worden said. "Do you have a hunch?"

"Those two guys might be Americans," Isen said. "It's conceivable that other agencies are working on this thing. I just want to take a look at the area they were in, see if I can't get any ideas."

"Captain Sherlock," Worden said.

Isen chuckled and took two pictures of Wolf from the bulletin board.

"Yeah, this isn't exactly the kind of stuff we learned in the infantry school, is it?"

Isen stuffed the pictures into a large envelope, then pulled on a baseball cap to keep the sun off his head.

"You carrying, sir?" Worden asked.

Because of an agreement between the Mexican and American governments, the Operation Sentinel soldiers were not allowed to carry weapons when they weren't in the field. This seemed ludicrous to Isen, whose orders were to use deadly force, if necessary, to stop Wolf. But he'd been in the army for a while, and he knew that logic didn't always explain everything. Besides, he'd already gotten into trouble once before because he'd used his weapon when some politician didn't think he should have.

"Nah, I don't think so," Isen said. "There'll be cops around, and I don't need the attention."

By the time he got to the site of the shootings, the police had already removed the bodies and were about to tow the car away. Two uniformed officers were leaning up against a wall nearby, smoking. When they took no notice of the

American bystander, Isen checked out the car. Nothing. There were stains on the street where one of the men had fallen, more stains in the back by the stairway where the other body had been found.

When the car was gone and the police presence had dwindled, Isen installed himself at approximately the spot where the driver's seat would have been. From there he spied the buildings in the area. The choice was almost too obvious. If these men had been looking for Wolf, they'd been watching the dilapidated hotel that stood just a few meters down the street, sandwiched between a cantina and a leather tack store. As Isen watched, one police officer went into the front door of the hotel. He emerged a few minutes later and continued to make his way down the street. There was a good chance, Isen thought, that the Mexican police did not make any connection yet between this crime and the manhunt going on across the country. But it would be only a matter of time, maybe a few hours, before the local authorities filed some sort of report and the Federal Judicial Police sent someone over to investigate. Surely they would think it odd that two gringos had been gunned down on this sad street, with no evidence of drugs around. That would get somebody's attention soon.

But Isen didn't have a few hours. He tucked Wolf's picture—faxed to him by Spano just that morning—up under his arm and walked to the hotel.

There was no one at the little desk when Isen went in the front door.

*"Hola,"* he called.

From upstairs, there was a response, *"Hola,"* followed by a long and unintelligible sentence.

Isen went to the staircase, dusty open steps from which the bottom three feet of banister had been torn away, and climbed. In the dark hallway at the top he met an old man who was locking the door to a room.

"Hello," Isen said slowly, self-conscious of his pronunciation. He'd found, on more than one occasion, that Mexicans who didn't want to be bothered with him would simply pretend that they couldn't understand his Spanish, which wasn't much of a stretch.

The old man shuffled past him, barefoot. Isen followed him down the stairs.

"You're a gringo," the man said when they were in the marginally better light by the desk.

Isen wasn't sure what to say to that; it was fairly obvious that the old man was right. "What did the police ask you?" Isen said, knowing that the question sounded suspicious.

"The police wanted to know if I heard anything, that's all," the old man said. "Why do you want to know?"

"I'm looking for this man," Isen said, opening the envelope. He pulled out the picture that showed Wolf with a beard. "Seen him?"

"No." But the old man was squinting. Isen wondered if he wore glasses, if he even owned glasses. He produced another picture of Wolf, an artist's conception of what the man in the photo would look like without a beard and mustache.

The hotel clerk squinted, struggling to focus. Isen moved the photo closer, then further away, trying to find the man's focal point. There was no reaction, and Isen was about to ask if anyone else worked in the hotel, when the old man spoke.

"His head is shaved now."

"What?"

"I said his head is shaved," the Mexican snapped, apparently offended that Isen had misunderstood him.

"You've seen him?" Isen asked.

"Someone who looked like that—something like that, I'm not sure—was here last night." The old man stuck an index finger in one ear and wiggled it about. "But he left. That's where I just was, to see if he was still here. I remembered him after the police left, and I went up to see if he'd left without paying, which is what most of these people would do."

Isen felt the swirl of adrenaline but did not interrupt.

"But he left the money he owed on the bed."

"Did you see him leave?" Isen asked.

"No."

"What time did you last see him?"

The old man pulled out the drawer to the desk and busied

himself with its contents, though it didn't look to Isen as if he was doing anything in particular. "I don't remember."

"Look," Isen said, "I don't have any money. Why don't you just tell me when you saw him last?"

The old man shoved the little drawer shut and looked at Isen. "An American with no money?" he sneered.

Isen started to leave.

"Around ten o'clock," the old man said to his back.

Isen turned around. "Is that it?" he asked.

"That's all I know."

"Thank you." Isen nodded and walked back out on the street. He decided to talk to the police and had gone only a few feet when the old man came out on the street behind him.

"I didn't tell you he had an accent."

Isen turned.

"A German accent, I suppose," the old man said.

The thing to do was to keep moving.

Wolf had walked around the waterfront for several hours after the shootings, eating breakfast in a small café that filled with dockworkers at seven o'clock. He dawdled over his meal for almost an hour, until the stares from the waitress, who wanted him to leave, became obvious to other customers. He didn't want to stay in Tampico—the shootings would attract *someone's* attention—but he had to make the afternoon call to Becht, and he didn't want to travel and chance being apprehended at an airport or car rental desk—he was too close. Besides, he was dog-tired.

Wolf took stock of the action so far: Although the brush with the Americans had been frightening, until someone connected him with the bodies, the investigators were no closer to him than before. He had four men in Tampico with him, five more up in Monterrey, and three in Washington. He would use the uncommitted men to continue the war if the incident in Washington fizzled. But he wasn't worried about that, yet. Almost all of the pieces were in place. What he needed now was another room, someplace he could sleep for a few hours. Then he and his men would link up and leave.

"Is there a hotel near here?" he asked the waitress.

The woman shot him an unfriendly glance, then motioned at an old man, probably the owner, who was propped behind the register.

"Excuse me," Wolf said to the man, trying to keep his voice low so as not to broadcast his accent to everyone in the place. "Is there a . . . hotel near here?" He inclined his head conspiratorially.

The old man caught the implication; he leered at Wolf and began nodding his head slowly as he fished for a pencil on the cluttered counter. He tugged a sliver of paper from a drawer and drew Wolf a map. "It is only an old house, but you can get what you want." He pushed the sketch across the table to Wolf, who slipped the man a few bills and retrieved the paper, stuffing it into his pocket without looking at it.

He found the house easily enough, and from a pay phone across the street he called the four men who were in Tampico with him. He picked a café a few doors down from the dirty clapboard rectangle and told the men to meet him there at eleven-thirty. Then he would call Becht, and the final stage of the plan would be in motion. It was eight forty-five when he walked up to the front door of the little house and explained to the woman there that he merely wanted a room.

There was a dark, dirty hallway leading straight back from the front room, and Wolf got the key to the last door. There was very little going on at this time of the day. Some of the all-night customers were being roused out by the girls. Wolf felt his way along the wall to the last door. As he tried the lock, there was a sound immediately behind him. He crouched, turned, and pulled his weapon all in one movement.

*I'm getting too jumpy,* Wolf thought. *I almost shot her.*

A Mexican woman, a girl really, stood behind him. She was small even for a Mexican woman, perhaps five feet or so. She stood barefoot, covered only by a stained dressing gown. Underneath, Wolf could see the outline of panties.

"Are you next?" she said conversationally, as if she were talking to someone in line at a grocery.

Wolf looked down at the floor, stared at the tops of her bare feet. He hoped if he acted shy she would go away. He didn't want to speak to her and have yet another person remark on his accent. But she mistook his hesitancy for coyness. She laughed at him, touched his face with one finger. He swept his eyes back over her body.

"I know what you need," she said. She put her hands under her tiny breasts and lifted them, as if for inspection, giggling again. But Wolf was tired, and frightened, and did not have the energy even for this.

"No. Go away."

The woman stuck her lip out, a child's pout. "You must like little boys," she said, swinging her hips as she walked down the hall.

A couple of hours later and three hundred meters away, Isen and Worden were walking down opposite sides of a small street, looking for some information as to where the German-speaking hotel guest had gone. When they reached the end of the block, they linked up on one corner.

"Think we should go back to showing the pictures, sir?" Worden asked.

Isen had decided that they wouldn't show the pictures to everyone they ran across. There was no telling how extensive Wolf's network was, and they didn't want to tip him off that a couple of Americans were looking for him. The local police weren't about to cooperate; Isen and Worden were simply not welcome there; and even if they had been, and even if they could get in, it was doubtful the police would devote much effort to run down leads developed by amateurs.

"I'm not sure," Isen said. "We're not making much progress. Spano will be here shortly, Colonel Reeves and the boys a few hours after that, and we don't have much to tell them."

"We can't even be sure Wolf didn't leave town," Worden said glumly. "He may be in friggin' Washington, for all we know."

Worden was as frustrated as Isen, but, as evidenced by his tangling with Fuentes and the local authorities, was less adept at controlling his anger. The fruitless search for Wolf seemed to be coiling him like a spring.

"Let's go over to that place you like and see what's shaking over there. Maybe part of our problem is that we should be staying in one place; moving around like this might make us miss him altogether."

Isen and Worden walked to the small lunchroom Worden favored—where he'd been picked up by the Mexican police—and got a table outside. At this time of morning, eleven-thirty, there was still a half hour or so when the building would shade part of the eating area. Isen didn't figure they would need that long to eat. They ordered some bread, beans, and rice, which the waiter served up in a minute from some large pots on a gas stove up against the outside wall of the building. Always wary of the water, they drank sodas.

"Thanks, Jesús," Worden said to the waiter in his just better than passable Spanish. Jesús, normally a happy man, did not smile.

"Not a good day today?" Worden asked.

"No," the waiter said. Though the place was as busy as it ever got, Jesús never hesitated to stop and talk, especially to the gregarious Worden, with whom he'd struck up a friendship of sorts.

"No, Señor Worden, today is not a good day." He put a dish he was carrying on the edge of their table and held it there with his leg as he mopped his brow. "One of the women is out sick, we had to throw away ten pounds of rice that the cook burned—ah, he is in love and cannot think straight." He waved his handkerchief in the air to signal his displeasure. "And now I have four foreigners, four gringos in there complaining that they want imported beer. German beer."

Isen's Spanish was good enough to follow the conversation, and he thought he'd heard the last remark incorrectly until Worden nearly choked on his drink.

"What did you say?" Isen asked Jesús, trying not to sound alarmed.

"The cook is in love . . ." Jesús began.

"No, no," Worden interrupted, recovered now. "The part about the beer."

"Oh, that." Jesús fluffed his handkerchief, then stuffed it into the back pocket of his pants. "There are four gringos in there who want imported beer. Does this look like the kind of place that has imported beer?"

Jesús turned away, leaving Isen and Worden staring at each other.

"I want you to go back to the command post and call Reeves," Isen said deliberately, glad to be speaking English again. "Tell him exactly where we are and what's happened so far. I'm going to stay here and watch these guys."

"What if they leave?" Worden asked.

"Then I'll follow them." Isen's mind was racing. There were just the two of them to start with, he was sending Worden away, and both he and Worden were unarmed. They needed reinforcements fast.

"After you call Reeves, contact the police and tell them what's going on here."

"They're not likely to listen to us. Even if they do, they'll probably give me some lame shit about us not actually seeing Wolf yet."

"Lie to them," Isen said. "Tell them we saw Wolf. We can't afford to be fucking around with this one, and we need some help."

Worden walked away briskly, trying to move fast without drawing an undue amount of attention to the presence of the only other foreigners in the place.

Isen looked at his watch. The little black numerals said 1140.

Heinrich Wolf felt sick as he dressed. He supposed it could be the surroundings—there was a strong smell of tobacco and urine in the room and in the hallway, and Wolf tried to hold his breath as he moved. Outside, he breathed hard and fast to clear his nostrils. But by the time he walked the short distance to the café where he'd told the men to wait, he knew that it hadn't been the whorehouse making him sick. It was fear. He wanted to have the other men around him, to protect him as he traveled out of Tampico and the search intensified—if that was possible. But he was afraid that the crowd might draw attention.

This close to the end, it had become a desperate footrace, and he felt himself hurtling toward the tape, lungs and legs on the verge of collapse, desperate with fear because there would be a winner, but no second place. Still, it was the most exciting feeling he'd ever experienced, and though he couldn't be sure, he thought he was still a step ahead of his opponent.

Isen spotted him as he was crossing the street. The man was as tall as Wolf was supposed to be, but he looked older than the subject of the artist's drawing that Isen was carrying around, and the glistening head made him look sinister. Isen pulled his cap lower on his forehead and turned half away from where the man approached. He picked up his spoon and lowered his head as if he were suddenly interested in the almost empty plate before him. Now the stranger was twenty feet away, walking as if he owned the street. And as the quarry approached Isen felt a peculiar emptiness at the thought that he was unarmed, while this one and the four men inside at the bar were, no doubt, all carrying weapons.

He looked up the street for Worden, but the NCO had left only a few moments ago and was probably just reaching the command post.

The man stepped up onto the raised outdoor patio. He wore a loose-fitting shirt, Isen noted, but not so loose that he could hide a pistol under there. Isen studied the figure, trying to determine where, besides in the bag he carried, he might have concealed a weapon.

Then the man looked at Isen. Like an animal caught in the headlights, Isen could only stare back. The eye contact lasted only a second, but in that time Isen felt naked and, for the first time in a long time, afraid of a man.

The man went inside to the bar and the four men who were waiting in there. Isen could not hear them, couldn't even tell if they were speaking German, Spanish, or English. But he could see that the newcomer wasn't happy, probably because the men inside had been drinking. As the fifth man bellied up to the bar himself, Isen took a sip of his soft drink and stole another glance down the street.

*C'mon Worden. Hurry up, hurry up.*

Somewhere else in Mexico was one of the most coldly efficient antiterrorist organizations in the Western world. But all of their training and sophisticated equipment and high profile status couldn't make the Delta Force appear where they weren't. Isen tried to compose himself, to plan for what he would do if the group inside left. If his hunches were right, there were five men inside who were responsible for the murder of almost two hundred people, and Isen was a bit rattled. When he looked up, Wolf had backed away from the bar and was motioning toward the door.

*Shit!* Isen thought, near panic now. *They're leaving.* There was little chance he could trail them through the town without being spotted. He looked down the street again, as if the looking could make Worden materialize.

*What the hell am I going to do even if Worden does show up?* Isen thought. *That will just make two of us who are all fucked up.* He began to feel a sinking in his chest. These men, objects of a two-continent manhunt, might get away—all because he was by himself, and unarmed. *I can't hit them with fucking chairs.*

When he looked through the window again, he saw one of the men leaving through a back door. His first thought was that they were splitting up, but then he remembered that the pisser was out back. *Divide and conquer.* Isen stood abruptly, stepped off the small porch, and made for the corner of the building. As he slipped around the side of the cantina, it occurred to him that Wolf and the others might have set up this ruse to get him out back, to smoke him out to see if he was a police officer. The thought that he'd been duped made Isen's stomach flip over neatly.

But the man was out there, relieving himself on the section of the outbuilding wall that served as a urinal. Isen approached him from behind, not even bothering to cover the noise of his footsteps. In a few seconds, the man would be done and would rejoin the others. Isen had to do something immediately. Now or never.

The man hunched his shoulders and adjusted himself as he zipped his fly. He was thus engaged when Isen spoke.

"Say, isn't that Heinrich Wolf in there?"

If there was any doubt as to the identity of the men in the bar, this man removed it. His eyes widened and his mouth dropped open in a caricature of surprise as he began to turn toward Isen. His mistake was raising his hands to fumble with something in his pocket.

Isen brought his leg up from the ground like a punter, swinging his hip and his arms to gain momentum. The instep of his right foot landed squarely on the soft tissue of the man's scrotum. The German seemed to explode at the mouth. He doubled over, spraying Isen with a mouthful of saliva. Once started forward, he never recovered but continued to fall until Isen had to jump back to get out of the way. The man went down face first, his hands still in his pockets, gasping for air like a desperate fish on a boat bottom. Isen pulled the hands free and found a small automatic and extra magazines. He whipped off the man's belt, twisted his victim's arms around in a double hammerlock until the forearms were parallel, then used the belt to fix them together. He turned the man over and used his own belt to bind the feet of the prostrate terrorist, who was sucking in air and crying with the pain. Isen wondered for a split second if someone could die from such an injury. Then he thought about the people on the airliner, and at Fort Hood, and in Germany, and on the beach. More than that, he had a growing sense that Wolf's whole operation would soon try for some climactic blow. It was no time to be circumspect.

"Too bad, motherfucker," he said. He took the dirty handkerchief that had come out with the pistol and stuffed it into the man's mouth. *"And* you gotta be quiet."

Isen dragged the man behind the outbuilding, wondering what he might do next. The odds were still against him, of course, but it was a great relief to be doing *something*. He had a pistol now, and he had the advantage of surprise. He straightened his clothes, checked the chamber of the small automatic, and walked back around to the front of the building.

Worden was standing amid the outdoor tables. Isen was surprised to see Ray Spano at the other corner of the building.

"Where are they?" Worden asked when he saw Isen peeking around the corner of the building.

"Aren't they in there?" *Stupid question,* Isen thought. *If they were, Worden wouldn't be standing in front of the open door asking where they were.*

Worden shook his head.

"One of them is tied up out back," Isen said, coming onto the raised patio. "We'll let the police get him."

"The police aren't coming," Worden said.

"WHAT?"

"The local police told me that they got a report that an American team captured all the terrorists up in Monterrey this morning," Worden said.

"I even told them that we didn't get Wolf up there," Spano added.

"Did you tell them that Wolf was *here?*" Isen felt a dark red rage creeping up.

"Yessir," Worden said.

"Okay, okay," Isen said, holding his hands up, a conductor waiting for quiet. "Let's do this. Tell Jesús that there's a man out back who tried to kill me. Tell him call the police, and don't untie the guy."

As Worden ducked inside, Isen looked at Spano. "What the hell are you doing here?"

"I was already in the air when you guys called about your sighting," Spano said. "Reeves and the rest of the team should be along in the next hour or two."

"We can't afford to wait," Isen said.

Spano nodded, decided it wasn't time to tell Isen about the gas bombs in Washington. "We've got to stop him. Shoot on sight."

Isen nodded. Later he would wonder at how quickly he'd accepted that order. At that moment, Spano's pronouncement only gave voice to a decision Isen had made on his own. Wolf had to be stopped. Immediately.

Isen scanned the street; there was no one around. This was a new situation for him; his experience as a tactician seemed of little help here. Should the three of them split up and cover more ground, or should they head off in the same direction? Worden came out just as Isen decided that there was safety in numbers. The three men jogged off the curb and into the dusty street, heading east.

"I brought a weapon this time, sir," Worden said. "I . . . uh . . ." He faltered, at odds with himself. Common sense dictated that they needed to be armed. But Worden had already brought down a lot of heat on them for making up his own rules.

Isen felt like a hypocrite. "Maybe there are times to ignore the rules," he said. The comment grated, but he lifted the pistol he'd taken from the first man and pulled back the action. He spied, within the chamber, deadly brass. "Who the hell knows anymore?"

Fifty meters down the road, a man stepped out of a side street. He and the soldiers spotted each other at the same time.

"Hold up," Spano said, slowing immediately to a walk. He couldn't tell if this was one of the quarry or not. But the man got one look at them, spun around, and started running. The three Americans raced down the street behind him, Worden out front, followed by Isen, then Spano, who was still contending with the effects of the bullet he took in his calf at the ambush.

"Hold back," Isen shouted to Worden. "Don't expose yourself around that corner."

The man they'd spotted had taken off down a narrow side street. Isen sent Worden in the same direction on a parallel alley, while he edged up to the corner building to take a look. When he was ready to peer around the corner, he lay flat on the ground, just as he had been taught at the infantry school. Whatever part of his head was exposed would be at the ground level, instead of where a shooter expected a head to appear. There were a few locals, no one else. Isen stood up and took a careful step out onto the avenue.

The first two shots were high, smashing into the wall a few feet above his head. Isen crouched and rolled onto his shoulder and back, turning over completely, keeping his eyes open and trying to spot his target in the spinning picture he had of the street. He scuttled toward a parked truck a few meters away, and he heard two more shots thud into the truck body. The townspeople were cleared off the street by the time he got his bearings.

"Mark, you all right?" Spano yelled from somewhere behind him.

"Yeah," Isen said, his voice a bark. "Can you see anything?"

Isen looked behind him for some sign of Spano. Then there was firing up ahead, then Worden's voice.

"I got one! I got him!" Worden was shouting in high excitement. "Come on up here."

Isen peeked around the edge of the truck and saw Worden, arms fully extended, pistol out in front of him, his weapon trained on a dark lump in the street. Isen ran up, staying close to the buildings and watching the rooftops. Worden was breathing heavily.

"I saw him shoot from inside that doorway," Worden said, flicking his head toward the building behind him. "I got him when he stepped out to fire again."

"Where are the others?"

"Don't know."

Spano came up from behind them. "I can't keep up with you guys," he said. "I'll watch this one and this street. Why don't you go a bit further?"

On the opposite side of the street there were only two more buildings before the edge of the town petered out into dry, litter-strewn lots. The building behind them was the last one on the near side.

"Go around back of those buildings," Isen said to Worden, indicating the ones opposite. "And I'll go in the front and see if anyone is in there."

Worden took off at a dead run for the corner of the last building, and Isen made his way up to the front entrance. There didn't appear to be any bystanders around; everyone had cleared out at the first sound of gunfire, he supposed. Isen stood beside the door, then quickly ducked in front of the opening and back again, trying to see what was inside. There was nothing but darkness visible. He pushed the door open with his shoulder, holding the pistol stretched before him with both hands. He was inside when the shooting started again. Because it was so loud, he thought it was inside, and Isen fired into the gloom at the end of the first-floor hallway he'd entered. Then he realized that the pounding was coming from out back. He darted through the front door and went around to the side where Worden had gone.

Jack Worden was on his back, eyes open, arms spread as in a crucifixion, with large holes in his chest and stomach. He was dead.

Isen was swept by a feeling that he was operating outside of himself, as if he were watching someone else carry on. He stepped over the body and chanced a look behind the building. There was a man running away through a trash-strewn yard. Isen raised his weapon quickly and fired. The man disappeared over a low board fence, and Isen thought he'd missed.

Heinrich Wolf thought that his lungs were on fire. He was running down a small embankment when he heard two more shots. When he turned around, Claus, one of the two men left with him, was tumbling down the same slope in a dusty ball. Wolf and Stoddard, the only other man left, went back to help him. The top part of Claus's shoulder was torn away, as if someone had snipped off the corner of a paper cutout of a man. Bone and gristle were clearly visible through the reddening mass of flesh and bits of cloth. Wolf fought back the urge to vomit.

Claus was on his back, his eyes closed tightly. Stoddard's face had collapsed in panic; he'd dropped his weapon in the dust.

"We must leave him," Wolf said to Stoddard.

The unwounded man, a fairly bright boy of about twenty, looked at Wolf as if he'd just suggested they sprout wings and fly to safety.

"We must get to a phone," Wolf said. When Stoddard still didn't respond, Wolf raised his hand and slapped the boy across the cheek, knocking him backward into the dirt.

"WAKE UP, YOU MISERABLE SHIT," he screamed. "THEY ARE RIGHT ON TOP OF US!"

As if to punctuate what he said, a voice from the top of the embankment called out to them.

"The police have you surrounded. Why don't you give up while you're still alive?"

*Americans,* Wolf thought. *It might as easily been the Soviets.*

Wolf looked around. There was no sign of movement in the miserable grasses and trash that stretched out behind them. "He's lying," Wolf said.

But when he looked at Stoddard, he saw that the American's bluff was having the desired effect. Stoddard had crouched down in the fetal position; his pistol lay a few feet away, muzzle down in the dirt.

Wolf stood up. "Are you coming with me?" he asked again.

Stoddard didn't speak. He stayed hunched over, his arms over his head. The head barely moved, shaking quickly from side to side. *No.*

Wolf stepped behind Stoddard, so close that he had to spread his stance to accommodate Stoddard's shaking legs.

*So many weaklings,* Wolf thought. *So many who do not have the courage to stand with me as I bend history to my will.*

He lowered the pistol until the blue steel was touching Stoddard's hair. *I will not let them ruin my plan.* He fired once, spraying the wounded Claus with blood and gore.

Wolf looked up the embankment. There was no sign of the American, but that wouldn't last long. He had to get to the car the four men had secured for his leaving Tampico. It was supposed to be nearby, out of sight. Then he would find a phone and make the call to Becht before driving away from the miserable city. Even if the American was bluffing about the police, the place would be swarming with them in no time.

"Give up, you're surrounded." The American voice again. There was no one visible at the top of the embankment. Wolf kept his eye on the sandy edge as he moved to his right, back toward the buildings and the small streets where the car was parked.

\*    \*    \*

Isen moved twenty yards to his right, to where a shallow wash had cut into the top of the slope. He squeezed into the little ditch, which was only slightly wider than his shoulders, and crawled forward to where he could see the men at the bottom.

Two men—apparently wounded—lay still just below where he'd seen the one man go over the edge. Isen thought he saw a shadow moving through the rangy undergrowth just past where the two men lay. He jerked his pistol free of the ditch and fired a shot at a range of about thirty yards. A geyser of dust leapt up behind the target. It was a man, and he stood up and began to run. Isen got off two more shots before the figure was shielded by a gradual turn in the embankment. Isen stood and slid down the bank, holding the pistol trained on the two men. One of them was clearly dead, shot through the back of the head. The other man, hit in the shoulder, was either dead or passed out from the loss of blood. Isen lowered his pistol and put his hand on the wounded man's neck. There was a pulse there, but a faint one. Isen couldn't make out, in the mass of red, where he might stem the flow; the blood seemed to be coming from everywhere at once. He tore the shirt off the dead man, wadded up the cloth and pressed it to the wounded man's mangled shoulder. He concentrated so intently on the wounded one that he almost forgot about the one who got away. Suddenly aware of his mistake, he turned—his hands still on the wounded man—and pushed at the other one, the corpse, with his foot, turning it over.

Mark Isen had seen some pretty terrible wounds in his time in uniform, but he never learned how to prepare for horror.

The man's forehead had exploded where the bullet had exited; everything above the eyebrows was open, so that Isen was peering into the cavity of the skull. He looked away instinctively, then forced himself to look back.

It was not Wolf.

That meant that the target, the dangerous man, was still out there, perhaps about to do whatever it was that Reeves was so afraid of when he told Isen to use deadly force. *Stop the man. Kill him.*

Isen looked down at the wounded one, a complete stranger, who was hanging on to life under his hands. He would bleed to death in ten minutes, maybe less. Isen glanced around, hoping for a police officer, Spano, someone.

Wolf came out of the low ground and entered the back of a dilapidated grocery near where he, Claus, and Stoddard had first heard gunfire. His left side was on fire where the bullet had torn into the armpit from behind; he could feel the stickiness already reaching the tops of his pants. His thoughts came at him disconnectedly, in an edgy rush. *Got to find something to dress this, losing too much blood.*

There were two old women sitting on the floor behind a counter in the back of the store, their fat legs stuck straight out in front of them. Apparently they'd taken cover there when the shooting started outside. Wolf came upon them suddenly, might have frightened them into a scream, except that he put his hand to his mouth.

"Where are the police?" he said in Spanish.

One of the women began to weep, her shoulders and arms rising and falling as she shook. Her companion said something to her—not comforting, but something sharp. The crying woman put a fist into her mouth to stifle her sobs.

"There is a police officer outside," the calmer one said, eyeing Wolf's wound. "He is standing over one of the dead *banditos.*"

Wolf walked toward the door, careful not to get into the light. He could make out a body facedown in the street. That would be Woethe, the trigger-happy Bavarian recruited by Becht and the first one to go down today. He scanned the area but could see no one else.

*I cannot wait here,* he thought. He looked at his watch; Becht was already waiting for his call. *Shit!*

He hustled back to the counter where he left the women. On the way he grabbed a folded piece of cloth from a table of fabrics. As he moved he worked the loose end of the cloth under his shirt to stanch the flow of blood. Looking down he saw a trail—thick black drops of his own blood—on the floor.

"Where is the other policeman?" he demanded of the women. There was no way, of course, that they could know exactly what was going on here; but his accent, something in his voice, his face, the wound, all conspired against him. The stronger woman, at least, seemed to have no doubt that Wolf was in the wrong. She stared at him but refused to answer.

Wolf was becoming dizzy, weak from the loss of blood, and he was long past playing games. He reached down, grabbed a handful of the soft flesh on the back of the old woman's arm and twisted viciously.

"Where is the man who was outside?" He bent down, his face—full of hatred and the fear of a cornered animal—only a few inches from hers. She spit at him.

Wolf brought his arm up sharply and hit the woman as hard as he could with the stubby muzzle of the pistol. There was a sickening sound, like eggshells breaking, and the side of her face opened up, spilling blood over her and Wolf's hand. He pushed her to the floor. By this time, the other woman, already hysterical, had begun to hyperventilate. Wolf put the pistol to her head.

"Be quiet," he seethed through clenched teeth.

Out of the corner of his eye he saw something move outside, across the street. He crept back to the front door and saw a man standing near Woethe's body. The man's back was to Wolf.

Wolf tugged the door open, took three steps into the middle of the street, and crouched into a firing position, holding the weapon in his good hand. The pistol rode up with the first shot, but his target was already staggering. Wolf paused to bring the weapon down again before squeezing the trigger twice more. In the bright sunlight, he could see the dust rising from the target each time a bullet struck home.

He took two steps toward the body, then backed away and turned to his right to head back to the car. Up ahead a man stepped out of an alley.

\*　　　\*　　　\*

Ray Spano had gone to look for help. He found one Mexican police officer, whom he sent around to where Worden had killed the first terrorist. He was off to find more help when he heard the three shots. He ducked into a narrow passage between buildings that emptied out onto the street he'd left moments before. When he stepped back into that street, his eyes were drawn to the two corpses on the right side, then to movement on the left. He raised his pistol instinctively and fired before he had gained a target.

Wolf saw the muzzle flash of the other man's pistol straight on, which meant, he knew, that he was looking down the barrel. He heard one round sing by his ear just before he pulled the trigger on his own weapon. Already weakened, he wasn't ready for the kick. His arm jerked back, and he staggered, the wound in his side screaming at him. But he had hit the other man, who was on the ground, crawling toward his pistol, which lay a few feet from him. Wolf staggered across the street and fell headlong against the building there. He could raise his pistol only to a level just above his belt, but he squeezed off a couple of more shots in the general direction of the man who'd shot at him. He was trapped up against the building; if he took a step out into the street the policeman would have him. He pushed against a door and almost fell inside as it swung open. He careened into a wall, stepped away, noticed a bright red splash of blood where he'd brushed the surface. He wanted to sit down, dress his wound, rearrange the cloth he was trying to hold against it. He stumbled back through the house and out the back door, still headed toward the car and the telephone.

Isen stepped into Spano's line of fire before he identified himself. Spano, who hadn't seen which side of the street Wolf had disappeared into, was not sure why he didn't shoot immediately. On such threads do the lives of soldiers depend.

"Mark," Spano said weakly. He was still in the street, though he'd managed to drag himself into the limited protection offered by the gutter. He'd turned around there to look for Wolf, but found Wolf gone. Shot through the same leg he'd been wounded in just recently, he was in blinding pain.

"Where are you hit?" Isen said as he ran across to Spano.

"Fuck that," Spano said, pulling his leg away from Isen's attention and waving him on. "Go get that motherfucker."

"Which way?" Isen ejected a magazine as he talked, pulling another from his pants pocket and slapping it into the weapon.

"I'm not sure," Spano said. "He was down there past those two bodies."

Isen nodded once, glanced at Spano's leg, stood, and trotted off down the street. The blood on the wall caught his eye, drawing him to a trail of red that led through one building. He pushed the door open carefully, stalking wounded prey.

The street in front of him swam in his vision as if in a great heat. Wolf stumbled and fell three times in the two blocks to where the car was parked. After the third fall he had to crawl to a trashcan and use it to pull himself up, like a child just learning to walk. Wobbling on his feet, he looked behind him just before he turned the corner. As slow as he had been, there was no one behind him.

He managed to stay on his feet for the last fifty or sixty feet to the car, stumbling heavily against the trunk when he did reach it. There were two small boys watching him from the window of a building a few feet down from the car. *I must be quite a sight,* he thought, *but I've won.* He tried to smile, but it came out as a sneer, and the two children disappeared back into the darkness.

Wolf fished in one pocket of his blood-soaked trousers for the key. It wasn't there. He had difficulty focusing, couldn't remember what he'd done with it. He tried again, thrusting his hand deep into the warm wetness of his clothes. This time, he found it. He opened the door and fell inside; the pain, all blue and steely, took him away for a moment.

The car wouldn't start.

There was nothing but a clicking when he turned the key. He pressed the clutch down farther, thinking that he hadn't engaged the start button. Still nothing.

He got out of the car and looked around the empty street. *I must not pass out,* he thought, pressing the bandage on his left side more tightly against the hurt. Black circles danced in front of his eyes.

He made it as far as the corner. On the adjacent street he spotted a sign for a public phone, fifty meters away. It might as well have been a hundred miles. He hobbled a few yards to a three-foot space between two block buildings where he rested and looked behind him. Still nothing. With one last great pull at his strength he made his way down the street, collapsing at the door of the little pharmacy with the telephone sign.

It was Saturday morning, and the shop was closed.

Wolf raised the bloody pistol and shot at the bolt lock. He missed the first time, shattering much of the door's glass. Then he pressed the muzzle right up against the door and fired again, splintering wood and metal. Inside, he found the old-fashioned booth, fell onto the bench inside, and pulled the telephone onto his lap.

Mark Isen was less than two hundred yards away when he heard the report of the pistol. He cocked his head, heard another shot. But he wasn't sure where they came from.

In the small maze of tightly packed buildings, the sound bounced off walls and street surfaces, slowed and twisted by the hot, fetid air. Isen stepped into the middle of the street and listened for another clue. There were no more shots.

Heinrich Wolf couldn't focus his eyes; he was feeling very tired. How comforting it would be to let sleep take him here—just a short rest while the rest of the town took siesta. But he couldn't. There was something urgent to do. *What is it?* His head hurt from the effort of focusing his eyes, his thoughts. Then he remembered. *Yes, Becht is waiting for me. I have retained control of the whole opera-*

*tion.* His mind swam with pictures of the Washington monument, with Becht's face as he stood by a phone somewhere. He struggled to grasp the receiver.

For the first time he could remember, he thought he might fail. *If we miss this opportunity we can always strike another day.* But there would be no time after this, and that made him sad. He closed his eyes as he gathered his strength for another assault on the telephone. But with his eyes shut he saw the face of the American girl he'd strangled, so he opened them again. He fumbled in his shirt pocket for the number he needed, dropped the paper on the floor. He tried to grab at it, but his fingers were useless.

*Be patient,* he told himself. *You haven't come all this way to be foiled by a telephone.*

But he was slipping away now, and he heard something else: footsteps behind him, an approaching crunch of glass underfoot. He looked at his hands, bloody palms open and facing up on his black-stained lap. Wolf's head slipped back, and he gulped hot air, eyelids fluttering. He felt himself spinning away into darkness, and from somewhere he thought he heard Becht's voice, calling him. But he didn't answer, couldn't find the strength. He only stared at the phone.

Wolf slipped from the bench, landing in a sitting position in the doorway of the booth. He felt someone lift his arm and tug at his side, pulling the cloth bandage free. The air felt cool on his wound, on his cooling blood running freely across his lap again. He rolled his eyes back; there was a man standing over him, smiling. The man reached over Wolf, listened to the dead receiver, let it drop. Wolf pulled up some reserve of strength.

"Are you an American?" Wolf whispered.

The man moved his lips, smiled again. Wolf thought he heard *"Nyet."*

By the time Mark Isen found Wolf a few minutes later, the terrorist had bled to death. Isen picked up the phone, heard nothing, then placed the receiver in its cradle.

Ten minutes later, the Mexican police were present in strength, directing one another on the dirty street, poking at the car, asking Isen improbable questions. Shortly after that, Colonel Reeves showed up, with his escort and liaison from the Mexican Judicial Police. These men, federal officers, knew exactly what was going on, and they quickly had things moving along briskly. Two of them were bent over the body, studying the paper an officer had found in the booth, pointing and nodding in tandem. They called Reeves over and spoke to him for several minutes. Reeves summoned one of his commo technicians and sent the man scurrying off with the paper the police had turned over.

"What was that about, sir?" Isen asked when Reeves joined him a moment later.

"We found some phone numbers, northern Virginia area code, from the looks of them, so we're sending them back to the FBI to see if we can't pick up the guys at the other end."

"What was so important to Wolf about reaching the phone?" Isen asked.

"He was getting ready to call somebody in Washington area, probably with instructions to set off chemical bombs at the Fourth of July fireworks," Reeves said.

Isen suddenly felt weak at the knees. His intuition about the holiday had been right, but he felt little sense of accomplishment. Wolf could easily have made the call; Isen had been far enough behind him. He looked at Reeves, and the Colonel seemed to read his mind.

"The Mexicans checked with the long distance operator. We don't think he made the call, Mark. Looks like he bled to death first." Reeves reached out and put his hand on Isen's shoulder. "It was close, but we won this round."

# 32

## North Carolina
*10 August*

MARK ISEN DROVE THE STATE AND LOCAL HIGHWAYS NORTH-east from Columbus, away from the interstate, so that he could get a glimpse of the real South. They passed through sleepy Georgia and South Carolina towns thick with the smells of pine and heat in the humid dog days of summer.

"I hate those interstates," he said. "They make the whole country look exactly alike. Besides, after seeing all that brown dust in Mexico, I'm enjoying all the green here."

Adrienne was content just to be away from work and the army for a while. She sat contentedly in shorts and a T-shirt, her feet up on the dashboard in front of her. She didn't say much, but she held Mark's hand as he drove or stroked his arm with her fingers. She was more content than she had been in a while.

They stopped for ice cream—it was too hot for lunch—just inside the North Carolina state line. Adrienne sat in a booth in the small shop, watching while Mark stood at the counter and ordered. He had come back from Mexico some-what changed. They'd both attended the funeral for Jack Worden; Mark had presented the trifold flag to the widow, who was a year younger than Adrienne. That had been a sobering day, but there was more to this change in Mark.

It was almost as if his experiences of almost getting screwed out of his career had opened his eyes. He was still philosophical about it. "I don't blame the army," he'd told her. "It was just a bad run of luck." He'd wound up with a letter of admonishment in his local personnel file at Operation Sentinel, but the bad paper would never get into his permanent records.

Mark told Adrienne everything he knew about what happened: all but one of the NDP men had been killed or captured in the two days before the holiday, the three missing bombs accounted for. Although convinced that the last man, a German named Becht, would not operate alone, the FBI was pursuing him vigorously.

The President had stood his ground and won the battle with the NDP, yet he was lambasted in the press and in Congress for what might have happened had those bombs gone off at the Washington fireworks, and he was forced to make some concessions to his opponents. One bone he tossed them was Operation Sentinel, closed down two weeks after Mark left Mexico. But by far the biggest irony was that the Pentagon, as part of its continued reduction of American forces in NATO, planned to reduce U.S. naval forces in the Mediterranean.

Adrienne said she felt sorry for the President, who had aged years during the spring and summer, but Mark pointed out that the old man hadn't caved in; he had not conceded a point to the NDP.

"That would have been small consolation," Adrienne had offered, "if they killed a couple of thousand people at the Fourth of July fireworks."

Finally, that was the image that had riveted the nation: the vulnerability of everyday American life. Heinrich Wolf, who had died with his dreams on the floor of a tiny Mexican pharmacy, had accomplished something truly remarkable: he had set in motion a rippling fear that disturbed the security of an entire nation. In cities and small towns all over the country, Americans now knew that they really were as vulnerable as the unfortunate residents of Beirut or Northern Ireland or the West Bank.

Mark's new pragmatism was an unexpected windfall for Adrienne, for he confided in her that he was going to spend more time looking out for himself—and for her. That was when she hit him with the West Point idea.

She didn't quite know what kind of response to expect from him. Mark wasn't given to theatrics (as she knew she was), but she thought that, at the very least, he'd be annoyed that she'd done all this without him. But after she'd explained her reasons, after she told him about graduate school and the chance to take a break, after she told him that she should get to pick some of his assignments too—he thanked her. Adrienne was stunned, and had she not been so elated, she would have been angry with herself for becoming so worked up about it beforehand.

Mark contacted the people at West Point whom he needed to see, scheduled interviews, then put in for leave. They would take their time driving up the coast, spending some time sightseeing along the way. Adrienne had found a military guest house on Governors Island that offered incredibly low rates to military people—just a few minutes by ferry from Manhattan. They planned on two nights there.

When Mark returned to the booth—carrying sundaes larger by far than what Adrienne had asked for—she had some papers spread out on the table.

"Put those monsters down," she said, "And let's look at these colleges again."

Adrienne had been pleasantly surprised when the two academic departments Mark was talking to sent them lists of the graduate schools he might apply to: forty different schools, all over the country. After seven years of being *sent,* it took Adrienne a while to believe that they were actually allowed to *pick* where they wanted to live. She never got tired of looking at the list and discussing the cities and college towns they could get to know.

Mark put the big plates of ice cream down on top of the lists. "You have to eat this before it melts," he said. "I'm trying to fatten you up so all those college boys won't be chasing you all over when you start going to the gym at the university."

"It seems much more likely that the little college girls will be chasing *you* around," she said over a mouthful of ice cream. "Oh, Mark," she said in a Scarlett O'Hara flutter, "tell me again how you won the war."

They teased each other back and forth for a while, and when people came in the shop and glanced at them, Adrienne pretended that she and Mark were just another couple of civilians on vacation, with no wars behind them and no separations ahead.

Mark told her about the Spanos, whom they were about to visit in Fayetteville. Adrienne was a little apprehensive; she knew that Spano was Delta Force, and she was afraid talking to him might tempt Mark to throw off this West Point thing—but she could hardly stop him from talking to his friends.

When they stood to leave, she noticed that he had a bit of ice cream on his lip. She kissed him there, licking the ice cream off, her hands on his upper arms.

"I love you, Mark," she said.

"I love you too, baby. And I'm very excited about everything in store for us," he said. "It will be great to spend this time together."

They walked to the car holding hands, and Adrienne allowed herself to believe that they would have a quiet life for a while.

Since Mark didn't know his way around Fayetteville, he called Ray Spano when they got to Fort Bragg. Spano met them at the officer's club, and from there they drove out to the Spano's home, where they were to have a barbecue.

"Yo, Diane, the warrior is home," Spano announced as the three of them walked around to the back side of the house and into the yard. He opened the gate in the tall board fence, then turned to Mark and Adrienne, "Watch out for my wife's stupid dog. He won't bite, but he'll slobber all over you unless you smack him one."

"I heard that comment about my pet," Diane Spano said as she came out on the patio. "I don't think you should give Rusty a hard time, since he's the only full grown male in the family who's always around to talk to.''

"As you probably guessed from the loving banter," Spano said to the Isens, "this is my wife, the lovely Diane. Diane, this is Adrienne Isen, lately from beautiful Columbus, Georgia, home of the infantry; and Mark Isen, conqueror of Mexico, scourge of villains, slayer of dragons, etcetera, etcetera."

Adrienne shook hands with Diane, a handsome, dark-haired woman who might have been a year or two younger than Spano. "Thanks for inviting us over," she said.

Mark took Diane's hand. "I feel like I know you, Ray. Ray talked about you so much. I was glad we got some leave time so I could finally meet you."

"My pleasure," Diane said. Then she kissed her husband. "Hear that, Ray? Mark knows how to fill out a leave request; I'm sure he could train you."

Spano, who had retreated into the house, appeared at a window, his hands clasped in mock prayer. "Lord, how am I supposed to protect the free world *and* be responsible for teaching this woman to appreciate the male species? It's too much for one man." Dropping his stage voice, he asked Mark and Adrienne, "What can I get you to drink?"

"Iced tea?" Adrienne asked. Spano nodded.

"A cold beer would be great right now," Isen answered.

"I hear you're on your way up to West Point to interview for an instructor's position," Diane said, sitting back on one of the wood frame chairs that dotted the large deck behind the house. There were toys strewn across the boards, but no sign of the children.

"I'm going to give it a shot," Isen said. "It would be a nice break."

"I hope you get what you want," Diane said, smiling, sincere, serious. She had small teeth and Cupid's bow mouth, and in spite of her smile, Adrienne wondered if she and Ray had the same fights she and Mark had—too much army, not enough home life. Ray Spano came out of the house then, holding a tray with three beers and a single iced tea. He bent over Diane and delivered one beer, a glass, and a kiss.

"Gawd," she said, throwing her head back, playful again. "I do love to have men wait on me."

"It's my chosen lot in life, babe." Spano gave one of the other bottles to Isen. "Hope you're not into glasses or anything," he said.

"It was nice of you to put us up for the night," Adrienne said.

Diane waved her hand. "No problem. Maybe we can come and visit you guys up at West Point. My family all lives up that way," Diane said. "In and around the city." Adrienne supposed she meant New York, and that it went without saying that *the* city was New York City.

"The same neighborhood they've been living in for three generations," Diane continued, "since they got off the boat. Ray and I go up to New York in the summer to these big family reunions, cousins by the dozens and all that."

"That's great," Isen said. "I'm an army brat, myself, and I always thought it would be nice to have a big family like that, all living near each other, I mean."

"Well, there are advantages to moving around," Diane Spano went on. "Ray and I manage to avoid most of the little family squabbles that take up so much time. When we get home, it's always a big deal, so people are on their best behavior."

"Except for your mother," Spano said.

"Except for my mother," Diane said, smiling at her husband. Then, to Mark, in a stage whisper, "She thinks I married down. A soldier, you know."

"She shoulda been grateful," Spano said. He had one hand on his hip, and the fingers of the other hand described a small circle, thumb to forefinger. A scolding stance. He was imitating, Isen supposed, his own or Diane's Italian American family. "I give-a Diane her first pair of shoes."

The Isen's and Diane laughed. This was a side of Major Ray Spano that Isen had not seen before. Spano, encouraged in his comic routine, continued in an exaggerated accent. "Now I'm gonna go inside and get the food ready."

"He gets a little giddy when he gets home from a trip," Diane said as her husband retreated. She wasn't just making an offhand comment. She had made a study of Ray

Spano and his habits. Married to a man who could never tell her anything about his work, Diane had managed to establish a complex system for figuring out when something was bothering him.

Though Adrienne had just met Diane, she found it easy to imagine that Diane and Ray had adjusted to the hardships his profession brought them. She realized it was a ridiculous assumption, since she really knew little about the Spanos, but it comforted her to think that such an arrangement was possible.

*All we need is a little time together,* Adrienne told herself. She had hoped for something like this military version of the suburban American dream before he went to war. But all the time apart was beginning to wear. She wanted a life where the two of them could come home in the evening and simply be together. There was something terribly corny and terribly desirable about this life on the back deck, with the barbecue warming up.

"Ready for another drink?" Diane asked.

"Please," Adrienne said, handing over her glass. When Diane had gone inside, Adrienne turned to Mark. "I think it's going to work," she said.

"What's that?"

"I think if we can get away from that army schedule for a few years, we'll be a lot better off."

Mark took her hand. "I know it's going to work," he said confidently. "And we'll both be happy. I'll learn how to relax, and we'll be together every night and on the weekends, and we'll take vacations."

"And we can get to know New York City," Adrienne added. "Maybe take one of those carriage rides in Central Park." She was filled up then, with love for this man whose life was so hard on her, and with the glistening new promise they had worked out—that they would try. He would settle down for a while and still be a soldier, and she would have him around. The tough jobs would be there when he came back to them.

Mark leaned over and kissed her on the cheek, on the eyes, and Adrienne realized she was about to cry.

"There now, don't cry," he said, wiping her face with

a roughened finger. "Our hosts will think we're out here fighting." He squeezed her shoulders and stood up.

"I'm going to go in and see if they need any help," he said. "You're all right now?"

"Yes, yes, I'm fine," she snuffled. "I'm just overcome with it all."

Mark turned away, and she called to him.

"And I'm happy too," she said.

"I am too, baby." He walked away from her, in through the sliding glass door and into the kitchen.


Inside, Ray Spano was cutting up ingredients for a salad.

"I didn't know you were so talented," Isen said.

"I like to keep current in a lot of skills in case I bag the army," Spano said. He looked around, Isen supposed, to see that the women were not in earshot before he continued. "Colonel Reeves told me something interesting about the deal down south when he was here yesterday."

"What's that?" Isen had been put off by the fact that he'd been left out of some of the follow-up work Delta did with the Mexican police and the State Department. Colonel Reeves had just about made him a hero in the report to the White House, but as far as the Delta Force was concerned, he was still an outsider, a curious bystander with no real need to know. Consequently he was trying to forget the excitement and put the whole thing behind him. But Spano had him interested now.

"Remember those two gringos who got themselves shot on the morning we found Wolf? Turns out they were Russians."

"What?" Isen felt lost.

"Yeah. The Mexicans found some evidence that pointed to the Soviets. They denied it, of course . . . held out for ten days until the Mexicans threatened to show the evidence to anybody who wanted to see it. They let the Ruskies cop a plea. They cooked up a story that these two guys were on their day off, and that they had nothing to do with what all was going down in Tampico. But get this . . . Colonel Reeves said the Mexicans told him that these two had been going around to banks in Mexico City and Tampico, asking for Wolf. The banks aren't talking, of course, but Colonel Reeves thinks that the Russians bankrolled some of his stuff, then got nervous when Wolf started to kill a lot of people. Maybe they tried to off him.''

"They were working together?" Isen asked.

"Up to a point. And somebody cut the starter wires on that car he tried to use to get away."

"This business is like some spy novel," Isen said, shaking his head.

"Yeah, maybe when you're teaching English up at Woo-Poo you can tell them all about how truth is stranger than fiction."

Isen sipped his beer, went away somewhere in his thoughts, came back. "I'm not sure we learned all that we needed to learn," he said.

"How's that?"

"Operation Sentinel got quashed for political reasons, so because we can say that the politicians did us in, we have no motivation to figure out what's wrong with the way we use force."

Spano looked at him curiously.

"Sometimes force is the answer," Isen said, "and we need to be good at it. But that's a dangerous talent. We've been almost too successful lately, so it's like we have this sharp sword: we know it's there in the scabbard, all sharp and hard and ready; and we've proven that we know how to use it; and lately it's been an effective way to fix things. The danger is that we're going to look for reasons to draw it, when it should be a last resort."

"Those concerns are for the politicians," Spano said. "Our job is more direct. We need a sword, right?"

"Right," Isen said.

"And somebody has to keep it sharp and keep in practice with it, right?"

"Yeah."

"That's us," Spano said. It was all true, of course, but it was also true that these were questions for the professional soldier to consider.

Spano liked Mark Isen—Isen was a three-dimensional person who was smart enough to see that there are a lot of ambiguities and few easy answers. But, for that very reason, he wasn't convinced that Mark would be a good choice for Delta Force. Spano believed that sometimes you had to pull the trigger and worry about the mess afterward. Colonel Reeves, however, wanted Isen on board, and he'd told Spano to make the pitch.

Isen was quiet again, and Spano couldn't tell if he was thinking about his upcoming interview, or if he was preoccupied with thoughts of Wolf, or if he was thinking about the future of their army. Still, an opening was an opening. Ray Spano began chopping carrots, all but drowning out the sound of his own voice as he began to talk in earnest about Isen's future.

Adrienne caught her breath in the minute before Diane came out to join her and started talking about the kids. Something about them both falling asleep up in the playroom. Adrienne was only half listening. She watched Mark and Spano through the screen door; the men were talking intently about something.

"It's normally too hot to sit out here, even in the evenings," Diane was saying, "but we got lucky tonight."

Inside, Spano was chopping something on a butcher block, the big knife he held flashing quickly before him, and the hammering sound drowned some of his words. Adrienne kept hearing Spano use the word *you*.

At first she thought she was being paranoid; after all, they could be talking about anything. She looked away, heard Diane evaluating the swimming pool at the officers' club, then looked back. She thought Mark had been looking at her out the window, but he turned his head quickly, and she couldn't be sure. Diane's voice faded in and out.

". . . if you get up here," she said.

"What?" Adrienne asked. "What about us?"

"I said they should have a lot of the new construction on post done by the time you get up here," Diane repeated.

"We're not coming here," Adrienne said.

"Oh, I know you're going to West Point, but Mark's getting the hard sell from Ray and Colonel Reeves, Ray's boss," Diane said. "They want him to come down here, now or after the tour up there. And from what Ray tells me, they'd be lucky to get him." She smiled at Adrienne as if she'd just paid them both a great compliment.

Adrienne got up and went to the screen door. Inside, Mark had his back to her, and Ray Spano was saying something about promotions in the special operations community. The two men laughed deeply together.

Adrienne retreated to the railing at the edge of the deck, where she felt something vital float out of her. She put her hands on the railing and looked out at the tops of the tall pines, etched like ink drawings against the horizon. Up above her, the darkness edged across the starred bowl of sky, like a curtain drawn from east to west.